SISTERS AT WAR

ACROSS THE SEAS 3

CLARE FLYNN

CRANBROOK PRESS

For the MIAMI gang – Anne Caborn, Clare O'Brien and Hilary Bruffell. Source of my sanity in 2020.

1

A PARTING AND A REUNION

MARCH 1940, THE ATLANTIC OCEAN

At some point his luck was going to run out. As a merchant seaman, Will Kidd was only too aware of the heavy losses sustained by merchant ships and yet, so far, he had come through the first months of the war with barely a sight of a German vessel. On the way south through the Bay of Biscay, towards Gibraltar, just two weeks ago, they had spotted the periscope of a submarine, only to find on closer inspection that it was a piece of driftwood. They had also identified a German warship off the south coast of Ireland but either it was running low on fuel and heading for home, unwilling for an encounter with a convoy, or somehow it failed to spot them. Either way, it sailed on without engaging. Such good fortune could not last forever.

This morning, Will was keeping watch as they headed back to England. The *Christina* was straggling along, heavily laden with cargo. Being low in the water, they'd been unable to sustain the eight knots the rest of the convoy were keeping to, and Captain Palmer had requested permission for them to continue alone. They were following a course as far from the Spanish and Portuguese coast as possible, as the risk of being sighted was less the further out to sea they were.

Will scanned the dark water around him with a practised eye, all too aware that somewhere out there, danger was lurking. The stretches closer to home were always the most perilous.

The *Christina* was an ageing tramp steamer. Will knew the ship like the back of his hand, having served on her between African ports before the war. The vessel was slow, cumbersome and would have been all too easily picked off trailing at the rear of the convoy. Better to take their chances alone, rather than slow the other ships down. But the problem of leaving the shelter of the convoy was that they only had a four-inch, low-angle gun, a relic from the last war. If a torpedo struck, they could be heading to the bottom of the sea before they had a chance to fire a shot back.

Night was falling. Will was near the end of his watch and looking forward to a few hours' sleep. At first, he thought he saw a pod of dolphins, then realised it was moving much too fast – a line of bubbles crossing the bows from starboard to port. Grabbing the voice pipe, he sounded the alarm whistle and within moments Captain Palmer was beside him on the bridge.

'Bring her about!' Palmer ordered and the helmsman swung the ship through ninety degrees. The captain ordered them to increase speed but, even at full throttle, the *Christina* was too slow for a U-boat, even a submerged one whose speed would be constrained by battery power.

As the captain reached for the steam whistle to alert the rest of his sleeping crew, Will saw the unmistakable phosphorescent trail of a torpedo as it narrowly missed the *Christina*'s bow, closely followed by another.

'Send an SSS with our coordinates,' the captain instructed the radio operator.

The first officer appeared on the bridge. 'Torpedo near miss off the stern.'

'Turn her again. To port, hard about ninety degrees.'

The *Christina* turned again so that the stern of the ship faced the attacker. Will was astonished. Three torpedoes and none of them on target. He could barely believe their luck. It couldn't hold out.

'Full steam ahead.' The captain was holding them on a steady course, hoping to put some distance between them before the U-boat fired another torpedo.

Will was the first to see the sub as it surfaced on the port side. He sent out an alarm as shells began raining down.

The radio officer was frantically sending out signals that they were under submarine attack; the Germans were targetting the ship's aerial masts. The only gun, better suited to anti-aircraft defence, was little use at the angle required to fire at a surfaced submarine.

Palmer continued to steer the *Christina* on a random zigzag path, to make aiming as difficult as possible for the German vessel, aided by the cover of darkness.

But the shelling had only just begun. The *Christina* shook and groaned under the onslaught of fire from close range. Shells exploded everywhere across the decks.

Will looked at Captain Palmer, awaiting instructions.

'Bastards.' Palmer's voice was grim. He grabbed the megaphone and gave the order. 'Abandon ship.'

The booming of exploding torpedoes continued. Water rushed down the companion ways. Steam shot up as a boiler exploded. Torchlights cut through the blackness of the night.

Everything was happening so fast. Will staggered along

the deck to supervise the lowering of the port lifeboat, under the constant bombardment from shellfire.

Looking back, he saw the captain flinging the confidential books overboard, consigning them to the depths, safe from German hands.

As the bosun climbed into the port lifeboat to ready it for lowering, a shell exploded on the deck beside them. Will watched in horror. The explosion killed the first officer instantly and sent the bosun and the lifeboat plunging headlong into the roiling sea. Blinding lights, confusion, noise, pitching back and forth. Will looked over the side but there was no sign of the bosun. Just a mess of shattered timber floating on the black void of the sea.

The Germans must have known that they were abandoning ship, yet the U-boat had fired regardless. Will and the rest of the crew followed Captain Palmer over to the other side where they managed to lower the starboard lifeboat and clamber on board, fumbling in the dark, lit only by torchlight. The waves crashed against the *Christina* and buffeted the lifeboat as it went into the water.

The boat moved away from the ship and the men watched as the German U-boat continued to hammer shells into the now-blazing hull of the *Christina*. It was sport – like throwing balls at a fairground coconut shy. Shattering. Blasting. On and on, remorselessly.

The pounding of the old girl was painful to the whole crew. A slow noisy torture. They sat huddled in the lifeboat surrounded by the cold sea, watching transfixed.

It took a full hour before the *Christina* gave a few earsplitting creaks, roaring like an animal in the jaws of a lion, before she finally succumbed and slipped beneath the waves. No one spoke. But there was a collective sigh as the vessel that had been their home disappeared.

The silence was broken by Captain Palmer reciting the Lord's Prayer. Thinking of their two lost comrades, the men joined in or bowed their heads respectfully, regardless of their religious beliefs.

Its brutal task complete, the U-boat slid away into the darkness. The destruction of the *Christina* had been performed with complete disregard for human life or the terms of the Geneva Conventions. The men, drenched with salt water, shivering from cold and shock, began to sing to keep their spirits up, before hoisting sail.

Will exchanged looks with Captain Palmer. They were the longest-serving on the *Christina*. Will could imagine what Palmer must be going through having lost his ship as well as one of his three officers and a valued crew member. Whilst not the fastest or most elegant of vessels, the *Christina* had been home to them for a long time and both men had many memories.

The lifeboat limped along, through mercifully calmer seas, in what the compass indicated was towards the north-west coast of Spain. Will sent up a silent prayer of thanks that his life had been spared in his first encounter with the enemy. He would be seeing Hannah again soon.

Less than one hundred miles from the coast, they were bound to be picked up – they all hoped it wouldn't be by a German vessel. The prospect of being taken prisoner and sent to a camp in Germany was their unspoken dread.

The survivors were hungry, weak and exhausted when, around sixteen hours later an Italian ship found them. The *Vigevano* was a merchant vessel heading north to the port of Cork in Ireland. It took the men on board, distributed blankets and hot soup, and agreed to make a diversion to drop them off in Penzance.

Will was leaning on the rails, staring out at the sea, when

he felt a tap on his shoulder. '*Amico mio.* I am so happy to see you again, my Aussie friend.'

Before he could turn around, he was wrapped in a bear hug by his oldest, dearest friend, Paolo Tornabene.

'Paolo, me old cobber. You're a sight for sore eyes! I never dreamt I'd get to see you again. Oh, mate!'

'*Il Capitano* Palmer, he say me you are here with him. I am so happy! *Madonna!* I happy you are alive.' He punched Will lightly on the shoulder. 'Come, I have some beers. We drink before my watch begins.'

The two men sat on the boat deck, their backs against the bulkhead, drinking beer. The air was cold, but they were sheltered from the wind by the mass of the nearest lifeboat.

'I hope that's the last time I end up in one of those.' Will jerked his head towards the lifeboat.

Paolo insisted on a blow-by-blow account of the sinking of the *Christina*. '*Molto triste.* I loved that ship. *Cazzo!*'

'Why did you leave the *Christina*?' Will asked. 'Captain Palmer told me you jumped ship.'

'No. I no want to leave *Christina. Certo,* is not the same without you, *amico mio,* but I like *il Capitano* and I was happy on the ship. But in Salala in Egypt I go ashore, and bad men attack me in the street one night on the way back to port. They take my money, beat me. When I wake up *Christina* is gone. I have nothing. When *Vigevano* come into port, I find a job on board. But you? *Il Capitano* say you go back to Liverpool to find your girl. Is true?'

Will grinned. 'I found her. I married her.' He chinked bottles with his friend.

'*Come!?* How is possible? She was already married, *si*? It was a lie?'

'She thought she was married, but it was illegal. She and that fella were married by his father. He was supposed to be a minister – but it turns out his wasn't a recognised church and he wasn't qualified to marry anyone. It was all a sham. The poor fella she thought she'd married turned out to be a queer.'

'*Mi prendi in giro*? You are joking me!'

'I swear to God it's true! The man never laid a finger on her.' Will grinned at his friend. 'He's called Sam. A good mate of mine now. A real decent fella. Gave my Hannah and her sister a home after...' Will swallowed and turned his head away.

'After what?'

'After her father murdered her mother. I got there moments after it happened.'

Paolo gasped. '*Ma, no*?'

Will nodded. 'He'd have killed Hannah's sister too, if I hadn't turned up in the nick of time.'

Will told his friend of the events of that dramatic night, culminating in the arrest of Hannah's father, Charles Dawson, and the fatal heart attack of her 'father-in-law', the man who had conspired with Dawson to marry Hannah to Sam. 'Anyway, the upshot was she was free to marry me.'

Paolo shook his head, his eyes wide. 'I am very happy for you, Will. *Molto contento davvero*. But the father of your Hannah? What happen to him?'

'He's dead, mate. They hanged him. And good riddance. He was the most evil man I've ever known.'

'*Noo...ch'e cazz...*' The Italian swore under his breath, incredulous.

'Hard to believe, right? We must be the only couple on the planet to each have a father hanged for murder. But in her old man's case it was justified.' He took another swig of beer. 'Look, mate, why don't you come back to Liverpool with me. You can meet Hannah and we can celebrate me surviving my first encounter with the German Reich, as well as share a belated toast to our marriage. I'd always hoped you'd be my best man.' He paused, thinking it through. 'Captain Palmer will be looking for another ship. Why don't I have a word with him and see if we can take you along too? You could jump ship when we get to Penzance. We could sail together again.'

Paolo's eyes shone and he chinked his beer bottle against Will's a second time. '*Bravo, amico mio*! Is a good plan. You think *il Capitano* agree?'

'He knows as well as I do, you're a decent man and a good sailor, Paolo. Don't know how long we'll have to wait for another ship, but they don't like keeping sailors ashore when Britain needs food and arms.'

'It will make me very happy to be away from this ship. Many of the men on board are *fascisti*. Not all of them, but I don't like to be with so many *amici di Mussolini*.

'Come and join the side that's going to win this war.'

Paolo looked sad. 'It will be soon, I think, that *Italia* will join the war with Hitler. I want to be away from the *Vigevano* before that happens. I don't want to be on the other side from you, *amico mio*.

'I'll drink to that,' said Will.

2

SISTERLY TENSIONS
ORRELL PARK, LIVERPOOL

Hannah dragged herself upright and swung her feet from the warmth of the bed onto the cold linoleum floor. She stretched out a hand to open the curtains. Not yet dawn, but a pale grey light was beginning to suffuse the gloom. Shivering, she reached for her candlewick dressing gown and shrugged herself into it, feeling in the dark for her slippers.

She made her way downstairs, through the silent house into the back parlour and scullery, where she drew back the blackout curtain, put the kettle on and set about preparing for the day ahead by lighting a fire in the grate.

Since the government had instituted rationing, she'd been trying to get used to unsweetened tea. So far, the regulations covered butter, sugar and bacon and she wanted to stretch what little they had. Glancing at the new buff-coloured ration book, she wondered how long before tea joined the list. With the steaming cup in her hand, she curled up in the threadbare nursing chair in the corner.

It was unusual for Hannah to be up before anyone else stirred. Their household at The Laurels was a strange one.

They were a collection of misfits, each with their own story. Nance and Sam had become a surrogate family to Hannah and her sister. In normal circumstances they would never have met.

The large Victorian villa was owned by Sam who had been the equally unwilling partner in a sham marriage to Hannah that their fathers had concocted. A match that was neither legal nor consummated, Sam having a preference for his own gender. He had been kind to Hannah, allowing her to stay on at The Laurels, taking her sister Judith in too, as well as Will when he was in port. Sam had promised them all that until the war was over, he would make no decisions about the house, and in the meantime was glad of the rent and their company in the big draughty property.

This morning was a rare chance for quiet reflection. Sipping the tea, she thought of Will. Perhaps her husband was also enjoying a cuppa as he kept watch on deck. She tried not to dwell on the dangers he was facing, and instead imagined their future together once the war was over.

If Hannah counted up the hours she and Will had spent together before marrying, they hardly amounted to anything. Yet, the moment they met by chance on the Liverpool waterfront, it was as though they'd known each other all their lives. Finding Will was like discovering a part of herself she hadn't known was missing. She hadn't felt the lack of him until he was in her life but then couldn't imagine life without him – even though they were apart more than together.

But pointless to dream of the future, when the war had thrown an impenetrable barrier in front of them. Even getting to the end of the month seemed an unreachable goal when she lived with the daily possibility that her husband might never return to her.

So far, the war was amorphous, remote – just words in newsprint or delivered over the airwaves in the sombre tones of BBC announcers or the nasty crowing of the loathsome Lord Haw-Haw. People called it The Phoney War – uneventful after the years of anxiety about the threat of Hitler's Germany and the universal expectation that the losses and traumas of the last war would be repeated immediately. Apart from the appearance of Anderson shelters popping up in suburban gardens, the enforcement of the blackout, the carrying of gas masks and the evacuation of children from the major cities to the countryside, there was little tangible evidence that Britain was at war.

But for Hannah Kidd, the war was far from phoney. The harsh realities that might take months to manifest elsewhere, had begun immediately at sea. Rather than the Royal Navy, it was the merchant navy which had been the first target of German aggression. Within hours of Prime Minister Chamberlain's declaration of hostilities on September 3rd, a German U-boat sank the passenger liner *Athenia,* voyaging from Liverpool to Canada, packed with women and children evacuees. One hundred and twelve passengers and crew were lost that night off the north-west coast of Ireland. This attack on a non-military passenger vessel marked the first evidence that the rules of engagement were there to be broken. It also marked, for Hannah, the beginning of acute anxieHannah ty whenever her husband returned to sea. Barely a day went by when there weren't reports of shipping losses, as U-boats picked off merchant ships carrying essential supplies from all corners of the earth.

Hannah's musings were interrupted by the door opening.

Nance, wearing a black lace negligée in defiance of the

cold, breezed into the room. 'I heard the kettle whistling. Tea in the pot, then?'

Hannah smiled. 'Morning, Nance. Just brewed.' She went over to the dresser and took down a cup and saucer, filled it from the teapot and handed it to Nance.

Nance's constant optimism mixed with a biting cynicism often made her entertaining company. Yet there was a crudeness and a lack of sensitivity about her that sometimes stretched Hannah's patience. And if truth be told, Hannah resented the way Nance and Judith appeared to have forged a friendship, cutting her out.

Nance had been the mistress of Sam's late father. Despite being left a small legacy by him, she remained at The Laurels, shelving plans to use her inheritance to buy a cockle store in Southend-on-Sea, due to the war. Whether Sam was reluctant to challenge Nance's assumed right of residence or, like Hannah, he'd become fond of her, wasn't clear. But he allowed her to stay on and she was part of the fabric of the house – even though she did little towards its upkeep.

Nance swung one of the chairs around to face Hannah and flung herself onto it dramatically. 'Blimey, it's cold enough in 'ere to freeze the balls off a—'

'Thanks. We can do without the rest.' Hannah passed her an overcoat hanging by the back door. 'Put this round you.'

'Ta, love. Couldn't sleep.' Nance glanced up at the clock on the wall. 'Bleedin 'ell. It's not even six o'clock yet.' She gave an enormous yawn.

'I couldn't sleep either.'

'What kept you awake then? Surely not the non-existent war?'

Hannah swallowed her irritation. 'It may be non-existent for us, but it certainly isn't for Will.'

'He'll be all right, love. Trust me, I've an instinct for these things. That man's a survivor. Like me. Knock us down and we get up again. Roly poly toys, that's what we are.'

Wishing Nance would disappear, Hannah gritted her teeth and said, 'I hope you're right.'

'Course I'm right.' The older woman leaned back in the chair and gave a dry chuckle. 'I always am. And this war that ain't even a war at all will be over before the year's out. You mark my words. That Hitler's all mouth and trousers! What with his screeching and screaming like a banshee and his horrible little moustache. Can't even grow a proper one. He's lost his nerve he has. I tell you he'll be scuttling away with his tail between his bandy legs before you can say Jack Robinson.'

Hannah said nothing in response to the diatribe. She didn't share Nance's optimism about Hitler's lack of staying power, but the last thing she wanted was an argument, which was what tended to happen lately when she disagreed with Nance. Even though Nance's outbursts were short-lived and bore no malice, Hannah hated conflict of any kind, after years of enduring her father's violent temper storms. It was important that they lived in harmony in this house with its motley collection of individuals, each here out of the kindness of their landlord's heart. Hannah didn't want to give Sam Henderson cause to ask her to leave. Besides, it wasn't only herself she needed to think about. There was also her sister, Judith – not to mention her wish to ensure Will had a home to return to between voyages.

Hannah had married Will Kidd the day before war was declared. For years, her existence had been governed by the iron rule of her father. Then, just as she'd been liberated from his control, the war had come along and imposed its own constraints. As a result, they had enjoyed only a two-day honeymoon before Will had to return to his ship. Thoughts of giving up the sea and them leaving together for his native Australia were halted by the declaration of hostilities. Torn between the desire to move back to Australia with his bride and his sense of duty, Will had chosen to stay in Britain and support the war effort by continuing to serve in the merchant navy.

The two women jumped when the front door crashed shut. A few seconds later, Sam Henderson appeared in the back parlour.

Their landlord looked exhausted, his blond hair ruffled and his overcoat collar turned up against the cold.

'What a long boring night.' Sam was volunteering as a fire watcher but so far there had been no fires to watch for. 'Any chance of a bacon sarnie? No time for a proper breakfast.'

Nance huffed self-righteously. 'Bacon's rationed. You'll only get one rasher.'

Seeing Sam's forlorn look, Hannah offered her own rasher to him. 'You need it more than I do, having to go to work after being up half the night.'

Sam blew her a kiss. 'You're an angel, Hannah.' He pulled a face at Nance.

Nance put the kettle on to boil again. 'I'm going to freshen the pot. Want some?'

Hannah nodded. Above them was the sound of running water. 'Someone else couldn't sleep.'

'Your Judith can't get into work early enough these days.' Nance sniggered. 'I wonder why.'

'What do you mean?' Hannah was uneasy. She glanced at Sam, but he was already heading for the door to go upstairs to wash and change. She laid the bacon rashers in the pan.

'Judith's been leaving the house before seven, missing breakfast, and she's not due at work until nine. You have to wonder what that's all about. Very fishy.'

Hannah felt a pulse of alarm. 'Where's she going, if not to work?'

'Oh, I'm sure she's going to work. Not necessarily directly though.' Nance raised her eyebrows and rolled her eyes comically. 'I reckon she has a gentleman friend.'

'Judith?' Hannah was incredulous. 'You're joking.'

'Why?' Nance looked affronted. 'She's young. She's pretty. Why shouldn't she have a young man?'

Hannah could find no answer. Had she been selfish, taking Judith for granted, seeing her as her supporter and confidante and not as a person in her own right? Judith had always been content with her job as a seamstress, intent only on avoiding their father's wrath. Yet now, freed from Charles Dawson's yoke, it was not only possible but even inevitable that she would want to spread her wings.

'You're right, there's no reason why she shouldn't have a boyfriend.' But inside Hannah was hurt. Why hadn't Judith told her? Once, they would have shared everything. Had Hannah been so caught up in her own worries that she'd stopped noticing her sister?

The kettle whistled and Nance busied herself making the tea.

'Hey! go easy on that sugar. We have to make it last,' Hannah said.

'I'm using your ration. Shame to waste it.'

'It's not wasted – we need it for baking.'

Nance rolled her eyes. 'You're such a spoilsport.'

'Not me. Blame Adolf Hitler.'

Nance sat down and pulled her cup and saucer toward her. 'All right, all right. I'll try and cut down a bit.'

'Never mind try. We have to do it. Otherwise no cake.' With a little laugh she said, 'It'll get easier anyway. They'll be rationing tea before long. Let's get back to Judith. You know something, don't you?'

Ever since Nance had discovered Judith's skill as a seamstress, she had cultivated a friendship with the young woman, bringing her treats and taking her to the pictures. In exchange, Judith happily altered Nance's clothes and made her new ones on the Singer machine they'd found when clearing out the room that was now Judith's bedroom.

Nance shrugged. 'She's not said nothing about a boyfriend, if that's what you're wondering. But she's got a spring in her step that wasn't there before. She's usually glum – sad even.'

Hannah thought for a moment. 'She's perked up a lot lately now you mention it.'

'It don't seem right to be meeting a man at this hour. But she can't be going to work.'

'Why not? Maybe they have a rush job. A wedding dress or something.' Hannah wanted to think the best.

Nance stared at her open-mouthed, eyes wide as saucers.

'What's the matter? What did I say?' asked Hannah.

Nance ran a hand through her peroxide blonde hair. 'Blimey. She ain't told you, then?'

A chill spread through Hannah. 'Told me what?'

'She ain't working at that place no more. Packed it in same time she changed her name.'

Hannah jerked the bacon off the burner and turned around. 'What on earth are you talking about?'

'Don't you two speak to each other at all these days?'

Hannah began pacing up and down the room, heart

pounding. What was happening? How could she be so unaware of her own sister? Nance was right – Hannah struggled to remember the last time she and Judith had talked to each other about anything significant. Not since their father's trial.

'You'd better tell me everything.' She pulled out a chair and sat down at the table opposite Nance. Sam's bacon butties could wait.

'It's not up to me. She should tell you herself.'

'No. Tell me now.'

Nance hesitated then said, 'After the trial and your father being hanged, Judith didn't like everyone knowing who she was. Not when it had been in all the papers. She felt uncomfortable with those women she worked with. Said she hated the way she'd catch them staring at her. And she knew they talked about her. So, she decided to change her name from Dawson and get another job somewhere no one knew her. A fresh start, like.' Nance fumbled in the drawer of the table, pulled out a packet of Woodbines and a box of matches and lit a cigarette. 'Didn't want to be known as the daughter of a convicted murderer.' Perhaps realising the remark was tactless, she added, 'After all, you got to change your name to Kidd when you got hitched.'

Hannah felt terrible. How could she have been so blind to what Judith had been going through? 'What's she changed it to?'

'Your mother's maiden name. Morton.'

'I see.' Hannah had never smoked in her life, but was tempted to ask Nance for a cigarette.

'You need to talk to her. Ain't right her keeping secrets from you.'

'Where's she working?'

'Education Office. In town.'

Hannah slumped forward, her head in her hands. 'I've been blind, haven't I?'

Nance gave a little shrug.

'Do you have any idea why she didn't tell me?'

Drumming her fingers on the tabletop, Nance thought for a moment then said, 'Maybe I'm speaking out of turn, but I reckon she thinks you're angry with her.'

'Angry with her? Why?' But inside, Hannah knew why.

'Because you think she could have done more to help your poor mother.' Nance held Hannah's gaze. 'I've told her a thousand times, if she had, you'd have had a dead sister as well as a dead mother.'

Nance's words were brutal but Hannah realised she was right. Dawson would have killed his daughter as well as his wife. It had been nothing short of a miracle that Will had turned up at the house in Bootle, determined to find out where Hannah was. Too late to save Sarah Dawson, his arrival had saved Judith's life.

'The poor kid blames herself for running upstairs when your dad attacked your mother. She decided – wrongly I'm sure – that you blamed her too.'

Hannah was filled with shame. It was true. She had blamed her. Not in so many words, even to herself, but in her uncrystallised, unarticulated thoughts. Her behaviour to Judith had changed since the trial, and Judith must have sensed it. How could she not? Hannah had used her worries about Will as an excuse to distance herself from her sister. But Judith would have known there was more to it than that.

Nance went on. 'The kid's enjoying her new job. Making friends. Being part of something. When she was a seamstress, she was stuck with three older women. There's a younger crowd at the Education Office.'

Hannah was crushed. How had she missed this? Why,

until today, had she ignored Judith's frequent absences at breakfast? Her sister only ever had a full cooked breakfast on Sunday, but normally she'd managed a piece of toast before leaving the house. Judith had changed so many things in her life and said nothing. Hannah was stung.

The door opened and Judith's head peered round. 'Going in early. See you tonight!' Then she was gone.

Hannah jumped up. 'Judith! Wait. I want––' But the sound of the front door slamming cut her short. She turned to Nance. 'Well!'

'Must be a fella.'

'But she said she was needed in early.'

Nance snorted. 'Come off it! It's the Local Education Office not the bloody War Office. She's a filing clerk not the School Inspector. No, love, she's got herself a man.' She said the last words with comic relish. 'And good luck to her, I say.'

HANNAH WAS WAITING in the front parlour when Judith came home. She called out to her sister to join her.

Judith came into the room, looking cautious and guarded. 'What are you doing in here?' She glanced at the fire, burning in the grate. 'You usually sit in the back.' It was almost an accusation.

'I wanted to talk to you. In private.'

'What? Now?'

'Yes. Now.'

Judith sat down on the chair opposite Hannah's and folded her hands in her lap.

Hannah was suddenly nervous. How had it come to be so strained and formal between them, when they had once been so close? She remembered all those hours, lying on their twin beds in the cramped bedroom in Bluebell Street, listening as their father shouted at their mother on the other side of the thin partition wall. They used to confide in each other, sharing a joint fear of Charles Dawson's explosive anger as he railed against womankind and pontificated on his own power as God's representative. But now, Judith was detached, distant, unreachable.

Hannah leaned forward, her voice catching in her throat. 'I hear you've changed your name.'

'Can you blame me?' Judith snapped at her. There was no attempt to justify herself or deny what Hannah was saying. 'You're Mrs Kidd now. Why should I be stuck with Dawson?' She shuddered as she spoke the name.

'I understand, Judith. I'm not criticising what you've done, I'm merely surprised that you said nothing about it. Surely you didn't imagine I'd be against the idea?'

Judith looked down, avoiding her eyes.

'And your job? You've changed that as well.'

Judith raised her gaze, a hint of defiance in her eyes. 'What of it? It's my life.'

Hannah winced. What had brought on this antagonism? 'I'm your sister,' she said, conscious of how lame she sounded. 'I have your best interests at heart.'

'Well there's no need for you to concern yourself with what you're quite right in pointing out are my interests. Now, if you're done, I'm going to wash my hands.'

Hannah could hear the sigh as the door closed behind her sister.

THAT EVENING, Hannah had no opportunity to resume the conversation, as Judith had accompanied Nance on a trip to the Carlton Cinema to see a Bette Davis film, *Dark Victory*.

Hannah preferred to remain behind in the empty house, enjoying the solitude and catching up on her reading.

When they returned, the film had clearly affected Judith. She refused her usual cup of cocoa and went straight up to bed. Nance rolled her eyes. 'It was a real weepie, that picture.' She snorted. 'Almost had me reaching for me hankie.'

'What was it about?'

'A woman with a brain tumour who falls in love with her surgeon. He'd tried to keep her – whaddaya call it? – negative pognotis from her. But she finds out and they get married anyway.'

'I think you mean prognosis.'

'That's what I said. Anyway she goes blind in the end and she knows that means she's only got hours left to live and doesn't want him to know, so she pretends everything's fine and gets him out of the house, then she goes upstairs and lies down on the bed and dies.'

'It sounds very depressing.' Hannah shivered.

'It was. Judith was bawling her eyes out. Mind you, so was half the cinema.'

'I'd better go and talk to her.'

'Nah! Leave the girl be. A good cry'll do her good. Get the cocoa on, love.'

3

A FAUX PAS

A few days later, unable to sleep, Hannah was up early, sitting with a cup of tea in the back parlour when she heard movements upstairs and Judith's footsteps on the staircase. She hadn't been able to stop thinking about her sister and how things had got to such a parlous state between them. She would seize the moment to talk to her again. Try to find a way to build bridges.

But Judith didn't come into the kitchen. Hannah heard the front door close quietly. She jumped to her feet. Without stopping to reason why, she grabbed her coat from the hallway and slipped out of the house, hatless.

Judith was already quite a way ahead of her and walking so quickly that Hannah almost had to run to keep her in sight. She went straight past the train station and proceeded down the hill towards Walton Vale. Clearly, she wasn't getting the train into the city centre where the Education Office was.

In spite of the early hour, there were plenty of people about on Walton Vale. To Hannah's surprise, Judith turned in between the metal railings in front of the large Catholic church and went inside. Waiting a few moments, Hannah followed her into a small porch, which gave onto a larger lobby, beyond which was the body of the church behind a thick oak door. There was no sign of Judith. Putting her ear to the door, Hannah listened, trying to establish whether there was a service taking place, although at not yet seven, that was doubtful. Heart thumping, she eased the door open, praying it wouldn't creak, and peered inside.

The church was dark, faint light filtering in through the stained-glass windows and a flickering glow from a couple of candles near the altar. At first, she thought the place was empty. Taking a tentative step forward, she saw Judith in the front pew of a side aisle. Hannah was about to join her, when the door to the sacristy opened and a cassocked figure emerged. The priest went straight to Judith's pew, took her hands in his and sat down beside her. While the distance and the gloom were such that Hannah couldn't make out his features, it was clear to her that he was a young man.

Fear gripped her. Was Judith having a clandestine relationship with a Catholic priest? If he was the man she'd been meeting regularly in the early morning, this was much worse than Hannah's worst imagining of an unsuitable attachment. Everyone knew Catholic priests were celibate, so how on earth had Judith got herself involved with one?

Her sister's head and the priest's were close together, and Hannah could hear the low murmur of their talking, but it was too far away to make out the words. A wave of guilt washed over her. What was she doing here, skulking at the back of a church, spying on her sister? Backing away, she felt for the door, pushed it open and slipped out of the church before she could be detected.

She ran all the way back to The Laurels. When she burst

into the house, Nance and Sam were drinking tea at the table in the back parlour.

'Where the Hell you been so early in the morning? Getting as bad as your sister.' Nance shook her head and handed Hannah a fresh cup of tea.

'I was following Judith.'

Nance looked at Sam, who put his hands up as if to say 'not my business'.

'You followed her? Did she see you?'

'No. I'm pretty certain she didn't.' She sank into a chair. 'But I feel terrible. Spying on her like that. I don't know what came over me.'

'Don't be so hard on yourself, Hannah.' Sam leaned across the table and patted her hand. 'You're only looking out for your sister. It's because you care about her.' He got up from the table, left the room and returned a moment later putting his coat on. When he returned, he said, 'Nance was just telling me about the name change and the new job. If Judith's keeping that kind of thing from you, you've every right to check up on her. After all you are in loco parentis.'

Nance chipped in. 'That's right, love. She's only seventeen after all.'

Hannah sipped her tea, relieved that Sam had also been unaware of what Judith was doing. She'd have hated to find out she was the only resident of The Laurels who was in the dark.

OVER THE FOLLOWING DAYS, Hannah agonised over how to tackle what she had begun to think of as 'The Judith Situation'. She became increasingly convinced that her sister was indeed having a relationship with the young priest. Sam's reminder that she was in loco parentis was particularly poignant. Their father had never been a good parent to them. In fact, he was everything that a father should not be – cold, violent, bullying. And their mother had been so cowed by him she had done little to protect her daughters until, when she finally woke up to the need to act, it was at the cost of her own life. It was up to Hannah now to take responsibility for her younger sister.

Hannah was completely mystified why, of all the young men available, Judith should set her sights on a man of the cloth. Hadn't their bigoted father done enough to put her off religion for life? Charles Dawson's zealotry, self-righteousness, his literal interpretation of the scriptures, and his conviction that women were worthless vessels there to do a man's bidding, had destroyed Hannah's belief in a merciful God. Her father's god was an angry one: the bringer of fire and brimstone, of vengeance and cruelty, with a complete absence of compassion. In Hannah's mind, religion and violence were inextricably linked. While she was prepared to believe Catholics might have a different approach, one thing she knew: they didn't allow their priests to conduct romantic relationships.

She had to nip it in the bud. Consorting with a priest could only bring more shame and scandal on the family. Angry, Hannah made her mind up. She must speak with this priest. He needed to do the right thing.

Setting aside the heap of potatoes she had been peeling, Hannah dried her hands, grabbed her coat and hat and ran out of the house, grateful that Nance hadn't witnessed her departure. She didn't want anyone trying to talk her out of this.

She hurried down the hill. As she crossed Walton Vale a group of women came out of the church.

'I need to see the priest,' she said. 'Where will I find him?'

'If you're quick, you might catch Father Edwards in the sacristy. If not, the presbytery's round the corner. The priests'll be there for their dinner.'

'There's more than one?'

'It's a big parish.'

Mumbling her thanks, Hannah went inside the church. She hadn't anticipated the possibility of there being more than one priest. The one with Judith had been too far away for her to see his face clearly – but she could tell he was tall, young and of slim build.

As she entered the nave, she saw a man of the same stature, wearing a cassock, standing below the pulpit with an elderly woman. It had to be him. He was a handsome man, with fine patrician features, and long tapering fingers. The priest placed his hand on the woman's shoulder in a final gesture and she turned and walked away down the aisle past Hannah.

Before the priest could disappear into the sacristy, Hannah called out, 'Father, may I have a word with you, please?'

He stopped, a smile on his face. 'I hope it's quick. There's a nice Lancashire hot pot waiting for me at the presbytery. I'll be hearing confession at five o'clock if you need more time. I could get here early and see you then.'

Hannah was surprised at her own courage. 'No. You need to talk to me *now*. It won't wait. It's about you and my sister.'

A frown creased the priest's forehead. 'Your sister? Do I know her? Is she sick? Father O'Donnell is doing home visits this afternoon. I could—'

'She's not sick. She was here with you early this morning. Right there.' She pointed to the pew.

'Ah, I see.' He stretched his lips wide. 'Judith said you wouldn't be happy.'

'That's putting it mildly. I don't imagine your bishop and the other priests here would be happy about it either.'

'On the contrary. They'll be delighted. They'll do all they can to help.'

Before Hannah knew what possessed her, she had whipped her arm back and slapped his face. 'Keep your hands off her. Don't you know she and I have suffered enough disgrace in our family already?'

The priest put his hand up to his face but his expression was kind rather than angry. 'I realise you've probably had more than enough religion in your life, Mrs Kidd. It is Mrs Kidd isn't it? But the Catholic church holds very different beliefs from those of your late father. And if the church is bringing comfort to Judith, surely you won't begrudge her that?' He looked at her intently, still holding his hand against his cheek.

Hannah's veins ran cold as the realisation seeped into her brain that she'd got the wrong end of the stick. 'You mean? You and she? You're not...?' Her voice trailed away. She wanted to curl up in a tight ball.

The priest began to laugh. He had a big laugh, warm and generous. 'I suppose I should be flattered that you might think that, but I can assure you, as a priest, I have foresworn any romantic involvements.'

'So why...?'

'Why were we meeting at such an early hour?'

Hannah nodded, but she already knew the answer.

'Your sister is considering becoming a Catholic, Mrs

Kidd. With the full knowledge of the parish priest, I am giving her instruction.'

'Oh, Father, I'm so sorry. What must you think of me?' She clamped a hand over her mouth.

'I think only that you obviously care a great deal for your sister. But I promise you, there's nothing untoward happening between us. Judith started coming to early Mass here a few months ago. She used to sit at the back and watch. One day she waited behind and asked me to tell her what being received into the Church would involve.'

'I see.'

'It's not a quick process. We like prospective converts to enter into it with eyes wide open, understanding all the implications. And, in Judith's particular circumstances, it's especially important that she fully understands her own motives.'

'So, does she understand them?'

'I believe she does. We agreed that she will begin formal instruction next week. I asked her to make sure she tells you first and she agreed to do so.'

'She did?'

He nodded gravely.

'I am very surprised at this, Father...?'

'Father Edwards.'

'Judith has never shown any interest in religion. In fact, both she and I grew up seeing it only as a source of pain and violence. What our father did in the name of religion killed all possibility of faith on my part and I thought it was the same for Judith.'

He said nothing at first, just looked into her eyes, then said, 'All God's children are different. Judith wants to find and believe in a different kind of God from the one your father purported to follow. The God I worship is loving and merciful. And Judith takes great comfort from knowing that your mother is now safe with him and the Blessed Virgin Mary.'

Hannah swallowed. Was he going to try and convert her too? The church was suddenly claustrophobic. The smell of incense was cloying and caught the back of her throat, as it mingled with the heavy scent from the vases of flowers and the wax of burning votive candles.

'Give her time, Mrs Kidd. Let Judith find her own words to explain how she feels. And rest assured she will be safe coming here. We are a very welcoming parish.'

Desperate to get out of the church, Hannah forced a smile. 'Very well.' Then she added, 'I'm glad I was wrong about what was going on between you. I apologise for misconstruing your intentions.' She looked up at him, embarrassed. 'And for slapping your face. I hope it didn't hurt too much.'

He grinned. 'I'll survive. Think no more about it. And God bless you.'

When Hannah got back to The Laurels, all thoughts of the conversation she needed to have with Judith were abandoned when she went into the back parlour and found her husband sitting at the table with Nance.

Dropping her handbag on the floor, not stopping to take off her coat and hat, she barrelled across the room and into Will's arms. He lifted her up and kissed her hungrily.

Nance got up. 'I'll be off then. Leave you two love birds to get on with it.' She left the room but neither Will nor Hannah noticed her go.

'I had no idea you'd be back today. I was so worried. It's been so long. I've not been able to sleep. I was afraid something had happened to you, but I didn't want to let myself think about it. Oh, Will.'

He stroked her hair. 'Something did happen. We were torpedoed by a U-boat and lost the *Christina*. Two good men went down with her. The bastards kept firing, blasting the hell out of us. They didn't let up, even while we were abandoning ship. She went down about twenty minutes after.'

'Thank God you're alive!' She clung to him tightly.

'It was awful. Honestly, Hannah, I thought we were all going to cark it before we could get into the lifeboat.'

'When did it happen?'

'About a week ago. We were picked up by an Italian merchant ship off the Spanish coast.' He pulled away and grinned at her. 'But you're not going to believe this! Who was on that ship but my old pal, Paolo Tornabene.'

'He was?'

'And the best bit is when they dropped us off at Penzance, Paolo came with us. He's going to sail again with me and Captain Palmer. Turns out he was bashed and robbed somewhere in Egypt and missed the *Christina* sailing. He hadn't absconded.' He lifted Hannah up and twirled her around. 'The old team's reunited.'

Hannah's face had transformed. She looked at him with incredulity. 'You're not serious, Will? You're not going back to sea after what's happened?'

'Of course, I am. As soon as Palmer can organise another ship.'

Hannah was distraught. 'But you've had your ship sunk from under you and you survived. You've used up your luck. How can you expect to get away with it if it happens again? And what about the two poor men who died?'

He pulled her close to him and kissed the top of her head. 'It's my job, my darling. If ships like ours didn't sail, no one would have food to eat and the country would have no weapons to defend itself. We all need to do our bit.'

'But you don't, Will. You're an Australian. We could go to Australia. That was the original plan. It's time we went back to it.'

Will sat down at the table and pulled her onto his lap, where her head rested against his chest. 'Australia declared war when Britain did. I'd still have to serve if we went back there.'

'Yes, but it's further from the Atlantic. There aren't any U-boats around Australia.'

Will sighed. 'We've been through this, Hannah. Please, I don't want to argue with you on my first day back. There are far better things we could be doing right now.'

4

A GUEST AT THE LAURELS

That evening, when Judith came home, she was as delighted as Hannah to find Will safely returned. She flung herself upon her brother-in-law and hugged him. 'My favourite sailor, back in port! We've all missed you!'

As she watched her husband and her sister, Hannah remembered with a sinking heart that she still had to have that conversation with Judith. But it could wait until later. Right now, all she wanted to do was savour every moment of having Will home again and seeing Judith smiling.

Will interrupted her reverie. 'I hope you don't mind, I forgot to mention it earlier, Hannah, but I've invited Paolo Tornabene to join us tonight. Not to stay. Just for some tucker. There's always plenty. I hope Sam won't mind'

'You obviously haven't heard of rationing.' Nance pulled a face.

'Sam doesn't do the cooking, so he won't care,' said Hannah. 'And rationing won't affect anything we're having tonight. It's only a stew and I'll fling in a few more spuds to stretch it out.' She looked pointedly at Nance and added, 'If it wasn't for men like Will risking his life you wouldn't have any stew in the first place.'

Diplomatically, Will said, 'I don't think any of you have met Paolo? He's Italian, from Naples, and his English is pretty good. We sailed together before Hannah and I met.'

Hannah noticed her sister has pursed her lips at the mention of a guest. Judith was always wary of strangers. Ever since the trauma of their father's trial, she hated meeting new people – although evidently that didn't include Catholic priests.

'We'd better eat in the dining room as we're such a big crowd tonight,' said Nance. 'And since we're having company, I'm going to make a bit of an effort and put on some fresh slap.' She winked at Will. As usual, Nance did little or nothing to prepare the meals – her limit was toasting bread, brewing tea and boiling the odd egg.

Hannah looked at Judith. 'Do you mind setting the table, Jude?'

Judith opened her mouth as if to protest but checked herself. 'Of course.' Perhaps her new-found interest in religion was already affecting her behaviour.

Sam Henderson arrived home soon after six and was delighted to welcome Will back. He listened intently as Will described the fate of the *Christina.*

'After what you and your Italian friend have been through, you must invite him to stay the night here too. As long as he likes, in fact. We can make up a camp bed in the front parlour.'

Will grinned. 'Kind offer, mate, but Paolo's already fixed up down at the Sailors' Home. There's a couple of other lads off the ship there. Anyway, he wasn't on the *Christina* with us when she was sunk. It was his ship that picked us up.'

'Well, if you're sure. But any friend of yours, Will, is always welcome at The Laurels.'

'That's bonza, mate. Poor old Paolo hasn't had the easiest of times. His girl was forced by her family to marry some old fella and she threw herself off a clifftop.'

Sam whistled. 'Poor chap. When was this?'

'About a year or so ago. He doesn't talk about it now, but he was very cut up at the time.'

As he was speaking, the doorbell resonated through the house.

'Can you let Mr Tornabene in, Jude, while I get the stew out of the oven.'

Judith threw her a sour look, but complied. A few moments later she reappeared, with the Italian behind her. Her face was transformed by a radiant smile and she appeared unable to take her eyes off Paolo.

As Will began making the introductions, the door opened, and Nance swanned into the room. She was wearing a red velvet dress with a neckline that barely contained her ample cleavage. Cherry red lipstick had been freshly applied and she was wreathed in a cloud of cheap perfume. 'Aren't you going to introduce me to your handsome friend, Will?' she said, looking Paolo up and down and evidently liking what she saw.

'Careful you don't catch a chill in that dress, Nance.' Sam rarely missed an opportunity to spar with Nance. 'There's quite a nip in the air. You don't want to get a chesty cough.'

'I have very hot blood,' Nance said, breathily. 'Being an Eye-tie, I imagine you do too, Mr Torna... I think I'll call you Paolo if that's all right with you?'

The Italian grinned. '*Ma certo.* Of course, *Signorina.*'

'And you must call me Nance, sweetheart.' She fluttered her eyelashes.

Hannah wished Nance wouldn't make such a spectacle of herself. She must be at least forty and it wasn't dignified. But as she carried the pot of stew into the dining room, she noticed it wasn't only Nance who was evidently appreciating the presence of their guest. Judith was transfixed.

Paolo Tornabene was a good-looking man. There was no denying that. Not as tall as Will, he had glossy, jet black hair, light olive skin and large brown eyes. Hannah could see why her sister would be entranced. She tried not to be annoyed. Falling for a man might quash Judith's present leanings towards the Catholic faith, and Hannah would be relieved about that. But on the other hand, she had an uncomfortable feeling about Judith falling for the Italian. Yes, he seemed a decent enough fellow and he was a friend of Will's, which was recommendation enough, but the last thing Hannah would wish upon her sister was to end up in her own situation, with a husband at sea during wartime. And worse still, as the man was an Italian, there was always the possibility that if Italy entered the war, he would become the enemy. As she started to eat, she told herself she was being silly. It was probably a passing crush. After tonight they may not see Paolo for some time. And hadn't Will said that since his girlfriend had died, Paolo hadn't so much as looked at other women?

But as the evening continued, Hannah's concern grew. While Judith and Paolo barely spoke to each other – Nance dominating the conversation and flirting outrageously with the Italian – there was no mistaking the furtive glances between them. Each took any opportunity to look at the other and if their eyes met, they both looked away only to look back again at the earliest opportunity. She wondered if Will had noticed too.

The meal over, Sam suggested they move into the front

parlour. Hannah began to clear the table, but Judith stepped behind her and untied her apron. Giving her a little push towards Will, she said, 'You've done enough. Go sit with your husband. I'll do the dishes.' She started to gather the plates.

Nance, oblivious as usual to the concept of helping out, slipped her arm through Paolo's, ready to steer him into the parlour. The Italian politely but firmly removed it and smiling broadly at Nance, said, 'I'll join you all in a few minutes, *Signorina,* but first I am going to help the lady to carry the dishes to *la cucina.*'

At that moment, Hannah realised that any hope of the attraction not being mutual was a vain one. With a worried glance at her younger sister, she went out of the room with the others, leaving Paolo and Judith to get on with it.

Nance had a face like thunder when the four of them sat down.

Will gave a little shake of the head. 'Strewth! I never thought I'd see that.'

'See what?' Nance's voice was surly.

'A hot-blooded Italian man offering to help do the dishes.'

'He didn't.' Nance's tone was waspish. 'He just said he'd help her carry them into the kitchen.' She started to get up from her chair. 'I'd better go and help her.'

Sam stretched an arm out to bar her passage. 'If an Italian man offering to wash up is a rarity, then Nance Cunningham offering has to merit a few paragraphs in the *Echo.*'

Hannah and Will laughed, and Nance looked indignant.

'For heaven's sake, sit down and leave them alone, Nance.' Sam lifted his hands in a gesture of resignation. 'If it's any consolation, Nance, I share your pain. I can see the attraction. And I've always had a weakness for sailors.'

'Sam! Stop it.' Hannah frowned at him. While the whole household was aware of Sam's preference for men, it was not something they ever referred to. If he pursued liaisons, it was away from the house and handled with discretion. Sam had already experienced the perils of being found out – he had endured blackmail and as a homosexual, he risked losing his job with the local council and even prosecution.

Hannah held up a copy of the *Radio Times*. 'I was going to listen to this – it's on in a few minutes. But maybe you'd rather not, Will?' She pointed to the entry, a half-hour programme on the Home Service about life aboard a merchant navy vessel.

Will pulled her onto his knee. 'If you don't mind, darling, it would be a bit of a bus-man's holiday. But if Nance or Sam want to hear it?'

Vigorous shaking of heads.

'I'd rather enjoy being here on dry land with all of you. Why don't I put some music on the gramophone?'

This proposal met with approval and soon the parlour was filled with the sound of Artie Shaw and *Begin the Beguine*.

It was more than twenty minutes before Judith and Paolo joined them, Judith carrying a laden tea tray, and Paolo with a brown paper bag from which he produced some bottles of beer. The three men and Nance settled to play a game of whist, but it was apparent that Paolo had his mind on other things. Hannah couldn't fail to notice that there was something happening between him and her sister. While they said nothing, they seemed unable to take their eyes off each other.

The card game was abandoned when it was time for the nine o'clock news on the wireless.

Sam fiddled with the dials, tuning the set to find the Home Service.

A disembodied voice filled the room. 'Here is the News.'

They huddled around the wireless. Nance looked bored and annoyed, Judith distracted, Paolo's eyes remained fixed on Judith, while Sam, Hannah and Will listened intently.

As the broadcast progressed, it became clear that this was no ordinary day. They listened in silence, even Nance, as Neville Chamberlain's voice came over the airwaves.

'Early this morning, Hitler added another to the horrible crimes that have already disgraced his name by a sudden attack on Holland, Belgium and Luxembourg.'

There was a collective sigh.

'Didn't anyone hear this earlier?' Nance spoke and was immediately shushed by the assembled company.

Hannah listened as words filtered through her consciousness.

'...some new and drastic action to be taken,' continued the Prime Minister.

She reached for Will's hand, remembering what had been said to Chamberlain in the House of Commons a few days before, by Leopold Amery, echoing the words of Oliver Cromwell to the Long Parliament hundreds of years earlier. 'Go! In the name of God, go!'

Over the airwaves, Chamberlain went on to explain that he had tendered his resignation to the King and that His Majesty had accepted and 'entrusted my friend and colleague Mr Winston Churchill to form a coalition government.'

The six of them listened rapt as he spoke.

'I have borne a heavy load of anxiety and responsibility.'

Chamberlain's voice echoed through the wireless set, resonant and declamatory, with an undertone of regret and sadness. As he spoke of Hitler as 'this wild beast' who must be disarmed and overthrown, they looked at each other, each wondering why it had taken until now for their former prime minister to show some fighting spirit.

The party broke up soon after, with Paolo refusing Sam's offer to stay the night and sleep on a camp bed.

'*Grazie mille*, Sam, but I have paid for the room at the Sailors' Home and I have much to do tomorrow.'

'I'll walk you to the bus stop. You might not find it in the blackout.' Judith was on her feet already.

'Sam, will you go along too?' said Hannah. 'I don't want Judith coming back on her own in the blackout.'

Judith threw her sister a dirty look but said nothing as Sam went to get their coats.

Nance, her expression as sour as a lemon, went straight up to bed, calling a goodnight over her shoulder, evidently conceding defeat to Judith.

As the door shut behind Paolo, Judith and Sam, Will took Hannah in his arms and kissed her passionately. 'At last! Let's get to bed right now, Mrs Kidd.'

Hannah needed no encouragement and they went hand in hand upstairs to their bedroom.

5

NO JOB AND A NEW JOB

Will set off after breakfast for the docks to meet Captain Palmer and find out if he had any news for him. Sam was still sleeping and Nance announced that she was going with a friend to New Brighton.

As soon as they'd gone, Hannah tackled Judith. 'I met a friend of yours.' She tried to sound lighthearted.

Judith frowned, puzzled. 'A friend? Who?'

'Father Edwards.'

'He came to see you?' Judith's eyebrows shot up.

'No. I paid a call on him.' There was no way she could avoid confessing. Better to get it over with. 'Look, Judith, I was worried about you. We never used to have secrets from each other.'

'You did actually.'

'What? When?'

'You and Mother never told me about you and Will. I only found out about him after you'd married Sam.' Judith had a petulant expression. 'You were planning to run away with him, and you didn't even tell me.'

'Jude, you know Sam and I were never properly married. So, don't ever call it that. And the reason I didn't tell you about Will was that Mother and I didn't want to put you at risk with our father. And at that point we were planning for me to get away to Ireland so I wouldn't be forced into that sham wedding. If Father had found out about Will wanting to marry me, you know what he'd have done.'

'You mean you thought I'd tell him? You thought I'd blab?'

Hannah sighed. 'Please, Jude, I don't want to argue with you. But look what happened when I told you about Aunt Elizabeth. I asked you never to mention her to anyone.' She was referring to their mother's sister, who had been forced out of the family's former home by their father when Judith was a baby. Charles Dawson had overheard Judith asking her mother about Elizabeth and in a violent rage had launched his first physical attack on Hannah.

Unable to deny the truth of that, Judith lowered her eyes.

Hannah continued. 'Let's not rake up all that horrible stuff about our father. The last thing we want is to have him come between us now he's dead.'

Judith pursed her lips but nodded. 'How did you hear about Father Edwards?'

Hannah felt her face reddening. 'I'm ashamed of this part, but you need to know I did what I did out of concern for you.'

Judith stared at her, eyes narrowed. '*What* did you do?'

'I thought you were meeting someone secretly. Nance told me you'd been leaving the house early in the mornings. She thought you had a boyfriend. Naturally I was worried.'

'Naturally? Why shouldn't I have a boyfriend? You did.'

Hannah looked down, lacing her fingers together. 'I know. I'm sorry, but––'

'But nothing.'

'I thought if you were keeping it secret it must be someone unsuitable. So, I followed you yesterday morning. I'm not proud of what I did, but I was worried.'

'No, you weren't. You were snooping. It's despicable. You actually followed me. Like... like you were some cheap private detective. Horrible. I can't believe you did that.' Judith jumped up from the table.

'I'm sorry.' Hannah swallowed. She needed to get it all out. 'I saw you meeting Father Edwards in the church. I'm afraid I jumped to the wrong conclusion.'

'Go on.' Judith's eyes were now narrow slits and her fore-head was creased with a deep frown. She slid back into her chair.

'I thought... you and he were...'

Judith's mouth shot open. 'No! You didn't! How could you think that?'

'There's no easy way to tell you this, so I'm going to spit it out. I went back to the church later on and confronted him.'

Judith's hand clamped over her mouth, eyes wide.

Hannah dropped her head. 'I accused him...oh gosh... this is going to sound terrible. I slapped his face.'

To Hannah's amazement, Judith burst out laughing. 'Good grief! You didn't! Where did it happen?'

'In the church.'

'Did anyone see? What did he do?'

'Fortunately, the place was empty. He took it very well actually. He laughed when he realised I'd misconstrued things. He seems a very decent man.'

Judith, serious again, said, 'He is.'

'He told me why you'd been meeting. He said he'd asked you to tell me about it.'

'I was going to tell you this weekend. You managed to get

in first. And if you'd been a bit more trusting and less suspicious, you'd have saved us both a great deal of embarrassment.'

'Are you serious about wanting to become a Catholic? I have to say, Jude, it seems to me that you and I have had enough religion to last us a lifetime.'

'That rubbish Dawson spouted wasn't religion. Far from it.' Judith never referred to their father as such, always using his surname, as if to deny any familial connection. 'The Catholic Church is a great comfort to me. Would you deny me that comfort?'

'Of course not. But to be received into the Church as a Roman Catholic is quite a drastic step.'

'I knew you wouldn't understand.'

'I'm trying to.'

'All you need to know is that I am doing this after lots of careful thought. It's part of my life and I have no intention of stopping.'

'I wouldn't dream of trying to stop you.'

'Good. Are we done then?'

Hannah had intended to broach the subject of Paolo too but it would be throwing fuel on the fire. Besides, it might prove to be only a short-lived crush. Yet somehow, she doubted that. She recognised love at first sight when she saw it. Hadn't she experienced the same instant attraction when she'd first met Will?

As though reading her mind, Judith pre-empted her. 'In case you're tempted to interfere between me and Mr Tornabene, there's no point. I'm going to the pictures with him tonight and I don't give a fig what you might think about it.' Without waiting for a response, Judith flounced out of the room and Hannah heard a bedroom door slam a few moments later.

· · ·

CAPTAIN PALMER, an untouched pint by his side, was reading the newspaper when Will walked into the pub. Palmer jumped up and went to the bar to buy a beer for Will, who sensed something was troubling his former boss.

Palmer took a slug of beer, then lit his pipe.

Will studied his face, wondering what was about to come, anxious that if the Master had already assumed captaincy of another ship, he might be about to say there was no place for Will, for Paolo or for both.

'I had a long talk last night with my wife.' Palmer took another gulp from his tankard and Will saw the older man was actually nervous.

'To cut a long story short, Doris doesn't want me going back to sea. Yesterday, I was offered a job ashore, based in Plymouth. It's a liaison role between the Royal Navy and the merchant marine.' He looked around to ensure there was no one near enough to overhear, then with a lowered voice said, 'I can't give you details as it's classified.'

Will gaped. 'You're kidding me, sir. You're giving up the sea? To be stuck behind a desk?'

'Doris has taken what happened to us on the *Christina* badly. She suffers from her nerves and since the kids left home, she's been lonely and finds it hard to cope.' He avoided Will's eyes. 'She's got no other family. I'm due to retire in three years anyway, so it's a good opportunity for me.'

Will struggled to take it in. 'I can't imagine you doing a desk job.'

'You're not the only one.' Palmer shook his head. 'But Doris needs me. It means I'll be at home every night yet still involved with the war effort. It could turn out to be an important job. It's in Plymouth at first, but I'll be in a good position for a job back here in Liverpool.'

'I see.' But Will didn't see.

'I know you're probably thinking I'm taking the easy way out, but if it were my decision alone, I'd be sailing again as soon I found a new command.' Palmer puffed on his pipe. 'And while it may be a desk job, it's a vital role. I'll be in the thick of things.' He spoke as if trying to convince himself.

'Yes, sir. I'm sure that's true. There's no one who knows as much as you do about ships and crewing. And now you've first-hand experience of being on the wrong end of a few torpedoes.'

Palmer smiled ruefully. 'I'm sorry I won't be sailing with you and Tornabene and the others again.' He shook his head. 'Look, Kidd, you'll have no trouble finding another ship – in fact the Master of the *Shelbourne* is looking for a Second Officer. I've already put in a word for you.'

Will gave Palmer a mirthless smile. 'Thank you, sir. Appreciate that.' He had a sinking feeling that he knew what was coming next.

'He won't take Tornabene though.' Palmer gazed into his beer. 'It's doubtful anyone will. Sentiment against Italy is worsening and people are worried it's only a matter of time before they join forces with Hitler.'

'But didn't Britain reach an agreement with Mussolini? Less than a year ago. I remember reading about it.'

'Since when can we trust Mussolini? He and Hitler are as thick as thieves.' Palmer's voice was tense.

Will knew the captain was right. He remembered the night before the war when the *Christina* was in port in Naples and he'd happened upon a gathering of the Blackshirts in a piazza in the city. Even though Will couldn't understand the words on their banners nor those they were chanting, the encounter had chilled him. They were certainly not men of honour. No, they were cut from the same cloth as Hitler.

Yet Paolo loathed everything about the Fascists. It was deep-rooted – if he'd ever had a chance to get near him, Paolo would have killed Mussolini. It was a bitter irony that the very men his friend despised could now deprive Paolo of his livelihood and his future.

'But, sir, I persuaded Paolo to get off the ship that rescued us! He gave up his job. He hates the Fascists as much as any of us do. You know he's totally trustworthy.'

Palmer shrugged. 'I know all that. But there's nothing I can do about it. I'd have happily taken him on any ship of mine, but I know him of old. Others don't. No master is going to have an Italian national on his ship. It's harsh. But it's a fact.'

Will ground his teeth. Why hadn't Palmer thought of that before he'd agreed to Will persuading Paolo to jump ship?

Palmer got to his feet, clearly uncomfortable, and keen to end the conversation. He took a slip of paper out of his pocket. 'I've written down the name of the Master of the *Shelbourne*. Over at the Canada dock. I don't know when she's sailing, but if you're smart, you'll get over there fast. The Captain is expecting you.'

PALMER WAS as good as his word. Captain Ryan was delighted to meet Will and arrangements were made for him to sign on with the *Shelbourne*. Everything happened so much faster in wartime.

'Sorry to hear about your last vessel, Kidd,' Ryan said. 'Sounds as if that Nazi would have been happy sending you all to the bottom. Palmer told me they didn't even give you time to evacuate and you lost a couple of men.'

'It was bad, sir. The first few torpedoes were well off target and Captain Palmer did a great job taking evasive action, but, in the end, we were sitting ducks. It was as if their skipper was angry about missing the shot to begin with and was determined to blast the hell out of us. God knows how much ammunition he used up.'

'Thank goodness most of you made it. And causing the Hun to waste ammunition helps the war effort.' The older man's eyes narrowed. 'But why didn't you have an escort?'

'We were in convoy but struggled to keep up. The *Christina* couldn't get past six and half knots. Captain Palmer asked permission to go it alone and the commander agreed.'

Ryan chuckled and clapped Will on the back. 'When it comes down to it, most of us would rather trust to our own wits and knowledge than follow orders – especially if they're coming from some ex-public-schoolboy in naval uniform for the first time.' He gave a little snort then said disdainfully, 'Some of the RN officers care more about saluting than running a ship.'

'I won't argue with that, sir.'

'In wartime, needs must. Not our place to argue.' He gazed over the dock for a moment. Then, seemingly only now remembering why Will was there, he said, 'Better get yourself home and say goodbye to your wife. On board by tomorrow afternoon, eight bells. We sail tomorrow night.'

Will had a heavy heart as he left the Canada dock. It was less than twenty-four hours before he had to be on board. Hannah wasn't going to take it well.

· · ·

DELAYING the moment of truth with Hannah, Will went first to the Sailors' Home. Telling bad news to two of the people he cared for most was not going to be easy. He found Paolo in the large mess room, talking to one of their former colleagues from the *Christina*.

The Italian jumped up as soon as he saw Will. '*Ciao*, Will, there is something I must tell you.'

'Same here,' Will answered. 'But you first.'

'Last night, I ask your *cognata*, how you say it? – your sister of law?'

'*In*-law.'

'*Si*.' He shrugged and waved his hand in front of him in a sweeping gesture. '*La bella* Judith. I ask her to come with me tonight to see a picture *al cinema*. And she say me yes. I go now to meet her.'

'Good on ya, mate,' Will said, grinning broadly.

'Do you go back there now? We go together?'

Will nodded and they set off. As they walked, Will was grateful that Paolo was absorbed in eulogising Judith.

'It is the first time I like *una donna* since my Loretta die. I didn't think it would be possible. But I like her soon as I see her.'

'I'd never have guessed, mate.' Will winked at his friend.

Paolo punched him playfully. 'Now you tell me what *you* want to say.'

The moment of truth. 'I saw Captain Palmer today.'

The Italian turned to look at him. 'He has a ship? We are going to sea again? Already?'

'No, Palmer's decided to retire. From the sea anyway. He's taking a shore job. Down in Plymouth.'

'Noo! *Davvero*?'

'Yes. It's true.'

Will drew a deep breath. There was no easy way to break the news. 'He recommended me to another Master––.'

'*Fantastico!*'

Will grabbed Paolo's arm. 'Hold on, Paolo, this fella only wants to take me.'

'Then we must find another ship. We sail together, yes?'

Paolo's eyes were smiling. Will felt sick that he was going to have to let his friend down. Badly.

'Hell, Paolo, I only wish we could, but it seems no one's prepared to take on an Italian. They all reckon it's only a matter of time before Italy declares war.'

Paolo swore. '*Madonna! Noo...!*'

'Look, mate, I feel really bad. It's all my fault for persuading you to give up a perfectly good ticket with that Italian ship. I'm really sorry.'

Paolo frowned. 'Don't be sorry, my friend. I would not meet the lovely Judith if I had not come with you. And if that *figlio di puttana,* Mussolini, is going to make Italy be at war then I don't want to be on Italian ship when he do it.'

'But what will you do, Paolo?'

'Maybe I find another master who is like *il Capitano* Palmer and happy to use an Italian who works hard. Or maybe I get other work. If Italy comes into the war they will need perhaps translators here in *Inghliterra*? Someone who is knowing all the words used on ships.'

'You could be right, mate.' Although Will doubted it, he was relieved that Paolo was taking the news so phlegmatically. 'At least Judith will be happy she's not going to have to say goodbye to you right after she's met you.'

'You think she likes me?' Paolo's voice was eager.

'Nah, mate. That daft lovelorn expression on her face was for someone else.' He clapped an arm around Paolo's shoulder.

'Really?'

'Really.'

'So, what is this ship *il Capitano* has suggested for you?'

'It's called the *Shelbourne*. Doing the Atlantic runs.'

'Have you signed the papers?'

Will stretched his mouth into a silent affirmative. 'That's the good news. The bad news is we sail tomorrow night. I have to break it to Hannah. She spent half the night nagging me about how she wants me to give up the sea.'

'Then why don't you? We can both find other work.'

'Half the Poms make out they can't understand the Australian accent, but somehow I don't think they're going to be recruiting Aussie translators any time soon.'

6

LETTER FROM AUSTRALIA

H annah sat in the back parlour, wondering what she could do to restore the peace with her sister. In the light of her own behaviour in following Judith and confronting Father Edwards, the onus was on her to make concessions. She went upstairs and knocked on Judith's bedroom door.

Inside, she found Judith sitting on the bed, her head in her hands.

'Whatever's the matter, Jude?' Hannah went to sit beside her sister, putting a protective arm around her.

'Nance says all my clothes are old-fashioned and Paolo won't fancy me. She thinks he only asked me to go the pictures as I threw myself at him.'

'For goodness sake, Jude! You daft ha'peth! The poor chap is completely potty about you. It's as plain as the nose on my face.'

Hannah suppressed her own misgivings about Paolo in the face of Nance's thoughtless cruelty. She squeezed her younger sister's hand. 'Nance Cunningham is consumed with jealousy. That's the top and bottom of it. She'd give her eye teeth to be going out with Mr Tornabene. In fact, she'd give her eye-teeth to be you, clothes and all. No amount of finery and plastering her face with makeup is going to convince anyone she's anything but an old trout.'

Judith giggled, then laid her head on her older sister's shoulder.

Hannah took her sister's hand, relieved to see Judith smiling after all the months of misery. 'Now let's have a look at what you can wear.' She moved to the wardrobe and took out a navy-blue dress. 'It's a bit severe but you could sew a pretty collar on. That would transform it.'

'You're right!' Judith bounced to her feet and went towards the wicker basket where she kept all her fabric scraps and sewing materials. 'I have the very thing here. I've been saving it for ages.' She brandished a piece of white broderie anglaise. 'Enough to make a Peter Pan collar. It will be perfect.' She flung her arms around Hannah. 'Thank you, Han!'

A surge of relief swept through Hannah. 'I'm happy you're happy. Now get a move on. You need to get it finished before your gentleman friend arrives.'

JUDITH WAS CLEARLY EXPERIENCING a mixture of excitement and acute nervousness as she waited for Paolo Tornabene to arrive at The Laurels for their trip to the pictures. She sat in the kitchen, watching while Hannah made a cheese-and-onion pie.

'Are you sure this dress doesn't look drab?' she asked. 'I've done my best with it, but Nance says I look like a waitress.'

Hannah closed her eyes and took a deep breath. Sometimes she'd like to give Nance Cunningham a good slap. The woman was tactless and unconsciously cruel.

'I've already told you, Judith, the frock looks perfect. You've completely transformed it with that pretty collar. Take no notice of Nance. She's jealous. She practically threw herself at Mr Tornabene and she's annoyed that he only had eyes for you.'

'You think he did? Really?'

'Really.' Hannah turned from rolling out the pastry and smiled at her younger sister. 'He's keen as mustard.'

'And you don't think the white collar makes me look like a waitress?'

'No. The collar is nothing like a waitress would wear. In fact, I'd say you look more like a film star.'

'Don't tease me.' Judith's expression was anguished.

'I wouldn't dream of teasing you.' Hannah wiped her hands on her apron and turned to look properly at Judith. 'Turn around. Let me check your seams are straight.'

Judith did a twirl and presented the backs of her legs for Hannah's inspection.

'Yes. All shipshape. As pretty as a picture. Your hair is lovely too. That style really suits you, swept back from your forehead.'

'Nance did it.'

'She's not all bad then?' Hannah was about to say something else, when they heard the sound of the front door opening and closing. Judith quickly moved over to sit at the table, and Hannah noticed she was breathing deeply to calm herself.

The door to the kitchen opened and Will put his head around. 'Is this reserved for ladies only, or can a fella get a cup of tea?'

He stepped into the room and the women saw Paolo

waiting in the doorway behind him. Will signalled to his friend to come into the kitchen. 'I ran into this fella on the way here. He seems to think a certain young lady has agreed to accompany him to the local picture house. I told him he had to be mistaken. My sister-in-law's taste is far too good.'

Paolo was twisting his knitted cap in his hand. He looked at Judith who grinned up at him.

'I'm pleased to say it's you who's mistaken, dear brother-in-law,' Judith said, her face radiant and her eyes locked on Paolo's. 'I'm very much looking forward to going to the pictures with Mr Tornabene.'

Paolo grinned back and then there was an awkward silence.

Will kissed Hannah, then turned to the others and asked, 'What film are you going to see?'

Paolo looked aghast. '*Mannaggia!* I forgetted to look.'

'*Return to Yesterday* is playing at the Carlton, down the road.' Hannah put the kettle on the hob and lit the gas under it. 'A famous Hollywood actor takes on a role in an end-of-the pier show in a seaside town and falls in love with the leading lady. Nance saw it the other day.'

'*Perfetto!*'

A long awkward silence followed. Tornabene and Judith couldn't take their eyes off each other.

Hannah exchanged glances with Will, then said, 'Why don't you take Mr Tornabene through to the parlour, Judith? The fire's lit and I'll bring you a cup of tea in a minute. You've plenty of time before the picture starts.'

Judith threw her a look of gratitude and the couple slipped out of the room.

Putting the finishing touches to the cheese pie, Hannah covered it with a cloth and turned back to preparing the pot of tea. 'How did you get on with Captain Palmer?'

A frown darkened Will's brow and he studied the surface of the deal table. 'He's decided to retire.'

'What? You didn't see that coming, did you?'

'It's a sudden decision. He's been offered a shore job. Says he's only taking it because of his wife. Apparently, she suffers with her nerves and gets distressed when he's away at sea.'

'I know how that feels.' Hannah's voice had a bitter edge. She pulled out a chair and sat down at the table, then, as the kettle began whistling, jumped up. 'I'll take those two their tea, then we can talk properly.'

She hurried about, setting the tray, then took it through to the waiting couple. When she returned, she sat down and reached for her husband's hand. 'What does this mean for you?'

Will rolled his hand around hers. 'Me? I'm fine. The master's recommended me to the skipper of another ship – a pal of his. It's Paolo who's been left high and dry. Palmer is adamant no ship will take Paolo on.'

Will's other hand formed a fist and Hannah could sense how angry he was.

'I feel I've let him down.' He let out a long sigh.

'How? Surely it's not your fault – he looked happy enough just now.'

'Paolo's the most decent man I've ever met. He ought to blame me for talking him into getting off that Italian ship, but he says he doesn't.'

'He knows you were trying to help him. But I don't understand why he can't get another ship. You're always saying the merchant navy is desperate for sailors.'

'No one wants to sign articles with an Italian. Everyone reckons it's only a matter of time before they enter the war on Hitler's side.'

'And you think he'll want to return to Italy to fight for them?'

Will gasped. 'Hell, no, Hannah! He hates Mussolini more than I do. He blames the Fascists for the death of his girl and despises everything they stand for.'

'What's the problem then?' She stroked the back of his hand soothingly.

'Every Italian is under suspicion. Palmer says no one will take the risk of having a potential fifth columnist on board their ship. Only someone who knows him personally would chance it.'

'That's daft.' Hannah gave a little snort of disbelief. 'What possible harm could he do on board a ship? He's hardly going to scupper it and drown himself in the process!'

'He could pass information to the enemy. On ship movements, planned routes, number and nature of ships in the convoy. That sort of thing.'

'Paolo? I barely know the man, but he strikes me as a most unlikely spy.'

'Of course, he isn't a spy.' Will's voice was uncharacteristically irritable, and Hannah drew her hand away. 'Sorry, my love, I didn't mean to snap at you. Only I don't know what work he'll be able to find, and I feel responsible.'

'He blames you?'

'No. And that makes me feel worse. To be honest, he's got his head in the clouds over your sister, so he's not even thinking about the practicalities of his employment.'

'You think he's serious about Jude? They only met last night.'

Will gave her a meaningful look. 'Sometimes you know in an instant.' He smiled at her and took her hand back and sandwiched it between both of his.

'I'm sure he'll find something else.' She locked her eyes onto his. 'And if neither your Captain Palmer nor Mr Tornabene are going back to sea, maybe it's time you took a leaf out of their book and made that decision too.' Clutching his hand tightly, she wove her fingers between his. 'You've nothing to feel bad about. You've done your bit. You could have lost your life when the *Christina* went down. Please, Will, find something here in Liverpool. Or we could go to Australia. That was always our plan. Why don't we do it?'

Will's mouth stretched into a tight line. 'I've already signed articles for another ship. The *Sherbourne*. On the Atlantic runs. Captain Ryan took me on at Palmer's recommendation.'

Hannah snatched her hands away, pushed back her chair and got up from the table, moving over to the range where she lit the oven. 'You've already signed? Without discussing it with me. When do you leave?' Her voice was quiet as she struggled to control her emotions and contain her anger.

'I have to be on board tomorrow afternoon. We sail the following day.'

She slammed the oven door closed and took off her apron, flinging it down on the table where Will was still sitting. She'd never expected it to be so soon.

'And when exactly were you going to tell me? Instead of all that blathering on about your friend.'

Will lowered his head. 'I'm sorry. I was trying to find the best way to break the news.'

'The only news I'm interested in hearing is about you leaving the navy.'

'We've been through this so many times before, Hannah. How can I leave when the country needs me? No one, including everyone in this house, would have any food on the table if we all downed tools and walked away from the ships. The factories would have no raw materials to make armaments. Everything depends on getting cargo across the Atlantic. You know that, my love.'

'Don't you "my love" me! You know I'd rather go hungry than have you risking your life crossing that ocean. How many ships have to be blown to smithereens before you understand that? Besides, it's only a matter of time until the Germans invade. They've pushed us out of Norway and they're already invading Holland and France. If they succeed, what hope do we have?' She was pacing up and down opposite him.

'You don't mean that, Hannah. Unless men like me carry on, then yes, you're right, this country will fall. But as long as we do carry on, we have a fighting chance of winning the war. Listen to Mr Churchill.'

'Mr Churchill be damned!' Her rage spilled over into tears and Will got up and gathered her into his arms.

Tornabene and Judith must have heard the raised voices as, instead of returning to the kitchen to say goodbye, the rattle of the front door signalled their departure.

Will stroked her hair. 'Please don't take it so hard, Hannah. What kind of man would I be if I wasn't prepared to do the right thing for King and country?'

Her voice was a whimper now. 'But you're an Australian. This isn't your country.'

'He's still my king and Australia's part of the empire, and England is your country and I now consider it my home.' Will took a handkerchief out of his pocket and began to dry her tears. 'You knew I intended to go back to sea as soon as I found another ship.'

Hannah sniffed. 'I didn't think it would be so soon. And I didn't think it would be without Palmer and your friend. If they can leave, why can't you? And if the navy's so desperate to find crew, why don't they keep Mr Tornabene on? If they can dispense with him, they could jolly well manage without you.'

Will sat down, drawing Hannah onto his lap, where she laid her head against his chest, her stomach hollow and her head pounding.

'We only have one night together,' she said at last, her eyes welling up again.

He smiled down at her. 'So, we'd better make the most of it. Don't let's waste time quarrelling. We have the house to ourselves. Come on.' He moved her off his lap and taking her hand, led her out of the room towards the staircase.

Two hours later the front door clattered open and Hannah heard footsteps in the hall. She glanced at Will's wristwatch lying on the nightstand, detached herself from her husband's arms and sat bolt upright. 'Goodness, it's already seven o'clock. That'll be them back and I haven't put the pie in the oven.'

'Who cares? They can feed themselves.'

'Don't be mean! And I don't know about you, but I could eat a house now. I'm absolutely starving.' She swung her legs over the side of the bed, dodging his outstretched hand as he reached out to keep her there. 'And I'd be jolly surprised if you're not ravenously hungry too.'

'Hungry for you.' He smiled up at her. 'You're a hard woman, Hannah Kidd. But I don't know what I did to get lucky enough to find you.'

She bent down and kissed him slowly. 'Nor I you.' Unable to stop herself, she added, 'Which is why, now I've got you, I want to hang onto you.' Flinging his trousers and shirt onto the bed, she clapped her hands and said, 'Come on. Chop-chop! We need to go and eat.'

'Chop-chop? You sound like a sailor.'

'Maybe that's what I should do – sign articles and sail off with you. It's the only way I'd ever get to see you. And, if anything bad happened, at least we'd be together.'

He pulled on his trousers. 'Nothing bad's going to happen. And much as it would be bonza to have you in my cabin every night, I don't think the life aboard would suit you, my dearest girl.'

Downstairs, Judith was at the kitchen sink washing the teacups, while Paolo stood beside her drying them. Judith turned when Hannah came into the room. 'I've put the pie in the oven.' She gave a knowing look to her sister. 'Looks like you were otherwise engaged.' Nudging Hannah, she whispered. 'Half your blouse is undone.'

Hoping their guest hadn't heard, Hannah swiftly did up her buttons and began to set the table. Addressing Paolo, she said, 'Just the four of us tonight. Nance is having her tea with her friend in New Brighton and we rarely see Sam at the weekends.'

Will came into the kitchen, his hair tousled and in need of a comb. 'How was the film?'

Judith and Paolo exchanged glances, each appearing to hope the other would answer. Eventually, Paolo said, '*Molto bello.*'

'What was it about?' Will persisted, a wicked grin on his face.

'Oh... about a man...' Judith looked at Paolo.

'*Si, si. Anche una donna,*' Paolo added.

'That sounds interesting. Both a man and a woman. You don't often get films with men and women in.' Will sat down at the table. 'Most unusual. And what did this man and this woman do? What was their story?'

Hannah gave him a playful flick with a tea towel. 'Don't tease them,' she said, sitting down beside her husband.

Paolo looked sheepish. 'To say you the truth, we did not see much of the picture.'

Determined not to give up his taunting, Will said, 'Really? Did you get there late? Or did you leave early?' He laughed. 'Or did you manage to secure the back row?'

'Leave them alone, Will. Who are you to tease others about snatching a few kisses while they can?'

WHEN THE MEAL WAS OVER, they retired to the parlour, where Will got the fire going. As they settled down to enjoy a game of cards, he jumped up. 'I'd forgotten. I have a surprise. Hang on a minute.' He went out to the hall, where he'd hung up his donkey jacket, returning with an envelope.

Three pairs of curious eyes fixed on him.

'This concerns you as well as Hannah,' he said to Judith. 'It's from a lady I knew years ago in Australia. Miss Verity Radley is the schoolteacher back home in MacDonald Falls. She virtually brought up my sister after our mum died, and she was your Aunt Elizabeth's best friend.'

Judith frowned, clearly unsure whether she should welcome this news or not.

Will reached for Hannah's hand. 'Remember I told you I'd written to her before we got married?'

'She took her time to reply!'

'The letter went to the Sailors' Home. I only found it when I called in to meet Paolo. All I said in my letter to her was that we were about to be married. I reckoned it wouldn't be right for her to hear about your mother's death before Lizbeth did.'

Paolo was looking bewildered. Hannah leaned forward and explained. 'Perhaps Will hasn't told you, but my aunt was Will's stepmother. She went to live in Australia where she married Will's late father.'

'*Grazie*. He tell me but I forget.'

Will brandished the letter. 'Miss Radley says Lizbeth is very much alive and is now married to my old cobber, Michael Winterbourne. Can you believe it?'

Hannah, impatient, asked for the letter. She unfolded it and began to read aloud.

MY DEAR WILLIAM,

You cannot imagine how much joy it was receiving your letter. I have thought of you so often and also of your poor, dear departed father and sister, God rest their souls.

For you to be married – and to the niece of my beloved friend, Elizabeth, is cause for more celebration. When I read your letter, I thought I would faint with happiness. I have always included you in my prayers and worried that something might have happened to you. Elizabeth told me it was your intent to become a sailor and when so many years passed without a word, I presumed you had left Australia for good – or worse – had perished at sea.

It is many years since our dear Elizabeth left MacDonald Falls. She moved to Sydney with her little boy, Harry, and I continued to see her every few months. Then two years ago, a miracle of God brought our friend Mr Winterbourne to Sydney and they renewed their acquaintance—'

. . .

WILL INTERRUPTED. 'RENEWED THEIR ACQUAINTANCE,' he repeated scornfully. 'Miss Radley obviously hadn't a clue that Elizabeth and Michael fell in love twenty years ago on the voyage out to Australia – only my old man stepped in and kept them apart.'

'Never mind all that, Will. Let me finish.' Hannah continued to read out the letter.

To my surprise and delight they decided to marry and now live on Mr Winterbourne's sheep station in the north of New South Wales. Alas, the distance means we are rarely able to meet. They invited me to spend Christmas with them, but I find the heat at that time of year wearisome and prefer not to travel during our summer. I hope instead to visit during the winter some time. I intend to forward your letter to Elizabeth so she can reply if she sees fit – which of course I sincerely trust she will. Forgive me for this course of action, which I feel is the appropriate one, in case Mrs Winterbourne should decide to draw a line under her past.

Meanwhile, please convey my kindest and warmest wishes to your wife. I hope and pray that one day I might have a chance to meet her and to see your lovely face again, dear William.

Your faithful friend

Verity Radley (Miss).

P.S. I am so proud of your attainments in the navy. An officer! Both your mother and father, God rest their souls, would be exceedingly proud of you too.

'I DON'T GET IT.' Judith was still looking puzzled. Why would Aunt Elizabeth want to draw a line under her past? Does she know about Dawson?'

Hannah glanced at Will, wishing now she hadn't read it aloud.

'I said nothing about what happened with your father and mother,' Will said. 'It's only right that you two are the ones who break the news to your aunt of her sister's death.'

'So, what does she mean then?'

Hannah looked at Will and whispered, 'You first.'

'Your aunt was married to my father and Dad was hanged for killing my brother.'

Judith gasped. 'You never told me.' She glared at Hannah.

'It wasn't my place to tell. I'm sure Will would have told you in the end.'

'So, we both had fathers who were convicted murderers?' Judith's expression was cold, and she looked at Will accusingly then, turning to Paolo, said, 'You must be feeling left out, Paolo. Or did your father swing for murder too?'

Paolo said nothing, staring down at his shoes.

Will spoke again. 'My elder brother was bad to the bone. He was the cause of my mum dying when I was twelve. He bashed her when she was expecting a baby. He was gone for about nine years then turned up out of the blue and attacked Lizbeth. I tried to stop him, so he stabbed me, and I nearly carked it. If Dad hadn't turned up in the nick of time and shot him, Lizbeth and I would both be dead. So no, Dad wasn't a murderer. Unfortunately, the court didn't see it that way.'

'I'm sorry, Will.' Judith looked sheepish. 'So? Hannah? What else?'

Hannah swallowed. She'd been dreading this moment but couldn't put it off anymore. Secrets were like poison. If she left this one any longer, when Judith eventually discovered the truth, she'd never forgive her for withholding it.

'Maybe another time, Jude.' She took a gulp of air.

'No. I'm fed up with you hiding things from me and thinking you know best. If you and Will know something else I have a right to hear about it *now*.'

Hannah reached for her husband's hand and Will squeezed hers to offer reassurance. No more secrets. Painful as it was, Judith needed to know the extent of their father's evil.

'Our father attacked Aunt Elizabeth. More than attacked her...he forced himself on her. Then he and Mother threw her out of the house. That's why she had to go to Australia and her name was never mentioned. It's why Father was so angry when you asked Mother about her. Mother blamed Aunt Lizzie at first, believing she was trying to steal her husband. But in the end, she told Will and me the truth.' Her voice faltered.

Judith's expression was closed. Hannah couldn't read her reaction at all.

Will picked up the tale. 'Your aunt had two children while she was married to my father. Both died as infants with diphtheria. Your mum believed the first child, a boy called Mikey, was not my father's son, but your father's.'

Judith spluttered in outrage and got to her feet, moving to stand in front of the fireplace. 'That's disgusting.'

Will's face was grim and he glanced at Hannah who nodded.

'When Lizbeth married my dad,' she was already expecting a child,' he said. 'I put two-and-two together and worked out she must have already been pregnant by the time she arrived in Australia.'

'But you said that she fell in love with your friend, Michael what's-his-name, on the voyage out. How do you know it wasn't *his* child?' Judith folded her arms protectively over her chest. 'And you said she called her child Mikey. That must mean the baby was your friend's.'

Will nodded. 'Yes, I suppose it could have been Michael's. He glanced at Hannah. 'But it seems to me, it's a question only your aunt herself can answer.'

'Why didn't you tell me all this?' Judith turned to Hannah in anguish. 'You always treat me like a baby.' Then to Paolo, tears brimming, 'What kind of a family must you think this is? Why are you still sitting there? You should go! Get away while you can.'

She ran out of the room and they heard the door to the kitchen slam shut behind her.

Hannah got up and was about to follow her, but Paolo put his hand out. 'Please. I go. *Posso?*'

Will nodded. 'Let him deal with it, Hannah. He's not the one who's been keeping her in the dark. You and I are.'

When Paolo had gone, Hannah said, 'I should have told her before now, shouldn't I?'

Will shrugged. 'I know why you didn't. She's been through enough pain with what happened with your father. You were trying to protect her from more. And since she was too young to remember Lizbeth, what was the point of raising all this when we didn't think we'd find her again?' He put his arm around Hannah. 'It's my fault, love. I handled it badly. I didn't think it through properly. I should have told you when we were alone and left it up to you to choose the right moment to tell Judith. I'm sorry I've caused trouble for you.'

Hannah got up and cleared away the card table. 'I don't think we'll be playing cards tonight.' She took Will's hand and led him to the sofa. 'And no need to apologise. Judith needs time to get used to it. She's angry at me. Her opinion of our father couldn't get any lower than it already was. I think she's embarrassed about Paolo hearing all that and worried it might put him off her.'

Will shook his head slowly. 'I don't think anything's going to do that. He's well and truly smitten.'

'I think you're right.' She drew his head down to kiss him. 'Anyway, I won't let anything spoil our last night together. And that letter was the best news I've heard since the war started.' She rested her head against his chest. 'I'm so happy that Aunt Lizzie is alive and well. I wonder if we'll ever get to see her again.'

Then she stiffened. 'Give me the envelope, Will.'

When he handed it over, she slumped into a chair. 'The postmark is months ago. That means Aunt Elizabeth doesn't want anything to do with us.' She looked up at him, anguished. 'Otherwise, she'd have written by now.'

Before Will could say anything, the door opened, and Judith and Paolo came in. Judith's face had transformed into a beatific smile.

Paolo spoke. 'Judith say me she never go to a pub before.' He jerked his head at Will. 'Why don't we take *le belle donne* to have a drink?'

Surprised, Hannah looked at Will, who nodded, and said, 'Top idea, mate. I've a thirst like a kangaroo in a bush-fire. Get your coats on, girls. Drinks are on me.' He squeezed Hannah's hand and said, his voice low, 'We'll talk about it over a drink.'

7

THE WINDSOR CASTLE

T he Windsor Castle

THE FOUR WALKED down the hill to the public house, *The Windsor Castle*, arms linked and Will and Paolo each with a blackout torch. Neither sister had ever been inside a pub and both were curious but nervous.

A large red brick Victorian building with a turret, it sat on the corner of Walton Vale. The lobby opened onto a pair of doors with etched glass panels. Will pushed open the swing door into the saloon.

The room was packed. To Hannah's relief there were several women present and most of them looked respectable. They found a table towards the back, away from the crowds gathered around the piano where a middle-aged woman, with hair cut short and tight over her skull like a bathing cap, was seated on the piano stool. She was wearing a purple twin-set that was too tight to accommodate her ample bosom. In response to a shouted request, the woman began pounding the keys as everyone sang along to *Kiss Me Goodnight Sergeant Major.*

The place smelled of beer and the fug of cigarette smoke, but Hannah didn't find it unpleasant. Behind the heavy blackout curtains, it was warm and brightly lit, a cheerful haven after the dark, empty streets.

The two men drank pints of bitter. The sisters were unused to drinking alcohol, so Judith played safe with a lemonade and Hannah agreed to try a small sherry. The sweet stickiness of the drink was warming and the kick from the alcohol helped her relax.

Hannah looked about the room. There was a large central bar which also served the public bar on the other side. There were a few soldiers in uniform in the other bar, enjoying their beers. Hannah craned her neck and saw it was full of men – mostly talking, a large group playing cards, and another clustered around a dart board. On the saloon side several couples were sitting at small tables – the younger ones flirting and talking, while some of the older ones sat side-by-side, staring into the middle-distance, the possibilities of conversation evidently exhausted long ago. But the biggest crowd was gathered around the piano enjoying the sing-song.

'Will tells me you won't be joining him on his new ship, Mr Tornabene,' Hannah said, wondering whether perhaps this was tactless. 'Do you have plans?'

She intercepted Paolo exchanging a glance with Judith.

'Please, *chiamami, Paolo.* May I call you Hannah too?' He pronounced her name without the H so it sounded like An-na and addressed the request more to Will rather to her.

Will said, 'No need to ask permission, mate, we Aussies don't do formalities. If Hannah's happy, I'm happy.'

Hannah smiled. 'Any friend of Will's is my friend too, Paolo.'

'Tomorrow I look for work and then for a place to stay,' said Paolo. 'Without a ship I cannot stay at the Sailors' Home.'

'What kind of work do you hope to find, Paolo? On the docks?' Hannah glanced at Will, hoping he might have something to say and wishing she had never broached the subject.

'I do anything. *Non m'importa.*'

'It's a pity you haven't been able to find another ship. Will you keep trying?'

'No. Not to sea again. *Finito.* No more.' He swung his hands in a gesture of finality.

Hannah took another sip of sherry and decided to let the matter drop.

Judith spoke then. 'Paolo isn't *ever* going back to sea. If they don't think he's good enough to serve on a British ship, then they don't deserve him.' She locked eyes with her new boyfriend and slipped her arm through his.

It seemed that her sister and the Italian already considered themselves a couple. Surely, things were moving too fast. Relieved that Judith wouldn't face the anguish with Paolo she herself faced while Will was at sea, Hannah was nonetheless anxious about her sister falling too quickly for a man who could end up on the wrong side in this war. A man with no immediate prospects. Hadn't Will said it could prove difficult to find *anyone* willing to employ an Italian?

She fiddled with the stem of her glass but said nothing more. She wanted to raise the subject of her aunt with Will and Judith and why, evidently, Elizabeth didn't want to have anything to do with them. But Will was so quiet. It was their last night together and he seemed almost morose. Was he anxious about his forthcoming voyage?

The music came to a halt with a flourish of keys and resounding applause. The pianist rose from her stool. 'That's me done! There's a port and lemon with my name on it.'

The crowd groaned in disappointment and made their way back to their seats.

At least now they wouldn't need to shout in order to hear each other.

'We need to talk about the letter from Miss Radley.' Hannah looked across the table at Judith and was relieved when her sister nodded her agreement.

Will downed the rest of his pint. 'In that case we need another round of drinks.' He got up to head for the bar again, but Paolo jumped up and protested that it was his turn.

'No, mate, I told you the drinks are on me tonight. You can do the honours once you've got some work.'

Paolo, affronted, started to argue, but they were interrupted by the arrival of someone at their table.

'Judith – and Mrs Kidd. I haven't seen you in here before.' It was the Catholic priest.

Mortified, Hannah felt the blood rush to her face.

'Father Edwards!' Judith was beaming. 'What a surprise. This is Will Kidd, my sister's husband and this is Paolo Tornabene, our friend.'

Will and Paolo shook hands with the priest and Will offered to buy him a drink. Father Edwards glanced into his glass which was almost empty, slugged the dregs down and handed it to Will. 'That's extremely kind of you, Will. Singing's thirsty work.'

Hannah wondered how she'd failed to notice him

among those gathered around the piano. Drinking beer and joining pub singalongs – Catholic priests did not behave as she'd expected.

Paolo fetched another chair and the priest sat down between Will and Judith.

'I must admit, Father, I didn't expect to find a priest in a public house.'

'Ah, once in a while, Mrs Kidd. It's often the best way to get to know my parishioners – especially those who don't often cross the threshold of the church.' He grinned. 'It's not unusual to find one of us priests in here. Just because we're men of God doesn't mean we don't enjoy the occasional pint, especially when we maintain to each other that it's all part of doing God's mission.'

When the priest smiled, he had an air of mischief about him. It was impossible not to be drawn to him. No wonder he had impressed Judith so much. He probably charmed people into joining his church.

'This is the first time either Judith or I have been in a pub.'

'And what do you think?'

'I rather like it.'

The priest gave her a thumbs-up sign then turned to address her sister. 'Will I be seeing you at Mass tomorrow, Judith? Maybe Mrs Kidd would like to join you?'

Judith looked at Hannah, then said, 'I'll be there.' She turned to Paolo. 'And Paolo will be coming with me. He's from Italy so he's a Catholic.'

'You'll be most welcome, Paolo. We have quite a few Italians in the parish. Where do you live?'

'In the Sailors' Home, but I leave the merchant navy and must find a job and somewhere else to stay.'

Judith fixed her eyes on Father Edward. 'Maybe you

know of someone who might be able to help Paolo find work around here?' She took the Italian's hand. 'He'll do anything, won't you, Paolo?'

'I'll certainly have a word and see if anyone can help.'

Will returned with the drinks and joined them at the table.

Father Edwards took his pint of beer and said, 'I've just learnt your friend is leaving the navy, Mr Kidd.'

'I wish he weren't. I've sailed with him for years and was looking forward to doing so again. This bloody war!' Remembering he was talking to a priest, he added an apology for his language.

The priest flicked his hand dismissively. 'I've heard far worse in my time.' He turned to look at Paolo. 'Is it because you're Italian? I'd heard they're getting very twitchy about the possibility of Italy joining the war.'

Paolo nodded. '*Si*. No ship will take me now. The government say no more Italians.'

The priest shook his head. 'A pity. Not all men align themselves with their country's leaders. I take it you have no truck with the Fascists?'

'No, never. *Sono tutti figli di puttane.*' He spat the words out angrily then raised his hands and looked first at Judith and then at the priest. 'I am sorry to say bad words, but I hate Mussolini and his men.'

Father Edward nodded benignly. 'I heard nothing, Paolo. Even though ecclesiastical Latin is close to Italian.' He winked at Paolo, who grinned.

They chatted on until Hannah began to feel impatient. She wanted to talk to Judith and Will about Aunt Elizabeth and what they should do. As much as she liked the priest and Paolo Tornabene, there was still a part of her that was uneasy about Judith falling under the influence of these two men who had so recently come into her life.

Eventually, Father Edwards pushed his chair back. 'If you'll all excuse me, it's time I had a word with some of the members of my flock in the other bar.' As he got up, he put a hand on Paolo's shoulder. 'I've spotted a man in the public bar who may be able to help you, Paolo. I'll have a word with him and be back in a moment.'

He moved away to the door to the lobby and disappeared.

As soon as he'd gone, Hannah said, 'About Aunt Lizzie. Do you think we should write to her?' She twirled a cardboard beer mat between her fingers as she waited for her sister's reaction.

'Look, it's up to you. Do what you think is right, Hannah. I don't even know her. I was a baby when she left, and she means absolutely nothing to me.' Judith looked over at Will. 'You know the woman best, Will. You're the best judge of what Hannah should do. It's all the same to me. As far as I'm concerned, she may have been our mother's sister, but she's a stranger who lives on the other side of the world. We'll probably never get to meet her, so frankly, I don't really care.'

'But she's our only family.' Hannah was dismayed at Judith's reaction.

'What good's that when she's in Australia? If you want to write to her, that's your decision. But don't expect me to get involved. I've other things to think about.'

Hannah exchanged glances with Will.

Will gave a little shake of his head, warning Hannah to drop the subject.

'Very well.' She knew better than to push Judith. 'I'll write to her via Miss Radley and tell her about Mother.'

Judith winced. 'As I say, it's your decision.'

'She has a right to know. Mother was her only sister.'

Judith gave a long sigh of resignation. 'Frankly, you'd be better to wait until this teacher lady writes to Will again and lets him know if Elizabeth wants to have anything to do with us. You could be wasting your time writing if our aunt isn't interested. Miss Thingummy won't forward your letter. Besides, if Elizabeth was interested wouldn't we have heard by now?'

Hannah grabbed Will's arm. 'It's occurred to me – if our aunt doesn't want anything to do with us, surely your friend Miss Radley would have written to tell you that, wouldn't she?'

'That's a good point. Not to have heard from either of them seems odd.'

'I'm certain Aunt Elizabeth will want to know us. And to be in touch with you again.' She appealed to her husband. 'Will?'

'I did walk out before Dad's sentence was carried out and I wouldn't go and visit him. She could be mad with me too.' He thought, then shook his head. 'No. Everything I know of Lizbeth is that she's a warm and caring person who would be overjoyed to hear from her nieces. It'll be hard for her to hear what happened between your parents, and the circumstances of her sister's death, but she's a strong woman. She lost two children in tragic circumstances. She stood by my old man when he was condemned to death. She'll be shocked and saddened by what's happened here, but she'll want to know. And she's got my mate Michael to care for her. He's a rock.' He squeezed Hannah's hand. 'I think you should write.'

Judith folded her arms. 'There's your answer then. Now can we talk about something else?'

'It's time we thought of going home. Remember, you have Mass in the morning,' Hannah said pointedly, annoyed with Judith, but determined not to argue with her.

They were about to leave when Father Edwards reappeared, accompanied by a stout grey-haired man with a luxuriant moustache and a smiling countenance. The priest introduced him as Alfonso Giordano. 'Mr Giordano has a grocery store and is a mainstay of the Italian community.'

After shaking hands with them all, Giordano spoke rapidly in Italian with Paolo.

While they were speaking, the priest explained to the others, 'Mr Giordano is chairman of the Italian club too. He thinks he can help your friend.'

The barmaid rang a bell for last orders and Giordano and Paolo shook hands again and the grocer returned to the public bar.

'I hope that was useful, Paolo,' the priest said. 'You can fill me in on what you've agreed after Mass tomorrow. Now I'll bid you all goodnight. The housekeeper won't be happy if I'm not back when she brings in the cocoa.' With that, he headed out of the pub, calling goodbye to parishioners as he left.

Paolo was grinning. 'I have a job! *Dio mio*, I have a job!'

8

DUNKIRK

W ill had been gone for three weeks and, as always when he was at sea, Hannah was anxious. With each passing day her fear grew greater when he didn't return. Each knock at the front door made her heart stop, only for her to be crushed by disappointment when her husband wasn't standing there. Several times, she stood at the bedroom window, watching as the bicycle bearing the telegram delivery boy laboured up the hill. She was barely able to breathe until he had cycled safely past. Then she would feel guilty, knowing her relief no doubt meant bad tidings for somebody else.

The progress of the British Expeditionary Force in France was a source of more worry – this time for the country as a whole. The war was going badly. Hitler appeared to be unstoppable and the BEF had been disbanded and was in retreat towards the coast at Dunkirk. This rapid loss of face and humiliating abandonment of the Front was a shock to the whole nation and augured badly for the war. If Britain was already being forced back across the Channel, was it only a matter of time before German parachutes fluttered down into English fields and landing crafts with tanks ploughed inland from English beaches?

It occurred to Hannah that the need to withdraw the troops from France might well explain Will's continued absence. It was possible the *Shelbourne* had been diverted to the Channel to participate in the evacuation. The thought of her husband not only trying to evade submarines, but actually heading straight into the heart of the front-line action, was chilling. Yet Hannah knew he was doing no more than countless others in these terrible times – including numerous ordinary citizens – owners of small boats, pleasure steamers, ferries, lifeboats and fishing vessels, making their way across the Channel under heavy bombardment from Göring's Luftwaffe.

At least relations between herself and Judith had improved. Her younger sister's blossoming friendship with Paolo Tornabene had transformed her. There was no trace of the dark moods that had oppressed her since the terrible circumstances of their mother's death and the subsequent trial and hanging of their father. The bad news from the Front appeared to pass Judith by, so focussed was she on her growing devotion to the Roman Catholic Church and – even more – to her handsome Italian boyfriend.

Paolo had settled in with the Giordano family. As well as offering him a job in his grocery store, Mr Giordano had introduced Paolo to friends at the Italian Club and one family, the Continis, had agreed to take him in as a lodger. A fifteen-minute walk now separated him from Judith, and he was often to be found at the kitchen table in The Laurels, joining the others for their evening meal and Sunday dinner. His contribution of food from the Giordano shop was a welcome addition to their rations.

Sam's work, and his duties as an air-raid warden, meant

he was rarely at home. On Saturday evenings, he always went out and Hannah knew better than to enquire where. When he was around, he got on well with Paolo, and Nance appeared to have overcome her initial outrage that Paolo and Judith had become a couple.

May drifted into June with still no news of Will.

In the queue at the butcher's one morning, the general consensus had been that, with this retreat from Dunkirk and the inevitability of France falling, it was only a matter of time before Britain, too, was forced to acknowledge the likelihood of a German victory.

'That Hitler's got us well and truly on the run,' said a large woman wearing curlers under her headscarf.

'If you ask me, love, we'll all be learning German soon,' said Mr Collins, the butcher, as he stamped the woman's ration book.

'And you'll be serving us those blooming German sausages.'

'Hope you know how to make sauerkraut,' he replied.

'Don't even know how to say it, let alone what it is, but I won't be eating any of that foreign muck. Not blooming likely! I'd rather starve.'

'We're practically starving already,' moaned another woman in the queue. 'Trying to stretch the tiny bit of meat we get is like feeding the five thousand. I wish it was all over. Bring on the German sausages. My Harry used to be in port in Hamburg all the time before the war. He sometimes brought me back a tin. Not bad at all when you get used to them.'

'You get used to anything in the end,' observed the butcher, shaking his head.

Hannah hated the defeatism that was so widespread but

told herself that if it meant an end to Will crossing the Atlantic, she'd sleep better at night.

That evening, Hannah was alone in the front parlour. Nance had gone to a dance and Judith was at the Italian Club with Paolo. Hannah sat in an armchair, waiting for the nightly news from the BBC and knitting a woollen hat for Will to match the socks and gloves she'd already made.

Keen to hear what Mr Churchill had said in the Commons that day about the evacuation of Dunkirk, Hannah put down her knitting and got up to fiddle with the wireless dials to tune in the Home Service.

As she listened to the radio announcer reading the transcript of Churchill's speech in the House, it was clear that while the man and woman in the street may be ready to give up the ghost, the Prime Minister certainly wasn't.

'*I have, myself, full confidence that if all do their duty, if nothing is neglected, and if the best arrangements are made, as they are being made, we shall prove ourselves once more able to defend our island home, to ride out the storm of war, and to outlive the menace of tyranny, if necessary for years, if necessary alone. At any rate, that is what we are going to try to do.*'

Hannah squeezed her eyes tightly shut. She couldn't bear it. That terrifying word 'alone' made her shudder. What chance did this little island have against the might of the Third Reich if forced to stand alone? She wanted to shut out his words. It was too upsetting. She started to get up from her chair to cut off the drone of the BBC newsreader's voice. But something about the words made her pause, before her hand touched the dial.

'*We shall go on to the end. We shall fight in France, we shall fight on the seas and oceans, we shall fight with growing confidence and growing strength in the air, we shall defend our island, whatever the cost may be. We shall fight on the beaches, we shall fight on the landing grounds, we shall fight in the fields and in the streets, we shall fight in the hills; we shall never surrender, and if, which I do not for a moment believe, this island or a large part of it were subjugated and starving, then our Empire beyond the seas, armed and guarded by the British Fleet, would carry on the struggle, until, in God's good time, the New World, with all its power and might, steps forth to the rescue and the liberation of the old.'*

The simplicity of the words and the rhythmic repetition of the phrases was mesmerising. The paralysing fear that had overwhelmed Hannah faded away. Even with the bland voice of the announcer, it was impossible not to be infected by Churchill's courage and determination.

She put down her knitting. His reference to the British Fleet had brought tears to her eyes. Her mind drifted back to the day war was declared – the day after she and Will were married – when he told her that he intended to remain in the merchant navy and their plans to travel to Australia would have to be postponed. He'd said to her then that if he failed to do his duty, he would not be the kind of man she could respect or love. Nothing could ever stop her loving him. But that meant loving *everything* about him, including the fact that he had chosen to undertake one of the most dangerous jobs in the country. Painful as it was to know that any day might be his last, she had to admit that if Will had failed to step forward he would not have been able to live with himself. Whatever tough choices he made, she must always find the strength to support him in them.

When the broadcast ended, Hannah went into the scullery and made a pot of tea. Sitting at the kitchen table, she prayed for the strength to get through this war and whatever challenges it brought to them all. Religion was not something she had much time for – not after the years of her father's fire-and-brimstone zealotry – but sometimes prayer was a natural instinct. The God she prayed to was not a Biblical construct, but some form of higher being, a force for good, a bringer of comfort, someone to confide in. It didn't matter whether her prayers were listened to: the act of unburdening herself was a relief in itself.

Her thoughts drifted to the other occupants of the house. Sam – exempt from the first round of conscription the previous year as he was twenty-seven and above the cut-off point of twenty-two – was terrified at the thought of being called up. Since the law determined that all men up to age forty-one were liable to be called up at some point, as a precaution Sam had registered as a conscientious objector. So far, with a relatively important role in the local authority and his volunteering with civil defence, he had not been called. Yet Hannah wondered, in the light of Churchill's determination to fight on, how long it would be before conscription was broadened and Sam's conscience put to the test. He would find it hard to defend his position in the absence of strong religious conviction or physical disability.

She finished her tea, washed up the cup and saucer and went to bed.

As she struggled to sleep, Mr Churchill's words played over in her head. Maybe that was the shove she needed. If this war was going to drag on, then she'd better do her bit. What were her options? Working in a munitions factory? Joining one of the forces? The idea of actually helping to make bombs and bullets made her feel sick. So, too, did the thought of doing anything close to the actual fighting. Perhaps she could train as a nurse? A radio operator? An ambulance driver?

Whatever she chose would mean Nance would have to pull her weight around the house, instead of taking it for granted that Hannah would shoulder all the housekeeping. Even Judith, with a full-time job, did more than Nance. Something was going to have to change. And if the country was about to crank up its defences against invasion, before long Nance too might be compelled to undertake some kind of war work.

THE FOLLOWING MORNING, Hannah stood at the sink in the scullery, gazing out at the back garden. The lawn was overgrown – whenever Will had been around, he would run the lawnmower over it as a gesture of thanks to Sam. It was a warm sunny day, so maybe she would have a go at tackling it this afternoon.

The tangled cluster of gnarled apple trees at the bottom of the garden had shed most of their blossom. A squirrel ran through the pink-tinged carpet and scampered up one of the trees, disappearing into the foliage. Whether Hitler and his armies invaded or not, the natural world would remain unchanged. Trees would blossom, bear fruit, shed their leaves. Birds would still sing in their branches. The sun would continue to shine and the seasons to pass. Yet humans pursued a relentless search for power and wealth, with a constant need for change and improvement – often with terrible consequences. Everyone had believed after the cataclysmic toll of the previous war, the lesson had been learnt – but maybe humanity was conforming to the same continuity that nature showed – in man's case, a periodic need for destruction. Hannah brushed a hand through her hair, telling herself not to be so pessimistic.

She was about to get on with her next task – scrubbing the kitchen floor – when a shockwave ran through her body.

On the other side of the windowpane was Will, his

expression jubilant, despite the all-too-evident tiredness around his eyes. Those eyes that Hannah wished she could gaze into until the end of the world. Those kind, loving eyes. He was holding a bunch of Sweet Williams in one hand while the other supported his duffle bag, slung over his shoulder.

Hannah burst through the back door and flung herself into his arms.

'Will, Will, thank God. I thought you'd never come home. Oh, my darling!'

He bent and kissed her tenderly, his arms tight around her body. 'We went to Dunkirk.'

'I thought that must be it. I guessed they'd probably sent you.' She reached a hand up and stroked his hair. 'Was it as bad as I heard from the news?'

'Probably worse.' He gave a dry laugh. 'We were under constant aerial bombardment. The noise was deafening. We took some damage, but we made it through. That's all that matters. We managed to bring a couple of hundred lads across.'

'You must be shattered. When did you get into port?'

'A few hours ago.' He gave her a broad grin. 'I shouldn't be pleased about this, but the Germans managed to take a chunk out of the propellers and damaged part of the hull. We limped home but she'll be in the graving dock for several days while they patch her up. So that means more time here with you.' He lifted her up and swung her round. 'Anyone else at home?'

Hannah grinned. 'No one. Nance suddenly had a series of pressing engagements when I mentioned that I wouldn't mind a hand with the housework.'

Will rolled his eyes then pulled her into the house. 'What are we waiting for then?'

9

IL DUCE SHOWS HIS HAND

I l Duce Shows His Hand

A FEW DAYS LATER, on the tenth of June, Mussolini stood on a balcony overlooking the Piazza Venezia and declared war on Britain and France.

Hannah and Will were alone in the house when the news came over the wireless and they looked at each other with mounting fear. Mussolini's declaration was made in the evening to take effect at midnight. What might this mean for Paolo?

When Judith arrived home, they broke the news to her. She took it calmly. 'Mr Giordano says the government will probably summon everyone to a hearing at a tribunal and they won't be too concerned with people who have never been involved with the Fascist party. He's lived here for years. And everyone knows Paolo's not a Fascist. He chose to get off that Italian ship to come here. He hates Mussolini. Once the tribunal hear that, he'll be all right.'

Hannah glanced at Will. 'I wish I were as confident as you, Judith.'

Will looked anxious too. 'I hope Judith's right, but Paolo deliberately left an Italian ship to come to England. That could be seen as him trying to infiltrate the country as a spy.'

'That's ridiculous!' Judith snapped. 'How can you say that? You're meant to be his friend.'

'I don't think he's a spy. Of course, I don't. I'd trust Paolo with my life. But that doesn't mean other people will think that way. All it takes is some tinpot official who wants to throw his weight about.'

Hannah interrupted. 'Will's merely saying you should prepare yourself for the worst. At the beginning of the war, they categorised Germans as A, B and C and the Cs were supposed to be above reproach. Yet the moment Hitler invaded France, they rounded them up too.'

'Yes. Even Jewish refugees. How stupid is that?' added Will. 'They act out of blind panic.'

Hannah tried to appeal to her sister. 'It's obviously a complete over-reaction and in time it will all be sorted out – but in the meantime the government is bound to err on the side of caution.'

'Why do you always think you know everything? Why do you always talk to me as if I were a child?' Judith turned on her heels and left the room, banging the door behind her. They heard her footsteps stamping up the stairs.

'I always say the wrong thing.' Hannah picked up a cushion and thumped it.

. . .

SOME DAYS LATER, Hannah and Will were sitting side-by-side, hand-in-hand, on the settee in the front parlour, listening to the gramophone, when they heard raised voices in the street outside. Moving over to the window, they watched a group of about half-a-dozen people rushing along Moss Lane, heading towards Orrell Lane. Some of them were carrying broom handles, garden rakes and other implements.

'What do you think they're doing?' Hannah reached for her husband's hand. 'What's happening?'

'I've no idea. Do you think I should go after them?'

'No. They're clearly up to no good.'

'Maybe they're workmen of some sort – off to a union meeting or something.'

'Why take tools to a union meeting? One of them had a cricket bat! And it's evening. No one holds union meetings at this hour.' Hannah gripped her elbows and hugged her arms around her chest.

Will shrugged and moved to the door. 'Don't ask me, love. I'm having a beer. Can I get you something?'

Hannah shook her head.

When Will returned with a glass of ale, she said, 'I'm worried about Judith. She had an instruction class at the church this evening and was going to meet Paolo afterwards. They were to eat at the Giordanos.' She looked up at the clock on the mantel. 'I suppose it's too soon to expect her, but...'

'She'll be fine.' Will stroked her hand. 'You have to stop constantly worrying about Judith. She's a grown-up now.'

'She's only eighteen.'

'What she's gone through will have made her grow up. Your sister is a lot older and wiser than perhaps you give her credit for.' He looked into her eyes as he stroked her hair.

'I know. I'm sorry. I can't help it.'

He drew her against him and began to kiss her.

The front door gave its usual opening rattle, before being noisily slammed shut. Nance appeared in the doorway of the parlour. 'Break it up!' she called. 'No canoodling in the shared rooms!'

Hannah groaned inwardly but said nothing.

Nance flung herself into a chair. 'You've never seen nothing like it. I've just walked up from the Vale and you know that Eyetie grocers where Judith's fella works? Jordan's or something?'

'Giordano's,' said Hannah, impatiently.

'They've only gone and smashed the windows in, haven't they?' She puffed her chest out. 'Broken glass all over the pavement. They've looted it too.'

'What?' Hannah leapt to her feet, Will not far behind her.

'They're saying the Eyeties are a load of bloomin' traitors and I happen to agree with them. The buggers are fighting for Hitler now and we don't need their sort round here. And that goes for your Eyetie friend too. He can sling his hook. As far as I'm concerned, he's not welcome in this house anymore.' Nance put her hands on her hips and glared defiantly at Will.

Hannah looked at Nance, horrified. 'Don't be ridiculous. Paolo's not the enemy. He despises Mussolini and everything the man stands for. That's why he's here and not over there.' She turned to Will. 'You'd better get over to Giordano's and see if they need any help.'

Will looked grateful, put down his glass of beer and hurried out of the house.

As soon as he left, Hannah squared up to Nance. 'And the same goes for Mr and Mrs Giordano. They've lived in

Liverpool for more than twenty years. Their kids were born here. Their eldest son is in the airforce. Those bullyboys should put uniforms on instead of smashing shop windows. They're a bunch of pathetic cowards.'

Nance looked abashed. Giving a little shimmy, as though she were about to dance, she said, 'I'll go and stick the kettle on.'

Before Nance could leave the room, the front door rattled open again and Judith rushed in, weeping.

'What's wrong, my darling?' Hannah rushed over and wrapped her arms around her sister. 'Where's Paolo?'

'They've taken him.' Judith's words came out in gulps and her face was awash with tears.

'Who's taken him? Taken him where?'

'The police.' Her voice was a wail. 'I don't know where.'

'What? What on earth did he do? Surely they don't think he was responsible for smashing the Giordano's windows?'

Judith's words were distorted by her sobs and came out in jerky phrases. 'I went – over there as – soon as – I heard the news – about the Italians being rounded up.' She wiped a hand across her face. 'But I was too late. They'd already taken him and Mr Giordano.'

Hannah turned to Nance. 'What's happened to that cup of tea? Put some sugar in Judith's.'

Subdued, Nance left the room.

Hannah sat on the settee and drew Judith down to sit beside her. 'Tell me exactly what happened.'

'They came and took them away in a Black Maria. Said that Mr Churchill wants all the enemy aliens locked up.'

'That's ridiculous. What about Mrs Giordano and her daughter?'

'They're still there. Terrified.' Judith started weeping again, her words coming out in little jerks. 'I was comforting her when the shop window shattered and people in the street started throwing bricks in. There was a big gang of them.'

'Oh, Judith! You were there! Are you all right?'

'Of course, I am. But we had to hide in the storeroom and lock the door.'

Hannah gasped. It was awful to think of Judith cowering in fear behind a locked door for the second time in her short life. Trying to sound calmer than she felt, she said, 'Will's gone down there to see if he can help.'

'I know. I passed him on the Vale. He said I had to come home as you were worried about me, so here I am, but I'm going back there. I have to help Mrs Giordano clear up the mess. I promised her I'd be back as soon as I'd told you where I was and explained to Father Edwards why I had to miss instruction. He's already gone over there too to help out.'

'Then you're staying here. It's better to leave it to the men. Another gang of thugs was heading down Moss Lane a while ago. It's not safe.'

'But I have to find out where they've taken Paolo.'

'In that case, you and I need to go to the police station.' Hannah took hold of her sister's hand and gave it a squeeze. 'I expect they just brought them in for questioning and once they've established they're nothing to do with the Fascists, they'll let them go.'

'Oh, Han, will you help me get him out?'

WHEN HANNAH and Judith got back to The Laurels, it was after eleven. Will, Sam and Nance were gathered around the kitchen table. Three faces turned to look expectantly at the sisters.

'They're taking them to an internment camp. Prisoners.' Hannah's voice was flat.

'What?' Will looked horrified. 'They can't do that!'

'They just have.' Hannah pulled out a chair and sat down.

Judith remained in the doorway. Her eyes were red raw and puffy. 'I'm going to bed. I've got to get up for work tomorrow.'

'Don't you want nothing? A cup of cocoa?' Nance was on her feet and moving to the stove.

Judith shook her head and muttered, 'Goodnight.' She closed the door behind her.

'She's taking it badly.' Hannah let out a long sigh.

Will went to her. 'Was he there? Paolo? At the police station?'

'Yes. But they wouldn't let us see him.' She stretched her mouth into a false smile. 'We did manage to establish that they're likely to be sent to the Isle of Man. But one of the policemen told Mrs Giordano that it was only a temporary arrangement and some or all of them may eventually be sent overseas.'

The three listeners all gasped.

'To the Dominions.'

'Damn!' Will voiced what everyone was feeling.

'How did you get on at Mr Giordano's shop?' Hannah asked.

Will tilted his chair back, his hands propping himself against the table. 'The place was in a terrible state. The bastards had shattered the plate-glass window and the door. They were getting stuck into looting the contents when I got there. Fortunately, several of us arrived at the same time, including Judith's priest pal, Father Edwards.'

Grinning, Will said, 'He takes no prisoners, that fella.

Apparently, most of the buggers doing the looting were his parishioners, so he told them he'd ban them from the Catholic Young Men's Society which would mean no more cheap beer. Said he'd expect to see the lot of them in confession.' Will started to laugh. 'I think he may even have threatened excommunication! Anyway, whatever he said did the trick. Within a few minutes, he'd got them sweeping up broken glass, re-stacking the shelves and nailing plywood over the windows.'

Hannah laughed, grateful for a release of the tension inside her. 'Good for Father Edwards.'

'So, what's happening next?' Will asked.

'They said once the men are installed in whichever camp they're sent to, they'll be working out a system for spousal visits. But the police made it clear that Judith wouldn't be included. Girlfriends evidently don't count.'

Hannah's lips tightened into a narrow line and she shook her head. 'Mrs Giordano was at the police station too and offered to take a letter or anything for Paolo on Judith's behalf. But she doesn't know when she'll get a chance to visit.'

'That's rough,' said Sam. 'Poor Judith.'

'And poor Paolo. With no one to visit him.' Will lit a rare cigarette.

'Judith's already told Mrs Giordano she'll go to the Isle of Man with her, even if they won't let her see him. She says she wants to support her.'

'She barely knows the woman.' Nance was scornful.

'Do shut up, Nance,' said Sam. 'You can be dreadfully insensitive at times.'

'That's not fair! I'm only speaking the truth.'

'Shut up!' All three chorused.

'In that case, I'm off to bed and sod the lot of you.' Nance flounced out of the room.

'They won't let Judith go to the Isle of Man, surely?' asked Will.

'How can they stop her? Anyone can buy a ticket for the ferry.' Hannah turned to her husband. 'Can't you have a word with your Captain Palmer and see if he can put in a word on Paolo's behalf? Didn't you say he's got an important role?'

'Palmer's in Plymouth. I've no means of getting in touch.'

'What about Mrs Palmer?'

'She went with him. They've rented their house out.'

'Then I'm going to talk to that priest tomorrow. He may be able to help.'

THE FOLLOWING MORNING, before Hannah left to find Father Edwards, Nance drifted into the kitchen, wearing her negligée, an unlit cigarette ready between her lips.

Hannah took a breath. 'We need to talk, Nance. You have to start pulling your weight with the housework. It's not fair to leave everything to me. It would be different if you were working, but I've had enough of doing it all myself.'

'You like it.' Nance's tone was categorical.

'I don't like it at all.'

'Why do it then? Before you moved in here, we got by without all that scrubbing and cleaning.'

'The place was filthy.'

'You're too picky, girl.'

'Sam allows us to stay here out of the goodness of his heart. The least we can do is repay him by making the place as nice as possible.' She paused, wringing out the dishcloth and wiping the draining board. 'If you don't like cleaning, you could do the shopping, laundry and cooking.'

'Cook? Me? Now you're cracking jokes!'

'I'm in deadly earnest.'

Nance shrugged her shoulders dismissively. 'I pay my share of the bills.'

'We're not talking about the bills. We're talking about doing your fair share of the work.'

'You've never said nothing before.'

'Maybe I should have, but I'm saying it now.'

Nance folded her arms. 'What is it you want me to do?'

'You can take your pick. I've made a list.'

'Give it here then.' She snatched the paper from Hannah's hand and scrutinised it. 'I'll do the shopping.'

'And? You'll need to do a bit more than that.'

Nance huffed.

'Don't push me, Nance, or I'll draw up a rota. This is your chance to pick and choose. I'm looking for you to offer to do two or three other things.'

'What the hell's brought this on?'

'I'm thinking of getting a job or doing something for the war effort.'

'What? Join the services?'

'Maybe. Or I might join the Women's Voluntary Service.'

Nance snorted in derision. 'They're a bunch of posh toffs.'

'I need you to take on some of the work here, so I'll have time to start looking for something suitable and making enquiries. And I imagine there'll be interviews.'

'And what if I decide I want to get a job too?'

'Then we'll need to have another look at what needs doing at that point.'

'Some of the bingo girls say there's going to be a big

armaments factory in Fazakerly. There's quite a few of us thinking of applying. You're not the only one who wants to do her bit.'

'You've never mentioned this before.'

'You never asked.'

'Well, as I say, once either of us starts doing something, we can review the tasks, but until then, you're going to have to choose three more things.'

'Does Sam know about this?' Nance looked triumphant, playing her trump card.

'Actually, the list was Sam's idea.'

Nance looked affronted. 'You been talking to him about me?'

'Let's just say he's noticed you don't pull your weight.' She hesitated, 'In fact he suggested an alternative.'

'And what might that be?'

'That you pay for a daily woman to do what you should be doing yourself.'

'Why the hell should I pay for someone to clean up? I don't make all the mess. And I can't understand why it has to be so bleeding spotless round here. A bit of muck never did no one no harm.'

'The rest of us don't happen to agree. And you are the only one who is neither going out to work nor doing any housework. In case you've forgotten, there's a war on. So, what else are you going to do as well as the shopping?'

'I'll tell you what I'm going to do. I'm going to speak to our landlord. He'll have something to say on this once he's heard my point of view. Oh, yes, Mrs Bossy Boots, Sam won't like it at all.'

The door opened. 'What won't I like?' Sam came into the kitchen.

Nance swung round. 'It's her. She's saying I have to help

with the housework. I don't know who she thinks she is, Lady Muck?'

'If anyone deserves the title of Lady Muck, Nance, it's you. The rest of us have had enough of you swanning around, doing nothing except washing your undies and painting your nails.' He looked up at the wooden clothes rack, where, as usual, Nance's stockings and lingerie were airing.

'I've never been so insulted in all me born days.'

'I'm sure you'll get over it.' Sam smiled at her. 'Hannah does everything round the house. I happen to think it's time you did your bit too. Now if you've said your piece, I need to get off to work.'

Hannah handed him a greaseproof paper parcel, containing his sandwiches.

'Thanks, Hannah, you're an angel. Have a good day, ladies!'

10

LOCKED UP

Paolo had expected to be questioned at the local police station, believing that once they'd established he was not a member of the *Fascio,* they would let him go. What happened was far from that.

He and Mr Giordano were put in a holding cell, along with a number of other Italian men. The plainclothes policemen who had made the arrests disappeared, leaving them in the custody of an abusive desk sergeant who was convinced they were all Fifth Columnists. Nothing they could say would rid him of that belief.

One Italian constantly repeated the fact that he had fought with the British army in the last war and had the medals to prove it. 'I've lived here for thirty years. I am a naturalised citizen. My wife's a Liverpudlian. All our children are British. You must let me go. There has been a mistake.'

'Shut your mouth, you filthy fascist pig or I'll give you something to shout about.' Addressing the constable who stood by with a gun, the sergeant added, 'Keep that pointing at them, in case they try any funny business. These Eyeties can't be trusted.'

Their cause wasn't helped by a pair of men in the cell with them offering up a Fascist salute and shouting '*Forza, Mussolini! Viva Il Duce!*' The other men – the majority – turned on them and told them exactly what they thought of Mussolini.

Paolo still believed it was only a matter of time before they were freed. After all, this was England. People here were reasonable and fair.

It was strange to be surrounded by people speaking his native language. The Giordanos spoke English in the shop and whenever he had brought Judith to visit them at home. The family he was lodging with – the Continis – always spoke in English as Ernesto Contini was married to an Englishwoman. Once, being surrounded by speakers of his mother tongue would have elated him, but now it was depressing. For the first time in his life Paolo struggled not to feel ashamed of being Italian. He loved his country. He missed his country. But he despised what Mussolini had turned his country into.

As night approached, all the men realised they were expected to sleep here in the cold cells, without so much as a blanket, let alone a bed. At least it was June and not December.

The following morning Paolo's spirits lifted when a line of uniformed policemen appeared in the passage outside the holding cells. Surely this meant they were about to be questioned in front of a tribunal and they would be allowed to return home – apart from the two genuine *Fascisti*. Those two deserved to be locked up for the rest of the war.

They filed out of the cell, one-by-one, only to be hand-cuffed and escorted from the police station by the back door.

More police were waiting outside. Paolo gazed back at the Victorian, red brick police station. He had walked past it between his digs and the Giordanos' shop so many times, never dreaming that he would be locked up in there.

Still handcuffed, the men were frog marched through the streets. Paolo wished he had stayed on the *Vigevano* and might now be sailing through the Mediterranean, home to *Napoli*.

Then he thought of Judith, his beautiful Judith, who had restored his belief in the possibility of love. Surely it was better to be here – even treated in this way – if it meant he was in the same city as her. Once he made his case to a tribunal, the whole disgraceful episode would be cleared up and he would be freed. But why were they forced to wear handcuffs like common criminals, when he knew the British believed a man was innocent until proven guilty? Was this what war meant?

It was a bitter irony that, once again, it was the damned fascists who were conspiring to ruin his life. It had been Loretta's Fascist party brothers who had made his first love marry an old man against her will. It had driven her to throw herself from a clifftop. Now, thanks to the filthy Fascists, he was to be parted from his new love, just as everything was falling into place for them both.

Walking beside him was *Signor* Giordano, his face taut in unfamiliar anger. Paolo knew how much the older man loved England and Liverpool. His grocery store was a hub of the community – not only for Italians, but for local people too. He was a regular at Everton games, as crazy about his adopted team as he had once been for his beloved Fiorentina. It was unthinkable for the police to treat a man like him – with his son serving in the RAF – in this manner.

There had been no opportunity to protest that they

were innocent. It was illogical for the authorities to assume that all Italians were fanatics. Occasional visits to the Italian social club had shown Paolo that, yes, there were supporters of Mussolini among them, but the vast majority were members of the club in order to maintain their links with the old country, converse in their mother tongue, and enjoy Italian food and wine on feast days. Whatever they thought of the benefits of their adopted country, the cuisine was not one of them – especially now with rationing.

Rice Lane ended and County Road began. As they approached his grocery store Alfonso Giordano gasped.

Where once there had been plate-glass panelled windows, with a perfectly crafted display of salami and hams, long packets of macaroni and spaghetti in colourful paper wrappers, *biscotti*, woven plaits of garlic and onions, and raffia-clad bottles of *Chianti,* there was now only a pile of broken glass, with plywood sheets nailed across the windows.

'Cazzo! Guarda che hanno fatto questi figli di puttane!' the grocer wailed. But there was no one to answer his question as to who was responsible. Paolo threw him a look of sympathy.

Giordano stopped dead and began to call for his wife. 'Maria! Maria!'

Immediately, one of the police constables threatened him with his truncheon and pushed him back into the line. 'Get a move on. No stopping.' Staring back over his shoulder at the destruction caused to his store, Signor Giordano let out a low moan, but had no choice but to keep moving.

As they neared the centre of Liverpool, crowds gathered on the pavements, shouting abuse as the Italians trudged past. Paolo, angry and humiliated, was stung by the injustice of it all. Where were they being taken? They appeared to be heading for the waterfront.

Among his fellow prisoners were young men, born in Britain, some of them with strong Scouse accents. Ordinary men who worked as waiters or porters in hotels and restaurants, while others, like Alfonso Giordano, were retailers or restaurateurs.

When they reached the Pier Head, they were marched along the dockside and taken into an empty warehouse. Trestle tables had been set up at the end of the room to process the internees. Paolo stood in line as they shuffled forward, one-by-one, to provide their name, place and date of birth and occupation. He decided to declare only his current employment as a grocer's assistant. If the authorities discovered he was an experienced merchant seaman, he might be seen as a higher risk. His plan appeared to be working and he was handed a card bearing the letter B and sent to join others including his boss, at the far end of the building.

Rumours were already rife. Word had it that those men perceived as most dangerous would be shipped abroad to the Dominions, while the rest would be placed in internment camps in Britain. The process for determining the level of risk appeared to be arbitrary, as one of the two vocal fascists were placed in the B group while the other was with the As. After a while, the supply of cards ran out. Any attempt to organise the internees was abandoned and the men were sent to join different queues at random. The whole process was chaotic.

Paolo sat on a wooden bench talking with Alfonso Giordano and Ernesto Contini, when one of the Fascisti shouted to an official, pointing at Paolo, 'Why he is with this group? He's a sailor with the Italian navy.'

One of the administrators called Paolo back to the table. 'Is that right?'

'No. I work in a grocer's.' He pointed at Giordano. 'I work for him.'

Another official pushed his way through the crowd. 'What do we have here?' He looked Paolo up and down and laughed. 'I know this man. He served with me on the *Christina*.' There was a slight trace of an Australian accent. 'He and his pal caused me to lose my bosun's ticket.' He glared at Paolo with a malevolent grin. 'He needs to get his just desserts. If ever there was a fascist, this man's one.'

Paolo's stomach lurched. Jake Cassidy. The bosun on the *Christina* before the war. Cassidy had hated Will Kidd with an inexplicable intensity. He had a penchant for violence which had eventually cost him his job. Captain Palmer had made sure no one else was likely to hire him on their ship.

'You lose your ticket because you make trouble, Cassidy.'

'Is that right, Eyetie? Well, I'm sure as hell going to make trouble for you. I can promise you that.' He curled his lip. 'I'm a military guard now. My job is to make sure scum like you don't go spying on the country and passing secrets to the enemy.' Cassidy turned to the man issuing the classifications. 'This man's from Naples and we all know what a hotbed of fascism that place is. I wouldn't be surprised if he was working directly for the Dootchy and his mob.'

Cassidy snatched the card from Paolo, handed it back to the clerk and stabbed his finger at the clipboard bearing the list headed A. 'Stick his name down there. That's more like it. "Enemy Alien" – he's definitely a Fifth Columnist.'

Cassidy lowered his voice and moved closer to Paolo. 'Not that it makes a whole lot of difference how we classify you, as the government's decided the whole bloody lot of you are going to be locked up. I want to make sure if there's any soft options, they don't apply to a traitorous bastard like you.' He gave a dry laugh, his face so close that Paolo could smell his foul breath. 'Something tells me you and I will have another opportunity to renew our acquaintance before too long, Tawneybenny.' Giving him a mock salute, Cassidy headed out of the warehouse.

11

BATTLES ON THE HOME FRONT

Will was arguing with Hannah. Their first ever argument. It was about her desire to do something for the war effort. Will saw it as unnecessary and a reflection on him. It was his job to care for her and provide for her. And hers to be here in the home.

Hannah pursed her lips. 'It's not about money, Will. You provide perfectly well for us. But I want to do my bit for the war. I want to volunteer.'

'Doing what? I don't want you working in a factory. Besides, you do more than enough here as it is.' He curled his hands into fists and placed them in front of him on the kitchen table.

'I was thinking of joining the Women's Voluntary Service. There are all sorts of things I could do to help.'

'I'm an officer now. I don't like to think of my wife having to go out to work.'

'It's not working, it's volunteering.'

Will saw the crestfallen look on her face and knew he was being unreasonable. His resistance was more out of fear of the future than any wish to prevent Hannah doing what she wanted. He told himself now was no time for injured pride. Their lives were changing. The war was not going to be short and it was not going to be easy. The reversals in France, the entry of Italy into the war and the continued refusal of America to get involved, made him feel powerless and angry. Everyone was saying it was only a matter of time until the Invasion began. A port as significant as Liverpool was bound to be in the front line of the aerial attacks that would likely precede it.

He shuddered to think of Hannah here in Liverpool without him when he returned to sea. He imagined her huddled inside the damp and leaky Anderson shelter in the back garden or squashed, terrified, into the cupboard under the stairs which she had cleared of the mops, brooms and buckets normally housed there.

Hannah placed her hands around his clenched fists. 'My darling, I realise it's because you'll worry about me. But would you rather I spent my days here at home worrying myself sick about *you*? At least if I'm doing a useful job, I'll have something to take my mind off it.'

He lifted his eyes and met hers. 'I'm sorry. I'm being unreasonable, aren't I? It's that I don't want you putting yourself in any kind of danger.'

'That's not my intention.' She smiled. 'I'm no dare devil. I won't be joining the services. I'm too much of a cowardy custard. But I'm sure I can do something more useful than cleaning the windows.' She gave a little laugh. 'Not much point in doing that anyway with the blast tape all over them.'

Will could feel himself weakening. He hated arguing with her. And he knew she had the stronger case.

Evidently scenting victory, Hannah grinned at him. 'The WVS are desperate for more volunteers. I went to a talk at the Orrell Park Ballroom the other day. When you were down at the dock.' She looked apologetic. 'I meant to tell you about it, but all the business with poor Paolo being put in prison, made me forget. Mrs Kennedy from over the road was there and a lady who works part-time in the Post Office, and Miss Taylor who lives in the house next door but one – you know, the big one with the beech tree in the front garden. Mostly it will be collecting clothes and sorting them for refugees, helping with evacuees – escorting them to their host families. Homeless children – some of the poor things are apparently in a terrible state and need to be cleaned up before anyone will take them in——'

'So, you'll be bathing children?' He smiled.

She rolled her eyes upwards. 'Disinfecting them in some cases. The rather grand lady who gave the talk said it's not for the faint-hearted. Some of them have never had a bath in their life.'

Hannah got up and put the kettle on. 'But we have to be prepared for anything. From making cups of tea – something I'm well-qualified to do – to collecting up pots and pans to be used to make weapons, painting blackout windows, digging vegetable plots, knitting and mending, educating people to re-use things and avoid waste. All very mundane – but very important.'

Will got up and went to stand behind her, his arms around her shoulders as he kissed her neck. 'Whatever they ask you to do, you'll do it perfectly. I'm very proud of you.' He drew her around so he could kiss her properly.

A few minutes later, they were drinking tea when Hannah said, 'I saw Father Edwards today. He's been trying to find out where the police have taken Paolo.'

'Why didn't you tell me right away?'

'Because there's nothing to report. He says most of the

men have been sent to the Isle of Man but he hasn't seen any names. It seems they put them all on a boat without any record of who was who.'

'That's an outrage. And completely against maritime law. Every ship needs a passenger manifest.' Will's thumped the table in anger.

'It's war. They can do what they like. Or they probably think they can. And as far as the government's concerned they're just a bunch of enemy aliens.'

'He's on the Isle of Man, then?'

'Not necessarily. Father Edwards said they're holding people in Walton Jail and in an internment camp on an estate of new-built houses in Huyton. There's also a cotton mill near Manchester. They seem to be sticking the poor souls all over the place – even racecourses! It goes to show how unprepared they were for all this.' Hannah narrowed her eyes. 'There's no excuse. We've known for years war was on the cards. I can't believe what a mess the government's making of it.'

'So, we've no idea where Paolo is?'

'Father Edwards believes most of the Italians have been sent to the Isle of Man and it's mainly Germans in Huyton.' She put down her teacup. 'But what's worrying me is that he says there's a plan afoot to send as many internees as possible overseas to Canada and Australia. The government wants them out of the way.'

Will jumped up out of his chair. 'Without even finding out if individual Italians are threats or not? How can they do that?'

'Who's to stop them?'

'Men like Paolo could actually be useful to the country if they kept them here.' He began pacing up and down. 'There's war work they could be put to. Even if it's only labouring. We could use them on the docks. And men like Mr Giordano – what possible danger could he represent? The whole thing's mad!'

Hannah bit her lip. 'I know. And I'm terrified about how Judith will react if they do send Paolo away. She's in a bad enough state already.'

'We should never have stayed here when war was declared. I should have got you and your sister to Australia as we'd planned. All this is my fault. We'd have been safe and starting a new life. And Paolo would never have come to England—'

'And never met Judith. That's like saying you should never have come here yourself because you'd have avoided the war, but we'd never have met. Would you have wanted that?'

He crossed the room and knelt at her feet, his hands on her knees, looking up at her. 'Never in a million years. If the choice was to live forever but never have known you or die tomorrow but have had what we've had together, I wouldn't hesitate for a second.'

'There's your answer then. And it's the same as mine. I'm sure Paolo and Judith feel that way too. She really loves him.'

Will drew up another chair, sat down and pulled Hannah onto his lap. 'He loves her too. I can see it. I've known him a long time and he's never been so happy as he is with her.'

Hannah gave him a sad smile. 'I can't help worrying about her though. Judith's not strong. Her life was wrecked by our upbringing and then by everything that happened in Bluebell Street that night when our father murdered Mother. I'd begun to believe she would never get over it –

until Paolo came along. She rediscovered hope and happiness and now it's being torn from her again.'

Will stroked her hair, breathing in the familiar smell of her, Hannah's breath warming his skin through his shirt. 'It seems hopeless now, but it won't be like this forever. Somehow, we'll all get through this war. We've had more than our fair share of troubles but when I look at you, my love, I see only goodness and love.' He looked into her eyes. 'Whatever obstacles the world throws in our way, we'll get past them.'

The back door swung open and Nance came into the room. 'All right! Break it up! This is a kitchen not a bedroom. All that snogging is enough to put me off me dinner.'

'Nothing puts you off your dinner, Nance,' Will said drily.

Ignoring him, Nance gave Hannah a triumphant look. 'I've got a job! Ta-dah!' She swung her arms out in a theatrical gesture.

Will raised his eyebrows at Hannah, who said only a cautious, 'Tell us more.'

'I'll be serving the troops down the NAAFI canteen.' She gave a little hip wiggle and winked at Will. 'All those lovely fellas! And they do say the way to a man's heart is through his stomach. Well, there'll be more men than I'll know what to do with, and all of them standing in line for me to take me pick. I can't bloody wait.'

'I didn't know you were hunting for a husband, Nance?' Will's lips twitched in amusement.

'Who said anything about a husband? The one I had was one too many. I won't be making that mistake again – not bloomin' likely.' She patted her newly coiffed hair. 'But all those handsome men in uniform, looking for a bit of slap and tickle and an extra portion of chips – how can a lady possibly refuse?'

Nance sashayed her way around the kitchen. 'Any tea in the pot?' She put a hand against the teapot and pulled a face. 'Stick the kettle on again, Hannah. Time for a fresh brew. Me dogs are barking.' She kicked off her shoes, stretching her stockinged feet out in front of her. 'Now that's one thing a man's good for – a nice foot rub. I don't suppose...'

'To quote your own words, Nance, "not blooming like-ly".' Will winked at Hannah, though he knew she wouldn't see the funny side. It was clear what was coming next.

'*So*,' Nance said, underlining the word. 'With my new responsibilities it's completely out of the question for me to be doing *any* housework.'

12

THE ARANDORA STAR

P aolo had no idea what was going to happen to him. Told to wait on one side, he watched as a long snake of men were herded like bewildered sheep onto the decks of a ship. It was called the *Lady of Man* so it was apparent their destination must be the Isle of Man. Signor Giordano was in the queue, but before it was his turn to board, the guards slung a rope across the gangway and directed the rest of the queue, Giordano included, back into the holding shed where Paolo and the other category A men were waiting.

After waiting there for several hours, sitting on the concrete floor, they were shoved into open lorries and driven back through the centre of Liverpool towards Walton again. Paolo's heart leapt, believing they were going to be freed. Instead, the vehicle swung between the heavy armoured gates and behind the walls of Walton Jail.

Not only were they prisoners, they were now to be incarcerated in a place used to house common criminals. He remembered Judith telling him that her father had been held here before being hanged for the murder of her mother.

Inside, they found out that the wing where they were to be housed had been closed, unused, since the days when suffragettes had been imprisoned there. There was to be no mingling with murderers and rapists. Instead, they would be kept in the company of bats and pigeons, surrounded by damp mildewed walls, and the stench of decay. No one, not even family or lawyers, was allowed to visit – the only exception being clergymen.

Paolo felt a surge of hope when he was led, under guard, into a small room, and found Father Edwards waiting to see him.

'How are you doing, Paolo?' The priest gave him a wry smile. 'I'll be expected to make a full report to Judith. As you can imagine she's far from happy that she's not allowed to visit you.'

'How is she?'

'She's fighting fit and blazing angry that this has happened to you.'

Paolo gave a huge sigh of relief. 'I worry that she not want to know me now they put me in the prison.'

'Far from it. She can't understand why you're in here.'

'She is not the only one who is not understanding, Father. Why they do this to me?'

'You and most of the other poor chaps in this wing. The trouble is, the authorities were completely unprepared.' Father Edwards leaned forward in his chair. 'Not about Italy entering the war – we all guessed that was coming – but the decision to imprison every Italian man in the country. It was a knee-jerk reaction and they are running around like madmen trying to figure out how to cope with you all.'

'*Pazzesco!* It is crazy.' Paolo's fists were tightly clenched. 'I could be working to help *Inghliterra*. *Odio I Fascisti*. I hate *il Fascio*.' His eyes pleaded with the priest. 'Can't you say them? I do anything. I work hard. I go back to sea. They need the sailors.'

Father Edwards shook his head. 'I'm sorry, Paolo. The decision has been made. No Italian nationals will be permitted to serve in the merchant navy. I am hoping that, once the government realises that this wholesale internment is impractical and counter-productive, they will review each case, and men like you will be allowed to return to the community and your jobs – or put to good work for the war effort instead of being locked away like this.'

Paolo heaved a deep sigh. 'And Judith? You think they will allow her to visit me soon?'

'I don't know.' The priest paused then added, 'Not soon I fear. They can't cope. You are one of thousands. If they move you to an internment camp it will probably be different. But while you're in here, the authorities claim they can't handle family visits.' He touched the Italian's forearm. 'And as an unmarried man you will be at the back of the queue, I'm afraid.' He sighed heavily. 'Meanwhile, Judith sends you her love.'

'She is angry with me?'

'Why on earth would she be angry with you?'

'Because I am the enemy.' He lowered his eyes, avoiding the priest's.

'Judith knows perfectly well which side you're on. She's not so fickle as to pay attention to the thick-headed stupidity of Home Office officials.' He smiled sadly. 'You've found a good woman there, Paolo. She loves you.'

'She say you that?'

'She did. She asked me to tell you that no matter what, and how long you are kept apart, she will wait for you.'

Paolo gave an involuntary sob and slumped forward, his head almost touching the surface of the table. Then he sat upright. 'Please tell her, Father, tell her I love her with all my heart, and I pray every day to see her again.' A rush of emotion flooded over him. 'She is the woman I want to marry. Will you tell her for me, Father?'

'That's something you should wait and tell her yourself. Let's pray that it will be soon. This whole thing is down to panic – people are very jumpy since Dunkirk. Once the war starts to go in our direction, they will change.'

'I have a very bad feeling, Father. I have fear. Bad, bad, feeling. You promise me, Father, if something happen to me, you tell Judith that I love her very much and I wish to marry her. But if I die, she must marry someone else. A nice Englishman. Someone kind. I wish her *solo belle cose*, a beautiful life.' He dropped his head.

'Come on, son! Now who's over-reacting? You won't be in this hellhole for much longer, I'm certain of that. They'll move you to a proper internment camp, then Judith can visit and, please God, you'll be released before long and can get on with your life together.'

Paolo gripped the priest's arm tightly. 'Promise me, *Padre*. If something happen to me you say her I love her, but she must find another man. Promise me!'

'I promise. But I'm sure everything will soon be fine. Your fears are natural. The treatment meted out to you all is disgraceful. Shameful. But it won't be forever. Now why don't we say a few prayers together?'

· · ·

AT THE BEGINNING OF JULY, the internees were moved again. Back into the lorries, and down once more to the docks. This time there was no turning back. A large ocean liner, the *Arandora Star* was waiting at the quayside. Paolo knew of the ship – once the world's most exclusive cruise liner, with accommodation for First Class passengers only. Now it had been transformed: its portholes covered, and the promenade decks boarded up. Paolo shuddered. It looked like a floating coffin.

'Where are you taking us?' Alfonso Giordano asked one of the guards while they waited to board.

Unfortunately, the guard was Jake Cassidy

'You're going to Canada.' Cassidy grinned. 'Gets *very* cold there in winter. Not the kind of weather you Eyeties enjoy.'

The news was a punch in the stomach. How was this possible? Why was it happening? No one even knew they were going. Canada wasn't the Isle of Man. There would be thousands of miles of ocean between him and Judith. How was he to get word to her?

Alfonso was outraged. 'I must say goodbye to my wife. I need to send a message for her to come here.'

'You're not off on your holidays, sunshine!' Cassidy snarled. ' What do you think this is? Bloody Blackpool? You're prisoners. Enemies of the state. Fifth Columnists and Fascists. If it were up to me, I'd line you up against a wall and shoot the lot of you. It'd be a damn sight easier and quicker.'

Paolo put a hand on Alfonso's arm to restrain him, knowing all too well how unwise it would be to provoke Jake Cassidy. Will Kidd had once spent a night in a police station after an unprovoked attack from Cassidy. The Australian former bosun had a violent temper and relished any opportunity to demonstrate the power of his fists. The only consolation was that Cassidy was not one of the guards who would be accompanying them on the voyage.

The Italians were taken on board and divided into two groups. Giordano and Contini were sent with the majority down to cabins on A Deck at the bottom of the ship while Paolo was sent to the middle deck. The ship also carried Germans – mostly members of the German merchant navy, along with Jewish refugees from Nazi Germany, thrown in among a small number of hard core Nazis and *Fascisti*.

Conditions on the *Arandora Star* were better than the men had experienced at any time since their internment. The soldiers guarding them were polite and friendly, the food was decent and some of them were even offered drinks from the bar by a crew used to serving the wealthy.

In the early hours of the morning, Paolo, attuned to the movements of ships, woke as the vessel sailed out of the port of Liverpool. The last time he had been on a ship leaving here, he had been a free man, doing the work he loved, setting off on a voyage that would take him to the African continent, as the *Christina* plied her way between ports, collecting and depositing cargo in a series of short hops. Now he was crossing the Atlantic on a ship that was carrying him far away from the woman he loved and wanted to spend his life with. Would he ever see Judith again?

Sailing up the Mersey, the Lancashire coastline disappeared behind them as they swung into the Irish Sea. Paolo could only just see the distant outline of the shore in the moonlight: the barbed wire defences by the sand dunes of Crosby. Further north and out of sight, he imagined the pine woods at Formby Sands.

The day before Mussolini brought Italy into the war, he

and Judith had taken the train up to Formby. Signora Giordano had made them a picnic, packed with little treats that rationing would have made out of the question and which only a specialist grocer could provide. 'That's the last of the salami,' she'd said. 'I've a feeling we'll not be getting more supplies any time soon.' Ignoring their protests, she'd put a finger to her lips and winked as she handed it over, smiling.

It had been a magical day. He and Judith had wandered hand-in-hand through the quiet woods as far as they were able, before roadblocks and barbed wire prevented them getting as far as the beach. They found a quiet spot and ate their picnic while gazing up into the trees, watching the red squirrels scampering along the branches. After they had eaten, they kissed, and the kissing made them hungry for more. Her lips were soft, responsive, as hungry for him as he was for her. They lay down on the picnic blanket and she eagerly urged him on. Perhaps he should have tried harder to stop. He didn't want to be disrespectful – said maybe they should wait, but he was weak, mad for her and, when he tried to sit up, she pulled him down beside her again.

Now as he thought back to what they had done – her little cry of pain when he entered her, followed by her holding him even tighter as the pain turned to pleasure – he felt a mixture of guilt and longing. He was glad they had made love, but it might prove to be their one and only time. Who knew how long he might be stuck in Canada? Who knew what the war would bring for each of them? The memory of that afternoon would fuel his thoughts and dreams until he saw her again. But more than anything, he wanted to marry her. To prove that his love for her was deeper than just desire. That it would endure. That she was the only woman he would ever love.

But now he had been forced to abandon her, without a

chance to say goodbye or ask her to marry him. Would he ever be able to do that now?

What lay ahead? The same dark dread that had engulfed him in Walton Jail weighed heavy upon him, as he tried to sleep.

THEY WERE off the north coast of Ireland when the torpedo struck. Less than twenty-four hours out of Liverpool. U-47 had one torpedo left and was returning to Germany, when the zig-zag course of the *Arandora Star* caused the U-boat captain to guess that it was an enemy ship.

At six in the morning, Paolo was asleep on the top deck. He was woken by a loud dull thump, as the missile smashed straight into the engine room, breaking the back of the ship. Men were thrown into the sea, spewed out like ash from a volcano.

In the chaos and shock that ensued, Paolo saw that some of the lifeboats had been damaged by the explosion. The ship was listing sharply, rendering the lifeboats on the uppermost side of the ship unlaunchable – swinging uselessly on their davits over the deck rather than the sea. Those that were usable were being lowered in a frenzy of panicked activity. Prisoners, guards, crew, and some of the men who had been pitched overboard, were pulled inside them.

Many of the Italians were too terrified to move. Paralysed. A number of elderly men appeared too frail and shocked to do anything; others were screaming that they couldn't swim. Most of the Italians were on the lowest deck and had further to climb through the ship towards safety, by which time most of the functioning lifeboats were full or on the water, requiring a jump. Some of the cabin doors on those lower decks had jammed as a result of the explosion, leaving men trapped inside.

The early morning air was rent with screams of '*Aiuto!*' – help me! – or desperate cries of prayer and pain. This motley band of mainly blameless men: hoteliers, caterers, hairdressers, waiters, shopkeepers, and doormen, were still in shock from being torn from home and family when they had committed no crime. Most were over fifty – several in their sixties and seventies – and now they were bewildered participants in a sea battle they'd never expected.

One of the crew handed Paolo a life jacket and he spotted Alfonso several feet away. The grocer looked wretched, his eyes hollow, his face gaunt. Paolo grabbed another jacket and pushed his way through the crowd towards his friend.

'We must get into a lifeboat. There are still spaces,' he told him. 'The ship is sinking. We must get in a boat now.'

But by the time he and the shocked Signor Giordano reached the last of the lifeboats, it was already full and being lowered towards the sea.

Paolo looked about. The ship was going down. His years as a seaman left him in no doubt. 'We'll have to jump.'

'I can't swim,' Alfonso said. 'I never learnt.' Around them, men were diving or jumping into the sea, but there were hundreds of others rushing around on the deck in a blind panic, fuelled by terror. German voices mixed with English, and Italian. Those deciding to take their chances in the sea seemed to be predominantly German – many of them merchant seamen like Paolo, or British guards and crew, while the elderly Italians stubbornly refused to budge, clinging onto the rails. They couldn't believe that it could possibly be safer in the water than here on the – now steeply sloping – deck.

'I'll help you.' Paolo tugged his arm, desperate. 'You *have* to jump. Please, Alfonso. I beg you. It's our only chance.' He indicated the water below where men were bobbing around. 'Look you can see how the water level has risen up the hull. The ship is broken. Trust me, I'm a sailor. It's going to sink.' He tried to control the fear in his voice.

But Giordano clung to the railings, his eyes brimming with tears. 'I can't do it. I can't. You go.' His face contorted in terror.

Paolo tried to help his friend to put on the life jacket, but Alfonso shoved him away. As he did so the life vest was grabbed by someone else. Below them, the sea was littered with debris, dead bodies, men swimming towards the lifeboats and a growing slick of black oil. The stricken vessel creaked ominously.

'No. No. I can't.' Alfonso's voice, barely a whisper, dripped fear.

'Please, come with me, Alfonso.'

'No!' He shook his head rapidly, the fear pulsing off him, his eyes wild. Go! Tell my Maria I love her.' He pushed Paolo towards the railing.

Paolo wasn't ready to die. Jumping was the only hope he would ever have of seeing Judith again, With one last pleading look at Alfonso, he clambered over the railings and let himself drop towards the waters below.

The fall lasted an eternity, although due to the listing of the ship it was not a great distance. Was this how it had felt for Loretta when she had jumped off that clifftop into the Bay of Naples? The air rushing by and the sea below. Slow motion. Time frozen. Then he was under the surface. He'd forgotten to hold his life jacket down, so it jerked upwards, ramming him hard under the jaw as he hit the water. His lungs were bursting. Darkness everywhere. Up? Down? He didn't know the difference. Pummelled. Sucked underwater. Disorientated. Confused. Blind.

As he was beginning to believe he must already be dead, Paolo burst through the water, buoyed up by his life jacket, popping like a cork as he broke the surface. He coughed out brine, his lungs screaming, his hair sticky with oil.

Alive.

Another jumper landed on top of him, pushing Paolo under again. This time it was only for a moment, but the impact was a painful shock. He had to get as far away from the ship as possible before it went down or he would be sucked under with it. No life vest could keep him buoyant in the face of the suction power of a sinking ship.

He tried to strike away from the *Arandora Star*, but struggled against the life jacket, which kept pushing his body upright out of the water or flipping him onto his back when he needed to swim forwards.

Ahead, he saw a life raft with two men spread-eagled on top, clinging to its surface which was slick with oil. He forced himself to swim towards it.

The early morning was chilly and the sky full of grey cloud, but being July and close to the coastline, the water temperature, although cold, was not freezing. The sea dragged at his clothing, weighing him down and making it hard to swim. Saltwater chafed his skin under the life vest. His back throbbed where the jumping man had struck him. Summoning every atom of strength and willpower, Paolo forced himself through the water.

He managed to grab one of the ropes on the edge of the life raft. There was no room on top and anyway the raft was slippery with the spilled oil from the ship, so he clung to the rope. A lifeboat appeared a few yards away and he turned to swim towards it. Thankfully it wasn't yet full. Two men dragged him inside. They pulled several more survivors from the water until the crew member in charge said they could take no more. All around them, exhausted men bobbed up and down in the sea, struggling to stay afloat. But before long each one succumbed to exhaustion and cold and disappeared beneath the surface, unable to fight any longer. The sounds of despair, the wails, the last prayers, mingled like ghost music around them, until the only bodies left floating were dead ones, buoyed up by their life vests.

Paolo looked back at the *Arandora Star*. The hole the torpedo had made in her stern had taken in so much water that now the bows were raised high out of the sea.

The captain and officers stood on the bridge, as well as a German merchant navy captain and an Italian priest, offering up prayers. Below them, men were desperately trying to clamber up the steeply inclined deck. Perhaps Alfonso Giordano was among them. The bows pitched higher. The ship was now pointing skywards, almost vertical, and men rolled down the deck, tumbling towards the sea like falling skittles. Paolo watched, numb, as the ship slipped quietly and gracefully beneath the water. A moment later the only trace of the former luxury liner was a black oil slick, floating corpses and pieces of wreckage. There was a deathly silence, as though the entire world had stopped, then a dull resonant boom as the ship's boilers exploded underwater.

Paolo turned to look at the other men in the lifeboat. Two of them were dead.

They lifted the dead men over the side to join the other lost souls. The boat drifted, passing more corpses, but there was no sign of Alfonso. Paolo offered a prayer for the soul of his friend.

The sea was calm. If the wireless operator had radioed for help, they would surely be picked up before long. Paolo continued to scan the water for Alfonso Giordano or his body but saw nothing.

About seven hours after the *Arandora Star* slipped beneath the waves, a Canadian destroyer came to their rescue. It took another three hours or so for all the survivors to be safely brought on board before they set sail for the coast of Scotland. Paolo had never been so grateful to anyone as he was to those kind and competent Canadian sailors. With a blanket around him and a warming tot of rum, he leant back against the bulkhead and sent up a silent prayer of gratitude for his deliverance.

TWO-THIRDS of the seven hundred Italians on board the *Arandora Star* lost their lives and around one-third of the five hundred Germans. Forty-two of the one hundred and seventy-four crew, including the captain and most of his officers, and thirty-seven of the two hundred army guards, perished with them. The disproportionate death toll among the Italians was probably due to their position in the ship and consequent late arrival on deck, as well as the more advanced age of many compared to the other groups. The relatively high German survival rate was due to the majority being, like Paolo, members of the merchant marine and hence familiar with life drills and safety procedures at sea. Yet the *Daily Express* reported soldiers speaking of *panic among the aliens when they realised the ship was sinking... The Germans made it clear that nobody was going to stand in their way of being rescued. But the Italians were as bad. The whole*

mob of them thought of their own skins first. The scramble for the
boats was sickening.

When Paolo read these words in the newspaper offered
to him by a guard in Greenock after they reached Scotland,
he burned with rage. The group that had the most significant percentage of survivors was that of the British soldier
guards.

13

IN LIMBO

I t was three days since the news of the sinking of the *Arandora Star* reached Liverpool and Judith was inconsolable. She didn't even know whether or not Paolo had been on board. There was no ship's manifest and Mrs Giordano's pleas for information to the police and the Home Office had produced nothing.

The newspapers said that Italian families had besieged the Home Office in London seeking information about their loved ones. Questions had been asked in Parliament, yet so far there were no satisfactory answers.

Hannah wished there was some way she could ease her sister's pain.

'We know there were survivors,' she said, sitting at the kitchen table, watching Judith push her food around her plate. 'If anyone was going to make it, it has to be Paolo. He's strong, he's young and fit and he's a sailor. He'll know the drill better than most of the others onboard.'

Judith said nothing, continuing to stare into space.

There was a loud knocking at the front door. Hannah went to answer it and found Father Edwards on the doorstep. She showed him into the front parlour. As soon as he sat down and started to speak, Judith appeared in the doorway.

'I have news of Paolo at last,' the priest said, his voice solemn. 'He's alive. He was brought ashore in Scotland after the sinking of the *Arandora Star*. As far as I can find out, he's fit and well. Sadly, it appears Mr Giordano was not among the survivors. I understand Paolo is being held in Greenock near Glasgow.'

Judith gave a whoop of joy that made Hannah feel ashamed for her sister in front of the priest. Mr Giordano and so many others would not be returning to their loved ones. But she said nothing to reprimand Judith. Hannah could understand all too well her sister's joy. But for Mrs Giordano this must be the worst day of her life.

'Where is he? Can I see him? Is he coming home to Liverpool?' Judith could barely contain her excitement.

The priest looked sideways at Hannah. 'I'm sorry, Judith, but it looks as if he's going to be sent away on another ship. The decision to deport stands.'

'What? Why?' Judith's voice was anguished. 'Surely after going through all that they can't put him on another ship? It's not right! Why don't they put him in a camp here?'

Father Edwards shook his head. 'As a young man capable of serving in the military, Paolo, like all the interned Italians of a similar age, is considered a risk. He's also a former seaman who has served in the Italian merchant navy. That's viewed as a serious threat to national security.' He winced as he spoke. 'I know it's nonsense, but the Home Office doesn't have the resources to check individual cases, so their response is draconian and doesn't discriminate between those who are genuine risks and those who aren't.

They want all the so-called enemy alien men out of the country as soon as possible.'

'Paolo's not an enemy!' Judith wailed.

Hannah put her arm around her sister. 'Where are they sending him? Canada again?'

'I'm making enquiries and if I find out I'll let you know at once – but no one seems to know who's making the decisions.'

Judith's face flushed, her eyes filling with tears of rage. 'It's cruel. Inhuman. Paolo's survived a shipwreck. It's not right to put him straight back on another ship.'

Hannah exchanged looks with the priest. 'It's not fair. I agree, Jude. It's really dreadful. But you need to accept there's nothing we can do about it. If they decide to deport him then you're going to have to get used to that. At least this time we know it's happening. That was the worst thing when he was arrested – not having a clue what they'd done with him.'

The priest nodded his agreement. 'I promise you, Judith, I will do everything I possibly can to find out what's going on. I'll also try to find out if arrangements can be made for you to see him before he's deported.' He lowered his eyes. 'But I have to warn you I think it's unlikely permission will be granted.'

Father Edward got up and reached for his hat, where he had placed it on the chair beside him. 'I must be going now. I have the unfortunate duty of breaking the news to Mrs Giordano that Alfonso won't be coming home again. Then I have to be back in church to hear Confessions before Benediction.'

His words must have made Judith realise belatedly that no matter how distressing the news about Paolo was, nothing could compare with the pain Mrs Giordano would be facing. 'I'll come with you,' she offered. 'I have to offer my condolences.'

'I think it'd be better if you left it until tomorrow. While Mrs Giordano will be happy that Paolo survived, right now seeing you might be rubbing salt into her wounds. Better to leave her daughter to comfort her today.'

HANNAH WAS glad she'd volunteered for the WVS. It took her mind off her constant gnawing fear for Will, who was back at sea again, the repairs to the Shelbourne having been completed. Her worries about the Atlantic crossings had been intensified by the knowledge of what had happened to the *Arandora Star* after the sinking of the *Christina*. Barely a week went by without news of merchant naval vessels sunk and lives lost. Hannah had to keep reminding herself that if men like her husband didn't risk their lives doing these dangerous Atlantic runs, the nation would go hungry and there would be no armaments to fight the war. Scant comfort.

She'd tried to convince Judith that Paolo being sent overseas on another ship so soon after surviving being shipwrecked, was no different from what Will was doing.

'For Will it's not just a one-off journey but back and forth. Every trip is a battle against the odds, Judith. Can't you see that?' It was hard not to believe that one day his luck would run out.

Judith was adamant. 'At least Will has a *chance* of coming home. Paolo, once he's gone, is out of my life until the end of the war, whenever that might be.'

Hannah was too weary to argue. Obviously, they were both suffering. Trying to compare whose situation was worse was a pointless exercise. All they could do was hope and wait.

In the end, Hannah had to accept that her sister was no longer capable of optimism. The only consolation Judith was willing to accept was whatever she received when she went to church. Hannah was never tempted to join her there, however much she liked Father Edwards.

The WVS work was interesting, and Hannah discovered she had a hitherto untapped talent for organisation. She would have liked to have worked with evacuees but instead, here in Liverpool, she was often called upon to comfort mothers desperately missing their evacuated children, as well as sorting and sizing clothing donations and drawing up duty rotas.

While annoyed by Nance's sudden decision to take a job and absolve herself of any need to do housework, Hannah had to admit it was a relief not to have her around the house so much. As Nance had never helped with the cooking anyway and, since starting work at the NAAFI, had most of her meals in the canteen there, Hannah barely saw her these days.

Hannah's failure to write to her Aunt Elizabeth preyed on her mind. Every time she put pen to paper something held her back. Writing would involve the unpleasant duty of informing Elizabeth that her sister Sarah was dead, murdered by her own husband. While it would involve Hannah having to dredge up the unhappy memories of those terrible events, though that was not the main thing stopping her.

At first, she couldn't work out what was the cause of her reluctance, before recognizing it was fear of rejection. The thought of getting in touch with her once-beloved aunt, only to be rebuffed, was horrible, but Hannah had begun to think it had to be a possibility. If indeed her mother had been right and Hannah's father had raped Elizabeth and fathered a child with her, then it was hardly surprising that Elizabeth would want to close the door on such a painful episode. She had been thrown out of the family home and forced to travel to Australia. Who could blame her for wanting nothing to do with such a painful past and such miserable memories?

The delay in writing the letter also meant Hannah was keeping alive the possibility that one day they might be reunited – holding that hope was better than risking being snubbed by her aunt and closing the door forever.

She'd tried to explain this to Will before he returned to sea, but he had looked at her as though she were crazy.

'Lizbeth would never shut you out. She's not that kind of woman. You've done nothing wrong. She might be mad with *me* for running away when my old man was in jail, but she'd never hold that against you. And I don't think she'd be angry with me either. Not after all this time. She's got a big heart. Just write the damn letter, Hannah. Stop torturing yourself.'

So, she'd promised she would but, as each day passed, she told herself she would do it the next. Perhaps if Judith had shown the slightest hint of enthusiasm for the idea it would have been different but, caught up in her despair over Paolo, Judith never appeared to give the matter a thought.

14

THE LONG VOYAGE

He was back in Liverpool, on the all-too-familiar waterfront. Paolo breathed in the salt air and watched the screaming seagulls swoop and dip in search of scraps of food.

He had received a cursory going over in the Scottish hospital. They had been interested only in whether he could manage to walk a few steps unaided and made no other attempts to check whether his time in the sea clinging to a rope, and then the hours sitting drenched and cold in an open lifeboat, had done him any lasting harm. Then they were all packed onto lorries and sent to a detention centre in a former cotton mill.

The conditions there were worse than in Walton, the overcrowding unbearable and the food indigestible. After three days, to Paolo's intense relief, the survivors of the *Arandora Star* were herded onto another truck and driven to Birkenhead, across the Mersey from Liverpool to be temporarily held in tents in Arrow Park military camp.

The internees were wondering where they would be moved next. The authorities were not forthcoming but had indicated that their stay in Arrow Park was to be a short one. For the *Arandora Star* survivors, it was a relief to be on dry land after their brush with death and they gave little thought to their next destination, other than guessing it would be the Isle of Man. The numbers of Italians were much depleted by the death of so many, particularly the older men, but spirits among the young ones were generally high and there was universal relief that they had escaped deportation.

Paolo often fantasised about bringing Judith to meet his family in Napoli, visualising her climbing the steep stone stairs up to their apartment beside him. He imagined his mamma opening the door, then screaming her delight at seeing her son again. He wondered how his elderly nonna would react to Judith. Of course, they wouldn't be able to communicate – Nonna knew no English and Judith knew no more than a few simple words of greeting in Italian – but he hoped his grandmother would love her anyway. He was certain his father would. How could he not? Papa always had an eye for a pretty face. As for *Mamma,* as long as Paolo loved Judith, that would be good enough for her.

He pictured his brothers and sisters – they'd be older, of course. It was three years since he'd seen his family and who knew how long it would be until the war was over? He imagined his little sisters staring at Judith in fascination, the older ones appraising her with critical eyes. His family would all come to adore her.

They'd sit around the big wooden table, all squashed up to make space for him and Judith, Mamma serving up *pasta al ragù* or a steaming bowl of *stufato,* bursting with the flavour of freshly-harvested vegetables. There would be wine, rough and ready, yet robust and tasty. Ripe, luscious *pomodori* grown under Mediterranean sunshine in the rich volcanic soils and tasting like tomatoes should taste, but never did here in England.

Later, he and Judith would walk through the narrow streets and he would show her the dark outline of Monte Vesuvio and the moon shining bright over the beautiful Bay of Naples. Then he would kiss her in the moonlight and slip a ring onto her finger and they would agree not to delay any longer to be married. Just long enough for Mamma to prepare a feast and for the priest to agree to perform the service.

Paolo never tired of this fantasy. It sustained him, helped him bear up when the dark moods enveloped him, helped him push away the haunting vision of Alfonso Giordano standing on that sloping deck, clinging to the metal guard rails and refusing to leave the sinking ship.

A few days after their arrival in Arrow Park, they crossed the Mersey again. Herded onto the quayside, instead of the ferry steamer for the Isle of Man, another enormous ship awaited them, the *HMT Dunera*.

Realisation dawned. It was hard to credit it, but the authorities were evidently going to have another go at exporting the *Arandora* survivors. The men looked at each other, fear and anger mingling with disbelief. Here they were, in the clothes they stood up in, all their belongings having gone down with the *Arandora*, about to face another long sea voyage through perilous waters.

There was no information forthcoming about their ultimate destination. Paolo thought it was likely to be Canada again. He knew enough about the sea and now enough about the persistence of German submarines, to assume that the old adage about lightning never striking twice in the same place were palpably untrue. While the prospect of repeating the horrors of abandoning ship was unthinkable, whatever happened, he would summon the strength to get through it, survive, and one day be reunited with Judith.

The brief time the internees spent on the *Arandora Star* had been a relatively good experience until the German torpedo struck, so nothing had prepared Paolo and the other survivors for the horror that awaited them on the *Dunera*.

They were joined on the quayside by a large contingent of German and Austrian Jewish refugees. The survivors looked at these men, envying their heavy wool coats, and their elegant leather suitcases and holdalls.

The British army guards assigned to accompany them to their unknown destination took pleasure in heaping degradation on the survivors, seemingly resenting the fact that they had managed to emerge alive from the attack on the *Arandora Star.*

The humiliation began on the quayside at Liverpool. Paolo's throat tightened when he saw Jake Cassidy among the mob of military guards.

'Well, well, we meet again, Tourney-Benny. So, you and all those other filthy Eyeties escaped from that ship. I've heard about what you miserable cowards did – shoving and pushing to get on the lifeboats. You're all scum!' Cassidy turned his head and spat onto the concrete.

Paolo refused to rise to the bait, knowing it was exactly what the man wanted. He stared ahead, avoiding eye contact.

'You won't get away with that kind of behaviour now. We're going to make sure of that.' Cassidy jerked his head in the direction of the ship. 'If we're unlucky enough to get zapped by a U-boat you lot are going straight to the bottom, where you belong.' He pushed his face close up to Paolo's so that his foul breath was under the Italian's nose.

Cassidy drew back and watched, arms folded, as an officer barked an order to the whole group of two hundred-odd survivors. 'Empty your pockets!'

The internees had no choice other than to comply. They watched, helpless as guards flung empty wallets onto the ground, after stuffing the contents into the front of their battledress, soon bulging with banknotes.

'You won't be needing English money where you're going and, after the war's won, you'll be sent home to Germany and Italy.' The officer was still not satisfied. Turning next to the Jewish refugees he said, 'Belongings out of bags and on the ground ready for inspection. Now!'

The *Arandora* survivors watched as their new travelling companions complied. Some of the Italians didn't even have a pair of trousers to wear and were still clad in the pyjamas or underwear they'd been wearing when the U-boat struck at six in the morning.

The officer kicked at a fine leather suitcase. 'Get it all out. I want to see what you bastards are trying to smuggle out of the country.' The guards pressed closer, naked bayonets at the tops of their rifles.

The internees unpacked piles of clothing and effects on the concrete as the rain drizzled down, soaking everything. They watched, helpless, as Cassidy and the other guards rummaged through their possessions, pocketing anything that caught their eyes, and leaving the clothes in messy jumbled piles on the wet dockside. Passers-by, including dock workers and policemen, helped themselves to any items of clothing they fancied. The army officer in charge watched but did nothing to prevent the theft.

'Five items. That will do you. Hurry!' The officer kicked at one of the heaps of clothing. 'It's going to be very cosy on board and we've no room for lots of luggage.'

The internees scrabbled to gather a few essential items, stuffing them back into their leather holdalls.

'Leave the bags. They're going in the hold. You'll get them at the other end,' barked the sergeant-major. 'Only what you can wear or put in your pockets.' He addressed the guards, 'Get the bastards on board.'

Paolo and the others snaked up the gangway onto the *Dunera*, flanked by their prison guards, still holding rifles with bayonets. No matter how badly they had been treated until now, this was the worst they had experienced. The soldiers were, like Cassidy, rough men, hard-faced, cruel. Later he discovered that many of them were former criminals released from prison to perform military service.

On board, the two hundred *Arandora Star* survivors were segregated from the other prisoners, shoved onto the end of the deck behind barbed wire to wait in the rain while the hundreds of other internees were boarded.

The humiliating ordeal from their welcoming committee was not over. The guards went among them, searching pockets for any remaining valuables, confiscating fountain pens, wedding rings, and wrist-watches. Paolo for once was glad he'd never had a chance to acquire such items, as around him his countrymen and the German survivors, mostly like him pro-British, were stripped of their valued possessions.

In Arrow Park he had become friendly with a young man, Guido Visconti, a former hotel manager, and the two stuck closely together.

From the open deck, the men were ushered by the bayonet-bearing guards down into the belly of the vessel, where they were barricaded into a cramped airless space, with blocked portholes allowing no natural light. The only way out was by means of a narrow stairway, access beyond behind a locked door.

Paolo exchanged glances with Guido. Were the ship to come under attack, they would be trapped, unless they managed to break down the door – a task likely to be impossible since the guards made it clear it would be constantly guarded.

'Are you thinking what I'm thinking?' asked Guido.

'We'd better hope the ship's captain knows what he's doing and keeps us out of trouble.'

'And if we're torpedoed?'

'If we're hit, then we say our prayers and prepare to meet our maker.'

'*Orcoddio!*' the hotel manager swore. 'They are going to let us die?'

'You heard the man when we were on the dockside.' Paolo gave a resigned shrug. 'No point in worrying about something we can't change.' He knew he didn't mean that though. If they were trapped down here unable to escape, he'd never see Judith again. He could never resign himself to that and would fight to the last breath to escape.

They were given no bedding and there were insufficient hammocks for everyone. Paolo and Guido were among the many who ended up sleeping under their overcoats on the bare floor, leaving the hammocks to the older men.

For Paolo, being on a ship was second nature, even though he had never experienced conditions such as these. The movement of the vessel rocked him into a familiar sleep. He sensed that the ship was taking a course due north, presumably in an effort to avoid the dangerous U-boat infested passages around Ireland. He imagined that they would eventually turn west to make the crossing over the North Atlantic to Canada.

They had been aboard about twenty-four hours when Paolo and Guido were pulled out of the line where they were waiting to use the latrines. A guard shoved them in front of him to an area of an upper deck where an enormous pile of the Jewish refugees' baggage was stacked. They watched, dumbstruck as two of the guards used their bayonets to slash the beautifully tooled leather of these expensive suitcases, letting the clothing inside tumble out onto the deck. 'Quick as you like. Over the side with it all.'

Guido started to protest but was rewarded with a blow across the shoulders with a rifle butt.

'Shut your mouths and get on with it. I want this deck cleared of all this filth before the day's out.'

The guards leaned on the railings, smoking and sharing dirty jokes while Paolo and Guido did as instructed, dumping case after case into the sea. The ship's wash now trailed clothing, like sombre-coloured bunting. If a U-boat needed an easy indication of where they were, it couldn't have asked for more.

BEING AFLOAT WAS NOT a familiar experience for many of Paolo's fellow passengers, as they discovered on the second night. Many of the men were seasick and Paolo was woken from sleep by the old gentleman in the hammock above him vomiting all over his legs. He told himself to be thankful it wasn't over his face.

The cabin soon became unbearable. Access to the latrines was severely limited by day and prohibited overnight. The men were expected to use buckets which filled rapidly. The stench of urine, excrement and vomit polluted the unventilated air. A breeding ground for dysentery.

At eight o'clock on the second morning, Paolo and his cohort heard a strange noise: a metallic rasping, like something being scraped across a giant cheese grater, followed by the loud boom of an explosion. Having lived through the demise of the *Arandora Star*, Poalo knew immediately that it was a torpedo. In a panic they all rushed up the stairwell.

The doorway at the top was locked as usual. Fearful for their lives, they charged it and managed to smash through one of the panels. The German who was in front was met by a bayonet, forcing him to retreat, his arm slashed and bloodied.

An angry voice boomed through the hole in the door. 'Get below! Drown like rats, scum!' The barrel of a gun pointed through the broken door panel.

Terrified, the men had no choice but to retreat back down the stairway. They sat on the floor of the stinking cabin, awaiting death.

But nothing happened. The torpedoes must have coincided with the ship's change of course into the next zigzag and they'd narrowly missed the ship, exploding beyond the *Dunera*. They had cheated death.

From that day on, the German former merchant sailors organised a duty rota, to keep guard, not only against the possibility of further torpedo attacks, but also against their growing fear of their soldier guards.

The men were subjected to frequent searches and confiscation of any remaining valuables, often accompanied by violence. Jake Cassidy was the worst offender. He took every opportunity to taunt, strike and humiliate. His primary target was Paolo, who was powerless to defend himself. A favourite tactic was to smash the butt of his rifle down on the bare toes of the detainees. Another cruel trick was for a smiling guard to offer an internee a cigarette. If the man accepted, which most of them – desperate for a smoke – did, they would beat them with a rifle butt. The fear of being attacked was often outweighed by the desire for a consoling cigarette, and as the guards did this separately, choosing different victims, this sport lasted longer than it might otherwise have done.

The commanding officer, Lieutenant-Colonel Scott, did nothing to prevent the misdeeds of the guards – indeed he sometimes participated in the ill treatment.

'You slimy Eyetie coward. How many soldiers and sailors did you shove out of your way to save your miserable greasy fascist skin?' was a frequent taunt.

The vessel was seriously overcrowded, with almost twice as many passengers as it was designed for. During the day, hammocks were forbidden and men sat or lay on the floor or on top of tables. The hatches were battened down, so they had no natural daylight, other than fifteen minutes on deck for supervised exercise.

One afternoon, when Paolo was doing his statutory daily exercise – consisting of walking in circles under the gaze of the guards – he found himself next to Cassidy.

The Australian curled his lip as he looked Paolo up and down. 'You're looking rather feeble these days, Tourney-Benny. The Old Dootchay won't be too happy with you. Time you built those muscles up. Let's have a hundred press-ups. Now!' He kicked Paolo and hit him across the back with his rifle-butt.

Weak with hunger, thirst and lack of proper exercise, Paolo struggled to do as ordered. Every time he faltered, the Australian landed a kick. Praying for strength, Paolo told himself to do it for Judith. He was near collapse by the time the whistle blew to signal the end of the torture. He vowed

he would work on his strength at every opportunity. He had
to build it back if he was going to survive.

Hygiene was a serious concern as a result of the
constantly overflowing toilet buckets. The proper latrines
were little better. Men had to use them by rota – there were
insufficient cubicles to support the numbers of prisoners. As
the latrines had no doors, the internees were forced to defe-
cate in full view of a long queue of their waiting fellows. The
saltwater used to flush the toilets swilled the contents out of
the bowls, covering the seats in a combination of excrement
and salt. There was no toilet paper and the situation wors-
ened as poor conditions and near-starvation rations led to
numerous cases of dysentery. No one was permitted to shave
– razors and hair combs were confiscated and one piece of
soap a week was shared – along with a towel – by ten men.

Paolo had never been so degraded and humiliated. Was
this what he had survived the sinking for? It would be easy to
allow this sub-human treatment to break his spirit, but he
channelled his shame into anger. He refused to give Cassidy
and his thugs satisfaction by falling into depression or
despair. Instead, he tried to focus his mind on trying to work
out where the ship was headed. During the brief periods of
exercise, he studied the sky and the position of the sun. After
eight days at sea, they were heading south. Canada was not to
be their destination and rumours began to circulate around
the ship that it was likely to be South Africa or Australia.

He passed the news to Guido. 'We have a long voyage
ahead of us, *amico mio*. Almost two months probably.'

Guido let out a cry of anguish. 'We'll all be dead if they
keep treating us like this.'

'We mustn't give them that satisfaction,' said Paolo. 'At
least Australia is warm and sunny. We'd probably freeze to

death in Canada in winter – especially if these same guards are to stay with us.'

'Surely not? They'll be needed back in England, won't they?'

'I hope so. The Australians can't possibly be as bad as them.'

Guido snorted. 'Your friend Cassidy is an Australian. He's the worst of the lot.' He pointed at Paolo's cheek which was scarred and reddened from a recent blow inflicted by the former bosun.

Paolo told him all Australians weren't like Cassidy – '*Lui non c'entra niente*. My friend, Will Kidd, is Australian and he's the best friend I've ever had. He and I sailed with Cassidy. Will hated him as much as I did. If you think Cassidy picks on me, it's nothing to how he was to Will. The difference was when we all sailed together, he couldn't show it.'

THE *DUNERA* HAD BEEN at sea for almost a month when they anchored at Cape Town to take on supplies. This was the ship's third stop and each time the men had hoped it was to be their final destination. After all South Africa was still a part of the British Empire, even if now a sovereign state, so why were they not disembarking there?

Paolo did not even get so much as a glimpse of Table Mountain, which he remembered nostalgically from his time sailing the Christina, as it was wreathed in mist during the fifteen minutes he was allowed on deck. He remembered the happy days when he and Will had sailed between different African ports, picking up and dropping off cargo as they went. He had loved the life on the tramp steamer, hopping back and forth, carrying whatever loads needed transporting. The colour and vibrancy of Africa had always appealed to him, the heady smell of ripe fruit and spices and the warm smiles of the people. All that was denied him now.

Perhaps it was moving into the relatively safer waters off Africa and the Pacific, away from the constant threat of U-boats, or the fact that some of the nastiest guards had jumped ship, but after Cape Town one or two of their guards softened their behaviour slightly. The savage beatings tailed off. But apart from occasional 'fruit days' when oranges and other African fruit taken on board were distributed, living standards didn't improve. The unsanitary conditions and poor diet had caused the men to lose significant amounts of weight. The bread they were served was full of maggots and the butter rancid. Their matted uncombed hair and ragged beards had rendered them unrecognisable from when they'd boarded the prison ship.

As for Cassidy, he didn't modify his attitude at all. If anything the closer he got to Australia the more he went out of his way to make life for Paolo hell.

15

A DEAD CAT AND A NEW FRIEND

 Dead Cat and a New Friend

THE FIRST BOMBS dropped on Liverpool at the end of July, the bombardment increasing as August began, mostly over on the Wirral, where the shipyards were. By late August, the raids were heavier and were now aimed at both sides of the Mersey. The occupants of The Laurels became accustomed to the wail of the sirens, the thud of the anti-aircraft guns and the thunder of explosions. Familiarity, however, didn't dispel the stomach-wrenching fear that gripped Hannah every time the early warning sounded. The rising wail ran through her body, the sound coursing along her blood vessels and tingling through her nerve endings.

On the occasions when Hannah and Judith were alone in the house during a night raid, they took to sheltering in the cupboard under the stairs rather than venturing into the garden to climb down into the Andersen shelter which, when it rained, accumulated water in the bottom, creating a sludgy swamp. The shelter, always cold and damp, was a haven for spiders and earwigs. The sisters put an old eider-down in the under-stairs cupboard to cushion them on the wooden floor and squashed together into what used to be a broom cupboard. It was preferable to sitting shivering on a wooden bench with their feet in a puddle.

Sam was often out on air-raid warden duty and Nance frequently stayed out all night after going dancing. The sisters knew better than to enquire where she went.

Since receiving the news about Paolo's deportation, Judith was no longer capable of casual conversation and passed her time sewing or studying her catechism – she was even more intent on being received into the Catholic Church. Hannah was concerned about her sister's state of mind. Her attempts to get Judith to talk about Paolo or her feelings about their separation were always brushed off. Judith had perfected the art of what Hannah thought of as her brave smile. She used this like a mask and wouldn't be drawn into revealing anything that lay behind it.

One evening, Nance sauntered into the kitchen as Hannah, Judith and Sam were eating supper. She had a way of walking that involved swivelling her hips in an exagger-ated manner, testifying to hours of careful study of the films she lapped up at the pictures. Hannah wondered why she bothered to use it when they were her only audience. It was probably now so deeply ingrained that Nance couldn't do otherwise.

She lifted the lid of the saucepan that was standing on the hob. 'No offence, but I'm glad I gets me meals free down the NAAFI and don't have to eat what you dish up out of the rations.' Her nose wrinkled. 'Mince again. What's it with this time?'

'Mashed potatoes and it's absolutely delicious,' Sam said, loyally.

Judith looked up from her plate. 'Really tasty. Our Hannah does a great job stretching the rations out. What did you have at the NAAFI that was so wonderful then?'

'Bangers and mash. Real sausages.' Nance's expression was smug. 'Got to feed the forces proper, haven't we? But the most exciting thing that happened to me today was I got to see the King and Queen.' She folded her arms across her chest and waited expectantly.

No one said anything.

'Aren't you going to ask me about it?' she said at last, pouting. Another tribute to the power of the silver screen. Hannah couldn't help wondering how, in this time of short-ages, Nance never seemed to run out of her signature crimson lipstick

Sam gave a sigh of resignation. 'I'm sure you're going to tell us anyway.'

'Their Majesties came to look at the bomb damage in Birkenhead and to visit the shipyards. To boost the workers' morale.' She spoke the words as though she had read the phrase in the newspaper.

Hannah finished eating and put her knife and fork down. 'And what were you doing over in Birkenhead?'

'I wasn't. Afterwards, they stopped by the NAAFI before they left Liverpool. It were top secret! They was no more than a couple of feet away from me.' She looked thoughtful. 'Surprising how short they were. Even him. Shorter than Sam here. And Queen Lizzie is a right little titch.'

Sam glanced at Hannah and rolled his eyes. 'I hope you didn't tell her that. She might have had you imprisoned for treason.'

'Less of your lip, Samuel Henderson. You need to show

me some respect. After all, I could have been your step-mother!'

Sam snorted, looked as though he was about to respond, but thought better of it. 'Time I was off on my rounds. I'm on first shift tonight, so with a bit of luck I may even get to sleep in my own bed later if Hermann the German gives us a break. Good night, ladies.' He scraped his chair back and left the kitchen.

'Oy!' Nance called after him. 'There's a dead cat in the front garden. Must be the old geezer's next door. Get rid of it, Sam, will you? Before it starts to stink the place out.'

Hannah didn't know the old man next door. She'd only seen him a couple of times when he'd appeared in his back garden while she was hanging out the washing. 'I heard the gentleman next door over the fence yesterday, calling for his cat. Do you think it's the same one?'

'Bound to be. It's the only ginger cat I've seen round here. Horrible scraggy little thing too.' Nance wrinkled her nose in disgust.

'How sad. I tried to speak to him but when I wished him good morning, he acted as though he'd been scalded and rushed back indoors.' Hannah began to clear away the plates.

'You sit down, Hannah, I'll do the dishes,' said Judith. 'You look done in.'

Hannah smiled her gratitude, then turned to ask Nance if she knew anything about the elderly neighbour.

'Why would I know? He's a bit too long in the tooth for me,' she said, winking. 'Not when I can take me pick of the boys down the NAAFI.'

'Must you always assume everything's about *that*?' Judith turned from the sink and threw Nance a look.

'*That's* the only thing what makes life worth living in this miserable bleeding war.' Nance patted the back of her hair with a hand. 'And I've always been partial to a man in uniform. You should come out dancing with me some time, doll.'

Judith jerked her hands out of the sink and without stopping to dry them, ran out of the room.

'What's got her goat?' Nance put her hands on her hips.

'In case it's escaped your memory, Nance, Judith's young man is on a ship sailing to who knows where, and she's worried sick about him.'

'Oh, yes.' Nance's face looked unusually contrite. She'd always had a fondness for Judith. 'Silly me. I didn't think.'

Hannah sighed and shook her head. 'You never do,' she muttered under her breath.

It was a few days later when Hannah thought of the next-door neighbour again. Sam told her he'd been unable to reach Mr Hathaway so had buried the dead cat under the apple trees in the back garden.

'In our garden?'

Sam grinned at her. 'The old boy's garden's a jungle. I'd need a machete to clear a space.' When Hannah frowned, he added, 'If he's not happy I'll have to dig the cat up again and rebury it for him. You wouldn't think there was a war on, and I have better things to do. Like digging human beings out of bombed-out buildings.'

Hannah squeezed her eyes tightly shut. She didn't like to think about what Sam must see when he was helping clear bomb damage.

After government advice at the start of the war had led to a tragic mass culling of pets, there were not so many left these days, and many that were still around were going hungry. Rationing did not extend to pets. Perhaps that was what happened to Mr Hathaway's cat. Had it simply starved to death? Unlikely. Cats were natural hunters.

On the way back from her shift at the WVS, Hannah looked up at the grime-encrusted windows of Mr Hathaway's house. They were so filthy, he wouldn't need to use blackout curtains.

Back home, she made a batch of scones, using milk that had turned sour when Nance had left it out after making tea. Hannah had lost count of the number of times she'd told her to put the milk back on the cold shelf in the larder. On the spur of the moment, she decided to set aside two of the scones and take them round to the elderly gentleman. It might cheer him up over the loss of his cat.

Hannah made her way up the path to the neighbour's front door, between twin lawns where the grass was knee-high and peppered with dandelions. She knocked on the paint-flaked door and waited for a response. She was about to give up, when the door creaked ajar.

Speaking into the narrow gap, she said, 'Mr Hathaway, I've been doing some baking and thought you might like a couple of scones. They're still warm.'

'What?' The voice was tetchy, and high-pitched for a man. 'Who are you? What do you want? Go away!'

Hannah decided to make allowances for his age. 'I'm from next door – Mrs Kidd. I'm one of Sam Henderson's lodgers. I thought I'd pop round and introduce myself and give you these scones.'

'Why?'

Hannah gave a little half-laugh. 'I thought you might appreciate some home baking.'

A bony hand shot through the gap in the doorway and grabbed the basket from her hands. Then the door slammed shut in her face. Swallowing her annoyance, she made her way back to the gate. Behind her, the front door creaked open again.

The old man was wearing black braces which held up his trousers from a waistband just south of his armpits. He was skin and bone and had very little hair left on his head, the top of which shone as though he had polished it. His shoes, in contrast, were scuffed and dull and one lens of his spectacles was cracked. She'd heard he was about seventy, but he looked much older.

His reedy voice halted her. 'My cat's gone. I think she's died. All that noise in the sky scared her.'

'You mean the air raids?'

'Is that what it was? I don't like it. Reminds me of the war.' He stood in the doorway, one hand holding it open and the other still clutching the basket of scones.

Puzzled, Hannah frowned. 'Oh, you mean the *last* war,' she said eventually. 'The raid the other night seemed to go on forever. When did your cat disappear?'

'A week ago. I think she went away to hide and die. That's what cats do when they know their number's up. They slink off to die somewhere else. Somewhere you won't find them.'

'I'm afraid you're right. Sam, our landlord, found a dead cat and buried it in our back garden. I'm so sorry. He said he'd put a note through your door.'

The old man stepped aside to reveal a sea of unread letters and leaflets covering the hall floor behind him. 'I never read anything that comes through the door. Nothing good comes of it.' He made a little noise, a half sob, as though only now processing Hannah's words about the cat. 'I liked that cat. She kept the mice under control.'

'I'm so sorry. Was she very old?'

'I don't know. She turned up one day and never left. Years ago. I lose track of time.'

'You must miss her terribly.'

'Yes. I do. She was a nurse you know.'

Hannah's head jerked back in surprise. 'The *cat*?

'What cat? I'm talking about my Flo.'

'Flo?'

'My wife.' He scowled at her as if she were an idiot. 'She worked over at the hospital in Fazakerley. Infectious diseases. She nursed my mother when she was dying of the scarlet fever. That's how we met. Then she died too.' He turned away.

'I'm sorry, Mr Hathaway.'

The man grunted then stepped back inside his hallway and closed the front door.

Hannah went home, glad that she'd made the effort to meet her strange neighbour. Was it the loss of his wife that had made him a recluse?

That evening, she'd tried to tell Judith about the episode, but her sister wasn't interested.

Nance, drinking a beer straight from a bottle, did have something to say. 'I can't think why you're wasting your time on an old geezer like him. What a bloody waste of a couple of scones. That's our rations you're throwing away on him. I could've had those.'

Judith looked up. 'Next time you take the trouble to make some scones, our Hannah will bear that in mind. In the meantime, put a sock in it, Nance!'

Nance's face registered surprise. She wasn't used to Judith snapping at her. 'I've never been so insulted in all me born days,' she said.

. . .

THE FOLLOWING MORNING, there was a knock on the front door.

Mr Hathaway handed Hannah the empty breadbasket. 'Very tasty,' he said and turned to go.

'Why don't you come in and have a cup of tea? I've just put the kettle on.'

His brows crinkled into a frown, but he stepped inside the hallway and followed her into the kitchen.

'How are you coping with rationing?' Hannah asked, casting around for something to say as she handed him his tea, noticing how his hand shook when he took it.

'The char handles it. She does the shopping.' He put down the cup and saucer and Hannah noticed he was missing two fingers on his right hand. She decided not to ask about it.

'And the cooking?'

He grunted. Hannah presumed that was a yes.

'It must be lonely for you. Being on your own. I suppose your cat was good company.'

He stared at her as if she were stupid, then turned his attention to his tea.

'Sorry there's nothing to go with that. All the scones are gone. And we've run out of biscuits, I'm afraid.'

He nodded. 'You married?' he asked. 'To that sailor?' Seeing her surprise, he added, 'I see people come and go. I keep an eye on things.'

'Yes,' she said. 'My husband, Will, is with the merchant navy. He's doing the Atlantic crossings. I worry terribly.' She tightened her lips.

'He's lucky to have a woman like you.'

Surprised, Hannah didn't know what to say.

'I had a good woman. Too good for this world. She gave

her life for other people. Cared about them more than she did about me.' He stared into his teacup.

'I'm sure that's not true.'

'She was my little darling. So pretty in her nurse's uniform.'

He seemed to be in a trance, so Hannah said nothing.

'I used to go to the sanatorium to visit Mother, but the real reason was to see Flo. Couldn't keep my eyes off her even though I was nearly twice her age. When Mother died, and I had no reason to keep going back to Fazakerley, I asked her to marry me. Didn't expect her to say yes.'

He hunched over the table, his eyes fixed on the inside of his teacup, as if he were seeing something inside it. 'Found out afterwards she only accepted me to get away from her family.'

'Her family?'

'From her father. He used to beat her. Maybe more than that.' He choked off a sob. 'She married me to be safe from him. Told me on our wedding night.' He looked up at Hannah, his eyes brimming with unshed tears. 'I promised never to lay a finger on her. And I never did. I was more of a father to her than a husband. The father she wished she had.' He bent his head. 'I never went back on my word. She was my precious little darling. But marriage meant she had to give up the nursing and that broke her heart.'

Hannah leaned forward and touched his hand. 'You are a very kind and good man, Mr Hathaway.' She hesitated for a moment. 'I know what it's like to be badly treated by a father. Your wife was fortunate indeed to find you. I'm sure you made her very happy.'

Mr Hathaway looked up. 'I made her safe. After what she went through, no one could make her happy.'

'I'm sure she cared for you very much, in her own way.'

Hannah felt a surge of compassion for the elderly man. 'How did Flo die? She must have been very young.'

'Twenty-nine. She caught the diphtheria. Funny, isn't it? Spent all her time caring for patients with infectious diseases only to have one get her too. When we married she carried on going back to the hospital at Fazakerley and helping out as a volunteer. She was desperate to help people. It was what she loved more than anything. And that's how she died.'

'Sometimes life can be cruel.' Hannah squeezed his hand again.

'The doctor said she had no fight left in her. Turned her head to the wall and waited to die.' The tears were now unabated, rolling slowly down his cheeks.

Hannah plucked one of Sam's clean handkerchiefs off the airing rack and handed it to him.

'If I could only have made her love me half as much as I loved her, she'd have found the will to live. But she didn't ever care for me. I was just her protector.'

Hannah's heart went out to him. 'I'm sure she must have loved you.'

The old man wiped his eyes again then put down the handkerchief. 'No, she didn't.'

'Then ask yourself this, Mr Hathaway. If you had known that at the time, would you still have asked Flo to marry you?'

'In a heartbeat.'

'Then waste no time on regrets and sorrow. Think of how you made part of her life better than it would have been without you. Love has many forms and I'm sure in her own way, your Flo loved you. Her last years were happier once she was safe with you.'

Mr Hathaway looked up at her. 'I'd give anything to have

her back. She'd be forty-nine now. But I bet she'd still be as pretty as the day I first clapped eyes on her.'

A few minutes later, Hannah accompanied the old man to the front door. As she was about to close it behind him, she saw someone coming up the street. All thoughts of Mr Hathaway vanished as she ran down the pathway to meet Will.

16

THE LAND DOWN UNDER

The *Dunera* with its cargo of emaciated and wretched men, reached Fremantle in Australia. Yet again, it proved not to be their final destination. Spirits plummeted and the men, Paolo included, started to think that this was indeed some kind of voyage of the damned. Would they be destined, like Wagner's *Flying Dutchman,* to sail forever without reaching land?

After crossing the Great Australian Bight, they approached Melbourne. This time, before docking, all sixteen hundred men were ordered to shave, but were given only eight razors to share them between them. Trying to remove weeks of growth with blunted blades was a desperate challenge and a last example of the vicious and baseless cruelty their jailers had meted out over more than fifty days at sea.

Once the ship docked, some of the prisoners, including Paolo and his two hundred fellow Italians, were ordered to disembark. Alongside them were ninety-four Germans – not the Jews but the category A prisoners who were considered to be dangerous – mainly ex-merchant seamen. The *Dunera* was to continue its voyage to Sydney, where the rest of the exiles would at last stand on dry land.

Paolo stood on the quay at Prince's Pier, overwhelmed with relief to be off the *Dunera* and away from Jake Cassidy, although with trepidation about what might await them. The sky was overcast and the temperature low enough for him to shiver. The men scrabbled about on the dock, trying to identify their own belongings from the much-diminished pile of garments that had been taken from them in Liverpool. But Paolo, like the other *Arandora* survivors, had no clothing to reclaim. He stood on the dock wearing the same filthy shirt and trousers he had worn since July. Scant protection against the chill of the Melbourne morning.

The men were shepherded onto a waiting train, to be taken to their internment camps at Tatura which, according to the Australian guards accompanying them, was a trip of just over one hundred miles.

The three-hour journey was a surprise to all of them and, at last, a welcome one. En route, the train stopped at Seymour, where the delighted men were served with tea and cake.

The Australian guards were casual and friendly, offering cigarettes to their prisoners and wishing them a cheery 'G'day.' To their surprise, none of the internees wanted to accept a cigarette.

One of the guards tried to press a cigarette on Paolo, but like all the men, he was terrified of a repeat of what the *Dunera* guards had done – offer a cigarette and then, if accepted, beat the unwitting recipient with the barrel of a gun. Even the heaviest of smokers had foresworn smoking on the voyage under these circumstances.

'Come on, mate, don't tell me you don't smoke.'

'I don't but even if I did, I don't want to be beaten.'

'Beaten?' The man jerked his head back in surprise. 'It's only a durry, mate. Not the crown bloody jewels.'

One of the other Italians, unable to resist the temptation of tobacco any longer, reached out and took the proffered cigarette. Instead of beating him, the Australian guard leaned forward and lit a match for him.

For the first time since leaving Liverpool, Paolo allowed himself to relax. He looked over at Guido and saw his friend was smiling.

After a few more minutes in which no repercussions were made against the smoker, more of the men gratefully accepted the proffered cigarettes and the tension in the train lightened.

'I thought it was supposed to be hot in Australia.' Paolo, shivering, addressed one of the guards.

'Strewth, it's autumn, mate. And in Melbourne it doesn't matter what the season's meant to be, you can get all four of them in a single day. Temperature's under sixty today but tomorrow could be down to fifty – or as easily up to eighty degrees.' The man leaned against the carriage wall, smoking. 'S'dry now. Could rain like the clappers in half an hour.' He gave an ironic laugh.

Paolo looked out of the window, taking in the scenery of this strange country. The land was flat and rather uninteresting – miles of farmland with the occasional clump of gum trees. But, after the squalid confinement of the *Dunera*, it was the Promised Land. Will used to talk about his Australian home in the Blue Mountains – a land of chasms, crags and spectacular scenery.

Paolo turned to the friendly guard, 'Are the Blue Mountains near here?'

The man shook his head. 'No, mate.' He called over to

his colleague, 'Blue Mountains are over near Sydney, aren't they, Clancy?'

The other guard nodded. 'New South Wales. 'Bout seventy miles from Sydney. My grandparents came from there. Reckoned it was a bonza place. Why you asking, mate?' He looked at Paolo with interest.

'I have a good friend who was born there. He also say me it is bonza.'

'Which town's he from?'

Paolo tried to remember. 'Mac... Mac...Falls. I forget.'

The guard grinned. 'MacDonald Falls?'

'*Si, guisto*! Yes. You have been there?'

'Me? I've never left Victoria, mate, but that town's where my folks came from. Moved down here when the mining dried up. Went into farming instead.' He stretched his hand out to shake Paolo's. 'Reckon, you're all right, mate. Name's Clancy. What's yours?'

'Tornabene, Paolo Tornabene.' Paolo accepted the proffered hand.

'You lot look like bloody skeletons. They told us to expect a bunch of dangerous war criminals and fifth columnists. Can't see it myself.'

'They give us little food on the ship. Always hungry. Now we all very thin. I work in grocery store and before I was sailor on British merchant ship.' Paolo indicated Guido on the other side of the compartment. 'He was hotel manager. And that old man there was a chef in a big London hotel.' He pointed out others: concierges, ice cream makers, barbers, café owners, teachers, musicians and a doctor. 'None of us is enemy of British. We all hate Mussolini and Hitler. On ship many Jewish men who came to England for escape Hitler.'

'That's bad, mate. Here in *Straya* we believe everyone

should get a fair go.' Clancy gave his head a thoughtful shake and moved on up the carriage.

The Australian countryside might be uninteresting, but Paolo decided the people were warm and welcoming. It was a judgement he wasn't surprised to make, based on his experience of Will Kidd.

Turning to gaze out of the window again, Paolo's thoughts inevitably returned to Liverpool. What was Will doing now? Was he safely in port or facing danger at sea? And what of Judith? Would she know he was here in Australia? Did she know he'd survived the sinking of the *Arandora Star* – or that he had been on it at all? She might even believe him to be still imprisoned in Britain. His fists curled into tight balls and he gritted his teeth. Regardless of the friendliness of their guards, he was still a captive and heading for incarceration. While nothing could be as bad as what he had endured on board the *Dunera,* he was destined for a prison camp and what lay ahead was unlikely to be *la dolce vita*.

THE CAMP at Tatura was constructed on a small hill and surrounded by a double row of barbed wire fencing with a gap between the rows. A collection of huts with corrugated iron roofs, Paolo imagined those roofs would make it cold in winter and hot in the summer. Remembering what the guard had said about the changeable Melbourne weather, he wondered whether it extended to the whole state of Victoria.

Inside the double-rowed perimeter fence, the Italians were separated from the Germans. The two sections of the camp were divided by barbed wire – and the barrier of language – although Paolo had found most of the Germans to be decent enough men and they had been able to communicate in English on the ship. The Germans here at Tatura were mainly merchant seamen like him, the German Jews, who had been the largest grouping on the *Dunera*, having continued on the ship to Sydney and from there to another camp at Hay.

To Paolo's relief, the accommodation, although spartan, was not as bad as any of the places where they had been interned in England. The beds were narrow and hard, but vastly superior to sleeping on the floor in the bowels of the *Dunera*, surrounded by vomiting men and dysentery sufferers, and having to queue for up to an hour to relieve oneself. Here, there were clean latrines in each dormitory block, as well as a large communal area for meals and socialising.

That first night, Paolo stood outside his hut, relishing being once more on solid ground. He'd never had trouble adapting to being at sea, until that last terrible voyage. Now, nothing would tempt him back to sea even as a passenger. Nothing except one day sailing back to Liverpool to find Judith. When would he see his *amore* again?

He gazed up at the vast blackness of the Australian night. The evening was cold: crisp even. Millions of stars shone bright in a dense, black velvet sky. The sky in the Southern Hemisphere was so much more beautiful than in the north. It was easy to understand why the Milky Way had been given its name, as it was so clearly visible, spilling across the dark sky like a huge splash of spilt milk.

Paolo took comfort in the thought that Judith might this moment also be watching the same heavens, before remembering that for her it would be daytime, and the night sky was entirely different where she was. The icy chill of fear clutched at his insides. He had heard enough news to know that her sky at night would be crisscrossed by searchlights, the stars blotted out by cloud or the smoke from exploding bombs. No matter how long this war lasted or how long he remained in custody, he swore that one day he'd be reunited with Judith. The only thing that had helped him survive that voyage of the damned was the rock-solid belief that he would one day hold her in his arms again.

AFTER THE PRISONERS from the *Dunera* had been at the Tatura camp for a week, they were told they would each be permitted to write a letter home to their loved ones. Paolo faced a dilemma. He wanted to write to his mother and father and assure them he was safe, even though he was on the other side of the world. Yet, more than anything, he wanted to write to Judith. He told himself that his parents would probably not even be aware he had left the merchant navy, let alone that he'd been arrested and interned in Britain. As far as they knew, he might be anywhere in the world. But that was no excuse. He owed it to them to tell them he was an internee but was safe. The realisation was slow to dawn. Italy was at war with Britain and its empire, including Australia. If he wrote to his family the letter would be routed via the Red Cross and might take months or possibly not reach them at all. Better to wait until later. He could write to Judith with a clear conscience.

This was the first time he had attempted to write a letter in English. As a child of a relatively poor Neapolitan family, Paolo, like many of his countrymen, had left school at the earliest legal age of eight years old. His first job was pushing a handcart full of vegetables for his father, until he had found a place as a cabin boy on a ship. There had never been any call for the written word. It was one thing to speak English, and quite another to put pen to paper. He stared at the empty page. Judith would think him stupid, ignorant, like a small child unable to spell. Her respect for him would evaporate. His face burned. He couldn't bear for her to think badly of him.

Picking up the pen he began to write. *Cara Mamma e Papà.*

17

IN DISTRESS

L iverpool's August ended with buildings along the length of the dock road on fire after heavy bombardment, leaving no doubt that Germany intended to cripple the city's role as the most strategically important port in the country. The attack left the landmark Custom House in flames, its central glass dome and roof structure hit by both high explosive bombs and incendiaries. As firemen worked bravely to tackle the blaze, a German plane swooped low, machine guns firing, injuring several of the firefighters.

All the docks took a pounding, as well as the districts of Everton and Crosby. Newspapers were heavily censored to prevent Germany getting confirmation of exactly where their bombs had struck, thereby enabling them to hone their accuracy and build up a detailed picture of the damage they were wreaking. Reports referred only to a town or district in the north-west.

On the streets of Liverpool, the damage was all too apparent, without the need for journalists. As 1940 went on, daily evidence of the work of the Luftwaffe was apparent from the windows of a bus, or a walk through the streets. Nights for the occupants of The Laurels were regularly interrupted by the terrifying wail of air raid sirens and a hurried dash into the garden to the Anderson shelter.

Mr Hathaway next door had no shelter in his garden and Hannah asked whether he wanted to join them in theirs.

'No, thank you, my dear,' he said. 'If I'm going to die, I intend it to happen in my own bed.'

Hannah tried to persuade him. 'I met a couple who were bombed out this week when I was at the WVS. If they'd stayed in their beds they'd be dead now. Their house was completely flattened. Absolutely nothing left of it. They were inside the shelter in the garden and it was buried under rubble from the house. The AFS men dug them out and the two of them walked out of the shelter without a scratch.'

'I'm pleased for them. A fortunate couple. I fought in the first two years of the war and know what it's like to be buried underground.'

Hannah realised that, as usual, he was referring to the Great War, not the present one.

He held out his hand revealing the missing fingers. 'That's how I lost my trigger fingers. They'd no use for me after that and I was invalided out in 1916. My lungs were damaged too.' He nodded. 'I was buried alive for twelve hours before they managed to dig me out. They had to wait until after a gas attack. I don't ever want to go through that again. I had enough of trenches and fox holes then and I've no wish to spend my nights in a hole in the ground in your garden, Mrs Kidd.'

There was no point in arguing with him.

The first couple of weeks of September were relatively

quiet and, to their relief, Hannah and Judith were able to
spend most of their nights in their own beds too.

But God – or Hitler – must have a cruel sense of humour,
as the next time Will was at home on shore leave, the
bombing began again and this time the target was far too
close for comfort and they had to move to the shelter. On
the night of the 16th and 17th September the sound of the
bombers was immediately overhead. She shook with fear as
the drone of the engines grew louder and clutched Will's
hand tightly.

Opposite them, an ashen-faced Nance was grasping
Judith's hand. Tonight, there was no sign of the older
woman's usual bravado. Wrapped up in a Persian lamb coat,
a gift from Sam's father, Nance was shivering despite the
mild weather. In contrast, Judith appeared to be in a trance,
oblivious to her surroundings and the aircraft noise.

'Too bloody close for comfort,' Nance said. German
engines roared overhead and they heard nearby explosions.
'That sounded like it were right on the doorstep. I don't like
this at all. Not one little bit.'

The ground beneath them shook to the dull booms,
followed by the screams of sirens.

'Poor Mr Hathaway must be terrified.' Hannah looked at
her husband. 'I tried to convince him he should be taking
shelter but he won't have it. Told me he'd rather die in his
bed.'

Will said nothing but gave her hand a squeeze.

'Can't say as I blame the poor old geezer.' Nance sniffed. 'I'd
give anything to be tucked up in mine. Preferably with a handsome man.' She winked at Will. 'Nothing like an air raid to
cramp your style. And you being stuck on a bleeding ship for
weeks looking forward to a bit of the other, and here you are in

a hole in the ground with me and Judith to spoil your fun.' She chuckled. 'Mind you, if it were only me here I'd tell you both to get on with it. Might be a bit of distraction from old Fritz up there, but we can't have you shocking our Judith, can we?'

'Do shut up, Nance,' Hannah snapped. 'Sometimes I wonder if it's all you ever think about. The rest of us are hoping and praying we can get through the night and live to see another day.'

Nance curled her lip. 'I'm only trying to inject a bit of cheer. Better than thinking about what's going off up there.' She pointed at the corrugated iron roof. 'It's as much as I can do not to wet me knickers.'

'Why don't you try and get some sleep, Nance? Then we can all try and get some shut eye.' Will pulled Hannah closer.

Somehow, they all drifted off to a fitful sleep, until woken by the All Clear siren. Tired and cold, they made their way into the house.

WHEN HANNAH DRAGGED herself out of bed the next morning to make the breakfast, she found Sam sitting with a cup of tea at the kitchen table.

'When did you get home?'

'Half an hour ago.' He gave a big yawn.

'You're not going into work this morning, are you?'

'Of course, I am. It's as bad for everyone else.'

'That's not true. At least we managed to get forty winks in the shelter, in spite of Nance doing everything possible to stop us.' She rolled her eyes. 'It sounded awfully near last night.'

'It was. It was in this road. Incendiaries on the roof of the

Carlton. I spent most of the night helping the fire bobbies put the flames out.'

'Nance won't be happy. That'll curtail her trips to the pictures.'

'Not for long. They'll have it fixed soon enough. Even if it's only with a tarpaulin. Where's Will? I saw his coat on the hook.'

'He's upstairs. I didn't wake him. He needs his sleep.' Hannah turned to take a frying pan off the shelf.

'No, he's not. He's right here.' Will came into the room. 'I woke up hoping for a cuddle with my wife only to find her side of the bed empty.' He moved over to Hannah and kissed her lightly. 'Not much of a welcome, what with sitting in a bunker with the Queen of the Cockneys in her fur coat, droning on and on.'

Sam grinned. 'Nance doesn't improve with acquaintance then?'

Will pulled out a chair at the other side of the table and sat down opposite him. 'She's harmless enough. But being stuck all night in a shelter with her is like being in a small room with a noisy mosquito. She's actually scared stiff of the bombing. I hadn't expected that.'

Hannah passed a cup of tea to her husband. 'It's not Nance I'm worried about. It's Judith. She didn't speak the whole time we were down there. It's as if she's in a trance. She's barely eating either.'

'Worried about Paolo.' Sam leaned back in his chair. 'Can't blame the poor girl. Just as they get together, he's carted off to the other side of the world. Has she heard from him yet?'

'He might not even be there yet.' Hannah frowned.

'When did they sail?'

'According to Father Edward, his ship left on 10th July.'

Will did a mental calculation. 'Even allowing for delays and diversions he should be in Australia by now. I'm sure Judith will hear news of him soon. Even prisoners of war are allowed to write home.'

Sam finished his tea and got to his feet. 'They've let some Italians internees go already. After that fuss they kicked up in Parliament. I don't imagine MPs took kindly to their favourite waiters and concierges being thrown in prison. Half the staff of the Ritz and the Savoy, I gather.'

Hannah melted a lump of dripping in the frying pan. 'None of that helps poor Paolo. He's on the other side of the world now. I can't see them exactly rushing to bring him back. Repatriating so-called enemy aliens is hardly going to be high in their priorities, is it?'

She hoped Will would contradict her, but he shook his head, his expression rueful.

When Sam left to go to his work at the council, Will moved over to stand behind his wife, wrapping his arms around her waist and laying his head on her shoulder. 'Come back to bed.'

Hannah smiled. 'As soon as I've cooked breakfast for you and Judith, and she and Nance have gone to work.'

'No breakfast for Nance then?'

'She's far too good for the miserable fare I serve up here. Now she's working at the NAAFI canteen she's enjoying free food and plenty of it. Doesn't stop her pinching any cakes or biscuits I make, though.'

'So, soon there'll be just you and me?'

'The house will be ours by eight. I was meant to be going door-to-door to collect aluminium saucepans with the WVS. I'm jolly glad you're my excuse to get out of that.'

'So that's all I am, is it? An excuse for you to avoid doing your bit for the war effort.'

She kissed him slowly. 'Does that seem like an excuse, Will Kidd?'

'That seemed like you may mean business.'

'Oh, I most certainly do.' She grinned at him.

'Good, as I intend to make the most of it.' He looked away, avoiding her eyes. 'We sail again tonight.'

Hannah groaned. 'But, Will, I thought you'd have a few days this time.'

'Herr Hitler has put paid to that. It's going to be like this from now on. Fast turnaround. They want the ships on the sea, not in the docks. It's load and unload then on our way.'

'Why don't they use another crew?'

'And where would we magic another crew for every ship? Look, my darling, at least we do get a night and a day together which is more than we'd have if I were in the army out in the desert or stuck in a training camp at the other end of the country.'

'Not when we have to spend the night sitting in an Anderson shelter listening to Nance moaning.'

'Who's moaning now?' He wove his fingers through her hair and drew her face towards him for another kiss.

HANNAH WAS DUSTING the bannisters on the Saturday afternoon after Will had left, when she heard muffled sobbing coming from Judith's bedroom. The door was ajar. Cautiously, she pushed it open.

Judith was lying face down on top of the counterpane, her body convulsing as she sobbed into her pillow. Hannah rushed over and sat down beside her sister on the edge of the bed.

'Oh, my poor darling. Have you had news about Paolo?'

There was no response.

'I'm sure he must be in Australia by now, Jude.' Hannah placed a comforting hand on her sister's back. 'Once he's there he'll be safe. In fact, safer than we are!'

Judith twisted herself onto her back, revealing tear-stained cheeks and red eyes. 'I went to see Mrs Giordano this morning. She says her friends with husbands and sons on the same ship had letters from them yesterday.' She sniffed and wiped a hand across her eyes.

Hannah went across to the chest of drawers, found a clean handkerchief and passed it to her sister. 'Well, that's good news. I'm sure you'll hear soon yourself.'

More sobbing. 'No, I won't. He doesn't love me. Otherwise he'd have already written.'

'Maybe they take turns to get a chance to write. There are probably lots of restrictions.' Hannah said, clutching at straws.

'Mrs Giordano says there's going to be an enquiry as... they were treated... so badly on board. Someone at the Italian club told her when the ship got to Sydney a British army officer went on board and was shocked at the conditions. Some of the guards were arrested.'

'You're afraid that Paolo might not have survived the journey?'

She was greeted by more sobbing and pulled Judith into her arms.

Judith jerked away. 'He's alive. He was taken off the ship at Melbourne and is in a prison camp near there. His landlord, Mr Contini, wrote to tell his wife he was safe and sound and so was Paolo. I heard it from Mrs Giordano when I went to see her this morning.'

Hannah stroked Judith's hair.

'What am I going to do?' Judith began to wail again. 'I love him so much, but I made a mistake. That's why he doesn't love me.' Judith pulled herself up into a sitting position and lowered her head.

Hannah had a horrible premonition of what Judith was about to reveal. 'A mistake? What kind of mistake?'

'When we went to Formby. We... we...' She looked up at Hannah. 'I'm going to have a baby.'

Judith's words were a knife through Hannah's stomach. After more than a year of marriage, Hannah was growing increasingly anxious that she had failed to fall pregnant. Judith, after one illicit adventure in the Formby woods, had managed that seemingly impossible feat. Anger and jealousy rose in Hannah's throat, bitter as bile. It wasn't fair. She turned away so Judith wouldn't see her reaction.

'You're angry. I knew you'd be angry. Look, Hannah, I did it because I love him. We got carried away. I'd no idea he was going to be arrested. I thought we would be getting married. And it was only once. I didn't even think it was possible to get in the family way if you only did it once.'

Hannah's fingers twitched at the hem of her apron. 'Oh, Jude.' She bit her lip and turned to face her. It was hardly Judith's fault that she and Will had failed to conceive. Taking her own grief out on her sister was unfair. She put her arms around her and Judith's tears dampened her blouse. As her sister wept, Hannah did some mental arithmetic. 'That was back in June. You must be four or five months gone.' She looked at her sister's thin frame. 'You're barely showing but that will change soon enough.' Shaking her head, she added, 'I should have known.'

Judith shook her head. 'It's not your fault. You've enough to worry about with Will being at sea and you're so busy with your WVS work and running this house. And you've never had a baby yourself. You can hardly be expected to recognise the signs.'

Hannah winced but said nothing.

'I went to the doctor. He says it's due in March.' The tears ran down Judith's cheeks again. 'What am I going to do, Hannah?'

'Does anyone else know?'

'I was going to tell Father Edwards, but I don't want him to think badly of me. I've let him down. I've let everyone down.'

'Father Edwards is a kind and understanding man. He knows people are doing all kinds of things they wouldn't do normally because there's a war on. I don't think he's the sort of man to curse you from the pulpit and call you a Jezebel,' she said, referring to the fire-and-brimstone religion of their late father. 'Why don't you talk to him?'

'I'll have to tell him in the confessional anyway.' Judith paused. 'Maybe that's how I'll do it. It will be easier telling him in the dark behind a grille, when I can't see his face. Even if he knows it's me. I've been putting off making my First Confession because I'd have to tell him what I'd done. But until I make my Confession I can't be admitted into the Church.' She rubbed her eyes again.

'And do you still want to become a Catholic?'

'More than ever. It's all I have now.' Judith's voice was fierce. She sucked her lips in. 'There is someone else who knows.'

Hannah guessed who that would be. 'Nance?'

Judith nodded. 'She wormed it out of me. She'd noticed my stomach.'

Hannah blushed, ashamed that she had failed to notice her sister's condition herself.

'And?'

'Exactly as you'd expect. She says she knows someone who'll help me get rid of it.'

'What?'

'Don't worry. I'd never do that. It's against the teachings of the Church.' Judith placed her hands protectively on her belly. 'This baby is all I have of Paolo.' Her lip trembled. 'I won't give it away to an orphanage either.'

'As soon as Will gets back, I'll talk to him. Maybe we can adopt the baby for you. You can't possibly bring up a child on your own, Judith. That way you'd still be close to it.'

Judith gripped Hannah's arm. 'Do you think that's why Paolo hasn't written? He thinks I'm loose. Nance told me that men always lead women on until they get what they want, then they walk away accusing the women of having no self-respect or morals. Nance says all men are hypocritical that way. Including Paolo.'

'Poppycock!' Hannah was surprised at her own annoyance. 'Nance knows nothing. She's the last person you should ever listen to about anything, except where to trade ration coupons and what's showing at the Carlton.' She looked at Judith sternly. 'If there's one thing I'm sure about, it's that Paolo Tornabene loves you, Judith. If he hasn't written, there must be a jolly good reason for it. Why don't you write to him, now you know where he is?'

Judith crumbled. 'I can't. I just can't. He doesn't want anything more to do with me. Can't you see that, Hannah?'

THE FOLLOWING MONDAY, Hannah was in the kitchen having a cup of tea with Mr Hathaway when there was a ring on the front doorbell.

'Who on earth can that be?' She took off her apron.

Mr Hathaway got up and moved to the back door. 'Time I was off anyway.' He gave her a wave and slipped out of the door.

It was Father Edwards.

Sitting in the front parlour, the priest bent forward, his hands on his knees. 'I think you know why I'm here, Hannah. And I'm not breaking the sacred confidence of the confessional as Judith told me you know about her delicate situation.'

'I do.' Hannah lowered her eyes.

'I went to visit Paolo when he was in Walton Jail. He asked me to give Judith a message. I told him I'd prefer he told her himself once he was free, but he said he had a bad feeling, a premonition something dreadful was going to happen to him.' The priest looked up at her, his gaze intense. 'We agreed that if there was a possibility that he might not return to Judith, I was to tell her he loved her and wanted more than anything to marry her, but if he didn't survive he wanted her to marry someone else.'

Hannah gasped. 'You think something has happened to him. You think he's dead.'

'No. As it happens I most definitely don't. But that places me in a dilemma. I told Paolo I would only pass on his declaration if he was never coming back to Judith. Now, it seems, as far as I can gather, he is very much alive. Yet he hasn't contacted her. If I were to tell her what he told me, it might make matters worse for her. I have asked myself why he hasn't contacted her? There are several of my parishioners whose husbands or sons were transported on the *Dunera* and every one of them, apart from Paolo, has written to reassure their families they are fit and well.'

'So, you think Paolo's had second thoughts about my sister.'

'No!' The priest's response was vehement. 'I'm absolutely certain what he said was sincere and that he truly loves Judith.'

'Then why?'

'I've been puzzling over it. I'm wondering whether it's fear.'

'Fear?'

'Is Will home, Hannah?'

Hannah shook her head; a cold chill gripped her insides whenever she thought of Will at sea and the ever-present possibility that he might never return. 'Why?'

'He's known Paolo a long time, hasn't he?'

'Several years.'

'Perhaps our Italian friend was afraid of transmitting his feelings onto paper and failing to express them to Judith's satisfaction.'

'I don't understand.'

'One of the fatal flaws we men have inherited from Adam is the sin of pride. I may be wrong, but half an hour ago I had a cup of tea with one of the women whose husband was on the *Dunera* and is now in a camp in New South Wales. She's a Liverpool girl and was highly amused by the letter she received from her husband. His spoken English is fluent, but he'd never been called on to write anything in it until now. He was a labourer on the docks and they've been married about twelve years. She saw the funny side and showed me one of the pages, telling me their six-year-old was a better speller than her Giorgio is. It made me think of Paolo. Giorgio wasn't worried about his wife laughing at his mistakes. After twelve years, he can take her love for granted. But perhaps Paolo, desperately in love, is afraid of Judith ridiculing his poor writing skills.'

'Judith would never do that.'

'Of course, she wouldn't. But he might not have been ready to take the risk. Paolo is an intelligent man but, like many of his fellows, he lacks much formal education. He might have baulked at the idea of the woman he loves thinking his letters were like those of a small child. I thought perhaps Will might know whether he'd ever been required to write in English on board ship.'

'I've no idea. I know Paolo was an experienced mariner but not an officer. Perhaps you're right, Father. How do we find out?'

'I've taken the liberty of dropping a line to an old friend of mine who's also in the camp at Tatura, where Paolo is held. Father Carvalho is a parish priest and studied English at university in Bologna. I've suggested he offers his services as scribe to any of the men in a similar dilemma to the one I suspect Paolo is going through. It will mean a long wait for Judith, I'm afraid, but I have a very strong hunch this is the crux of the matter.'

'Father Edwards, you're a genius.'

'Now how about you stick the kettle on, then we can put our heads together and see if we can find a solution to young Miss Judith's problem.'

'You're not going to throw her out of the Church?'

The priest grinned. 'She's not the first and certainly won't be the last young woman to step off the path of right-eousness.' He hesitated a moment. 'I'm going to tell you something now, Hannah, that I've never told anyone else before and I'm telling you, only because the people concerned are both dead. I know I can rely on your absolute discretion.'

She nodded, curious.

'I was born on the wrong side of the blanket, as the saying goes. I've no idea who my real father was. My mother married the man I knew as my father when I was a baby. He was a widower with four children under ten so it was, you could say, a marriage of convenience. He was a good husband to her and took care of us both, so it all worked out for the best.'

'How did you find out your dad wasn't your real father?'

'He died soon after I became a priest and Mother told me the truth. It had been preying on her conscience, and once he was gone, she couldn't stand to keep it secret any longer.' He smiled. 'Especially once I'd become a priest.'

'It must have been a shock to you.'

Father Edwards tilted his head to one side. 'Not really. I'd often wondered why I was the only one in a family of dark-haired siblings to have hair the colour of pale straw.'

Hannah felt a new respect for the man and his honesty. 'I'll go and put that kettle on.'

Hannah returned with the teapot. 'I did suggest to Judith that perhaps Will and I could adopt the child.' She poured him a cup and handed it to him.

'Now why on earth would you be doing that? Judith and Paolo will make fine parents once they're together again. And you and Will are surely going to have children of your own.'

'No sign of that, Father. In over a year of marriage.' She looked away, embarrassed.

'Early days, Hannah. Early days. And what with your husband being away at sea, it's not surprising.'

She looked down. 'I suppose you're right.' She raised her eyes. 'I'm not in Confession but I'm going to admit I felt a twinge of jealousy when Judith told me her news. It seemed so unfair.'

Father Edward put down his cup and saucer. 'You wouldn't be human if you didn't feel that way.' He smiled. 'Now, I've had a couple of thoughts I'd like to put to you.'

'Yes?'

'Firstly, I think Judith needs to tell her young man he's

going to be a father. If my hunch is right, he's going to be overjoyed. There's no question in my mind he'll stand by her.'

'But how can she hold her head up as an unwed mother?'

'That's my second thought.' He put his tea aside and leaned forward. 'I could marry them.'

'Yes. After the war's over and Paolo returns. That could be years away.' She frowned and shook her head.

'Have you heard of a marriage by proxy, Hannah?'

Her frown deepened. 'By proxy? No.'

'It's allowed by Canon Law of the Roman Catholic Church. It's designed to be used in circumstances where one party is unable to be present. Unfortunately, it is not recognised by the law of the land. Under Canon Law such a marriage depends on both parties being willing, so Paolo would need to give his mandate. I'm far from certain that it would be approved by the civilian authorities but it would mean they are married, most importantly of all, in the eyes of God.'

'You could do this?'

'I'd have to take it up with the Archbishop. Obviously, I'll have to discuss it with my colleagues in the parish first. No promises, but this could offer Judith some hope.'

18

RETURNED TO SENDER

Hannah had no idea how long it had taken for the envelope to reach her, but its message was stark. The name and address written in her own hand had been crossed out and the words 'Return to Sender, Addressee deceased' were scrawled across the front in a spidery script. Her heart sank. Miss Radley had been her only hope of reaching Aunt Elizabeth, and now the poor woman was dead. Although she had never met her, Hannah was saddened by the news, remembering the kindness of the teacher's words in her letter and the affection Will had for her.

Hannah opened the drawer in the little writing desk in the front parlour and took that first and only letter out and read it again. How sad she had never had the chance to know Miss Radley and now with her death all possibility of finding Elizabeth was gone.

'What are you doing?' Judith came into the room.

'My letter to Miss Radley in Australia has been returned. The poor woman has died.'

Judith's brow creased. 'Died? How?'

'I don't know. The unopened envelope was marked Deceased.'

'Was she very old?'

'No. According to Will she would have been in her fifties now. And in good health when he last saw her. But that was about fifteen years ago.'

'How sad.'

'It means we'll never find Aunt Elizabeth now.'

'That's rather pessimistic, Hannah. There must be something in Miss Radley's house with Aunt Elizabeth's address on. Letters or papers. When Will is home next you should ask him who might know, so you can write and make some enquiries.'

Hannah tried to conceal her surprise that her sister was actually showing an interest in the subject. She couldn't help wondering whether Australia had become more interesting to Judith now that Paolo was there.

Hannah steeled herself and asked the question. 'Have you talked to Father Edwards about your predicament?'

'Yes.' Judith lowered her eyes.

'And?'

'He's written to Paolo, enclosing a letter from me.'

Hannah was surprised. 'You've written to Paolo? I thought you told me you couldn't bear to.'

'That was before I spoke to Father Edwards. He's convinced Paolo believes I won't love him any longer now that he's a prisoner of war. A lot of the internees are ashamed that they're seen as the enemy. Paolo might not want me to feel obliged to stand by him, especially now he's on the other side of the world.' She reached for Hannah's hand and squeezed it. 'But none of that matters to me. All I want is to be with Paolo and to be married to him and have this baby.' She stroked her tummy. 'As soon as Father

Edwards gets confirmation from him, our marriage can go ahead by proxy.'

'The Archbishop gave his permission?'

'Not exactly.' Judith blushed and looked down again. 'He said it isn't legal as far as the government is concerned and would not be recognised by the civil authorities or registered as a legal marriage.' She looked up again and smiled. 'But I would feel that God recognised it and that's what counts for me. I'm going to change my name to Tornabene so our child will carry its father's name.'

'But it won't be legal.' Hannah was dismayed. 'In the eyes of the law you'd still have an illegitimate child.'

'Father Edward has spoken to a solicitor friend and he says...' She fumbled in her handbag and pulled out a piece of paper and read from it. 'Something called *The Legitimacy Act of 1926* means that if a couple have a child out of wedlock but subsequently marry, that child is automatically legitimised. And nobody needs to know.'

'So, the wedding won't actually be a marriage by proxy?'

Judith looked evasive. 'God would recognise it and so would Paolo and I and Father Edwards – that's what matters to me.'

'But as soon as it's announced that the priest has performed a proxy marriage... won't he get into trouble?'

'No, because it won't be announced as such. He describes it as a blessing of our union. I don't give a fig about the law – what good was the law to Paolo? Stuffing him in prison, almost drowning him, then sending him to the other side of the world on a ship in savage conditions.' Judith's voice was fierce.

'But do you really want to go through this when your husband-to-be isn't present?'

'I'd much rather he was here to stand by my side, but it's

not his fault that he can't be. And if it's a choice between our baby being illegitimate or my being married with an absent husband, I'll choose marriage any day. We will do it again properly after the war.'

Judith folded her arms and Hannah knew better than to attempt to argue.

'If he's home when we do it, do you think Will would stand in for Paolo?'

'He'd be honoured. But you know he's not in port very often.'

Judith nodded. 'That's true. I want it to happen as soon as we hear from Paolo, maybe I'd better ask Sam to do it – but I want you to know Will would be my first choice. When we do it properly one day, Will is obviously going to be Paolo's best man anyway. That's for sure.'

Taken aback by her sister's transformation from abject despair to calculated planning, Hannah was relieved that Judith was now certain about the depth of Paolo's feelings.

THE FOLLOWING DAY, when Judith was at work, Hannah rushed through her chores and headed down the road to the church to see the Catholic priest. She found him next door in the presbytery. A stern-looking housekeeper showed her into a chilly room with linoleum flooring and no fire in the grate. Several wooden chairs stood against the walls and she guessed it was a waiting room for parishioners. She sat down nervously.

A few minutes later the young priest arrived.

'I'm sorry to receive you in here, Mrs Kidd,' he said. 'It's rather bleak. Only The Boss, as we call him – Canon O'Leary – is meeting with the ladies of the Catholic

Women's League in the parlour. I imagine this is about Judith?'

She nodded. 'I'm concerned this proxy marriage could get you into trouble.'

'She told you it isn't legally binding?'

'Yes. So, I can't see the point of doing it.'

'As I told you, Mrs Kidd, Church law does recognise this ceremony as a marriage, even though the state doesn't. To be honest, Archbishop Downey is sympathetic to the idea of it being introduced as a wartime measure, but it seems there are more pressing concerns than the plight of young women such as Judith for the government and Parliament.'

He rubbed his hands together. 'Heavens above, but it's chilly in here. We can only light one fire with the rationing and shortages.'

'Don't worry on my account. I'm used to the cold.'

'Judith has given me her solemn word that when Paolo is eventually free and returns, they will conduct a full legally-recognised marriage before they live as man and wife. And, according to the law, the child will be legitimised by such a union.'

'You're telling me this will be a sham wedding.' She gave a sigh.

'Not as far as God and the Church are concerned. Why do you say that?'

'Because I was once supposedly married with similar claims.'

The priest frowned and leaned forward in his chair, his hands on his knees. 'Go on.'

'My father compelled me to marry someone against my will and the marriage was carried out by a supposed man of God who was anything but. My father and the groom's father were both members of a religious sect that was more about lining their own pockets than worshipping God. It's one of the reasons I have no truck with religion myself.'

Father Edward looked pained. 'I'm sorry to hear that, Mrs Kidd. I presume it's not Mr Kidd you refer to?'

'No, and I'd rather not mention who the man was since he was as much an innocent victim as I. And I can assure you my real marriage is completely legal.'

'I don't doubt it. And so too will be Judith's, as soon as her intended is home. Meanwhile doing this will give them both some comfort during the terrible pain of separation.'

Hannah got up. 'Thank you, Father. I feel reassured.'

19

A KIND OFFER

P aolo was suffering from the blues. While the Tatura camp and its Australian guards were a marked improvement on the horrors of the *Dunera*, he was overcome with remorse about his pride preventing him from writing to Judith. He'd made enquiries about whether he could write to her now but was told he must wait.

As his fellow prisoners began to receive replies from their families in England, he felt even worse. Watching them reading their letters and hearing their whoops of joy was torture. There was no sign of anything from his own family in Napoli and he suspected that if they got his letter at all, it would not be for a long time and the chances of his hearing anything from them before several months had elapsed were equally remote.

Like all the men in Tatura with close relatives in Italy, he worried constantly about how his family was coping. He knew there was heavy bombing of the major cities in Britain and he imagined the RAF would be retaliating over Germany and Italy. It was sheer agony to think that British bombs might now be raining down on Napoli just as

German ones were targeting Liverpool. He loathed Benito Mussolini and his cursed alliance with Adolf Hitler with every fibre of his body. Yet it had been the British who were ultimately responsible for the death of men like his friend Alfonso Giordano by sending them on that fateful voyage to Canada – even if it was a German torpedo that sank the *Arandora Star*. It had been British soldiers who had maltreated them on the *Dunera*. And the British government who had decided to intern innocent men in the first place.

As the internees acclimatised to life in the camp and began to build a community in Tatura Number Two camp, Paolo increasingly kept himself apart. His envy of the other men as they read their letters from Britain evolved into resentment – even though he only had himself to blame. Resisting calls to join in games of football, participate in the camp choir, art classes and other activities, he shunned company, choosing to walk alone around the perimeter fence for exercise and spend the rest of his time staring list-lessly into space. Why had he ruined everything with Judith?

When he told his friend from the *Dunera* about Judith, Guido had laughed and responded, '*Chiodo scaccia chiodo,*' – saying Paolo would soon get over her. This lack of empathy irked Paolo, and from then on he avoided Guido too.

The only man he talked to at any length was the Australian guard, Clancy, the man he had chatted to on the train from Melbourne. Clancy's accent reminded him of Will's, and his relaxed and approachable manner put him at ease. Paolo also wanted to ensure he kept up his English. The older internees tended to speak Italian. The ones closer to Paolo's age were mostly born in the United Kingdom and Paolo felt unsure of himself at their confident slang-filled English.

'You like to keep yerself to yerself, mate, don't you?' Clancy said to him one afternoon. 'Fancy a smoke?' He offered the packet to Paolo.

'Thanks you.'

'You don't need the "S" on the end when you put the "you" after thank. Only if it's on its own. *Thank* you or thanks.' Clancy spoke slowly in a matter-of- fact manner.

Paolo nodded. 'Thanks.' His features creased in a rare smile.

'If you don't mind me saying, cobber, you seem a bit miserable. I know it can't be much fun being locked up in here, but it won't be forever. Your pals all seem to be finding ways to keep busy.' He jerked his head in the direction of the football game. 'I thought you Italians liked soccer. You must be the exception.'

'I like to watch more than to play.' Paolo took a long draw on the cigarette.

'You got a girl over in England?'

Paolo nodded.

'She written to you?'

Paolo shook his head and turned away. 'I think she find somebody new. No girl want to go with the enemy. She forget me. And it is *colpa mia* - my fault. I didn't write to her.' He put his head in his hands. 'I fear she laugh at my bad writing *Inglese*.'

Clancy chuckled. 'Thought it might be something like that. Next time you get the chance to write I'll give you a hand, mate. Not that my writing's Shakespeare, y'know. But it's better than nothing.'

Paolo looked up, hope in his eyes. 'If I tell you what I want to say her, you write it for me?'

'Reckon I can.' Clancy gave him a comforting hand on the shoulder. 'I should have some time tomorrow.'

The following day, Clancy approached Paolo. Grinning broadly, the guard dug in the pocket of his uniform and pulled out an official-looking brown envelope. 'This came today for you. Sorry, pal, but we have to read them first. That's the rules. Two letters – one from a priest and one from your girl. She's even put a photie in for you. She's a looker, mate!' He gave Paolo a thumbs up.

Paolo scrambled to his feet, his eyes shining. He held the photograph of Judith to his lips and kissed it, then leapt in the air, arms waving above his head in a frenzied dance, adrenaline racing through his body. '*Madonna Santa! Mi vuole ancora bene!*'

'Haven't a clue what you're saying, cobber, but I think I get the gist!'

20

A CEREMONY AND A ROW

The letter from Paolo giving his consent to a marriage to Judith by proxy arrived in late November. It was accompanied by a letter to Judith which Paolo said had been translated for him in the camp. The use of an intermediary must have tempered the words the young man used to convey his feelings, but the sentiments were clear enough. He loved Judith absolutely and couldn't wait to know they were married – even if remotely and not yet in the eyes of English law – and he was overjoyed that they were expecting a child. He apologised for not being able to be by her side but was with her night and day in his thoughts.

Judith read the letter over and over again until it was in danger of falling apart. Two days later, Father Edwards was to conduct the proxy ceremony. As expected, there was no possibility of Will being there to stand in for his friend, his ship having sailed a few days earlier.

'You don't mind that I asked Sam, do you?' Judith said on the morning of the ceremony. 'I want to be able to call myself Mrs Tornabene as soon as possible.'

'I understand,' said Hannah, as she brushed her sister's hair. 'What are you doing about a wedding ring?'

Judith looked stricken. 'I didn't think of that. Obviously, Paolo can't get me a ring.' Her lip trembled. 'I should have thought about that. Maybe I can make one out of fuse wire or something.'

'Wait here.' Hannah left the room and returned moments later with a small leather box.

Judith opened the box and gasped at the gold band nestled in the velvet interior. 'Grandmother's wedding ring! Of course. Why didn't I think of that? Are you sure you wouldn't mind? After all, Mother gave it to you.'

'I've never worn it. Will bought my wedding ring. Go on. Try it on.'

Judith took it out of the box and slipped it onto her finger. 'It fits perfectly. Are you sure you don't mind me having it?'

'Jude, I wouldn't have offered it unless I was sure. You've as much right to it as I. Mother would have been very happy to know you were wearing it. And although we never knew our grandmother, I'm sure she'd be happy too.'

THE PROXY WEDDING ceremony was a small affair. The only guests were Sam, Nance, Mrs Giordano and her daughter Felicia, Mrs. Contini, Paolo's former landlady, and one of the other parish priests. Rather than in the main body of the church, they gathered in the Lady Chapel – a side chapel dedicated to the Blessed Virgin – at a time when the church would be empty in the evening, after Confessions and Benediction had finished. There was no Mass as part of the proceedings – a relief to Hannah, Sam and Nance. But Father Edwards was dressed in his full vestments and made an effort to make the ceremony as special as possible. As Sam stepped forward with the ring on Paolo's behalf and the priest intoned the blessing, tears welled in Hannah's eyes. Both Italian ladies were weeping. Even Nance looked moved.

The party returned to the Laurels, where Hannah and the Italians had pooled rations to put on a small spread, supplemented by some sausage rolls that Nance had managed to smuggle out of the NAAFI. The occasion was topped off by Sam, who had managed to obtain a bottle of sherry so they could toast the bride and absent groom.

THE NEXT MORNING AFTER BREAKFAST, Nance sat down opposite Hannah and Sam at the kitchen table. Judith had gone to Sunday Mass. Nance looked uncharacteristically happy, lounging sideways in her chair, one elbow propped up on the table. She lit a cigarette then drained her cup of tea.

Hannah got up to clear away the plates, knowing there was no possibility of Nance offering to help.

'You seem awfully perky today, Nance,' said Sam. 'You've had the biggest grin plastered over your face since you came in the room.'

'I'm a naturally cheerful person,' Nance said, admiring her freshly varnished crimson fingernails.

'Come on, pull the other one. There's something you're not telling us.' Sam exchanged a glance with Hannah as she filled the sink. 'And I know you're going to tell us 'cos you never manage to keep anything secret.'

Nance looked offended. 'I'm a very discreet person, I'll have you know. No need to remind me that careless talk costs lives.' She picked up the teapot and poured more tea into her cup. 'But as it happens, I have a young man and he's taking me out this afternoon.' She assumed a nonchalant air that did little to disguise her evident excitement.

'A young man? He must be a bold lad.' Sam raised his eyebrows. 'How young?'

'Old enough to know what he's doing but young enough to have plenty of energy to do it.' She gave her shoulders a little wiggle and pouted at Sam.

Hannah turned back to the dishes. She hated it when Nance talked that way. Why was she always so cheap and sordid?

But Sam was enjoying himself. 'So, what's this bright spark's name and where did you find him? The Royal School for the Blind?'

Used to Sam's teasing, Nance flicked his arm with the tea cosy. 'I'll have you know, Samuel Henderson, Tom's as fit as the butcher's dog. He's twenty-nine and is in the RAF.'

'Wants to experience the sins of the flesh before the Luftwaffe get him, does he?'

'I imagine he's well acquainted with them already. He has a wife and two kids down in Devon.'

'Nance! How could you?' Hannah couldn't contain herself anymore. 'How could you be so cruel as to tempt a man who's only separated from his family because he's risking his life for his country? That kind of behaviour is despicable.'

'Get you, Mrs Fancy Pants Kidd! You trying to tell me you believe your old man doesn't have a girl in every port? In your dreams! Maybe you can do quite happily without a bit of the other for weeks on end, but I'll bet my bottom dollar, your old man can't. Or won't. They're all the same those sailors.'

Without pausing to think, Hannah swung around from the sink and slapped Nance hard across the face. 'How dare you?' She pushed open the back door and rushed out into the garden, where it was icy-cold with a heavy frost.

She stood shivering under the bare branches of the apple tree, trying to calm down, her hands rubbing up and down her arms, her feet stamping on the rock-hard ground.

The back door opened, and Sam came out. He was wearing his coat and was holding hers. 'Here, get this around you, Hannah. Ignore Nance. You know she's playing games with you. She knows as well as I do that Will wouldn't so much as glance at another woman.'

Hannah was crying now. 'He used to once. I mean ... he used to have a girl in every port.'

'Maybe he did, but that was before he met you, sweetheart. He worships the ground you walk on.' He pulled Hannah into his arms and cradled her head as she wept against his shoulder.

After a few moments, she drew her head away. Sam offered her a handkerchief and she dried her eyes. 'Oh, Sam, I miss him so much. This awful war. I don't think I can bear it anymore.'

Sam smiled at her. 'Of course, you can. You're a strong woman. The strongest I know. Nance only says what she does because she knows you'll rise to the bait. We all have our own way of coping. Nance's is to have as much fun as she can to cover up that she spends most of her time absolutely terrified. You know what she's like during a raid.'

Hannah nodded. 'I shouldn't have lost my temper. Do you think I hurt her?'

'Only her pride. She's had stronger blows in her time. A slap from you won't do her any harm. And she did ask for it. She went too far this morning.'

Hannah drew her coat around her and turned towards the house. 'I'd better go back in and apologise.'

'It'll have to wait. She's already gone out. Says she's doing a shift at the NAAFI this morning so she can have the afternoon and evening free to see her fellow. By the time she staggers home tonight she'll have forgotten all about it.' He slipped his arm through Hannah's. 'Now why don't we stick the kettle on again? Judith will be back from church soon. I'll peel the spuds for lunch.'

'You'll do no such thing, Sam. Sunday's the only time you get to put your feet up. I'll do the spuds and you can sit and talk to me while I get the joint in the oven. Mr Brown put a nice piece of beef by for us this week.'

'You have the butcher eating out of your hands, Hannah.'

'Not really.' She laughed. 'It might have something to do with the fact that I gave Mrs Brown half a dozen apples. She's going to bake them with some of those blackberries I picked on the railway bank.'

'That was weeks ago.'

'She bottled them. Saving the rest up for Christmas.'

'Christmas.' Sam shuddered. 'What kind of Christmas will we be having this year? Do you think Herr Hitler will respect the season?'

'I doubt it. He seems determined to hammer Liverpool into the ground.' Hannah bit her lip. 'All I want is for Will to be home but there's about as much chance of that as of Nance becoming a nun.'

Sam laughed. 'Good grief. Can you imagine her as a nun? She'd be seducing all the altar boys and slugging down the communion wine.' Seeing that Hannah wasn't laughing, he added, 'We can always time our Christmas to whenever Will gets home.' He picked up one of the potatoes Hannah was preparing to roast and tossed it in the air, catching it. 'After all, it's not as if you and I and Judith ever celebrated

Christmas when our fathers were around. Just another day of misery.'

Hannah nodded. 'I used to walk along our street in Bootle and peer through the windows to see what a lovely time other people were having. The carol singers stopped knocking at our door after my father threatened to throw a bucket of water over them. If anything, Christmas was even more miserable than other days. We had to kneel in front of him on the cold floor while he read from the Old Testament and screamed at us that we would end up in the eternal flames of Hell if we appeared not to be paying full attention or if we were unable to recite the verses we were meant to have learnt by heart.'

'Grim!' Sam shuddered. 'I have Nance to thank that my father confined his tub thumping to that chapel and didn't bring it back home. He'd either shut himself in his study with a bottle of whisky, checking how much cash he'd managed to extort from his gullible fellows, or he'd be upstairs with her.'

'At least your father wasn't a murderer.'

'Both men were evil hypocrites.' Sam shook his head. 'How did we get onto this awful subject?'

'Maybe because we never have.' Hannah reached over the table and squeezed his arm. 'You are the only person who understands. I could never speak to Judith about it. It's as if she's wiped her memory of all the horror and who can blame her?'

'You know Nance isn't as bad she pretends to be, don't you?' Sam looked at her intently.

'Pretends to be?'

'She had a rough time with her husband in London. He was a violent drunk. Not unlike your father. But he didn't dress it up in all the religious claptrap. When she moved up here it can't have been much fun for her going on the game. But it was that, steal or starve. And I think she was actually genuinely fond of my father for giving her an escape route from the brothel. And the old man was definitely fond of her. He lavished enough presents on her. Like that fur coat she never has off her back once the mercury drops.'

'You think she misses him?'

Sam gave her a tight-lipped smile. 'All Nance really wants is to find herself a nice steady chap and settle down. The lipstick and face paint is part of an act to cover up that the poor woman is actually desperately lonely.' He sighed. 'That's why she picks on you about Will. You've got what she wants. A man who loves you and who'd crawl a thousand miles on his hands and knees to get home to you.'

'But why on earth does she throw herself at married men? I still can't believe how she's bragging about seeing a man who has a wife and children. That's no way to find herself a husband.' She spooned some dripping out of a pot and put it into the oven to heat up in readiness for roasting the potatoes.

Sam shrugged. 'She's no spring chicken. Perhaps she lives in hope that one of her fancy men will fall for her and give up his family. Or maybe she's living a fantasy where she's in her twenties and meets a dashing airman. And as for her new lover, he knows every time he climbs into his cockpit it could be his coffin so he's grabbing what pleasure he can too.' He smiled at her. 'Who am I to judge?'

Feeling ashamed, Hannah turned to open the oven and put the potatoes inside, then slipped the small joint of beef onto a lower shelf. She didn't want to get to the subject of Sam's own proclivities.

Her blushes were saved by the door opening and Judith coming into the kitchen.

.   .   .

DECEMBER 1940 BROUGHT a lull in the bombings and the occupants of The Laurels began to hope that perhaps the reprieve would last through Christmas. Judith was now visibly pregnant and complaining of backache and swollen ankles. She had given up her job at the Local Education Office and reverted to working as a seamstress – not in her old firm but taking in work at home. Although clothing wasn't yet rationed, there wasn't an abundance of choice and many women turned to her to take their clothes in or remodel them. She also had a lucrative sideline in making wedding dresses. It might be a long time before she could be reunited with Paolo and she wanted to set money aside to care for herself and the coming baby. Hannah suspected her sister was also considering the possibility of going out to Australia to join him – although this had never been mentioned.

Nance's courtship by the RAF officer was never put to the test as Nance never spoke of him again, though she was still out most evenings, supposedly meeting friends in a pub or going to the cinema.

21

AN UNEXPECTED OFFER

After docking, Will had only six hours before he was due back on board the *Shelbourne*. Turnaround times were as fast as possible, as getting supplies in and out of the port of Liverpool was of paramount importance. He was determined to make the most of the brief time he had ashore, planning to head straight to Orrell Park and Hannah.

Coming down the gangplank at the Prince's Dock, he was shocked to see his former boss, Captain Palmer, waiting on the quayside.

'We need to talk, Will.'

'Captain Palmer!' Will shook the former Master's hand. 'Good to see you, sir, but please don't think me rude – I can't stop to talk. I've only a few hours in port and haven't seen my wife in four weeks.'

Palmer put a hand on Will's shoulder. 'Actually, it's Commodore Palmer now. When you hear what I have to say, I think you'll agree that it's very much in your and your wife's interest. In fact, I'd like to speak with her too. I've already taken the liberty of sending a car to collect her. But first of all, we need to talk in private.'

Will's jaw dropped.

'Come with me. It's a few minutes' walk. Save your questions until we get there.'

Will, puzzled and a little annoyed, knew better than to argue. They walked beneath the overhead railway and headed up Chapel Street, turning into Rumford Street towards a new office block behind the Town Hall.

Palmer indicated a side doorway that looked like a fire exit. Inside, the walls were bare concrete, with nothing but a metal guard rail and concrete steps leading down to what must be the basement. The sharp smell of fresh paint hung in the air.

Palmer preceded Will down the stairs into the bowels of the building. 'Seven foot of concrete over our heads and walls three feet deep make this the safest building in Liverpool.' He pushed open a door into a large room where naval ratings were painting the walls and men were laying yards of cable. 'Welcome to Derby House. Before long, this place will be a hive of activity. Telephones, signalling equipment, radio interceptors. This will be the joint forces command centre. Not only the Royal Navy but the RAF, and the Marines will be here too.'

Will looked around the empty and featureless concrete room. 'But how? Why?'

'We will be monitoring the western approaches to Britain. We're going to track every enemy convoy, every submarine wolf pack, every airplane, that threatens our shipping routes.'

'But isn't that what you're doing in Plymouth?'

'The Admiralty and the War Office think Plymouth's too vulnerable to bombing and since the bulk of our merchant shipping comes through the port of Liverpool it makes more sense for us to be located here. This bunker is purpose-built.'

Will scratched his head. 'I still don't get it. Why are you showing *me* this?'

Palmer smiled. 'Because I want you to join us, Kidd. You know more about merchant shipping than most of these Navy chaps. I want someone with a merchant navy back-ground. Someone familiar with the Atlantic shipping routes. You'll have to transfer into the Royal Navy Reserves, wear the uniform and all that.' He clapped him on the back. 'I've cleared it all with the Admiral. He will be stepping down when we start up here in Liverpool and I don't know who his successor is yet but apparently it's all sorted.' Palmer looked at his wristwatch. 'Now we need to get moving or we'll arrive after your wife does. I've asked her to meet us in a nearby café.'

When the two men emerged from the bunker into the daylight, Palmer turned to Will. 'No mention of what you've seen or heard today to anyone, including your wife. All she needs to know is that it's a land-based role that's part of the war effort.'

Palmer's assumption not only that Will would accept the position but the way he had involved Hannah in it, made Will feel manipulated and resentful. As they walked through the streets, his annoyance mounted.

Palmer looked at him sideways. 'You're awfully quiet, Kidd. I thought you'd be excited.'

'I'm not doing it.'

'Not doing what?'

'Working down in that bunker, giving up the sea. Pushing a pen or whatever it is you expect. I'm a seaman. I'm not suited to that kind of work. So, I'm saying no.'

They had reached the café and Palmer took Will's elbow and steered him to the back of the room and a table away from other people. 'I'm staying in the Adelphi tonight but to be honest I still feel far more comfortable in places like this. Let's thrash this out over a good cup of tea.'

WHEN THE UNIFORMED man knocked on the front door, Hannah's heart missed a beat. But the man told her Will was in port but only for a few hours and he wanted her to come to meet him in town as he couldn't leave the docks.

Excitement at the prospect of seeing her husband at last, mingled with bitter disappointment that it would be for such a brief time. Hannah got into the motor car behind the driver and they headed towards the centre of the city.

She leaned forward and started to question the young man who told her he was a naval rating and a driver for senior officers.

'But why on earth are you driving *me* then? Are you sure it isn't bad news? Is my husband missing?'

'Sorry, ma'am, but I don't know your husband. I'm under instructions from Commodore Palmer.' The man stared ahead, making it clear the conversation was closed.

They pulled up outside a café near the docks. Hannah pushed open the door into the steamy interior and saw Will near the back, deep in conversation with an older man. Noticing the empty cups in front of them, Hannah wondered how long they had been talking, and forced away her irritation that she hadn't been here for every moment her husband was on dry land.

She approached the table. The café was deserted apart from the woman behind the counter and one or two dock workers grabbing a quick break – a cup of tea and a piece of bread and dripping. Will jumped to his feet and wrapped her in his arms. Hannah glanced at the other man, who had risen to greet her. Will motioned for her to join them at the table and she repressed her annoyance at having to waste time with this stranger.

'This is Commodore Palmer, Hannah, the former Master I served under on the *Christina*.'

The older man reached out a hand to shake hers and she gave him an unwilling smile.

'I won't keep you long, Mrs Kidd,' Palmer said. 'I know you'll want to make the most of Will's brief shore leave. But I need to tell you what I've proposed to him.'

Impatient, she said, 'What?' Her tone was brusque, but she didn't care. She wanted Palmer out of here so she could be alone with her husband.

'I'm now a landlubber but working for the Royal Navy Reserve. I can't tell you any details as it's classified information and this is a public place. I would like Will to join me as part of my staff here in Liverpool, but he's expressed reluctance. I'm rather hoping you might persuade him otherwise. It will mean he loses the extra £10 per month he gets now in War Risk pay, but there are opportunities for rapid promotion once he finds his feet.'

Hannah's mouth fell open. 'You want Will to work here? In Liverpool? On land?'

The commodore nodded.

'So, he can live at home? Come home to me every night?'

'That's the idea. Although I can't promise he won't have to work at night occasionally but you'll get to see much more of him than you do now. And importantly you'll know he's safe from the clutches of Admiral Dönitz and his wolf packs.'

She could scarcely believe what Palmer was saying. She

turned to Will. 'And you're not sure?' She stared at him, dumbfounded. 'You're not sure?'

Will looked uncomfortable. 'I am sure actually. I've turned the job down. Look, Hannah, of course I want to be here with you. But I'm a sailor. I belong on the sea. I can't see myself behind a desk, poring over charts and tables and all that kind of thing. The work I do now is what I've always done. And it matters. It keeps the country fighting.'

Hannah's mouth fell open, her throat dry. The room was hot and stuffy. What was Will saying? All those lonely nights, longing for him to be there in the bed beside her. The chance for that to end was being offered to them on a plate, yet he preferred to carry on going to sea, risking his life, being apart from her. He'd rather continue to put her through the constant anguish of knowing that each day might be his last.

Anger coursed through her. Pushing back her chair, she ran out of the café and stumbled in a half-run along Bath Street, blind to where she was going.

Will caught up with her, grabbed her arm and pulled her towards him, holding her against his chest as she sobbed into the rough wool of his jacket.

'I'm sorry, Hannah. I didn't mean to upset you like that. You know I want to be with you. I think about you all the time. Only how can I give up the sea when I've just got my Mate's Certificate?'

'You've no idea, have you?' She jerked away from his hold, hammering her fists against his chest. 'It's easy for you. When you're at sea you're occupied all the time. You're doing your job. You're constantly on the move. There's no time for you to dwell on us being apart or on what might happen to you. You don't know what it's like for me. Every single morning I wake up thinking will this be the day I get the news that you're never coming home again. Every single night, I lie awake in bed with a cold space next to me where you should be. Every day there are a million things I want to talk to you about, ask your advice, hear your voice, feel your hands touching me.' She stepped backwards, looking at her husband, her eyes raking his.

'I can't talk to Judith. She's in her own world. All she cares about is having her baby and seeing Paolo again. Understandably. I'm terrified she's going to decide to go to Australia and I'll be left alone.' She kept her eyes locked on his. 'But you know what? If Judith does decide to go, I'll probably go with her.' She closed her eyes, shocked at her own words but fuelled by anger and frustration. 'I want to get away from this dreadful city where nothing good ever happens, where every night we all face the terror of air raids.' She took a gulp of air. 'It's not even as if I'm afraid of being killed – only of it happening without you being here to hold my hand. That's what I can't bear – that we could both be killed in this ghastly war, but we won't be facing it together. We'll both be alone.'

Hannah fought back the furious tears and looked up at him, clutching the lapels of his pea jacket. 'That's why I can't understand why you won't take this job. You'd still be serving the war effort. Commodore Palmer clearly thinks it's important work and you'd be well suited to it.' She stared at him, waves of anger overwhelming her. 'I remember you telling me that Palmer chose to give up the sea because of his wife. Because he loves her. Yet you won't do it for me.' Overcome with emotion, she could say no more.

Will took her in his arms again and held her. He dropped his head and kissed the top of hers. 'My dearest love. You are the light of my life. I would do anything for you.'

'But you won't. You won't do this.' She moved her head back to look at him again, trying to read what he was thinking in his eyes.

'I will. Of course, I will.' He stroked her hair away from her forehead. Taking a handkerchief from the pocket of his jacket, he dried her eyes. 'I'll go back now and tell Palmer I've changed my mind.'

Hannah felt the weight and pressure float away from her. 'You mean it?'

'Yes.' He reached down and took her hand in his. 'You matter more than anything to me. I was annoyed that he was trying to manoeuvre me into it. I was annoyed that he sent that car to get you. And most of all I was annoyed that he's taken up two precious hours of my shore leave that I could have spent with you. But none of that matters. Let's go and tell him I've changed my mind. But you understand it's not immediate, Hannah. It'll happen sometime in the new year. Until then, I have to go back to sea.'

Hannah bit her lip.

'It's only for a couple of months. Two or three more trips. We can cope with that, can't we?'

She nodded. Hand-in-hand they walked back towards the steamy windows of the dockside café.

DREAMING OF NAPOLI

After the initial flurry of letters into the camp at Tatura, the frequency of mail in either direction, diminished dramatically. Evidently the powers that be had wanted to ensure relatives were made aware that their menfolk were safe in Australia and that was as far as it went.

The authorities made a distinction between prisoners of war and internees. The former were compelled to work and the latter were paid for their labour. Paolo was attached to a group of internees who worked in nearby fruit farms and was saving every penny he earned.

There were rumours in the camp that some of the category B and C internees would be released soon and allowed to return to Britain, and several men were applying for entry into the United States. So far, Australia maintained that while they were ready to continue holding the interned men, they were not prepared to allow those considered suitable for release to remain in Australia, bypassing the usual immigration criteria.

All this was of academic interest only to Paolo, since he

had been unfairly classified in Liverpool by Jake Cassidy as a dangerous Category A fascist. His efforts to get this reviewed were rebuffed and here in Australia he had no means of proving that he had never been a member of the *Fascio*. His past service on an Italian merchant ship placed him in the same position as the many German seaman in the adjacent camp. His only consolation was hearing from Clancy that Cassidy had disappeared from the army on arrival in Australia, presumably fearing the risk of court martial, and was wanted for desertion.

'*Non ci credo*,' said Paolo. 'I don't think that is why he leave army. I think he always intend to come back here to Australia. Always his plan. Free ticket. Cassidy is very bad man. Bad like Mussolini. He will do bad things again now he is home in Australia.'

'You reckon? Bit of a bushranger, eh? You know where in *Straya* he's from?'

Paolo shook his head. 'I never talk with him. Even when we are in crew of *Christina*. He was bad man then too. After ship sink from German torpedo, *il capitano* give him bad report so he cannot get job on other ship.'

'Stone the crows! Sounds like the British government locked the wrong man up, mate. Don't seem right for a decent fella like you to be behind barbed wire and him walking the streets a free man.'

'I hope he does not come here.' Paolo shuddered at the thought.

Clancy lit a cigarette. 'You any idea how big this country is? It's a ruddy great continent, mate. Easy for people to disappear. Specially in the outback.' He blew out a long plume of smoke and leaned against the wooden wall of the hut. 'You can rest assured you've seen the back of that bad penny.'

. . .

NEWS SURFACED before the end of the year that a Captain Julian Layton of the Pioneer Corps was coming to Australia from England and would be visiting the camp to investigate the men's experiences on the *Dunera*. Hope that his classification might be reviewed revived in Paolo. Sentiment in Britain had swung from wholesale enmity towards internees to a growing awareness of the injustices perpetrated upon a largely blameless and harmless group of men. But as 1941 dragged on, there was no sign of the officer, and the dispirited inmates began to wonder whether the captain's existence and imminent arrival had been announced merely to appease them and he wouldn't be coming at all.

There was considerable continuing anger over the treatment they had endured on the *Dunera*, as well as about the theft of their valuables, money and other effects. There was no sign of any redress for these injustices, despite the questions asked in Parliament. Requests from the British government for Australia to allow wives and children of the lower category internees to be allowed to join them fell on deaf ears. Meanwhile, by the end of the year, most of those internees who had been kept in Britain, rather than shipped off to the Dominions, were being freed – around ten thousand of them.

At Tatura, as the year drew to a close, the temperature rose, and the air became oppressive and unbearably stuffy in the tin-roofed huts. Sometimes it was so blisteringly hot under the tin roofs that they dragged their mattresses outside and slept under the stars. The landscape surrounding the camp became arid and dusty and, when there was a wind, red dust blew everywhere, including inside the huts, making the camp bleaker. While conditions

were significantly better than the savage cruelty of the
regime aboard the *Dunera*, it was poor consolation to these
men who had been unceremoniously dumped in Australia.
The design of the camp didn't help either. The huts ran from
east to west so that their long sides got the blazing northern
sun in summer and the chill winds from the south in winter.

Clancy again was a source of comfort. 'Look, mate,' he
said to Paolo one morning. 'You were lucky to end up here in
Tatura. The lads off your ship who went on to Sydney got
sent north of here into western New South Wales. There's a
bigger camp up there at Hay.' He scratched his chin. 'You
don't wannna be in Hay. Hottest place in *Straya*. Over a
hundred degrees in the daytime. It's like being on a grid iron
there. And cold enough to freeze the balls off a kangaroo at
night. They can go months with no rain. Clouds don't make
it far enough inland, so there's nothing between the dry
earth and the blazing sun. You'd fry up there, son. As for
those pasty-faced Germans next door. Believe me, you're far
better off here.

Paolo tried to feel grateful, but it was hard. Yet, now that
he was certain Judith still cared for him, he was ready to join
in activities with the other inmates. He was welcomed into
the football squad, enjoying playing alongside his fellow
Italians against a team of Germans from the adjacent
compound. He passed time playing cards and worked hard
to improve his English by reading books from the growing
camp library. Books were in greater demand than any other
luxury among the internees, some of whom came from
academic backgrounds, with writers, poets, musicians and
philosophers among them. Whenever they had visits from
the Red Cross or the Quakers, books were always top of the
list of requested luxuries.

Paolo was determined to treat his captivity as an opportunity to plug the many gaps in his poor education. This was easy to do at Tatura with the camp inmates creating what became known as *The Collegium Taturensium* which offered a varied syllabus of lectures and talks from philosophy to art history. Paolo lapped these up, as well as the frequent musical concerts.

When Christmas 1941 arrived, the camp divided between those determined to use the day as an excuse for some good cheer and those whose isolation from hearth and home became more acute with the festival. Paolo bounced between the two states. It was hard to capture a sense of the season, when here in Australia it was summertime and the usual Christmas motifs seemed oddly out of place for those hankering for fir trees and all the festive trimmings. Nonetheless, there was a carol concert from German and Italian POWs and a musical recital which the Jewish internees – among whom the most musically gifted were concentrated – put on in a generous spirit of goodwill. A delegation of women from one of the local churches had collected items to make Christmas food parcels for the inmates and this too helped lift spirits across the camp.

Paolo walked around the perimeter on Christmas morning, wondering how Judith would be spending the day. By now, she must be six months pregnant and his eyes filled with tears that he wasn't able to see how her body was changing. He imagined placing his hands over her swollen stomach to feel the baby kick, as he had witnessed his father doing when Paolo was a boy and his mother was pregnant with one of his sisters.

He fished in his pocket and pulled out the dog-eared photograph of Judith. His wife by now, surely, in the eyes of God and the Church. She had explained that their marriage would not be recognised by the law but as far as the law of the Church was concerned it was valid. In the photograph she was smiling – that smile he loved so much which lit up her whole face, banishing her usual solemn expression. In Judith there was none of the natural flirtatiousness of so many of the Italian girls he had known with their self-conscious awareness of their own powers of seduction. Judith's shyness, modesty and artlessness had charmed him from the moment he had laid eyes on her.

When would this war end and free him of his incarceration? How long before he could hold his beloved against him, feeling her heart beating against his? How long until he could hold their first child in his arms? He kicked at the ground impatiently, sending up a cloud of dusty earth. It was intolerable being shut away behind barbed wire fencing, like a dangerous animal. Sometimes the injustice of it all overwhelmed him.

Looking beyond the wire, Paolo stared at the featureless flat land, its monotony punctuated only by the occasional gum tree and, more distant, the regimented rows of an orchard of apple trees. A couple of kangaroos were grazing in the distance on the sun-parched grass, near a dried-up creek bed. What would Judith think of this godforsaken place? This big flat land with its extremes of temperature, its peculiar wildlife and its big empty skies? It was alien to him. He struggled to imagine ever feeling at home here. It was too vast, too open and too featureless to ever charm him. He was glad she'd never have to experience it.

Instead he pictured the Bay of Naples, transporting himself to gaze out over the azure sea from up on the Vomero. He tried to recreate in his head the perfect blue of the water in the bay below, the city spread out and, on the other side of the curving bay, the splendour of a fiery sun rising from behind *Monte Vesuvio*, its twin humps dark against the roseate glow of a dawn sky. He pictured boats bobbing in the bay, colourful in the afternoon sunshine. He imagined the twinkling lights of the ancient city against the black of a cloudless night. He tried to recreate the memory of the familiar smells of roasting coffee, of *melanzane alla parmigiana* in heavy pans, the salty aroma of fish in the street markets, the sweetness of fresh vegetables piled high on market stalls, the drifting stink of volcanic sulphur when the wind was from the east.

One day. He swore he would stand hand-in-hand with his love and their child on the Vomero. One day. It was the only thing sustaining him through this intolerable separation. They would have their baby christened in the church of Santa Isabella. His sister Carlotta would be the godmother and his brother Mario could stand as *padrino*. Perhaps old Padre Camillo would still be alive to conduct the ceremony. That would make his mother very happy.

But who would be alive in this imagined scenario? By the time he was able to return to Napoli who knew how it would be? What if Mussolini and Hitler were to triumph? What if bombs flattened the beautiful city of his birth? Worse – what if German bombs destroyed Liverpool, killing his wife and child? He squeezed his eyes tightly shut and struck out with his fist against the wire fence, his flesh tearing as the barbs penetrated. The blood flowed from his hand into the dusty earth below.

No! It was senseless. This torture he was inflicting on himself. He needed to be strong, not weak. He needed to focus on staying healthy and alive. Most of all he needed to hope and trust in God that good would triumph and one day soon his dreams would be realised.

23

CHRISTMAS UNDER FIRE

Christmas 1940 in Liverpool was even more miserable than Paolo's in Australia. On the night of 21st December, Hitler and Goering gave the city an early Christmas present, sending one hundred and fifty bombers to attack in two waves. The bombing started at seven that evening and lasted throughout the night until soon after five in the morning.

Nance had gone out for the evening, Will was undertaking what Hannah hoped was his final voyage, and Sam was rushing all over the place in his role as an air warden, putting out the fires from the incendiaries, dropped ahead of the heavy bombing to guide the path of the bombers.

A high-explosive bomb breached the walls of the Leeds and Liverpool Canal. Millions of gallons of water escaped, causing extensive flooding of the surrounding area and leaving the canal dry. That night, the concert hall, St George's Hall, was in flames, the building burning above the heads of hundreds of people sheltering in its basement, trapped, until they could be evacuated by firemen.

Hannah and Judith huddled together inside the

Anderson shelter in the garden, cold and damp and utterly terrified as the pounding shook the ground, sending shock waves through their bodies.

One hand holding her swollen stomach protectively, Judith clutched Hannah's hand with her other, her whole body shaking. Hannah had been afraid that Judith's nerves wouldn't hold up under the terror of the bombing and her despair at the continued separation from Paolo. But Judith was stronger than she appeared. With each explosion, her eyes hardened with determination that she and her unborn child were going to get through this.

'Where's Nance gone tonight?' Hannah asked when the skies quietened after the first wave.

'Her fellow took her dancing.'

'Her fellow?'

'The RAF chap from Devon.'

'She's still seeing him?' Hannah was shocked. 'The one with the wife and children? I thought that stopped almost as soon as it started.'

'No. Whatever gave you that idea?'

Hannah realised she had never had any confirmation of this assumption. 'After we argued about it, she hasn't mentioned him... I thought she'd seen sense.'

Judith's lips stretched into a grim non-smile. 'I expect she decided to keep mum about him. Didn't want another penny lecture and a slapped face.'

'She told you I slapped her?' Hannah looked away.

'No. But Sam did.'

The blood rushed to Hannah's cheeks.

'You really should go a bit easier on her, Hannah. We all have our own way of coping during this ghastly war.'

Indignant, Hannah gasped, 'But a married man with a family?'

'A grown man, responsible for his own actions. You can't lay the blame entirely at poor old Nance's door. All she wants is a bit of affection. Only God can judge her, not us.'

Before Hannah could respond, another explosion reverberated through the ground, and the curved corrugated iron walls of the shelter vibrated. Hannah moved closer to Judith, wrapping her arms around her, the two of them locked together in a tight embrace.

The next explosion seemed to come from beyond the city, further inland, and the sisters drew apart again.

'Sounds like it's Manchester's turn.' Hannah took a long deep breath. 'Do you think we dare to move back indoors? I'd really like to be in bed.'

Judith thought for a moment. 'Shouldn't we wait for the all-clear? Or at least give it a few minutes more. If it stays quiet, we can go inside.' She took Hannah's hand. 'But can I come into bed with you? I don't want to be on my own if the planes come back.'

'Of course.'

Half an hour later with the bombers presumably having moved on, they were safely tucked up in Hannah's bed. Each tried to sleep but the adrenaline from the raid had pushed them beyond it.

'When's Will due home?'

Hannah sighed. 'Within the next three or four days, I hope.'

'It will be so good for you to have him here in Liverpool all the time. What a stroke of luck that his old boss has a job for him.'

Hannah hadn't told Judith how close Will had been to turning it down. 'I still can't believe that this living hell may soon be over. I can cope with bombs. I can cope with spending nights in that miserable damp old shelter. I can even cope with the separation – after all, *you* have to. But honestly, Jude, I don't think I can stand the constant gnawing anxiety of Will being at sea any longer.'

WHEN THE SISTERS went downstairs to prepare breakfast the following morning, they found Sam at the kitchen table. His face was streaked with dirt and his eyes were bloodshot.

He managed a grim smile as they came into the kitchen. 'That was quite a night.'

'Thank God you're safe, Sam.' Hannah touched the top of his head. 'I can't imagine what it was like being in the midst of it. It sounded like the worst raid yet. Was it dreadful?'

'No time to think really. Or to be scared.'

Judith eased herself into a chair beside him. 'What did you see?'

'I spent a couple of hours up on the roof of Lewis's.'

Hannah filled the kettle and lit the hob. 'On the roof! What on earth for? You must have been a sitting duck.' Lewis's department store was one of the many jewels in Liverpool's crown.

'Chucking incendiaries off.' He grinned. 'And then a bomb caused a fire on the top floor, so we had to put that out. To be honest, there was no time to think. We all just got on with it.' He brushed his hair back from his brow. 'Warehouses burning all over the docks. Some poor devils in a fire truck drove straight into a bomb crater as it blew up in front of them. All of them killed. There was a bus garage flattened. I had to walk most of the way back this morning. Anfield took an absolute hammering.'

Judith stood to lay the table. 'Sometimes I think it's worse being down in the shelter and not seeing what's going on up above. But I can't believe how brave you and your pals are, dashing all over the city. And as for chucking bombs off the roof of Lewis's...' She closed her eyes, shaking her head.

'Some poor souls in a public shelter copped it.' Sam got up and walked towards the window. 'In Anfield. A direct hit. One of the bobbies told me there are over seventy dead, poor souls.' He gazed out over the garden. 'Seeing all this destruction and death made me even think about joining up when I was walking home this morning.'

Judith and Hannah both gasped.

He smiled. 'But hating what they're doing isn't going to encourage me to do it back to them. Yes, I'd happily murder Hitler and Goering, but I wouldn't want to inflict that kind of carnage on ordinary Germans. I imagine most of them are like us. Trying to get on with their lives.'

'They voted the Nazis into power,' said Hannah acidly. 'They have to shoulder some of the blame.' She lit the grill and laid slices of bread under it.

Sam shook his head and tightened his lips. 'What kind of place is Liverpool going to be once this is all over? Bootle is devastated. Whole streets flattened. In the council we're keeping the statistics and almost half the houses there are either destroyed or damaged. All those streets of tightly packed Victorian terraces.'

'Bluebell Street?' Hannah looked up. 'Have they hit that?'

Sam nodded. 'I'm afraid so. Where your old house was, there's now a pile of rubble.' He looked embarrassed and had been clearly worried about breaking this news to the sisters.

'Good,' said Judith. 'I'm glad it's gone. Nothing but a house of hate. The Germans have done us a favour.' She got up and went to the door. 'See you later. I'm going to have a lie-down. I'm tired after last night.'

When she had gone upstairs, Hannah looked at Sam. 'Judith still won't talk about what happened there. But it wasn't all bad, you know. When our father wasn't there – which was a lot of the time – Judith and I were close. Much closer than we are now, if I'm being honest. She used to have such a sense of mischief. We talked so much. And until that terrible day, he was light on her. He saved his outbursts for Mother and me.'

She turned to look out through the window to the rain-sodden back garden. 'But she's right. It's better that the house has gone. So much violence and evil and if Will hadn't arrived in time, Judith would have been sharing Mother's grave now.'

Sam put an arm round her shoulder. 'But he did, and she isn't. Instead she's in love. She'll soon be having her baby. A new life to help blot out the old.'

Hannah nodded. 'I know. But what kind of world is this to bring a child into, Sam? Do you think we're going to make it out the other side? I really struggle to see how we're ever going to defeat Hitler. We're the last ones standing. How can we possibly hold out? And if we do, at what cost?'

'I'm sure eventually the Americans will have to stop sitting on the fence. If they come in and give us a hand the Germans will have no chance. And don't forget the Soviet Union. If Hitler falls out with Uncle Joe, he could soon be fighting on two fronts. That's going to stretch him. And our RAF boys saw the German fighter planes off. Don't despair, Hannah.'

Hannah reached for Sam's hand and gave it a squeeze. 'You're a good man, Sam. Where would we all be without you? For a girl forced to marry the wrong man, I couldn't have done better than you.'

'I enjoyed our brief non-marriage. Life here with you was a jolly sight better than the days when it was my father, Nance and me. Remember what a pigsty this house was until you wrought your magic?'

Hannah smiled. 'I hated having to go door-knocking for your father's awful phoney Church. When he wasn't looking, I used to throw his hateful pamphlets in the bin behind the library. I was terrified he'd find out. Anything was better than knocking on doors and trying to tell housewives that they were destined for damnation if they didn't abandon their evil ways.' She gave a half laugh. 'Now that it's all in the past it's almost funny. But then it was like living in a dark tunnel. You helped make it a bit brighter, as you were always kind to me. And never laid a finger on me.'

'And you kept my dirty little secret.'

'Don't let's talk about the past anymore.' She squeezed his hand again before letting it go.

'Any day now Will is going to be home for good. I'm looking forward to it so I can imagine how you must feel.'

'I know. I can't help being afraid though. Every minute Will's at sea I live in fear. I'll only relax when he walks through that door.'

'How does he feel about it? About becoming a landlubber?'

Hannah bit her lip. 'He obviously wants to be home and with me, but I know he doesn't want to give up the sea. He has a misplaced sense of duty. No matter how much he's been told that the work he'll be doing back here in Liverpool – whatever it is – will be of national importance, he's still convinced that unless he's doing what he's been trained to do for most of his adult life, he'll somehow be a coward. And he hates the idea of joining the Navy Reserves.'

'Then he must think I'm an even bigger coward. He knows that, if it comes to it, I'll refuse to serve altogether.'

'You're no coward, Sam Henderson. You're every bit as brave as Will. You risk your life night after night. What were you telling us about standing on the roof of Lewis's throwing bombs off? I'd be scared enough standing up there in peacetime. How can you even suggest you're a coward? Anyway, your council job is surely essential too?'

'One would think so, but I have one overwhelming thing against me – my youth. There are plenty of ageing accountants they can drag out of retirement to work again so they can send me off in a uniform.' He looked rueful. 'I reckon it's only a matter of time.'

'What will you do?'

'They'll drag me before a tribunal, and I'll have to explain the grounds for my being a conscientious objector. With luck they'll view my work as an ARP official as being sufficient for an exemption. If not, then I may have to join the Non-Combatant Corps.'

'It's daft,' said Hannah. 'Liverpool is a war zone. You're doing much more than a lot of conscripted men.'

'Let's hope, if it comes to a tribunal, they'll see it that way.'

24

STORMS AT SEA
LATE JANUARY 1941

The *Shelbourne* was positioned among more than thirty other merchant vessels, all gathering in the outer bay at Halifax, Nova Scotia. The ships were full to the gunwales with much-needed food, raw materials and munition supplies for beleaguered Britain.

Halifax was the regular rostering point for ships embarking on the dangerous Atlantic crossing. The bay was sheltered from the worst of the weather and, even in the coldest periods, the waters there never froze, thus avoiding the need for icebreakers.

Will was eager to set sail for England and the prospect of a few days' shore leave before he began his new job with Commodore Palmer at Derby House. Yet, despite his keenness to get underway, he was uneasy. There was the ever-present threat of enemy action – that the British convoy of merchant ships would be spotted and preyed upon by one of Admiral Dönitz's U-boat wolf packs or by the Luftwaffe. They would be like ducks bobbing about in a fairground game, easily picked off, forced to abandon their sinking ship and, if they were lucky, rescued by one of the other vessels.

If they weren't, headed for a cold, dark, unmarked grave at the bottom of the Atlantic.

Will's worries, and those of the other officers aboard the assembled ships, were intensified when they saw that their only armed escort was an elderly merchant vessel, the *Navaho*, now converted to a gunship, with a single 12-pounder gun, a couple of anti-submarine guns and a few machine guns on the bridge. The chances of it successfully staving off a U-boat attack, let alone taking the battle to the enemy, were next to non-existent. For her part, the *Shelbourne* had only a single 12-pounder anti-aircraft gun, operated by a Royal Artillery officer. Will, as well as the ship's first officer, Pettigrew, had received some rudimentary training in its operation, so that they would be able to assist with re-loading ammunition. Neither was keen to put it to the test.

Every voyage across the Atlantic carried the risk of attack. Every ship had to take its chances. They had no control over enemy action but had to rely on the sustaining power of hope – or, for the religious, faith. But spotting the presence of U-boats was far from easy and many attacks came without warning. Before a captain and his crew could respond, the damage was already done. The German submarines had the advantage of speed over most merchant ships, as well as the ability to dive.

Even if there were no means of knowing about the presence of the enemy, a good sailor knows exactly when the odds are stacked against him as far as the weather is concerned. The darkening sky, a falling barometer and a freshening easterly wind did not augur well. Already it was squalling within the shelter of the bay and every instinct told Will the wind would be blowing significantly harder beyond the headlands. Setting sail now would result in the convoy sailing straight into the heart of a fierce storm.

Before the war, the *Shelbourne* had been accustomed to slow hops through warm waters, making leisurely progress between Caribbean ports, collecting and dropping off cargo. It was ill-suited to the harsh cold waters of the northern ocean, loaded to capacity with steel and timber and with nothing to protect it against a rapacious enemy except a single anti-aircraft gun and the dubious security of the convoy. Like many merchant sailors, Captain Ryan included, Will believed that they would fare better taking their chances on their own, using the captain's expertise and initiative. In convoy they would be under the directions of a Royal Navy commodore, struggling to keep up and, if they did, they'd form part of a larger, more visible target. But the powers that be in the navy and the War Office thought they knew better, and merchant vessels were forced to comply. Maybe once he was installed in Derby House, Will would understand the reasoning better.

His doubts were reinforced when he saw the captain. Ryan's normally inscrutable face was transfigured by deep frown lines and the traces of suppressed anger. His shoulders dipped as though weighed down by worry. Usually he stood straight as a ramrod.

Turning to Will, Ryan said, 'Damn fool Navy Board says we can't sit out the storm. They've insisted on no change to our timings. No good sailor would get underway in these conditions. It's asking for trouble. Those fools don't have enough experience and understanding to read the weather properly.'

His words came as no surprise to Will. Contempt for the regular navy was widespread amongst merchant seamen, who considered their counterparts spent too much time in pointless drilling and theory, and not enough at sea.

He gestured towards the vessel beside, a converted collier called *Rochester Lass*. 'Looks bad, sir. That ship over there must be more than thirty years old. Can't see her being able to manage more than six knots in fine weather, let alone when sailing into the heart of a storm.'

'I served on her myself years ago as Second Officer.' Ryan's expression was grim. 'She was well past her best even then, and that was when we were only doing short runs carrying coal between the north east and London. God knows how she'll cope.' He cast a practised eye over the ship. 'Low in the water too. The whole lot of us are over-loaded.' He shook his head, then, his voice brisk, added, 'The *Shelbourne*'s coped with worse though and she'll cope with this.'

Will wondered if the master's sudden display of confidence was for his benefit. But he had no qualms or nerves about the nature of the job and its responsibilities, after more than twelve years at sea and having gained his Mate's ticket without difficulty. The war meant there were many Royal Naval officers with a fraction of his experience and significantly younger. But he doubted the *Shelbourne* had seen worse. Nothing came close to the cruel challenges of the North Atlantic in winter, especially in an ocean patrolled by packs of U-boats under a heavy sky where fighter bombers could emerge from the clouds at any time. Since the fall of France, Germany's access to the French Atlantic coast had significantly increased the range of the German navy and the peril they represented to British shipping.

Half an hour later they were underway. As soon as the convoy left the protection of the outer bay, they met the full force of the wind like a massive punch in the stomach. The

motley collection of ships sailed into the gale. With the light
fading and the sky darkening, the flotilla steamed straight
into a snowstorm, further impairing visibility. The Atlantic
churned beneath them, an icy cauldron in which the ship
pitched and twisted as they tried to move ahead. Any
attempt to form themselves into the Navy-recommended
column formation was futile, and the jumble of vessels
spread out across the heaving sea, trying to avoid colliding
with each other in the almost non-existent visibility.

Will had never known conditions like these before. The
crew were powerless against the might of nature. Out of
control, the ship tossed about like driftwood, instead of a
seventeen-thousand-ton cruiser. The convoy soon became
scattered, and with such poor visibility it was impossible to
see the other ships. By now, the sky was black, with no sign
of sun, moon or stars. Will stood on the frozen deck, noting
the significant fall in temperature since they had left Halifax. The other vessels in the sizeable convoy were out of
sight. With no other ships to guide their course, no visible
stars and planets to aid navigation, they were forced to use
dead reckoning to estimate where they were.

The captain addressed Will and the First Officer, Pettigrew. 'Do your best to hold a steady course and pray we get
through this. Maintain six-and-a-half knots until we catch
up with the convoy.' As always, there was authority in the
way Ryan spoke, but Will could see the strain and anxiety in
the older man's eyes.

The *Shelbourne* battled its way through the storm, which
showed no signs of abating. It was a watery hell. Sleep was
impossible for officers and crew as everyone laboured to
hold the ship on course through the heaving elemental
chaos. In his head, Will kept repeating Hannah's name like a

mantra. Get through this and she will be waiting for you on the other side.

The storm lasted ten days before the weather began to improve and the wild seas to calm. By the time the *Shelbourne* emerged from the maelstrom, Ryan and his men were close to collapse. But now, as they neared the Western Approaches new dangers awaited them. They may have come through the battle with nature but now they faced the danger of U-boats, which peppered the sea looking for targets. The battered, bruised and overweight *Shelbourne,* moving at a slow, lumbering pace would be easy prey. By now they were in range of the German long-range bomber planes, stationed in western France.

On the second morning after the storm ended, Will was on watch and saw a single aircraft flying towards them low above the water. It was a four-engined craft, black against the lightening sky. Definitely foe. Using the steam whistle, he signalled the alarm. The aircraft began to circle, keeping at a distance, as Ryan gave the order to ready the gun, but hold fire. There was no sign of the rest of the convoy. Had they even made it through the storm? How far ahead were they? Where was the Royal Navy when you needed them?

Will scanned the sky with binoculars. 'I think it's a Fokker Wulf Condor, sir. I can't see the markings, but it has four engines and looks the right size.'

'If it is, it's bad news. He'll be calling the wolves in.' Raising his voice, Ryan gave the order, 'All men on alert for U-boats. Start zig zagging.'

Sweeping his binoculars over the surface of the sea Will could see no sign of periscopes.

After circling a while at a distance, the Fokker swung towards them and came straight at the ship, engines roaring.

A chill went through his body as Will saw the bomb doors were open.

'Open fire!' Ryan ordered, and the anti-aircraft gun burst into life, firing until the angle of the plane's approach prevented it. As the German plane passed overhead, it let forth a burst of machine gun fire, aiming straight for the bridge, then dropped the first bomb, toppling the mast, before circling aft and opening fire again.

Will witnessed it all as if he were watching a movie unfold. Unreal – yet all too real. The *Shelbourne* shook with the force of another exploding bomb – this time smashing through the aft deck straight into the engine room. The ship jerked to a halt as the power to her pistons failed. Another bomb struck, skimming off the surface of one of the hatches before bouncing into the sea where it exploded, taking out part of the port side. The Fokker turned, then roared back the length of the ship from stern to bows, raking the deck with machine gun fire. The aft deck was on fire, and Will realised with horror that the stokers in the engine room wouldn't have stood a chance. The artillery officer was slumped dead over his gun. Out of the corner of his eye Will saw Pettigrew staggering away from the bridge, blood pouring from his face and chest. Scattered around the deck, crew members were in a frenzy of activity, around the burning hole in the deck, as they tried to stop the spread of the fire.

With a groan like a wounded animal, the *Shelbourne* listed to port. Will looked up and saw the Fokker receding into the distance. He scrambled along the deck to where Captain Ryan was supporting Pettigrew. It was clear the man was in his last throes.

Ryan barked an order to Will to check on the state of the engine room and the damage to the aft deck and sent the third officer to establish the condition of any other injured men.

The lower decks were already filling with water as Will waded towards the engine room. As he drew nearer, two blackened dismembered bodies floated towards him. The engine room had taken the full force of the first bomb blast. It was a charred shell of tangled metal and burning coal. There was no possibility anyone had survived the impact. Water was rushing in through the gash in the port side. The ship was listing badly.

When he got back on deck, he found Ryan attending the injured. The captain looked up.

Will shook his head. 'None of the poor sods down there stood a chance, sir. There's nothing left. The engine's smashed to smithereens and all crew dead.'

'Chief Engineer too?' Ryan looked stricken.

Will nodded. 'It's too dangerous trying to recover any of them. The water's rising.'

The third officer appeared at that moment, the bosun behind him.

'Lifeboats?' Ryan asked.

'Blown off the davits in the explosion,' Carew shouted, even though now in the absence of the plane it was uncannily quiet. Will realised Carew's ears must have been damaged. 'One boat's broken up and the other blown off into the water in the explosion, but it seems to be all right. Two men have swum out with a rope to stop it drifting away.'

'Life rafts serviceable?'

'Getting them into position now, sir.'

Captain Ryan closed his eyes for a moment, before saying the words no master ever wants to say, 'Prepare to abandon ship. Move the wounded to the boat deck. Fast! Get them onto rafts.'

Everything happened quickly from then on. The chief steward was dispatched to gather what provisions he could find, but returned empty handed, saying the galley was completely submerged. Officers and crew moved rapidly as Ryan checked each of the four surviving wounded sailors, calling out orders for the less badly wounded to be lowered off the ship using the rafts. Pettigrew was still clinging to life, but it was clear it was only a matter of time. The radio operator lay beside him, already dead. Will and the bosun organised the remaining men as they began to abandon ship. The men clung to the life rafts as they struggled to climb into the lifeboat.

Eventually everyone but the captain, Will and the dying Pettigrew, was in the water, aboard the lifeboat or on one of the rafts. Will sent up a silent prayer of thanks that at least the sea was mercifully calm.

On the deck, Ryan was holding Pettigrew's hand. The officer had lost so much blood he already appeared cadaverous, his skin pallid, lips blue and eyes glassy. Ryan looked up at Will. 'He's not got long now.'

'Captain, you need to get yourself off. Everyone else is in the lifeboats. One man is on a raft. Robertson's trying to get a response to our SSS on the portable transmitter. We need to abandon ship now, sir.'

'I'm not leaving Pettigrew. Get yourself off, Kidd.'

Will looked around, desperate. How could he convince the captain that Pettigrew was a lost cause and he must save his own life? 'Let's lift him onto the other life raft. If she goes down, he can float off as the water moves up.'

Ryan shook his head. 'We can't. He's too injured. I won't leave him to die alone. Go, Kidd! Think of your wife.'

As he spoke, the *Shelbourne* made a screeching sound, like the scream of a banshee, as part of the bulkhead gave way and the ship listed further to port. Before they could argue any more, Will, the captain and the dying officer were thrown sideways and hurtled down the deck at speed, towards the waiting sea. Will's last thought was of Hannah, before he was plunged into the depths of the ice cold Atlantic.

25

NEW YEAR 1941

F ollowing the Christmas bombings, January was a quiet beginning to the year, with fewer air raids due to adverse flying conditions.

Hannah was occupied with her duties at the WVS, mainly helping to find accommodation and clothing for families bombed out of their homes. Her heart was filled with sorrow and pity for them. Many of the affected families had little enough to start with and were now reduced to the clothes they stood up in. Yet through it all, Hannah never ceased to be impressed by the positive spirits and buoyant humour of her fellow citizens. The more bombs that fell, the more Liverpool's defiance of Nazi Germany grew. Many Liverpudlians' poverty and living conditions were already so bad that being bombed out of house and home didn't seem so much worse.

One morning in mid-January, Hannah was sorting through piles of clothing, looking for something to fit a little girl whose family had returned from a public air-raid shelter to find their tenement flat reduced to a heap of rubble and a large crater in the ground. The girl was about eight and unwashed: dirty-faced, wearing grubby clothes and worn-down shoes that were clearly too small for her. Hannah dug through the pile of garments on the table in the church hall and found a woolen jumper, a warm tartan kilt and a set of underwear. One of her colleagues was in charge of shoes.

Hannah held the garments up against the child. 'It looks as if these will fit.'

The girl grinned. 'The jumper and skirt'll do, Miss.'

'You need the undies too. All your clothing has been destroyed.'

The child giggled. 'There was no more clothes at home anyway, Miss.'

Puzzled, Hannah said, 'You must have had a change of underwear.'

'No, Miss.' The little girl looked surprised to be doubted. 'Not till the weather's better. Me mum sews us into it for the winter.'

Hannah gathered the items of clothing up and put them into a bag for the child to take away with her. She and her family would be sleeping in the church hall tonight.

Later, Hannah opened the door of The Laurels, eager to recount the tale of the little girl's permanent underwear to her sister. As soon as she entered the house, she sensed something had happened. Pushing open the door to the front parlour, she froze on the threshold. Commodore Palmer in his naval uniform was seated stiffly in an armchair, his peaked cap in his hands. Opposite him a nervous Judith looked pale as a ghost and avoided Hannah's eyes.

The blood drained from Hannah's face and she felt unsteady on her feet. The commodore, now standing, suggested she sit down. Hannah sank into the seat next to

Judith who reached for her hand. Snatching it away, Hannah wanted to cover her ears, close her eyes, shut out everything she knew Palmer was about to say to her.

She had to speak first. 'I know why you're here. I need to know, is there any hope?'

'I'm sorry, Mrs Kidd. I wish there was some crumb I could offer you but there isn't.' He lowered his eyes, avoiding hers. 'Will's ship went down and he went with it.'

It was a lie, a mistake. He had to be wrong. 'But this was to be his last trip. How can he be gone?' She struggled to find words. 'Will's survived a sinking before. You know that – you were with him. Someone could have picked him up as happened with the *Christina*.' She looked at him desperately.

The Commodore stared at the cap in his hands, rotating it between his fingers. He spoke as though reciting a prepared speech, laying out the facts for her. 'Will's ship went down in the North Atlantic. The *Shelbourne* was separated from the rest of the convoy during a bad storm. An air attack broke the ship's back and took out the engine room. One of the other ships in the convoy eventually picked up the survivors in a lifeboat. Will was not one of them. He and the captain were still on board attempting to get the seriously injured First Officer off the ship and into the lifeboat. Tragically, they were too late. It was an act of incredible bravery.'

Rage bubbled inside her. 'An act of incredible stupidity!'

The moment she had dreaded ever since the war began more than a year ago had finally come. In a matter of days Will would have been safely home with her. He'd sailed the seas for years. He'd survived a sinking and other attacks .They were supposed to be properly together for the first time since marrying. Instead he was lying at the bottom of the icy cold waters of the Atlantic, drifting through unfathomable depths in inky blackness.

Hannah dug her fingernails deep into the palms of her hands, wanting the physical pain to match the loss and grief swamping her. She fixed her eyes on Commodore Palmer. 'Why couldn't you have got him out sooner? You were already here in Liverpool – why couldn't you have got him to start this new job immediately? You could have saved him. You could have stopped him doing this last voyage.'

Palmer's face contorted. 'Believe me, Mrs Kidd, I would give anything for this not to have happened. I could do nothing until Will's transfer to the Reserves came through. And even if I could have done, I doubt Will would have agreed. I think he saw this last crossing as a way to say goodbye to the sea.'

Hannah gasped. 'A way to say goodbye to me too!' Unable to hold them back any longer, the tears flowed, then soon became great gulping sobs. Her skin was on fire, her nerve endings exposed and raw. She couldn't breathe, speak, do anything. Make it all stop. Wind back time, go back outside the house and come through the front door again. Find everything as usual. Stand at the sink in the scullery washing vegetables, counting the days until Will was back with her again.

But Will was never coming back.

All she wanted was to die too. To be with him in death. Now. Here. Away from a world that was cruel and alien. To slip into the maws of death, as Will had slipped beneath the waters of the ocean.

Judith's arms around her. Hannah had no idea how long she had been holding her.

The commodore spoke quietly to Judith, then, leaving

Hannah to her sister's attempts at comfort, he slipped out of the house.

HANNAH SPENT sleepless nights and days lying listless in bed, refusing to eat, speak or leave the house.

Judith had never seen her sister like this, even after their father murdered their mother, or when she had been forced into marriage to Sam and separation from Will. No matter how low she had been dragged, Hannah had found a way to bounce back, a way to stay positive. With Will's death, she had lost the will to live, had given up on life and entered into a catatonic state.

After several days, and with Hannah showing no sign of getting better, in desperation, Judith ran down the hill to the church to ask Father Edwards to call at the house and try to get through to her sister.

'Your sister is not my parishioner, Judith. Why would she listen to me?'

'Because she respects you. She likes you. Please, Father, I'm in despair. Please help her.'

The priest frowned. 'I can only suggest she turns to God for comfort and that may not be a message she wants to hear.' His face was grim. 'But I'll try. I'll do my best.'

Back at The Laurels, Judith went into the bedroom to tell Hannah that the priest had some to see her and wanted to pay his respects. Hannah rolled over in bed, turning her face to the wall and pulling the blankets up over her head. Judith was forced to go downstairs and tell Father Edwards it was a wasted errand.

'Give her time, Judith,' he said. 'Eventually the human spirit finds a way to carry on living. The grief will remain, but I'm sure your poor sister will find a way to pick up the pieces. Soon she will have a niece or nephew to distract her. You'll need her support when the baby comes. That will give Hannah a new sense of purpose. I'm going to say Mass for her this evening. You too can offer up your prayers for her. God will hear you. You must trust in Him.'

He raised his hand and made the sign of the blessing over her. *'Dominus vobiscum. In nomine Patris, et Filii, et Spiritus Sanctus,'*

After she'd shut the door behind Father Edwards, Judith sat down at the kitchen table, her head in her hands. In a matter of weeks she would be having her baby. How was she going to be able to go to the maternity home in Crosby and leave Hannah in this state? She'd been relying on her sister to get her through this scary time and now Judith felt utterly alone.

The kitchen door opened, and Nance came in. 'What was the God-botherer here for?' The older woman pulled out a chair and sat down at the table.

'Father Edwards came to talk to Hannah but she refused to see him. She hasn't been downstairs since she heard the news. It's six days now.'

Nance nodded. 'It's rough for the poor kid. He were a decent fella that Will. She'd done well to hook him. Good looking and all. She and I may not get on that well, but I wouldn't wish that on me worst enemy. Never mind, eh, once your nipper arrives it'll give her something else to think about.' She rolled her eyes upwards. 'I 'spect it'll give us *all* something else to think about – screaming its little head off in the middle of the night.'

Judith was affronted. 'Don't have a go about the baby before it's even born, Nance. That's not fair.'

Nance got up and went to put the kettle on, giving Judith an affectionate pat on the back as she passed her. 'I'm actually looking forward to meeting the little blighter when it gets here. Bring a bit of life into this place.'

IN THE END, it was Mr Hathaway from next door who got Hannah out of her torpid state. He knocked on the door one morning, bearing a small china bowl with a hyacinth. Judith, who didn't know him other than to wish him good morning over the garden wall, stood in the open doorway, her face puzzled.

'I've come to see Mrs Kidd.'

'My sister is unwell, Mr Hathaway. She won't see anyone. Perhaps you don't know but her husband has been killed.'

'I do know. That's why I'm here.'

'If the plant is for her, it's very kind of you. I'll see that she gets it.' She leaned forward to take the bowl from him.

The old man edged away. 'I'll give it to her myself. Where is she?' He looked over Judith's shoulder, his eyes scanning the hallway. 'I miss her.'

Judith, surprised, said, 'We all miss her, but I'm afraid she doesn't want to talk to anyone. Even me.'

Mr Hathaway moved towards her. 'She'll see me.' He called out, into the interior of the house. 'Mrs Kidd. It's me. Mr Hathaway. Please let me speak to you.'

To Judith's astonishment, Hannah's bedroom door creaked open and she appeared at the top of the stairs. She was wearing her dressing gown, her hair hanging in unkempt strands, her face gaunt and thin. She descended the stairs in silence, moved past Judith and went into the back kitchen, signalling to Mr Hathaway to follow.

The elderly neighbour gave Judith an I-told-you-so look, then moved past her towards the rear of the house, shutting the kitchen door behind him. Judith was left standing in the hall, then went through into the dining room where she had set up her sewing machine on the dining table. For a moment she was slightly affronted that this old chap whom she barely knew, had her sister's trust and confidence, but she pushed her resentment away. Hannah had at last returned to the land of the living.

'I BROUGHT YOU THIS. Thought it might cheer you up a bit.' Mr Hathaway handed the pot of flowers to Hannah.

'Cheer me up? Can flowers do that?' She pulled out a chair and sat down, abandoning the pot on the draining board.

'No. I suppose not. But they might at least make you realise that people care about you and miss you.'

Hannah looked away, staring past him at the window and the garden beyond. It was raining.

'Life goes on, Mrs Kidd, and it's time you came back to it. You're not like me, with no one to care about me until you came along. People need you. That sister of yours will be having her baby before long. She's alone too, isn't she?'

Hannah glanced at him, recognising his tact about Paolo being interned.

'I'm sorry about what happened to Mr Kidd. He looked a fine handsome fellow. But please believe me. The pain and loss and grief will never go away. But you will find a way to carry on living. You're a good strong woman. So many people rely on you. Your sister, Mr Henderson, and the other woman who lives here. Mr Henderson tells me you do great work with the Women's Service or whatever they call it these days. And you've helped me more than you can know. I've missed our talks. Our cups of tea together. You brought some joy into my miserable existence.' He touched her hand as it lay palm-down on the deal table. His fingers were bony, his papery skin cold. 'In fact, I was rather hoping you might make me a little cup of tea now.'

Touched by his kindness, Hannah got to her feet and filled the kettle, setting it on the hob and lighting the gas under it. She looked at the hyacinth. 'I'm sorry I was rude to you. It was kind of you to bring me this.' She picked up the pot and put it in the middle of the table.

'I plant the bulbs every year. Cheers me up when they come out.'

They drank their tea in silence, then Hannah reached across the table and took the old man's hand. She looked into his eyes. 'Does the pain ever get any easier? Did it for you?'

He considered her question. 'I don't think the pain lessens, but we get more able to bear it. At the beginning it's the shock. You refuse to believe the person you've loved so much is gone forever. The unfairness of it all. Your whole life loses all meaning. Everything changes.'

'Yes,' she whispered. 'Shock. Yes, that's exactly it. My body has been in shock. And I'm so angry. At God. At Hitler. At the German pilot. At Mr Churchill.' She gave a little sob. 'And most of all at Will himself.' She brushed away the tears. 'Does that sound dreadful of me to be angry with him?'

'No. I was exactly the same. My Flo had saved so many lives, only for her own to be taken. I was angry that she refused to stop visiting the sanatorium. She put herself at risk. I felt she didn't care what happened to her and that must mean she didn't care about me.'

'That's what I think about Will. He insisted on doing one last voyage. We could have managed without the money for a few weeks.' She stared down at her hands. Her fingers were woven tightly together. 'If only I'd been more insistent.

But I was so happy that he'd agreed to take that new job. I was over the moon.'

Hannah uncurled her fingers then squeezed them into two tight fists. She took a sip of tea, realising how parched her mouth was. 'He'll never walk through the door again. Why, oh why, didn't I beg him not to go?'

'Because you loved him so much. Hard and cruel as it is to accept, your husband died doing what he loved. You need to be proud of him. He was a brave man. A hero. It's because of men like him the rest of us have any chance of seeing this war through.' He looked at her, eyes sincere. 'Hard as it is to acknowledge, Mrs Kidd, your husband could have returned safely only to be killed by a bomb on the bus back from his new job. People are dying all around us. At least in my war it was men over there in France and Belgium. Now it's old folks and mothers and little children.'

This was the longest speech she'd ever heard Mr Hathaway make, but he was still in full flow.

'Life is unfair. Once we accept that, it gets easier to live it.' He leaned forward, looking straight into her eyes. 'You taught me that, Mrs Kidd. Your kindness to me helped me to begin to enjoy the world again instead of punishing myself. Life is always going to be lonely and poorer without the person we love. But ask yourself, if you had a choice between the brief time you and Mr Kidd had together but with all this pain and grief, or never meeting him at all, what would you choose?'

Without hesitation, Hannah jerked her head up. 'I treasure every moment I spent with Will. Every last moment.'

'There's your answer. Grief and sorrow are the price we pay for the sweetness of love. Maybe we pay it after years of happiness or maybe after only a brief time together. But if we truly love someone, we all pay that price in the end.'

'You are very wise, Mr Hathaway.' She gave him a weak smile.

'And unlike me, my dear, you'll always have the knowledge that your husband loved you as much as you did him. I used to see him from my parlour window, when he came home on shore leave. He'd be running up the hill from the Vale, even with a heavy bag. Couldn't wait to get home to you.'

Hannah smiled through the tears pouring down her cheeks. 'Really? He did that?'

The old man nodded. 'He most certainly did. I used to say to myself who could blame him. Wherever that young man is now, he's watching over you and I bet he's willing you to get yourself up and out there again, doing what you do so well. Taking care of people. Being kind. Sharing that beautiful smile of yours. Bringing light into people's lives.'

Hannah took a deep breath. The scent of the hyacinth sweetened the air and she took another breath, savouring it. New life. Mr Hathaway was right. She must go on. Pick up the pieces and be here for Judith and the baby. Now that she would never have a child of her own, she had to be even more strong and protective of Judith and her child.

Life must go on.

26

NEW LIFE

A few days after Hannah emerged from her self-imposed isolation and started attending to her WVS duties again, she received another visit from Commodore Palmer. He had come to enquire after her well-being, and to explain what she could expect in terms of a widow's pension following Will's death.

'I'm embarrassed it's so little, Mrs Kidd. Life is going to be hard for you.'

Hannah swallowed. It was going to be hard for her whether the pension was meagre or generous. Money was the least of her worries. After all, there had always been a struggle to make ends meet as she grew up. The once successful coffee trading business started by her grandfather was in decline even before her grandfather's death and her father's incompetence and neglect had driven it further into the ground. Any income it did produce was spent by Dawson and Sam's father, funding their phoney religious enterprise or, in her father's case – as Hannah had discovered later – paying for the services of prostitutes and pursuing other illegal money-making ventures. Hannah and

Judith had grown up without comforts, badly dressed, poorly fed and without small pleasures. The things she enjoyed cost nothing financially – walking on the sands at Crosby, secretly reading books from the library, lying next to Judith on their narrow beds in the tiny Bootle bedroom, talking of their hopes and dreams and telling each other stories.

'I'll manage, Commodore Palmer. Money isn't important to me.'

'I'd like to help.'

Hannah looked at him blankly, wondering how he thought he could possibly help, wishing he'd go and leave her in peace. Seeing him sitting there in his naval uniform with a thick stripe on his sleeve, his oversized great coat and his cap with its insignia on the settee beside him, made her think of everything she had lost, imagining Will sitting there in a smart new navy blue uniform. She said nothing.

'I'll get straight to the point. I'd like to offer you a job, Mrs Kidd. It will require you undertaking a period of intensive training and it's based on the assumption that you will be accepted into the Women's Royal Naval Service, the Wrens. You'll have to be interviewed by a selection panel, but I can't imagine why you wouldn't pass muster.'

She gaped at him, shocked.

Before she could say anything, he continued, 'The work is top secret. It's based here in Liverpool. In the same location where Will would have been working. It will, of course, be different in nature from what he would have been doing.' He pursed his lips. 'But you are an intelligent, articulate woman and we have some roles I think you would be well suited to.' He coughed. 'I can't tell you exactly what is involved, until you're on board, but we would train you in new skills such as telephony, or transcription. And the work is of national importance.' He leaned forward, looking intently at her.

'I don't know what to say.' Hannah was genuinely shocked.

'Then say yes. I can arrange for you to be seen by the selection committee as soon as possible. Although I'm sure it will be a foregone conclusion since you come with my recommendation.'

'But you don't even know me. You know nothing at all about me.'

'You'd be surprised how much I know, Mrs Kidd.' He gave her a tight smile. 'It's my business to find out. Besides, even if I didn't...' He tilted his head sideways. 'I knew Will well when we served together. I can honestly say, he was one of the finest men I ever had the honour to sail with – once he put his mind to it.' He gave Hannah a rueful smile. 'Believe me until he did, we had our moments. Sometimes Will Kidd was his own worst enemy. Impetuous. But once he knuckled down, he was a great sailor and a man I'd have trusted with my life. He was also an extremely good judge of character and the fact that he married you is the best endorsement for you I can imagine.'

Hannah drew her lips together tightly, trying not to give in to tears.

'So, will you do it, Mrs Kidd? Will you come and serve your country? The work you would be doing would be a wonderful way to honour Will's memory and whilst it's too late for him, you would be playing a part in saving the lives of many other men like him.' His brow creased with a frown. 'I'm going to be honest, things are not going well for our convoys in the Atlantic. I don't need to stress to you how critical this work is. We can't bring Will back, but we can do everything in our power to prevent as many other men as possible succumbing to Admiral Donitsz and his wolf packs in future. You could play a small but significant role in doing that.'

Hannah was still stunned. She thought for a moment then said, 'Thank you, Commodore. I am honoured by the faith you put in me, but I can't. There's my younger sister to think of. She's expecting a baby next month. She's entirely alone as her husband is overseas.'

'In Tatura Alien Internment Camp, Australia.' Palmer smiled. 'I told you I make it my business to know certain things. But don't worry, Mrs Kidd. Paolo Tornabene is a good man without a Fascist bone in his body. I feel personally responsible for him, as your husband and I, together, persuaded him to leave his ship, throw in his lot with us and come to Liverpool. I bitterly regret that. It was a foolish mistake. I put sentiment before reason. I should have known that as an Italian citizen he would be vulnerable should Italy enter the war.

He sighed. 'If I hadn't taken this job, Paolo and Will would have sailed again under my command. It weighs heavily on my conscience.'

'Don't say that,' she said, quickly. 'If Paolo hadn't left that Italian ship, he'd never have met my sister. Their situation may be dire, but neither of them regrets it.' She paused. 'You are high up in the navy, Commodore. You report to an admiral, don't you? Can't you do anything to get Paolo released so he can come back here? Back to Judith and their baby when it comes?'

The commodore looked down, avoiding Hannah's eyes. He seemed embarrassed. 'I will try, but I'm not optimistic, Mrs Kidd. It seems there is paperwork indicating that he was a paid-up member of the Fascists.'

Hannah rolled her eyes. 'The only organisation Paolo

was a member of was the Italian Club. According to Judith and her friends in the Italian community, almost all Italians joined. It was a social club. For some of them it made it easier to maintain contacts at home in Italy. Very few had any truck with Mussolini, least of all Paolo Tornabene.' Her words to the commodore were delivered coldly. 'Paolo hates Mussolini with every bone in his body.'

'I understand, but it's not just about links to the Fascists. I know what you've said is true, Mrs Kidd. We've locked up ice cream vendors, waiters and men who'd applied to join the British armed forces. It's a huge sledgehammer applied to a very small nut.' His face was stern. 'But in Paolo's case, prior to the Giordano grocery, his last employer was the Italian merchant navy. Under the Home Office guidelines Paolo Tornabene has two things working against him. Firstly, his time residing in Britain is very short. There are men who have been here more than twenty years who have been interned. And coming here straight from service on an Italian flagged ship makes him doubly suspect. That puts him automatically in the A category as the assumption is that he must have knowledge of enemy marine services.'

'That's ridiculous!'

The commodore looked surprised at the strength of Hannah's reaction. 'I agree. I'm sure, eventually, sense will prevail. But what I'm trying to explain to you, Mrs Kidd, is that Paolo is a long way down the pecking order. His case will require individual review and there are men with far fewer question marks against them who are likely to be released first.'

'Can't you pull any strings?' Hannah was surprised at her own pushiness.

'I'm doing what I can, but it's not going to be easy and it's certainly not going to be fast.'

Hannah was deflated. Getting Paolo back in England to be with Judith would make life dramatically better for her sister, and if Hannah herself were to attempt to build a new life without Will – something that still seemed an impossibility – improving her sister's lot was the first step.

Palmer leaned forward in his seat, elbows on knees, eyes fixed on hers. 'So, Mrs Kidd, will you come and work with us?'

'I need time to think about it, Commodore. And it's completely out of the question until my sister's baby arrives. It's due next month. If Paolo were to come home it would be easy for me to accept, but I have grave doubts as things stand right now.' Her eyes met his. 'But I promise you, I will talk it over with Judith and let you know.'

'I'll need an answer before the end of March. I can't keep the post open any longer than that. We began operations this week and by early April we need to be fully staffed, trained and operational.' He got up and moved towards the door. 'Please think about this very carefully, Mrs Kidd. You would be making an immense difference to our country.'

He seemed about to say something else, but evidently decided against it. Had he been intending to tell her it was what Will would have wanted? If he had, she'd have said no to him on the spot. As it was, she reiterated that she would give his proposal more thought.

Hannah and the commodore were at the front door when something occurred to her. 'If it's impossible to get Paolo home, there may be another way.'

He turned to look at her, curious.

'You could arrange for my sister and her child to travel to Australia.'

Palmer seemed taken aback. 'She'd go all that way? Alone? With a small baby?'

'I believe she'd go anywhere on earth to be near Paolo.'

'You do understand that Paolo would still be interned?'

'Yes. But Judith could visit him, surely. They've released thousands of interned men here in England already, and the others who are still locked up behind wire fencing are at least permitted to have visits from their wives.'

'We both know that Judith is not legally married to Paolo.'

Hannah gave the naval officer a cold stare. 'Gosh, you really do know everything, don't you? However, in the eyes of God and my sister, they're married. They had a proxy marriage service officiated by a priest—'

'Which has no legal standing in Britain.'

Hannah bit her lip. 'Well, it should have.' She opened the front door for him. 'Proxy marriages are recognised in other countries and under the canon law of the Catholic Church which is what matters to my sister. In wartime, with couples separated, it's scandalous that they're not accepted here.'

'I'm inclined to agree. I'll see what I can do, Mrs Kidd.' He shook her hand. 'Please think about my offer.'

HANNAH DIDN'T MENTION Palmer's visit to Judith. She didn't want to get her sister's hopes up about the commodore arranging a passage for her to Australia. The idea of Judith leaving her too was more than Hannah wanted to bear. Yet it would be selfish to stand in her way. Judith would give anything to be with the man she loved.

Hannah justified her silence by telling herself it was better to wait until the baby was born. Judith might feel very differently then. Besides, it was not as if Judith had ever articulated a desire to go to Australia. But Hannah knew her almost as well as she knew herself and was sure that it was only a matter of time before her sister voiced a wish to join Paolo there.

FEBRUARY WAS A QUIET MONTH. Bad weather curtailed the ambitions of the Luftwaffe, and Liverpudlians continued to enjoy a respite from the devastations they had experienced in the run-up to Christmas. But everyone sensed the lull of February 1941 was merely a stay of execution.

Sure enough, on the night of 12th March, the German bombers returned with a vengeance. The hardest hit areas were on the opposite side of the Mersey in Birkenhead, which was pounded non-stop in a night of sheer terror.

While it was quieter in Orrell Park, Hannah was woken by the sound of nearby explosions.

She went to wake Judith to suggest they retreat to the relative safety of the Anderson shelter. As she crossed the landing, she could hear her sister moving about.

Hannah walked into the bedroom.

'It's happening!' Judith's eyes were wild and filled with blind terror. She was on the far side of the bed, bent double, clutching her stomach with one hand and leaning forward, gripping the edge of the bed with the other. She looked up at Hannah, pleading. 'Help me!'

'We need to go down to the shelter, Jude.'

'No time!'

'You have to. For the sake of the baby. We'll be safer down there.' As Hannah approached, she saw that Judith was standing in a puddle of water on the polished wood floor.

'No time,' Judith repeated, gasping, and gulping in big mouthfuls of air. 'It's coming!' she screamed.

'Of course it's not.' When their little brother was born, it had taken long painful hours before their mother was delivered of her short-lived baby. Charles Dawson had sat downstairs reading religious tracts in the front parlour and forbade Hannah to summon a midwife or doctor. Desperate, her mother issued instructions to bring towels and water and a clean sheet to wrap the baby in. Hannah did so and her mother ordered her to leave the room. Hannah sat on the edge of her bed in the adjoining bedroom, listening to the sobs and screams of pain, until, at last, she heard her father leaving the house, slamming the door behind him. She ran next door to beg Mrs Crompton their neighbour to help. The baby, when it came, was tiny, blue, and although the efforts of Mrs Crompton, a mother of ten, eventually got the boy breathing, Timothy was a sickly baby and died in infancy. Was this going to happen again?

Judith's eyes were wild. 'Help me onto the bed. Please! Hannah!'

Hannah shook her head. 'We could be up all night. Maybe all day tomorrow too. Do you remember what they told you at Park House?' she said, referring to the maternity home run by nuns in Crosby where Judith was due to be admitted for her confinement. 'The nuns said your contractions could go on for hours. I can run to the phone box and call them. We could get a taxi to drive us there. The nuns will know what to do.'

Judith bent double, grabbed her sister's arm. Her nails dug deep into Hannah's flesh. 'There's an air raid going on. We can't get a taxi. Don't be daft.' The nails dug harder and Judith roared, chilling Hannah. Through clenched teeth, Judith said, 'Stop arguing and help me onto the bed. It's coming – now!' The last word was howled rather than spoken. A trickle of watery blood ran down her leg under her nightdress.

Hannah stared at Judith, paralysed. Their roles were reversed. Despite the pain Judith was in control, and Hannah was helpless and panicking.

'Get some towels. I need to push.' Judith's voice was ragged.

Hannah stood rooted to the spot.

'Do it, Han. Now!'

Hannah rushed across the landing and grabbed a handful of towels from the linen cupboard. Was Judith about to lose her baby? It was too soon. Several weeks too soon. And it was coming too fast.

She laid a towel under her sister's legs. As she eased it into place, she saw Judith was right. The crown was already visible. 'I can see the top of its head, Jude,' she gasped. 'You're right. It's coming.'

'Of course, it's coming. It's going to tear me in half.' Judith reached for Hannah's hand and squeezed it so tightly that Hannah had to bite off her own cry of pain. Sweat poured down Judith's face. Hannah took in a great gulp of air and moved to cup the emerging baby's head in her hands, instinct taking over.

Judith's screams changed in a way that chilled Hannah to the core. Was her sister about to die? Her eyes were rolling as she entered a semi-conscious state in which the only reality was the pain. No one could possibly survive this intensity.

As Judith struggled to push, they heard the roar of German planes and the echoing thunder of explosions. If giving birth didn't kill Judith would the Luftwaffe kill them all?

The baby's head was now half-out and Hannah gently

took it between her hands and urged Judith, weak and delirious, to keep pushing. With a blood-curdling scream and a super-human effort, she gave another push and Hannah eased the head out and wiped away the creamy film from the baby's eyes and face with a cloth. With a final supreme push Judith released the rest of the body into the world. Hannah wrapped the tiny baby in a towel, slippery as a sea creature, and placed her in the arms of an exhausted and near comatose Judith.

'It's a baby girl, Jude! You have a daughter. You brave, clever brilliant thing!' Hannah wiped her sister's soaking wet face with the edge of a sheet. She glanced at the alarm clock on the bedside table. Two-thirty in the morning. Now she needed to cut the cord.

ONE OF THE maternity nuns from Park House arrived the following morning, in response to the telephone call Hannah made after the raid was over and Judith and her baby were sleeping.

The nun, Sister Monica, examined the baby and said all was well with the child. 'Such a rapid labour is extremely rare but it can result in a very healthy child. Any baby so energetic that it pushes its way out that quickly must be fit and strong.' She indicated to Hannah to join her outside on the landing. 'It's Mother I'm concerned for. You might imagine that giving birth so quickly would be an advantage, but it's not. A normal birth gives mothers time to adjust to the pain of contractions as they build up and get stronger. Your sister had to cope with it happening instantly. I can't begin to imagine how much of a shock that must have been to her system. She's a brave girl. It must have been agony.'

Hannah swallowed. 'Is she going to be all right, Sister?'

'I'm sure she is, but the doctor will be here soon to give her a check and I'm going to ask him to keep an eye on her. She's had a terrifying experience and it may take its toll. Going through a rapid labour is hard enough anyway but to do so during an air raid and without a midwife or doctor...' She shook her head. 'You did extremely well, too, Mrs Kidd. Thanks be to God that you were with her. You should be proud of each other.'

After the nun had taken her leave, Hannah went back into the bedroom. Judith was ash-pale. The baby was sleeping quietly in the makeshift cradle Hannah had fashioned, using a drawer. It would do until she was able to collect the cot that one of the ladies of the WVS had offered.

Judith opened her eyes. 'Get us a cup of tea will you, Han? As sweet as you can manage.'

At the bedroom door, Hannah turned back. 'What are you going to call her?'

'Sarah. After Mother.'

Hannah smiled. 'Perfect.'

27

A NEW JOB

While Hannah was in the kitchen making the tea for Judith, the door burst open and Nance stumbled into the room. Her face was black with soot and her hair grey with dust or ash. Beneath her hairline were traces of dried blood. Her coat was torn and stained and her stockings were in shreds.

Hannah gasped. 'Oh, my goodness, Nance! What happened?'

'I was at my friend's in Birkenhead. We went into the public shelter when the raid started. I've never been so scared in me life. It went on and on. Right overhead. Explosions everywhere.' She banged her hand against the side of her head. 'The street what the shelter was in got clobbered, and the roof fell in on top of us.'

Hannah's hand flew up to her mouth. 'You took a direct hit?'

'Not direct but bloody close. The wall of one of the houses collapsed and part of it fell on the shelter roof.' Nance collapsed into a chair, kicking her shoes off. 'Blimey, Hannah, love, I thought I'd copped it. I really did.'

Hannah poured her a cup of tea. 'Here, get this inside you, you poor thing.' She was about to tell Nance what had happened during the night at The Laurels, when a mewling sound came from upstairs. Nance's mouth dropped open.

Hannah gave her an apologetic smile. 'As you can hear, we have a new tenant. A baby girl, Sarah Tornabene. Born extremely quickly in the middle of a raid.'

'Crumbs. Born already?'

'Less than an hour from when labour started until the baby arrived.'

'Blimey! You delivered it?'

'I did what I could, but it was all down to Judith. She was in agony. The midwife said rapid births are very distressing for the mother. I felt utterly useless. Honestly, Nance, I thought Jude was going to die..'

'Don't run yourself down. I bet you did more than you think. And knowing you were there with her would've made all the difference to her.' Nance gave her a pat on the arm.

Hannah was taken aback at the sudden unexpected kindness. 'Do you want to go and have a peep at the baby?'

Nance frowned. 'Maybe it's better if I leave it a bit.' She took a sip of her tea. 'Don't want to get too fond of the kid.'

'Whyever not?'

Nance took out a cigarette, lit it and drew down hard, releasing a wreath of smoke from the depths of her lungs. 'I'm going away. Made me mind up when I were in that shelter waiting to die last night.'

'Going away? Where?'

'Canada. I reckon there's a future for me there. I doubt there'll be a stone left standing in Liverpool and London before long, if those bleeding Kraut bombers have their way. No thanks. I'm out of here.'

Hannah was stunned. 'But how? When?'

'Next week. I've been offered a job. I was going to say no, as I don't really fancy dodging the U-boats to get there – specially after what happened to your old man. But last night in that shelter I changed my mind. I'd rather take me chances on the open sea than be a sitting duck here.' She took another long draw on her cigarette. 'My pal in the airforce pulled some strings for me. I'm going to be working on an air base over there where they train up our RAF boys.'

Hannah was open-mouthed. 'Doing what?'

'What I do now. Brightening up the boys' days with a smile and bit of a giggle while serving them up their grub.'

'And they'll ship you all that way? Aren't there any Canadian women who can do that?'

Nance rolled her eyes. 'I told you, my pal pulled some strings. He's going out there too. He's going to be testing our lads. The Canadians do the training, but Terry is going to be an examiner.'

'Is this the same chap with the wife and kids in Devon?'

Nance hesitated then said, 'The same, but there's no wife and kids.' She took another drag of her cigarette before stubbing it out. 'I made up that bit to wind you up. You can be a right judgmental cow at times.' She gave Hannah a grin and a wink. 'As it happens, I'm quite fond of the old boy.' She reached into her battered handbag and pulled out a small photograph and handed it to Hannah. 'That's my Terry.'

Hannah looked at the picture. To her surprise, Terry was a round-faced man who appeared to be in his fifties. Thin strands of hair were combed over a shiny scalp in a vain attempt to conceal his baldness. He looked like Oliver Hardy. Judging by the expression on Nance's face she clearly adored him, so Hannah quickly said, 'He looks a nice chap.'

'He may be no Cary Grant to look at but he's the kindest fella I've ever met. Treats me like a princess he does.'

'Are you going to get married?' Hannah struggled to contain her surprise.

'That's the plan. Eventually.'

'I see. And...'

'You're going to ask me if I'm sure there's no wife and kids, aren't you? I know it's hard to believe that a gem like Terry is still a bachelor, but he was so devoted to his flying, there was no time for courting.' She smiled, almost bashful. 'He calls me his little Cockney and I call him my knight in shining armour.'

Hannah tried not to laugh. It was strange to witness this sentimental side to Nance, with none of her usual armoury of barbed comments and without her habitual tendency to be hard-faced and cynical. Then she remembered what Sam had said about Nance wanting nothing more than to find a husband and settle down with him. For his sake she hoped Terry could afford a housekeeper, as it was impossible to imagine Nance turning into a model housewife. Unless true love had that effect on a woman. Somehow Hannah doubted it.

'Congratulations, Nance. It won't be the same at The Laurels without you.'

As March moved into April the first signs of spring appeared, after a cold winter characterised by frost and freezing fog. Daffodils brightened the gloom of the back garden. There was no more than the occasional minor air raid thanks to heavy cloud.

This relative calm was a relief as Judith, debilitated after the gruelling birth, struggled to cope with her small baby.

Hannah found herself having to deal with the increased laundry and spent hours boiling nappies and sterilising bottles. Judith's attempts to breastfeed were painful and short-lived.

The longer her separation from Paolo continued, the less Judith appeared able to handle it. Hannah's hope that baby Sarah would prove a welcome distraction for Judith didn't materialize. Though she adored her new baby, Judith was constantly weeping at the injustice of her husband being locked up on the other side of the world. She hadn't heard from Paolo since Christmas, due to the restrictions on the internees sending letters and the slowness and unreliability of the transportation of international mail.

It was hard for Hannah not to feel resentful. Judith showed little understanding of Hannah's grief. It was as if she expected Hannah to get on with her life. Whereas Judith, parted only temporarily from Paolo, should be indulged and pitied. Resisting the temptation to let fly at her sister, Hannah bottled up her resentment and grew increasingly lonely.

Because her husband had been more absent than present throughout their marriage, surely it should make the loss easier to bear – but the opposite was true. Will's death had hollowed her out, creating a huge cavity inside her, a dull ever-present ache. This background pain would, without warning, be replaced by a sudden sharp agony of grief that burst out and took her unawares in the middle of washing the dishes or sorting garments for the WVS. Sometimes her despair was so acute that she contemplated going down to the railway embankment and jumping in front of a train.

.   .   .

The time came soon for Nance Cunningham to say goodbye to the other occupants of The Laurels and set off for her new life in Canada. While there had been little love lost between Nance and Hannah, Nance's presence had supplied a balance between the sisters, perhaps delaying Hannah's realisation that she and Judith had moved far apart since the death of their parents.

The growing gulf saddened Hannah, along with the realisation that, while she and Judith loved each other, they had little in common. Nance represented a completely alien world to both sisters, which had drawn them together.

The day Nance left, they all gathered in the hallway to bid her farewell – including Sam who had delayed his departure for the council office.

'Are you sure you don't want us to come down to the Pierhead with you, Nance?' Sam asked as he passed her coat from the hall stand.

'I hate goodbyes. My Terry's meeting me off the bus so he'll carry me case. It's a bleeding nuisance that Exchange is closed. Quicker to jump on a bus than go all round the loop to Lime Street.'

'Then I'll walk down to the Vale with you and carry your case to the bus stop. It's the least I can do.'

'You're a real gent, Sam.' Nance gave him a broad smile, though her lip was trembling. 'I can't believe I'm leaving this place. After all this time.' She looked around the hall with its brown anaglypta and spidery cracks in the ceiling, as though trying to commit it to memory. 'Still, I'll have a place of me own in Canada. I'm sure it'll be far grander than this old dump.' She gave a chuckle, but Hannah could see she was struggling to control her emotions.

Hannah held out a hand to shake Nance's and found herself being pulled into the other woman's arms. Trying not to splutter at being drowned in cheap eau de cologne, Hannah hugged her back. The Laurels would never be the same again.

HANNAH HAD BARELY GIVEN Commodore Palmer's surprising job offer further thought. A new job was the last thing on her mind, even though she was all too conscious that times were going to be hard in the days and months to come, with Judith unable to take in sewing due to the demands of motherhood, as well as the cessation of Nance's contribution to the household purse. Hannah's WVS work was unpaid and the pension that came as a result of Will's death was modest to put it mildly.

When she did give it some thought, Hannah was ambivalent. The prospect of taking up work in the place where Will had been due to serve terrified her —it was impossible to believe she could ever be good enough or clever enough to do the kind of work the commodore had in mind. Her education had been patchy at best and it seemed inconceivable that the Navy could seriously require her services. Surely, it could only be a token gesture from Palmer – he probably expected and hoped she would say no and had only made the offer to assuage his guilt about Will. Yet he had said he'd checked her credentials with the WVS, so she must be doing a reasonable job there – even though Mrs Grundy, the lady in charge, was a bit of a battle-axe and rarely gave praise. But most of all, Hannah was frightened that being in the building where her husband should have been working would fill her with such sadness, such bitterness and such an overwhelming sense of loss that she would be unable to function.

Commodore Palmer needed her answer. Time was

running out. As she sat in the front parlour, knitting a cardigan for Baby Sarah, the door opened and Sam came into the room. He moved across to warm his hands in front of the sparse fire, then sat down in a chair opposite her.

'So?' he said.

'So, what?'

'Have you made up your mind whether to take the mysterious job?'

'How do you know about that?' Hannah put down her knitting.

'Judith told me. She doesn't think you should do it.'

'Really? She hasn't said that to me.' Hannah was surprised her sister had even considered it worth mentioning to Sam. Since the baby's arrival, Judith had been very self-absorbed.

'I happen to disagree. Taking that job could be the best thing for you.'

Hannah studied his face, wondering what he was about to say.

'I think it would make you feel better. You'd be making a difference. Helping other men doing the dangerous cross-ings that Will did. You can never bring Will back, but you might play some small part in saving other lives, in helping to prevent more women from facing widowhood.'

Hannah glanced down at her knitting pattern to avoid his gaze. 'And supposing I don't care about other people?'

'But you do. Otherwise, you wouldn't do what you do for Judith, for Mr Hathaway and for the WVS. Mr Hathaway told me the other day that your kindness to him has changed his whole outlook on life.'

She stared at Sam, disbelieving. 'He said that?' She felt a rush of emotion and looked away into the thin flames of the feeble fire.

'And what about Judith? How would she cope if I was out at work every day, in town.'

'It'd do her good. She's far too dependent on you and you make it too easy for her. It's time she did more for herself. I'm fond of the girl but she doesn't know how fortunate she is, with a healthy child and a husband who may be absent, but at least she knows he's safe. Sometimes I'd like to give her a big kick up the backside for the way she takes you for granted.'

Hannah stared at Sam, shocked at the vehemence of his last remark.

'Judith needs to concentrate on being a mother to her child and not expect you to be a substitute mother to her. When I think what you've had to go through and the way you have to shoulder it all yourself it really bothers me.' His eyes were kind but the set of his mouth was stern. 'Judith takes advantage.'

'Sam! That's not fair. She had a frightening time giving birth during a bomb raid – not to mention the dreadful painful labour she had to endure.' As she spoke, she felt herself blushing. But Sam wasn't like most men to whom she'd be wary about mentioning such matters. And judging by his expression he was taking what she had to say in his stride.

'I've asked Commodore Palmer whether he could fix for Judith to go to Australia if he can't arrange for Paolo to be freed and sent back here. Nance got a passage to Canada so I can't imagine why Judith shouldn't be able to get one to Australia. If they won't let Paolo go, it's the least they can do.'

'There you go again. Putting Judith before yourself again.'

Hannah bit her lip. 'I'm not. It's not like that at all.' Suddenly tearful, she scrambled in the pocket of her apron for a handkerchief. 'It's because I don't think I can bear it anymore.' She squeezed the hankie in her fist, forcing herself to hold back the tears.

Sam moved over to join her on the couch and put an arm around her. 'You can tell me anything, Hannah. I consider you to be my dearest friend.'

Hannah was touched. 'It's seeing Judith with her baby. Knowing that she and Paolo will one day be a proper family with a child of their own. She has a future while I have nothing.' She looked away. 'I hoped to have a child myself but now it will never happen. I've lost the love of my life and I don't think I can bear it any longer. Judith spends one afternoon in the sand dunes with Paolo and ends up expecting a child while I completely failed during more than a year of marriage. If I'd had a baby, I'd still have a part of Will, but I have nothing. Absolutely nothing.' She gave a gulping sob and Sam pulled her closer.

'My poor dear girl. I had a feeling it was something like that.'

'I feel terrible telling you this – even thinking it. I'm being uncharitable towards my own sister. Jealous. But, oh, Sam, I can't help it. If she goes to Australia, I wouldn't have the constant reminder of my own failure to become a mother. It's mean-spirited of me.' She wiped her eyes. 'And anyway, if she went out there, I'd miss her. The baby too. I'd have nobody.'

'You'd have me. I know it's not much, but I do care about you, Hannah. If Judith does go to Australia, I'll be sad to see her go. But nowhere near what I'd feel if you were to leave too. And I'd have to get rid of this place. No point me rattling around here on my own.'

Hannah took his hand and leaned her head against his

shoulder. 'Thank you, Sam. You are as dear to me as if you were my brother.'

'So, will you?'

'Will I what?'

'Go and tell that Navy big shot that you'll take his job. And never mind about sorting Judith out. It's time she sorted herself out. She's more than capable. That girl's stronger than you give her credit for. She went through hell with the murder and the trial and she emerged stronger. She got herself that job at the Education Authority without you even knowing, let alone sorting it out for her. She even changed her name without telling you. No. Judith is perfectly able to look after herself, if you'd leave her to get on with it. She can wash her baby's nappies as well.' He smiled and shook his head.

'Yes. I don't know how that's come to be my sole responsibility.' She rolled her eyes, smiling.

'So, you'll take the job?'

'I'll do it.' Hannah smiled back at him, but there was a hollow fear in her stomach at what might lie ahead.

TWO DAYS LATER, Commodore Palmer arrived again at The Laurels. Hannah received him in the front parlour, turning on the electric bar heater as she hadn't yet laid the fire. She told him that if his offer of a post was still available, she would be happy to accept.

'Delighted to hear it. The committee has approved your appointment in principle but would like to meet with you – just to make sure you don't have two heads – or a German granny.' He gave a little chuckle. 'I'll arrange it for tomorrow. Then you'll need to get fitted for a uniform and we can have you in training on Monday.'

'Is this normal, Commodore?'

He looked puzzled.

'I mean you recruiting junior staff like me.'

'Everyone has to be vetted.' He tilted his head to one side. 'But, no, you're right. It's not usually my purview. I think you know why I'm doing it.' He reached for the leather attaché case he had placed on the sofa beside him. 'As to the matter of your sister and her husband, I may have good news on that front too.'

'Paolo can come home?'

'I'm afraid not. As expected, I hit a blind alley on that one. But I can get your sister and her baby on a ship out there and have arranged for the Australians to accept her as an immigrant. It will take a bit of time. Possibly months. Lots of red tape. But it will happen. Once the war is over and Paolo is released, the pair of them can decide whether to remain out there or return here.'

'Oh.' The blood drained from Hannah's face and she shivered. Perhaps she had thought it was an impossible task and now that Judith could indeed be leaving England her stomach clenched. 'Gosh. It's actually going to happen?'

'Unless you or Judith has changed your mind.'

'No. I'm just trying to take it in. My sister going to the other side of the world.' She took a gulp of air. 'It was always me who wanted to go out there – what with Will being Australian and telling me so much about the place. And our only other relative, my Aunt Elizabeth, is out there. Now it will be Judith who gets to go. She'd never been in the least interested in Australia. How the world has changed in such a short time.' She looked up at the officer. 'I'll let her know. I hope it will be a big relief for her. I am extremely grateful to you, sir.'

Palmer rose to his feet and tucked his case under one

arm, his peaked cap in his other hand. 'Can you take a bus into Liverpool tomorrow morning? The interview panel is based at the Adelphi Hotel. Do you know it?'

Hannah nodded. She'd never been inside such a grand building.

'Ask at the desk for Chief Officer Nugent. Nine o'clock prompt.'

The commodore gave her a little salute and moved towards the door. 'Welcome to the team, Mrs Kidd.'

WHEN HANNAH TOLD her sister the news about the voyage to Australia, Judith flung her arms around Hannah's neck and gave her a vibrant smile – a rarity since her separation from Paolo.

'When are we going? When do we leave?' Judith was bouncing on her heels.

'You mean when are *you* going? I'll be staying here. I've accepted the commodore's offer. I'm going to join the Wrens.'

'What?' Judith's face fell. 'You can't. You have to come too.'

'Don't be silly, Jude. This is my home. I can't leave. There's nothing for me in Australia now. We'll never find Aunt Elizabeth. You'll be with Paolo. You have a new life to build there. My life is here in Liverpool.'

'No! You have to come. I can't possibly go all that way on my own.'

'You won't be on your own. You'll have Sarah.'

'She's a baby! And that's exactly why I can't go without you. I can't cope with her on my own. It's impossible. And I can't go on a ship alone. All that way! I'll be terrified. You have to come.'

'I can't. I'm starting the new job on Monday.'

Judith's looked horrified. 'Don't be ridiculous. What can you possibly do for that Commodore fellow?'

'I told you. I'll be in the Wrens. I'll be trained to do all kinds of things. Operating a telephone switchboard, for example.'

'No, Hannah, no! Please. You can't. You have to come with me. I can't possibly go without you.' Judith began to sob. 'And I so want to go. I want to be with Paolo. You have to, Hannah. I need you, and Sarah needs you. We've no idea how long Paolo will be in the internment camp. I can't be alone in a strange country. How can you possibly be so selfish?'

LATER THAT DAY, Hannah slipped through a gap in the fence into Mr Hathaway's garden and knocked at the back door. The old gentleman was bent over the crossword in the newspaper and his face lit up on seeing Hannah through the window.

'I've come for some advice.' She sat down opposite him at the rickety table.

'From me?' He looked both pleased and astonished. 'What advice can I possibly give to a sensible and confident lady such as you?'

'Not so confident these days.'

'Come on then, girl, spit it out.'

Hannah told him about the commodore's job offer. 'All being well, I start work on Monday.'

'That's very sudden.'

'Not really. I've had a long time to think about it. I finally said yes this morning.'

'Marvellous. Your husband would have been proud of

you. I certainly am. And I can't wait to see you in your uniform.'

Hannah gave him a smile. 'You're very kind, Mr Hathaway.'

'So why do you need my advice?'

'My sister doesn't want me to take the job. She wants me to go with her and the baby to Australia. She doesn't think she can cope on her own.'

'She's going to Australia?' His mouth dropped open. 'My goodness, me. How has she arranged that?'

'My husband's former boss is high up in the Navy. He's managed to sort it for her. Judith is desperate to be close to her husband, even though he's unlikely to be released before the war's over. Maybe she feels being in the same country will allow her to put pressure on the authorities – but mostly I think she just wants to be near him, even if it's on the other side of a wire fence. I don't blame her. I'd be the same.'

'I see. But why does she want you to go with her?'

'Judith's always relied on me. She's nervous at the prospect of a five week voyage, particularly the first part with the risk of attack.'

'And she thinks you can fend off the Germans?'

Hannah smiled. 'I think it's more about the company and helping care for the baby. And about being in a new country where she'll know no one.'

'Then maybe she ought to wait until the war's over.' He looked at her intently. 'Look, Mrs Kidd, your sister can't have it both ways. Either she's desperate to see her husband, in which case nothing should stop her, or she needs to wait. There's no reason to drag you into this. Least of all now when you have a new opportunity. Do you really want to do this job?'

'To be honest, I don't know.' She twisted her wedding ring round on her finger. 'I've no idea what it will entail as it's all top secret. But I want something – anything – to fill up the great yawning hole in my life.'

'And going to Australia wouldn't do that?'

'There's nothing there for me. Other than Judith. I have an aunt somewhere but no idea where. Taking this job is a way to be connected to Will. If he'd lived, he would have been stationed in the same place I'm due to be working in. And there's you and Sam. I'd hate to leave you both behind. Sam says he'd have to give up the house if I went to Australia. I don't want that to happen.'

'Then you must stick to your guns, my girl. Young Judith will have to find her own way forward.'

'And you don't think it's selfish of me?'

'Certainly not. Sensible, not selfish.'

Hannah got up and went to the back door. 'Thank you, Mr Hathaway. You've been a great help.'

CLANCY WALKED over to where Paolo was sitting on the step of his hut, grinning and holding a letter in his hand.

Joyful, Paolo tore it open, eager to read what Judith had to tell him. He wondered whether it was news that their baby had arrived, but reasoned that the delay in the post from England meant even if it had, the news wouldn't be in this one.

The excitement of hearing from Judith turned to pain when he read the contents. His best friend was dead, killed in an enemy attack in mid-Atlantic.

Anguish and sorrow engulfed him. He and Will had shared so many experiences in their time on the *Christina*.

He sat cross-legged on the edge of what had become the

sports pitch in the camp, close to the wire, under a clear starlit night. From the distant huts he could hear the faint sound of music as the camp orchestra played. Everyone would be in the mess room listening to the performance. The violinist was playing *O' Sole Mio* and Paolo was transported to Naples by the familiar music. No one could see him here. No one would come looking. Tears appeared unbidden and Paolo brushed them away. Why? Why? Why?

He thought of Jake Cassidy, now on the run like several of the no-goods who had been guards on the *Dunera*. Little more than common criminals. Why should a man as evil as Cassidy live when Will Kidd, the best of men, had died?

Paolo's faith in God was being sorely tested by this war. Religion had sprung more from habit than conviction, and now he asked himself how a supposedly merciful God could let such things happen.

28

IN THE CITADEL

Hannah was convinced she had failed to pass muster as the commodore had termed it until, at the end of what she was sure was a disastrous interview, Chief Officer Nugent, had stretched out her hand and said, Welcome to WAC.'

'WAC?' Hannah echoed.

'Western Approaches Command.'

'I've passed?'

'With flying colours, Mrs Kidd.'

Hannah had gulped. How was it possible? During the interview she'd been forced to admit that, apart from a part-time job helping with the book-keeping in her father's coffee firm and her voluntary work with the WVS, she had no working experience.

CO Nugent must have sensed her shock as she smiled and said, 'Don't worry you'll be trained on the job. Everything's happening very fast these days.'

. . .

Two days later, Hannah took a quick look in the mirror and adjusted her new Wrens' hat. It was true what everyone said: the Navy did have the best uniforms. The cap was jaunty and smart, her double-breasted jacket and pleated skirt, neat and trim. But Hannah felt no pride in her reflection. This new version of her – Ordinary Wren Kidd – would never be witnessed by Will. Some might say he would be looking down on her from heaven, but Hannah doubted it. For there to be a heaven there had to be a kind and caring God. Not one who would sink and drown her beloved husband after only a year of marriage.

Even if Will were looking down at her, she wasn't sure he'd approve of her smart new uniform. Hannah remembered the day they had argued over her volunteering for the WVS – how might he feel about her taking a full-time paid job in the services? How might he feel that she would be working in the place – she now knew it was Derby House – that he had been due to serve in? Whatever he might think, she was doing this in his memory, and was determined to make him proud.

Back downstairs, Judith, bottle-feeding the baby, looked up at her, took in the new uniform and sniffed. 'Look at you. The cats' whiskers.' There was amusement in her voice, and Judith seemed a little less hostile than before. Was she beginning to come around?

Hannah bent down and kissed the top of the baby's head. 'Be good for your mummy, little darling.'

Judith gave a reluctant smile. 'The uniform does suit you. See you tonight.'

'Wish me luck!' Hannah paused in the doorway, looking back.

'I won't go that far.'

. . .

CONSULTING the piece of paper Chief Officer Nugent had given her, after the rather scary interview last week, Hannah turned into Rumford Street and approached the large stone edifice that was Derby House.

Once past the guards and inside the building, Hannah, heart thumping, descended the stairs into the nerve centre of British Atlantic operations.

A young woman in naval uniform was waiting for her at the foot of the staircase.

'So, you're the new girl. Kidd?' The Wren was small, her hair neatly set in waves, her mouth bright with carefully applied lipstick. 'I'm Wren Telephonist Baker but you can call me Penny. Let's get a cuppa, then I'll give you the tour of the Citadel as we call our home down here in the bunker. I gather you're going to be in the Map Room and one of the girls there will show you the ropes.'

Hannah was staggered by what she saw as she followed Penny. The basement of the Derby House office building was a vast rabbit warren. In subterranean rooms, uniformed staff, some wearing earphones, were seated in front of switchboards. Others were patiently transcribing whatever they heard over their headphones.

They passed a locked door with an armed guard standing sentinel outside.

'No one's allowed in there except the man on duty. He gets locked in for his shift. All Top Secret.' Wren Baker put a finger up to her perfectly shaped lips.

'What's he doing?' Hannah stared at the locked door and the expressionless face of the armed guard.

'This place operates on a need-to-know basis. Your section head will brief you on everything essential for doing your job.'

The next half hour passed in a whirlwind for Hannah. They moved through room after room, past ranks of women sitting side-by-side, moving their hands at super-fast speed, pulling plugs in and out of holes on giant switchboards.

The largest room, the Map Room, was saved to last and Penny said goodbye on the threshold, telling Hannah to go in.

Inside was like a Medieval market, buzzing with people. Uniformed staff, some wearing earphones, were seated in front of telephones or other mysterious-looking equipment, while others pushed long pointer sticks across giant maps of the Atlantic Ocean or stuck pins and magnets onto huge boards on the walls or covering oversized tables. Another group was noting information on smaller charts around the room. Above them, on a raised dais, a group of uniformed officers was huddled together around a table, in hushed discussions.

The Map Room was dominated by a giant wall, painted black and divided into a grid of small squares. On the right-hand edge Hannah recognised the silhouetted outlines of the coasts of Britain, France, Spain and North Africa. Over the upper border was what she imagined must be Iceland, Greenland and the Arctic, and on the far left was what must be the Canadian coast. The majority of the wall was a vast black space with a few airplanes, ships and submarine shapes stuck there with magnets. Hannah bit her lip and stared at the expanse of black ocean dissected by its white painted grid. In which of these small squares had Will's ship, the *Sherbourne*, been struck? Which small anonymous spot held his unmarked grave?

Looking up, she saw a gigantic ladder on wheels, attached to the top of the wall on a metal rail, enabling it to slide back and forth across the giant map. Standing on the top of the ladder was a Wren, one hand holding onto the ladder, the other stretching out to place a submarine on a square of the map. There was another ladder on an adjacent wall, manned by a WAAF, this time in front of a series of enormous blackboards, also divided into small squares, filled with symbols and numbers in chalk. The tops of the charts were marked as Convoy Escorts, Non-operational Aircraft, Aircraft Symbols, and other arcane designators. Around the room were other Wrens and WAAFs and a few RAF officers.

Commodore Palmer greeted her, his usual charm replaced by a clipped businesslike detachment. 'Wren Trainee Kidd.' He gave her a curt nod. 'You'll be working in here once you've been trained. You'll shadow Leading Wren Plotter Harris.' With a slight dip of his head he indicated a woman leaning over the large table in the centre of the room. 'I'll leave you in her capable hands.' Without a further word he was gone.

Leading Wren Harris was in her forties and was brisk and businesslike. She launched straight into her introduction of operations.

'The big map on the wall is the Aircraft State Board. We plot the location of all our aircraft, convoys and escorts as well as enemy planes, ships and submarines.' She turned back to the table and the enormous map of the ocean in the centre of the room. Ships were positioned at various points across the surface, manoeuvred by a pair of Wrens using long wooden rakes. 'And that's the Situation Map. We plot our convoys, escorts, enemy subs, and aircraft. The idea is to have an up-to-the-minute picture of the entire North Atlantic.'

Leading Wren Harris pointed upwards. Hannah looked

over to where the woman was indicating: a glass panelled office, overlooking the whole room. 'That's the chief up there. Sir Percy Noble. He runs the whole show.' She lowered her voice. 'He's an Admiral. And we had Mr Churchill himself visiting last week.'

Hannah swallowed. How was she ever going to be able to do the kind of work going on here?

Leading Wren Harris gave her a broad grin. 'It looks harder than it is. Don't you worry, Wren Kidd. You'll soon get the hang of it. We build up a constantly updated picture of the entire ocean and everything on it so we can protect our boys and get them safely home. We track the German wolf packs, so we can predict movements and patterns, send the RAF boys in to hunt them down and help our ships evade the enemy.'

'But how?'

'You don't need to know that. At the moment you'll be watching and learning until we see how capable you are. You've signed the Official Secrets Act?'

Hannah nodded.

'You must never so much as breathe a word outside this room about what you see and hear in the Citadel. You'll be trained to understand these maps. How to position ships and subs and planes. Well, not the planes usually. The WAAFs do that. But we all work closely together here. It's not that hard, once you get a hang of the grids. After a while you'll know immediately which square is which. And you'll be shadowing me at first.' The woman picked up a submarine shape from the table. 'We use white ones if the position is an estimate. Black ones when it's verified.' She held up the shape of a ship. 'These red ships have been hit by a torpedo.'

Hannah blanched. This was all too real.

'Things may be going Hitler's way at the moment but

we're going to win this. There are so many clever people working here, I'm absolutely convinced we'll send the blighters packing. It's a matter of time.' She gave Hannah a quizzical look. 'You lost your hubby out there, didn't you?'

Hannah nodded.

'I'm sorry. That's why we're going to win this war. We simply have to because of men like him.'

Why hadn't all this intelligence and interception helped Will? A wave of nausea rose inside her stomach. This was too much. How could she do this work?

But how could she not?

HANNAH FLUNG herself with growing enthusiasm into her work inside the Citadel beneath Derby House. There was no time to dwell on her own loss, when every day she was forced to confront the losses of so many others. Every time she carried a transcribed message to the Chief Petty Officer Wren leaning over the map table, and saw her using the long rake to remove a ship sunk by a U-boat, Hannah knew other women would soon be facing the terrible news she herself had still not fully accepted.

The 4th of April, when half of the Atlantic convoy was sunk, was a particularly distressing day. Spirits in the Map Room were low, but no one let their guard slip. If anything, the more things went against the convoys, the stronger the determination and resilience of the workers in the Citadel. But Hannah couldn't help thinking that, short of a miracle, the Allied ships on the Atlantic were fish in a barrel.

The losses were sometimes offset by enemy submarines being sunk or aircraft shot down – but it was clear that, so far, Hitler was winning the Battle of the Atlantic. Every lost ship was a tragedy, but there was no time to dwell on it or to feel downhearted.

Her only regret about her new role was that her acceptance of the job had driven a wedge between her and Judith. Constrained by secrecy from giving her sister even the most minor details about the nature of the work she was doing – or even where she was doing it – Hannah could only tell her that the role was important to the war effort.

'So was the work you were doing at the WVS. I don't see why you had to get a full-time job. I've got more than enough to do trying to manage with a tiny baby, without having to take on your share of the housework. Do you realise how little sleep I get? I have to wake up for feeds throughout the night.' Judith's eyes bored into her.

Hannah bit her tongue before she could tell Judith she ought to have thought of that before she let Paolo have his way with her. Instead she said, 'We need the money, Judith. My widow's pension isn't enough for us to live on, and you're not able to take in any sewing at the moment. If it weren't for Sam's generosity in letting us live here rent-free I don't know what we'd do.'

'We'd go to Australia. That's what we'd do.' Judith glared at her sister.

'For heaven's sake. How many more times? You can go to Australia whenever you want. After all, it was I who got the commodore to obtain the permissions. You know I'm not going with you but I'm not stopping you going. And I've told you I'll give you my savings for the ticket.'

Judith scowled, then flounced out of the room, Sarah in her arms.

At times like these Hannah doubted herself. Underneath the petulant behaviour, Judith was fragile, and Hannah felt protective towards her. But she remembered how Mr Hath-

away had said that she had to live her own life without
trying to live Judith's as well. Judith and baby Sarah had a
future – even if it might seem impossibly far away while the
war was going badly. Hannah had nothing, and needed to
build a life for herself without Will. The long days at the
Citadel at least kept her mind occupied and prevented her
dwelling on her grief.

As well as the terrible losses in the Atlantic, Hitler's
appointment of Rommel to lead the Afrika Corps was
enabling Germany to reverse the Axis losses in the desert of
North Africa. With the fall of Greece to the German powers,
April produced a seemingly endless list of bad news.

Liverpool may have got off lightly so far in 1941,
compared to London, but everything changed in May.

Hannah returned home late on the evening of May 1st.
She was in bed when the sirens sounded just before eleven
o'clock. She pushed her feet into her shoes, grabbed her
dressing gown and the eiderdown off the bed and went
across the landing to Judith's room where she could hear the
baby crying.

'We need to go down to the shelter,' she said. 'Or at least
under the stairs.'

Judith nodded, a look of resignation on her face. She
gathered up a blanket to wrap around Sarah and followed
her sister downstairs.

They decided on the shelter as there would be more
room to spread themselves out and settle Sarah. To their
intense relief the raid was short-lived and the all-clear
sounded just before midnight.

By now, the sisters were accustomed to spending the
night in the back garden. With Nance gone, there was more

space in the shelter. It was still cold, damp and musty, but Hannah felt safer than being squashed in the cramped space under the staircase.

Despite the brevity of the attack, there was a lot of damage done that night. When Sam appeared the following morning, he told Hannah and Judith the sad news that the casualties included twelve ladies of the WVS who had taken a hit in the rest centre where they were preparing meals for the homeless. While none of them were personally known to Hannah, the fact that she had been a volunteer herself made the news even more poignant.

Judith's look of fear caused Hannah to ask herself again whether her decision not to go to Australia was sound. There were others who could take on the work she was doing, yet no one could replace her as Judith's sister and Sarah's aunt. Shouldn't she be putting her loyalties to family ahead of country?

That was clearly what Judith felt, as she frequently pointed out that, while she hated Hitler with a passion, she had no love for the British government after their dreadful treatment of Paolo.

The following night, the raids, aided by a full moon, lasted four long hours. The Docker's Umbrella – the Overhead Railway that ran the length of the docks and was vital for their functioning and for the transportation of workers, was badly damaged. The entire cityscape of Liverpool was changing daily. Whole areas were completely flattened, and services destroyed, as tons of bombs and incendiaries rained from the skies in an apocalyptic inferno.

HANNAH MOSTLY WORKED DAY SHIFTS, but from time to time she was required to work late into the evening. On such occasions, if there was a raid on, she had to remain at The Citadel as it was too dangerous to attempt to return home through the conflagration.

On the evening of 3rd May, the sirens sounded for another raid. Wren Telephonist Baker – Penny – whom Hannah hadn't seen since her first day at the Citadel, joined her over a cup of tea in the building's small Naafi canteen.

'Bad luck,' said Penny. A bit of a rush on today. I've a feeling we'll be in for an all-nighter.'

'My sister will be terrified if I don't come home,' said Hannah. 'She and her baby will be alone in the house. Our landlord is on fire-watch duty. I hope Judith goes into the shelter.'

Penny said, 'That's one thing I don't have to worry about. There's only me at home now. Dad died in the last war. He was a merchant sailor. Sunk by a German torpedo in the Irish Sea. There was just Mum, our Kevin and me. When this war started Kevin went into the Royal Navy and was killed at the beginning of last year. His ship was escorting a convoy. Losing him as well as Dad just about finished Mum. She died of a heart attack during the raids in November.'

'I'm so sorry, Penny. That's dreadful. Your whole family gone.'

'I was working on the switchboard at the Automatic in Wavertree. When the war started, I moved to work in the main telephone exchange in town, then they recruited me to work here. I thought it would stop me dwelling on Mum and Kevin dying and I like to think I'm doing my bit. How about you?'

Hannah told her about Will. When she got to the part about Judith wanting her to go to Australia with her, Penny had a different view from that of Sam and Mr Hathaway.

'If I were in your shoes, love, I'd jump at it. A whole new life away from all this death and destruction.'

'But as you say, by working here, we're doing our bit.'

'Family first, love. Once they're gone you can't get them back. I had a fella I was courting before the war. Name was Len. Met him when I was at the Automatic. He's out fighting in North Africa now. Before he went, he wanted us to get engaged, but I broke up with him. I couldn't go through the pain of losing someone again.'

Hannah was shocked. 'Did you love him?'

Penny shrugged. 'Who knows? After our Kev died, I pushed Len away. I don't want to get close to anyone anymore – at least not until the war's over. He asked me to get hitched when he was due to be posted overseas. Reckon otherwise we'd have drifted apart anyway. Or maybe that's me trying to make excuses.'

Changing the subject, she gave Hannah a bright smile. 'You going to grab a bunk while there's a chance?' she said, referring to the small dormitories where there were bunkbeds for overnight stays or to catch a brief rest during lulls in activity.

'Last time I tried that, the Commodore came after me, insisting he needed me to find him a particular chart.'

Penny nodded. 'They love to do that. If I get a bit of a break I come in here and have a cup of tea and read my book.' Face down on the table in front of her was a book with a black dust jacket, *No Orchids for Miss Blandish*.

Hannah hadn't read a book since before Will died. Once, that would have been unthinkable. When she'd first moved to The Laurels, when Sam's father was alive, she'd persuaded Nance to pick up books at the library for her as there were none in the house. Amos Henderson, like her own father, had banned all reading apart from the Bible. Nowadays, she was free to do as she wished, yet never seemed to have enough time to settle to a book. With a daily bus journey she had time to concentrate – although so often on the morning trip she stared out of the window at the growing bomb damage – and with the blackout, it was often too dark to read on the way home.

'I've nearly finished it. Very American and rather rude. Penny raised her eyebrows. 'Although the author's British. You can have it when I've finished. But don't blame me if you find some of it awfully shocking.' Penny winked. 'I'm working my way through all the piles of books Mum left. There's enough reading matter in our house to keep me going for the rest of my life.'

'Thank you. That would be wonderful. I've never read a book like that. I've always tended to stick to the classics.'

'Prepare for an education then.'

It was after five in the morning before the all-clear sounded. Hannah had worked through the night and as a result was told she could stay home until her shift started the following day.

Soon after six she left Derby House and set off on foot to get a bus home. It was immediately apparent that the night-long raid had utterly crippled Liverpool. Huge piles of rubble and masonry filled the streets where once grand Victorian municipal buildings stood. Roads were broken up by gaping holes and craters. Streets of elegant shops and department stores had been flattened. Famous landmarks were destroyed or disfigured, including the Customs House, now missing its domed roof.

As she made her way through the blighted city centre, she passed other people, heading into town to start work.

How many of them would find their offices or warehouses standing?

A crowd of people was gathered by a bus-stop. Hannah walked on, thinking that it would be pointless to wait with so many ahead of her and the possibility that some of the route might be blocked.

Dust hung heavy in the air, blotting out what should have been a clear spring day. How many families had lost loved ones during the night? How many homes had been destroyed while their occupants cowered in shelters?

She wondered whether to get a train. Since the collapse of the viaduct leading to Exchange Station in the Christmas bombings, the trains on the line from the city to Orrell Park had been diverted and it meant a long trip around the northern extension. Hannah, anxious to get home to Judith and Sarah, guessed sections of the track might have been damaged during the night and she didn't want to be stuck in a part of the city she didn't know.

She made up her mind to walk, hoping that a bus might come along if she followed the route. She had reached the junction with Stanley Road and Scotland Road and guessed that she still had about an hour's walk.

Increasing her speed, she hurried past bomb sites, trudging along between buildings with their windows blown out and roofs gone, clambering around piles of glass and rubble where the pavements had once been. Liverpool was alien and unrecognisable.

Out of nowhere came an earth-shattering, ear-splitting explosion. Deafened, heart pounding, convinced she was dying, Hannah instinctively flung herself down on the ground, heedless of the glass and shrapnel beneath her.

This wasn't a normal bomb. It was louder and more

violent than anything Hannah had ever encountered. She lay face down in the dirty street, waiting to die.

No warning. No sirens. Nothing. A sudden volcanic eruption. Between bombed out houses, she could see flames leaping skywards. It was coming from the docks. Cradling her head in her arms she lay, waiting for death as dust and particles showered down from the sky.

She had no idea how long she lay there, head on arms, body rigid, terror freezing the blood in her veins. A hand took her arm and helped her to her feet. The man who pulled her up was speaking to her, but Hannah couldn't hear him. Had her eardrums shattered? She stood help-lessly, watching the man's mouth form silent shapes. He moved off, evidently satisfied she was unharmed. She walked on, heedless of her torn stockings and filthy skirt. It was only after she reached Walton Vale that she was aware she'd lost her uniform cap. Gradually, her sense of hearing was returning, though it still felt as if she were listening though thick cotton wool.

Turning into Orrell Lane, Hannah realised she had dropped Penny's book. She'd need to buy her a new copy, though she had no idea where she'd get her hands on one, let alone spare the money to pay for it.

Walking up the hill she met an exhausted fire watcher returning home. 'What was the big explosion?' she asked him.

The man shrugged. She strained to hear his reply. 'Not a clue. All the telephone lines are down.' His eyes looked dead and Hannah shuddered to imagine what he'd been through during that long night while she had slept, safe in her underground bunker.

As she turned the corner by the Orrell Park Ballroom, heading towards The Laurels, fear engulfed her and she began to run towards her home. The windows were all blown out, the roof had collapsed and the side wall had vanished, revealing what had been Judith's bedroom. The iron bedstead dangled precariously from broken floor-boards over an enormous crater where Mr Hathaway's house next door had stood.

'No!' she screamed. 'No!'

Not Judith. Not beautiful baby Sarah. Not kind Mr Hathaway. Hannah stumbled through the gap in the wall where the gate had once been, staggering round the rear of the building to the Anderson shelter. It was intact. She scrambled down the steps, hoping and praying that her sister and niece would be there. It was empty.

Distraught, she climbed out again. Why hadn't Judith gone to the shelter? Why hadn't she herself been here to make her? Hannah looked around her, desperate.

Keep calm. Don't panic. Think!

If Judith had been in bed when the bomb struck, given that the bed was still there, might she still be alive?

And the under-stairs cupboard? Could they have been sheltering there? Hannah ran across the patch of lawn, now covered with pieces of shrapnel and pushed open the back door. Inside was chaos. The kitchen ceiling had fallen in and the side wall facing Mr Hathaway's house had disappeared, along with the range oven. The bedroom above, which had been Sam's, had deposited its furniture into the kitchen. Hannah clambered over the rubble into the hall. The stairs were intact as was the cupboard beneath. But there was no sign of her sister.

She was about to go upstairs when a voice yelled at her.

'Get out of there. It's not safe, Hannah.' Sam was standing on the other side of an open gap in the hall floor.

He reached a hand out and took hers, pulling her towards him. 'The hall ceiling could come down any minute.'

'Judith!' she cried. 'Where's Judith? The baby?'

'They're safe. They're in the Orrell Park Ballroom. The WVS are looking after them.'

She flung herself into Sam's arms, tension rushing out of her. Huge tidal waves of relief enveloped her as Hannah buried her head against Sam's chest. He gripped her arms and steered her out of the house.

Outside, they clung to each other, like ivy to a stone wall, Sam breathing words of reassurance.

Looking up and seeing again the void where next door used to be, Hannah stiffened. 'Mr Hathaway?'

'He'd have known nothing about it. A direct hit.'

She began to cry. Soft quiet tears. 'He always refused to go into the shelter. Said he couldn't bear being underground. I think it was the trenches in the last war, about the thought of being buried alive.' She pulled away from Sam and walked to where the garden fence had once been, looking down towards the edge of the crater. 'But he's been buried alive anyway.' A horrible thought occurred to her. 'He might still be down there, under the rubble. He might still be alive.'

She started to move towards the hole, but Sam held her arm. 'He's not alive, Hannah. Poor chap will have died instantly. There won't even be a body left to recover. I'm sorry. I know how fond of him you were.'

'He wanted to be with his Flo. He will be now.' She said a silent prayer for the soul of the old man. 'I want to see Judith now.'

'I'll walk you down there.'

She looked up at the shell of the house. From the back

she could see that the top floor was barely there. 'Do you think they can repair it?'

'If the foundations are solid. But with that crater next door I doubt it.'

'Oh, Sam, I'm so sorry. What will you do?'

He shrugged. 'What will *you* do?'

The moment Hannah had seen that missing wall where Judith's bedroom had been, she made up her mind. 'I think you know what I'll do, Sam.

29

MAJOR LAYTON AT TATURA

I t was not until late spring that Major Layton, the officer sent to investigate the *Dunera* voyage by the Home Office, finally arrived at Tatura. After landing in Sydney in late March he had been sent back to Melbourne and then on to Canberra to meet army and government officials. His arrival coincided with increased concern back in England about the treatment of the men on the *Dunera,* with more questions raised in Parliament. The recently appointed Home Secretary, Herbert Morrison, was anxious that the matter be cleared up as quickly as possible and reparation made. Layton, who had been promoted to major during the voyage out from Britain, was in no doubt that, as the Home Secretary's representative, he needed to act quickly, hoping he would have the matter resolved within a couple of months.

In preparation for the major's arrival, after the morning roll call, before they began work, the internees at Tatura were addressed by the camp commander, who distributed forms for them to complete to declare their losses.

Paolo took his compensation form and scanned it

quickly. They were expected to itemise their losses from clothing to valuables. He'd lost nothing. He'd had nothing to lose except his pride and his dignity, but there was no place on the form for that. At the end was a stern warning that false declarations would result in heavy penalties including up to four years' imprisonment with hard labour.

'*Bastardi!*' his friend Guido waved the paper angrily. 'First they rob us, starve us, treat us like dogs, and now when they say they make amends they make threats instead.'

Paolo shrugged. 'Just fill in the form. I am tired of fighting them.'

The men of Tatura, as well as their colleagues in the camp at Hay, put in their claims. Sixteen hundred separate compensation requests, mostly from the Jewish refugees who had arrived at the ship with luggage, were submitted for Major Layton to deal with before he could focus on which, if any, of the men merited release. He had already stated that the camp at Hay, with its bestial heat, was not a suitable place to intern anyone other than genuine prisoners of war and had demanded that the internees be moved to other camps. Many of them were transferred to Tatura.

Eventually, the major began the lengthy process of interviewing each individual inmate to determine their level of risk. So hasty had been the panic-driven roundup of so-called enemy aliens, and so ill-researched the MI5 classification of the men in those fevered days after Mussolini had declared war, that it was apparent that most of the internees in Tatura, were innocent victims. The majority of men in Camp Two were tradesmen, many from the hospitality business. Their reasons for leaving their Italian homeland had been largely economic – refugees from poverty who had worked hard to build a new life in Britain. When thousands of similar prisoners had already been released back in

Britain, there was scant justification in continuing to hold them prisoner here in Australia. Layton made the return of the Italian internees his priority.

Layton made an immediate offer to repatriate the older Italian men, too old to present a threat. Expecting a deluge of requests, he asked for volunteers, and was surprised when no one stepped forward. For these men, after the traumatic events of the sinking of the *Arandora Star* and the near miss of the torpedo attack on the *Dunera*, the last thing they wanted to do was get on another ship. Better to sit out the rest of the war in the relative comfort of Tatura camp.

Life in the camp was not so bad. The food was excellent, with a plentiful supply of lamb and fresh vegetables and a number of talented Italian chefs, from the best London hotels, operating in the camp kitchen. Paolo by now was running the camp store, drawing on his brief experience working for Alfonso Giordano. As internees, rather than prisoners of war, the men were paid for the work they did on local farms and were more than happy to spend this in Paolo's store. Each week, he would draw up a list of goods to be ordered from Melbourne and delivered to the camp. The profits were used to supplement the wages of those men who had volunteered for the least appealing duties such as cleaning the latrines and keeping the camp clean.

By late June it was Paolo's turn to be interviewed by Major Layton. He was stricken with nerves at the prospect, as he admitted to Clancy.

Clancy took out his pack of cigarettes and lit one. 'If you ask me, mate, soon as he meets you, he'll know you're no more a fascist than Winston Churchill is. Then once he knows you've a wife and kiddy who are poms, case closed.'

Paolo entered the hut where the major had his temporary office. Major Layton, born into a German-Jewish family which had migrated to England in the late nineteenth century, was well qualified to do this work. He was a fluent German speaker, and had worked before the war arranging the transfer of Jewish refugees from Germany to Australia and Britain. Word had quickly spread around the various camps at Tatura that he was a decent man, determined to do whatever he could for the internees, good-looking with kind eyes and a neatly clipped moustache.

He gestured to Paolo to take a seat in front of his desk. 'Tell me about yourself Signore Tornabene. How did you come to be in Britain?'

'*Mr* Tornabene. I wish to be English. I marry girl from Liverpool.'

Paolo told him about his time as a sailor, his decision to leave the Italian ship to rejoin the crew he had believed his former captain was reconstructing, and how that had failed to come about.

The major interrupted. 'Yes. I have here a letter from Commodore Palmer.'

'He is commodore?' Paolo's eyes widened.

'Yes. You have a very important friend, Mr Tornabene. Commodore Palmer speaks highly of you and confirms that it was at his suggestion you left the *Vigevano* and came to England.'

Layton shuffled papers in a file on the desk in front of him. 'I also have a letter here from a Father Edwards, a Catholic priest, stating that you are a member of his parish and you and your British fiancée intend to be married as soon as you are reunited.'

'We have proxy marriage. In God's eyes we are married now. But I want also in eyes of law.'

Layton smiled. 'And there is a child. A daughter?'

'Sarah. Now will be three months old.' Paolo looked

down, sadness rushing over him as it always did when he thought of the child he had never seen.

'If it were up to me, Mr Tornabene, I'd let you out of here immediately, but unfortunately I am constrained. Unlike your fellow countrymen who are now too old for military service, and in the light of your past employment in the Italian merchant marine, the British government still classifies you as being of higher risk.' He tapped the manila file. 'Everything in here indicates this not to be the case, but my hands are tied.' He looked apologetic. 'But don't despair, the situation could change as the war progresses. Meanwhile, are you treated well here?'

'Yes, sir. The camp is very good. We are fed well. I am learning many things. We play sport. I sing in the choir.'

'Very good. Look, I'm dreadfully sorry about the treatment you men received on the *Dunera*. Shameful.' He looked Paolo straight in the eyes and the Italian could see he was genuinely sorry.

'Paolo nodded. 'If I were still in England I would be free now? They say most Italians released.'

'Possibly. Although your age and history count against you. But, yes, you might have been released to serve in the Pioneer Corps. Most of those men from the internment camps here who have been repatriated have done so in order to join the Corps.'

'Why not Pioneer Corps here in Australia?'

His palms raised, Major Layton said, 'Again, it's outside my control. The Australian government don't want it. However, I am trying to negotiate with them regarding using suitable internees in some form of non-combatant labour corps, doing essential work here in Australia, freeing up Australians to join the military. But it's early days. All I can say, Mr Tornabene, is be patient.' He stretched out a hand.

'Before the year's out, all being well, your wife and daughter will be in Australia too. So, even though you will still be in here in the camp, you will at least have the consolation of knowing they are safe and close by. I'm also going to recommend to the camp commander that you are granted permission to formalise your marriage, once your fiancée is here, if you so wish.'

Paolo stared at him, dumbstruck, trying to absorb the import of his words. 'You say me Judith and Sarah are coming here? To Australia?'

'It looks that way. I thought you would know. Commodore Palmer is arranging it. I have no information about when they are due to sail but I imagine your family will be here before too long.'

Major Layton scraped back his chair, got to his feet and stretched out a hand. 'A pleasure to meet you, Mr Tornabene. And my good wishes for the future.

'WHAT'S UP MATE?' Clancy strode across the camp to where Paolo was, as usual, pacing the perimeter fence. 'Thought you'd had a letter from your sheila. Why so glum?'

The shock of Major Layton's news had been replaced by misery that Judith and Sarah would soon be tantalisingly close, yet unreachably far.

'My Judith she want to come to Australia. But the camp commander and Major Layton tell me until war is ended I am prisoner because I am dangerous to Allies. I am a sailor and was in Italian merchant ship so government think I am spy for Mussolini. They do not care that I hate all Fascists.' His expression was gloomy. 'So, if Judith come, I cannot see her.'

Clancy gave him a playful nudge. 'Come on, fella, buck

up. It's good news she wants to come out here. She must love you to bits. And you won't be stuck in here forever.'

'She have small baby and no job, no money, no place to stay. She know nobody. And her sister not want to come to Australia with her.'

'And what do you think, mate?'

'I want to see her. Every minute, every day I am thinking of her, but I don't want her to be alone. If sister not come, I wish Judith to stay in England. I have fear if she is on a ship and Germans torpedo.'

'Well, her sister can't stop the U-boats, mate.'

'I know.' Paolo squeezed his eyes tightly shut. 'I want her to stay in Liverpool until war's over. I want her and my baby to be safe.'

'You told her that?'

'I will say it when I can write a letter.'

'Listen, mate, while this bloody war's on she's hardly going to be safe in England. They've been getting hammered by the German bombers.'

Paolo was wretched. Clancy was right. If only Judith's ship could get past the wolf packs, she and the baby would safer here in Australia – and he might even get to see her at a distance through the wire fence.

'I am going to be crazy with only letters coming *a ogni morte di papa* – how you say in *Inglese* – only when the moon is blue. Judith say me she is angry with her sister. She is very unhappy.' He smashed a fist into his open palm.

Clancy put a steadying hand on Paolo's arm. 'If it's a place to stay she needs, I might be able to help you, son. My missus is mad about kiddies and our boys are both grown and gone now. I'll see what she reckons to your girl and your bub staying with us. I reckon my Sal would be glad of the company. Our two boys are serving in the army and neither's hitched yet so there's no grandkids. Sal would love to fuss over your sheila and your bub. Your sister-in-law too, if she changes her mind and decides to come. Let me ask the missus and I'll let you know.'

Paolo grasped Clancy's shoulders. 'You do that for me?'

'Not just for you. It'll be a real treat for Sal.' Clancy gave him a broad grin. 'No promises, mind.'

30

NEW WORLD

OCTOBER 1941

T he surface of the ocean rose and fell like a sheet of fabric being shaken. Its dark blue was unbroken all the way to the horizon, except close to the ship, where the water churned into a white-capped wash, revealing a turquoise green near the roiling surface. The ship created its own waves, which radiated outwards to join the crumpled blue velvet beyond. It was close to sunset, yet between the towering clouds the sky was still blue, soft and pale near the horizon, turning to a rich azure above.

As Hannah watched, leaning on the rails of the deck, the underbellies of the clouds darkened and seemed to move closer to the surface of the sea, forming themselves into a straight-bottomed horizon, mirroring the real one below them. Their tops and insides were now suffused with pink. The darkness would come soon. The sea changed to a dull gunmetal grey, shading to a richer colour of ink close to the ship. She gazed, transfixed, as the bank of clouds assumed the colour of the ocean. Above it, Hannah saw the bright spot that was the planet Venus. It was as though it were following the ship, maintaining the same fixed distance, a sharp shining pinprick in the night sky.

During the first days of this sea voyage, Hannah and Judith had been paralysed with fear that a German U-boat might spot them as they traversed the dangerous waters between Liverpool and South Africa. It had seemed too much to expect that they could run the gauntlet of the Reichsmarine and escape without harm. But neither woman voiced their fears. Judith seemed to be willing the ship to speed through the seas to bring her and Sarah as fast as possible to Paolo. For Hannah, every time she looked over the side or through a port-hole she was conscious of what had happened to Will. Every shadow on the surface or bird in flight chilled her to the core, fearing it might be a submarine or a warplane.

But now a sense of calm had taken hold of her.

Tomorrow they would reach Australia. She couldn't help a sense of disappointment that her first sight of the continent would be Melbourne, where they were to disembark. She would have preferred to arrive in Sydney, to experience the scene that Will had so often described to her.

Hannah had never tired of her husband's stories of growing up on a homestead in the bush and his time as a young man newly arrived in Sydney from the Blue Mountains, trying to get his first job as a cabin boy on a merchant ship. She had held in her mind's eye a picture of Sydney Harbour as Will painted it in words for her so many times, when she had lain in his arms and they imagined a future together after the war. The water of Sydney Harbour would be a deep cobalt blue, under a cerulean sky unsullied by clouds. She had envisaged herself and Will, standing hand-in-hand on the deck of a ship sailing past the newly built harbour bridge – he had been as eager as she was to see the great bridge for the first time.

But tomorrow when they stepped onto Australian soil in Melbourne, Hannah knew that, for her sister, it would be as significant as Sydney would have been for herself. Judith would be disembarking on the same quay where, about a year ago, Paolo had stepped off his ship. She would be experiencing the same sights he had seen, travelling through the same countryside he had.

Hannah already felt like an unwanted guest. Paolo had arranged for them to stay in the home of one of his prison guards. She thought this arrangement a little odd, but reminded herself that it was Britain which had decided to intern Paolo and the other Italians, not Australia. Judith had a reason to be there in what sounded a small country town. Hannah had none.

Leaning on the rail of the ship as the night sky darkened to an inky black, she saw the clouds dissipate. Venus had disappeared, and a myriad of bright stars now filled the heavens. Hannah prayed that she might find contentment here in her husband's homeland. Happiness was no longer a possibility – a sense of calm, of peace, was all she craved.

She owed this voyage to Commodore Palmer. Hannah didn't know how he had managed to get her released from the Wrens, how he got them on this ship, why he reluctantly allowed her to leave Derby House just as she had learnt the ropes and the need for the work they were doing at the Citadel was daily becoming more critical to the war effort. She supposed it was his abiding guilt over Paolo's incarceration and Will's death. Possibly intensified by an acknowledgement that both these events had been precipitated by his own decision to leave the sea in order to be with his wife. And of course he knew the sisters had lost their home and he appreciated that Judith, with a small baby, was in a fragile mental state.

Everything had changed for Hannah on the morning of 4th May, when she decided she must move heaven and earth to get Judith and Sarah out of Liverpool even if that meant leaving with them. With Mr Hathaway dead and Sam's house a ruined shell, there was little to keep her in Liverpool except the work she was doing. But how she had come to love that work! Those few weeks had given her a reason for being when her life had become devoid of hope and joy. Knowing that her contribution, no matter how small, might be making a difference had helped her keep functioning. In a way, Hannah had half hoped that her request to the commodore would have been refused.

She didn't blame Judith for wanting her to accompany her to Australia. Until now, neither sister had left Liverpool since moving there from Northport as small children. Undertaking such a massive journey and building a life in a new country, was scary enough without doing so alone with a small baby. But for Hannah, now that it was happening, finally being in Will's birth country, without Will, was going to be agony.

In contrast, Judith showed mounting excitement – eager to see Paolo, to introduce him to their daughter and touch him again – even if it had to be at a distance and through a barbed wire fence.

PAOLO WAS in a state of heightened tension and excitement. Pacing up and down his hut, he alternated between fear that Judith might feel differently about him when she saw him again, and joy that after more than a year they would at last be reunited. The long months of captivity, and particularly the gruesome conditions on the *Dunera,* had taken their toll. How would Judith react on seeing the premature greying of his once jet-black hair around the temples? His face was gaunt with lines etched into his forehead and the sparkle had gone from his eyes. He had put a little weight back on since being at Tatura but was still skinnier than he had been when they were last together. Why would a woman as beautiful as Judith want a man who looked like a spectre? He had built back his muscle strength by playing football and digging vegetables on the nearby farms where camp inmates were taken to work. But this made him appear thin and wiry rather than well-toned and fit.

Clancy was amused by Paolo's doubts. 'If your sheila's as good a woman as you say she is, then she'll love you whatever you look like, mate. I don't reckon she's the flighty type if she's prepared to come all this way to be near to you, when you can't even live together.'

'You think so?' Paolo's brow furrowed but his heart lifted.

'Bigger question for me is that by coming down here it looks like your missus has decided for you that you're both staying here in *Straya*, even after the war's over. How you feel about that, mate?'

'I dreamed always of returning to *Italia* and showing Judith my beautiful city of *Napoli*. But, my friend, I will live in a desert or a hole in the ground if I can be with her.'

Clancy grinned. 'It won't come to that, mate. You could do a lot worse than this country. It's God's own. Plenty of opportunity in *Straya* for those who work hard. A fair go for everyone. And once you're out of here you can always live by the sea, or in the city – which is actually the same thing, as our cities are all on the coast.'

The two men sat and smoked in silence for a few minutes before Clancy spoke again. 'When they let you out of here, you want to head over to Melbourne then. There's docks and ships and plenty of places to work. Reckon half of this lot will end up there.' He jerked his head in the direction of the wooden huts. 'Those that don't go back to Pom Land. Anyway, the missus has been scrubbing our place from top to bottom to get ready for your Judith and her sister. And she's stoked at the idea of having a bub in the house. Not sure I'm looking forward to the broken nights myself. I may volunteer for some extra shifts here, mate. For a bit of peace and quiet.'

Paolo took his friend's hand. 'I cannot say you how much I thank you, Clancy. You are my friend, not my prison guard. *Un vero amico*. When this war is finish and I am free, I buy you many beers.'

Clancy laughed. 'The day you get out, mate, it'll be my shout.'

WHEN THEY STEPPED off the train in the town of Tatura, Hannah's doubts resurfaced. It was a small rural station with a wooden station office and a small goods yard. The sun was already hot even though it was before eleven. Her clothes were damp and the fabric of her dress clung to her legs.

'Now what?' she asked Judith, realising they were the only people who had got off the train. 'Do you have the address?'

Judith shook her head. 'I thought someone would meet us.'

The baby woke up and started to cry.

'Wait here.' Hannah pointed to a wooden bench. 'It'll be cooler over there in the shade. I'll try and find out where we need to go. Mrs Clancy isn't it?'

Judith nodded, her face strained as she tried to soothe the baby.

Hannah walked inside the station office as a woman in her fifties hurried through the doorway from the street, wiping perspiration from her brow. 'Mrs Tornabene?' she asked.

Relieved, Hannah offered her hand. 'I'm Hannah Kidd, her sister.'

'Thank goodness. I saw the train leave and was worried you might think we'd forgotten all about you. I'm Mrs Clancy, but everyone calls me Sal.' She shook Hannah's hand.

'Then call me Hannah. Judith and the baby are through there on the platform. Sarah has just woken up.'

As soon as Sal Clancy set eyes on Sarah she stretched out her arms. 'May I?'

Judith happily handed the still blubbering baby over.

'Aren't you a little darling?' Sal grinned at Judith. 'Terry and I are stoked to have you staying with us. He never stops talking about your husband. It sounds like you've got a good fella there.'

Judith flushed with pleasure.

'Come on, let's get you home and get you settled. 'We're a little way out of town so I brought the horse and cart thinking you might have a lot of luggage.' She looked at the two suitcases. 'But it looks like you haven't.'

'Our home was bombed back in May. We've been living in a church hall since then.'

'We heard you poor things had it bad. But your whole house?'

'Our landlord's,' Hannah said. 'Still standing but unin-habitable. Next door was completely destroyed. Just a big crater in the ground.' She glanced at Judith. 'I wasn't there when it happened and fortunately Judith was in the shelter in the back garden.'

'Crikey! I'd no idea it was as bad as that. I suppose they don't put it all in the papers. You poor souls. That Hitler has a lot to answer for.' She handed the baby back to Judith. 'Well, don't you worry, chicks, you're safe from him here.'

The Clancy house, a ten-minute drive in the horse and cart, was a single-storey brick structure with a gabled iron roof and a covered veranda running around three sides. There was a neatly tended garden in front.

'It isn't much. But it's home. I raised my two boys here. It'll be good having young people in the house again.' Sal Clancy gave the women a broad grin. Her face was tanned and lined and her hair rather straggly. Her sturdy body looked muscular, as though used to hard work.

Inside the house, it was cooler, with a welcome ceiling fan in the room into which their hostess led them. She turned to Judith. 'I imagine you need to change the baby. There's a bathroom over there.'

She touched Hannah on the arm. 'I'll show you both to your bedroom once we've had morning tea. Sound good?' She was on her way towards the kitchen when she turned and added. 'I hope you and your sister don't mind sharing a bedroom. But it's a decent size and there's a little room right off it where I've set up a cot for the bub.'

IN THE EARLY EVENING, Terry Clancy came home. A tall rangy man in khaki shorts and shirt, he shook their hands with a firm grip.

He grinned at Judith. 'You're even prettier in the flesh. Your husband's a lucky fella, Mrs Tornabene. Right now, he's as nervous about seeing you as a bloke with a bloody knee in a shark tank. Thinks you might have gone off him. I keep telling him you wouldn't have come all this way if you weren't still keen on him, but he won't believe it, poor bastard.'

'When will I be able to see him?' Judith's voice betrayed her anxiety.

'Our Sal will take you up to the camp tomorrow and I'll make sure he's waiting by the perimeter fence. You'll be able to have a bit of a chin wag and let him see the bub. That's the best we can manage at the moment. I'm working on the camp commander but he's a bit of a go-by-the-rules kind of bloke. But yer fella got on well with the big man down in Melbourne, Major Layton. Sent here by your Home Secretary to investigate what happened to the boys on the *Dunera*. I reckon he'll do what he can to help you both.'

'This Major Layton, when is he coming?' Judith leaned forward.

'Hard to say but he comes up quite often. He's been arranging for the boys over in New South Wales in the camp there at Hay to be moved. We're getting a lot of them here. He's a busy man is the major.'

Mrs Clancy brought the meal to the table, apologising that it was only a simple shepherd's pie with zucchini fritters and peas. Hannah and Judith looked at each other in delight.

'No apologies, Mrs Clancy, I mean Sal. We've been used to rationing,' said Hannah. 'This will be a real treat!'

Judith was wide-eyed. 'Ooh, it smells delicious.'

'I'd heard you had rationing. That must be awful. Trying to stretch things out.'

'It's not only about stretching them out. Some things you can't get at all. Like oranges and fresh eggs. We have to use powdered eggs.'

Sal Clancy wrinkled her nose. 'Well, you'll get plenty of fresh eggs here as we keep our own chooks. Bacon and eggs for breakfast then, girls?'

Judith grinned from ear to ear.

'I think we're going to put on weight.' Hannah smiled, glad her sister had cheered up.

'Where's the ankle biter then?' Terry Clancy looked around as though expecting seven-month-old Sarah to stroll into the room.

The sisters looked at each other, until Hannah realised what he meant. 'Oh, you mean the baby!'

Judith, looked slightly affronted, and said, 'She's asleep.'

Mrs Clancy tapped her on the arm. 'Take no notice, Judith. Terry means well – I'm afraid you'll have to get used to how we Aussies talk.'

Both sisters, exhausted by the journey and overwhelmed by the plentiful food, retired early to bed.

Hannah was almost asleep when she heard muffled sobbing from the other bed. 'What's the matter, Judith?'

'I didn't think I'd feel like this.'

'Like what?' Hannah tried not to sound impatient.

'So sad. I think it's worse. Being here. Knowing he's so close but not being with him.' She made a gulping sound. 'At least in Liverpool everything around us was familiar. Everything's so strange here. So hot and dusty. What if I don't like it, Hannah? I won't be able to go home.'

Swallowing her irritation, Hannah said, 'At least you came of your own free will and you're at liberty to move around. Paolo had no choice in the matter. And you've told me a thousand times all you want is to be near him.'

'I know.' Another sob.

'Look, Jude, you're tired. You'll feel better once you've had some sleep. Mrs Clancy will take you to the camp tomorrow and you'll be able to see Paolo and show him Sarah. And we've just had the most delicious meal I can ever remember eating. You have so much to be grateful for. It's only tiredness making you feel that way. Now please, try to get to sleep.'

'I'm sorry. You're right. Mr and Mrs Clancy are being very kind. And I know it's worse for you. Coming to this awful hot dusty place just to be with me.' She reached across the divide between the beds and took Hannah's hand. 'But you're much stronger than me. You cope better.'

'Goodnight, Jude.'

Hannah rolled over onto her other side and stared into the darkness. She doubted she was stronger than her sister. Right now, all she wanted to do herself was give in to tears too. Tears for everything she had lost and left behind. Tears for Will and the family she would never have.

31

A WEDDING

Paolo was on edge. He had walked up and down beside the barbed wire fence since the approach of dawn. There was a hot wind and the dust blew up and into his eyes. His face was probably dirty but he didn't want to go back to the hut to wash it again in case Judith turned up with Clancy while he was gone. She'd think he didn't care about seeing her. Better red dust on his cheeks than have her doubt his joy at seeing her again.

He watched the road leading to the camp from the town. Every time a cloud of dust indicated the approach of a vehicle, his heart leapt inside his ribcage. But every time he was disappointed when it turned out to be one of the other guards arriving, a truck bringing in supplies for the camp kitchen, or the weekly delivery of goods for the store Paolo ran. He had paid over some of his hard-earned cash to get someone else to take in the order today and stack it on the shelves. How could he possibly do it himself when he needed to be here, keeping sentinel for Judith?

Then there she was. Climbing out of Clancy's pickup, their baby in her arms, turning to wave goodbye to Clancy as he drove on through the gates into the camp. Paolo watched her walk towards him, her hair shining, her blue printed cotton dress pretty as a picture.

'*Che bella!*' he said aloud to himself. He clutched the wire, using it to support his legs, fearing they might buckle under him. How long had he waited for this moment? How often had he doubted it would ever happen? How much did he love her? To see the woman he loved, body and soul, walking towards him under the Australian sun, even though he had imagined it so many times, made his head want to explode. Her displacement from Liverpool to the arid Victorian countryside was so hard to comprehend. She was a strange and beautiful being transplanted to an ugly place.

'*Che meraviglia!,*' he whispered. 'Oh, my beautiful Judith, I love you so much. I have missed you every moment.'

She held up the baby. 'Here's your daughter, Paolo. Here's Sarah.' She dropped a kiss on the baby's head. 'Meet your Papa, Sarah.'

The double rows of wire fencing were too far apart for them to touch, and they had to raise their voices to hear each other. It was a beautiful agony, being so close and yet so far.

Paolo drank in Judith's face and that of the baby, who was placidly studying him. 'She is beautiful like her *mama*.'

'She has her Papa's eyes.'

'Can you forgive me?' he said.

'For what? There is nothing to forgive.' Judith looked taken aback.

'For leaving you. For not to be with you when you are needing me.'

Judith frowned. 'You don't regret that we have a baby, do you?'

'*Mai!* Never! I am happiest man in this camp.' He

grinned broadly. 'I am a father. Now I need to be legally a husband and to ask you properly.' He was so close to the wire fence that the barbs caught on his clothing. 'Will you marry me, Judith?'

'Nothing will make me happier.'

Neither of them noticed when the gate to the camp opened again and Clancy emerged, carrying a folding wooden chair and a large umbrella. 'Reckon you'll be talking for some time, so you'll need this, Judith. Something to sit on and keep the sun off you and the bub. The wind makes it seem cooler but that sun's powerful.' He retreated again inside the camp, leaving them alone to catch up on everything that had happened during the fifteen months they had been apart.

JUDITH VISITED the camp every day, pushing the pram with Sarah, for the bittersweet meetings with Paolo across the fence. About a month after her arrival in Australia, Major Layton surprised the couple by persuading the Australian authorities to allow Judith a special dispensation to enter the camp in order to be married to Paolo. The camp commander let them use the mess room and the camp's Catholic chaplain agreed to conduct the ceremony.

As far as Judith was concerned, they were already married in the eyes of God, but she was eager to stand beside Paolo to swear their marriage vows. Sam standing in at the proxy marriage service was no substitute.

As she held baby Sarah in her arms, Hannah watched her sister standing next to Paolo. Judith's eyes were sparkling and there was no trace of the nervousness and misery that had characterised her behaviour back in Liverpool. She was wearing a dress she had made herself before leaving

England – Sam, who seemed to know everyone worth knowing, had managed to procure the pale-yellow silk. Not quite
the wedding gown, veil and long train Judith would have
liked, but nonetheless a pretty frock that set off her dark
hair and now glowing skin.

When the priest pronounced them man and wife, Paolo
kissed Judith so passionately that the priest shuffled his feet,
embarrassed, and coughed loudly. The congregation – the
Clancys, Hannah, men from Paolo's hut, a couple of the
camp guards and Guido, Paolo's friend from the *Dunera* –
applauded loudly, with some of the Italians cheering.

The camp commander had given them dispensation for
a small party and permitted Paolo to order in beers for the
men and sherry for the women – although Hannah was
amused to see Sal Clancy drinking a beer straight from the
bottle as the men did.

The camp musicians played a few tunes and Paolo was
able to dance for the first time with his new bride. After the
first dance, and to the amusement of all present, he danced
around the floor holding his baby daughter.

While it was wonderful to see her sister so radiantly
happy, Hannah couldn't help a pang of envy. Her own
wedding to Will had been a hurried affair, soon after her
father's execution and on the eve of war being declared. But
she would give anything to travel back in time to that day, to
have Will standing beside her and to be able to look with
love into his eyes once more.

Life was not going to be easy for Judith though. The
young couple would be married in name but not yet able to
live as husband and wife. Once the ceremony ended, Judith
would have to meet her husband only through a barbed
wire fence again. The war had now lasted two years and
there was growing unease that it might yet spread to the

Pacific if the Japanese continued to behave with such aggression. It could last for many years more. A long time to be separated.

At least they were all safe from the horrors of the Liverpool air raids. Now they were here on the other side of the world the memories of the devastation of the May Blitz were just that – memories – not something to survive and fear daily. Judith and Paolo had a future together. It may take time, but it was there waiting for them to step into. For Hannah there was nothing.

32

A NEW BEGINNING

A week after Judith and Paolo were married, while Judith was making her now daily visit to the camp perimeter, Hannah was in the kitchen helping Sal prepare vegetables for the dinner. It was fascinating to learn the names of so many unfamiliar vegetables, and to have such a plentiful supply of fresh meat and dairy products.

As she removed the stalks from silver beets, she looked up from her task and said, 'Sal, I haven't said anything to Judith, but I'm going to leave Tatura.'

Sal put down the knife she'd been using to peel the potatoes and wiped her hands on her apron. 'Can't say as I'm surprised, but I'll be really sorry. Where will you go? Surely not back to England?'

'No. I came here for good and I intend to stay in Australia. But I want to go to Sydney and then to the town where my late husband was born.'

Sal pulled out a chair and lowered herself into it. 'D'ya know, Hannah, I never even thought to ask if you'd been married. You're so young and fresh-faced. I never dreamt you were a widow. What happened?'

'I was married just over a year when he was lost at sea. On his last voyage. Will had accepted a land-based job after twelve years in the merchant navy. He was sailing back to Liverpool from Canada for the last time when his ship was bombed by a German plane and sunk. Several of the crew survived. Will and the captain were trying to rescue the injured first officer when it went down.'

Sal stared at her, eyes welling. 'You poor lamb. That's a real tragedy. And you say he was about to leave the navy?'

Hannah bit her lip. It was always so painful to talk about what had happened. 'He was only a few days from home.'

She tore the leaves of the silver beet away from the stalks. 'After he died, I wanted to stay in Liverpool. I loved my work there. I joined the Wrens and was working in the place where Will was due to work. But when the house was bombed and my dear friend next door was killed and Judith and Sarah had such a close shave, I decided to come out here with her. She's younger than me and has always been very dependent. We didn't have a happy childhood.' Hannah wasn't going to go into the circumstances of their parents' deaths and was relieved when Sal didn't ask.

'And your fella was an Aussie?'

'Yes. From a place called MacDonald Falls in the Blue Mountains.'

Sal frowned. 'I think that's where Terry's folks came from. His grandparents I believe. The Blue Mountains are meant to be pretty.'

'I have an aunt in Australia too. She emigrated here when I was a little girl. I was very fond of her. That's how I came to meet my husband. She was his stepmother. I look very like her. By one of those wonderful quirks of fate, Will saw me in the street thought I was her at first.' Hannah smiled, remembering the moment of their meeting.

'So, your aunt's in MacDonald Falls?'

'No. After Will's father died, she moved away and remarried. We lost touch. I was trying to trace her via her friend who was the schoolteacher in MacDonald Falls but the lady died. My letter was returned unopened.'

'I see. And now you want to do some detective work to find your aunty?'

'I'm going to do my best, but I don't hold out much hope. Australia is a huge country.'

'Yes, but there's not a huge population. You never know, you might track her down. But if not?'

'I'll find a job. I used to be a bookkeeper before I was married. And I have a reference from the navy for my short time in the Wrens.'

'You'll do fine over in Sydney. Never been there myself but I know it's a beautiful city and there should be a lot of opportunities for a clever woman like you. When do you plan to go? And more to the point, when are you going to tell your sister?'

Hannah sucked in her lips. 'I'm dreading that to be honest. Judith will try to persuade me to stay and I can't do that. I don't want to argue with her. She's going to be fine here with you. It's only a matter of time before she and Paolo will be able to live as a family then they won't want me around anyway.' Hannah swallowed. 'I have to live my own life. Make my own future.'

Sal shook her head slowly. 'I reckon you're dead wrong about Judith. That girl's been through a lot, and yes, maybe she's leaned heavily on you until now, but she loves you and she understands you have to build a new life. You ought to tell her, Hannah. She deserves to hear it from you. And you may be surprised at her reaction. Judith has Paolo to rely on now and Sarah to care for, just as you always looked out for her. How old are you, Hannah?'

'Twenty-two.'

'Are you fair dinkum? That's far too young to be a widow.' Then she grinned. 'You won't be for long. Some handsome fella will come along and snap you up.'

'No.' Hannah picked up another bunch of silver beet and slashed her knife along the edges of the stalks before ripping them away from the leaves. 'I'll never marry again. No one could possibly replace Will.'

'But don't you want a family? Children?'

'I wanted Will's children, but it never happened.'

'Give it time. You might feel differently one day. You don't have to fall head over heels with a man to marry him, bear his children and have a good life.'

'Perhaps not. But nor do you have to marry at all to have some kind of life. There are other ways. Many women lead fulfilling lives without husbands.'

'Not that many.'

'And many women are miserable in their marriages.' She was thinking of her mother but didn't want to say so.

'Fair point, I suppose.' Sal looked up and smiled. 'Whatever you do, Hannah, I reckon you'll make a good job of it. You're a fine woman and it's been an absolute pleasure to get to know you. I'm going to miss you when you're gone.'

Sal Clancy got up, came around the table and put her hands on Hannah's shoulders. 'And don't worry about that sister of yours. She's more than capable of looking after herself.' Sal gave her a hearty hug. 'Now, are you going to tell her or not?'

. . .

THAT EVENING, Hannah broached the subject of her leaving with Judith.

Judith's lip trembled and Hannah squeezed her eyes tightly shut, breathing in. She should never have listened to Sal. But then she felt Judith's arms around her.

'Oh, Hannah, I don't know what I'll do without you. But I know there's nothing for you here in Tatura.' She placed a hand against Hannah's cheek. 'I'm a big girl now and I'll have to manage without my big sister.'

Relief surged through Hannah. 'Oh, Judith!'

'You've been so good to me and I know at times I've been selfish, and it would be even more selfish of me to try and persuade you to stay. But what will you do? You aren't thinking of going back to Liverpool?'

Hannah gave her a sad smile and shook her head. 'There's nothing for me in Liverpool now. And the thought of getting on a ship and doing that long voyage again is more than I can bear. And how could I possibly put two oceans between us, Jude? No. I'm staying in Australia. That way I will get to see you and Sarah and Paolo from time to time.'

'Where will you go? What will you do?'

'I've absolutely no idea what I'll do. But I'm going to go to Sydney. I want to stand in front of that harbor Will told me so much about and see what he meant about it being the most beautiful place in the world.' She smiled again. 'It will be an adventure.'

Judith's eyes filled with tears. 'No one in this whole wide world deserves to be happy as much as you do, Hannah. You sorted out my life for me. Now it's time to find yours. And I know whatever comes up, you'll make the best of it.'

'I may even get to find Aunt Lizzie. I'll certainly try.'

'And you must promise to write to me at least twice a week.'

'I promise.'

THREE DAYS later Hannah left Tatura.

She chose to go alone on foot to the station, begging Judith not to accompany her.

'If you were standing on that station platform, I might lose my nerve. And the thought of standing around waiting for the train is too awful. I'd rather say goodbye here.'

Judith, reluctantly, after a tearful farewell, left the house at her usual time, taking Sarah to the camp in the pram she'd bought with the cash Paolo had saved up.

Sal also cried, wiping her tears away with the edge of her apron. It was a rare display of emotion from the usually phlegmatic woman.

'There'll always be a welcome for you here, Hannah Kidd,' she said. 'If things don't work out, don't be too proud to come back to Tatura.' She hugged her warmly. 'But I have a feeling you're going to do fine, young lady. And don't you be worrying about Judith either. I'll keep her under my wing.'

As Hannah walked down the pathway, Sal called out, 'Don't forget to write!'

With a farewell wave, Hannah forced herself not to look back as she walked briskly into the small town. Sal Clancy had been like a mother to her in the weeks she had been here. And as for Judith, it was hard to imagine the sister who had been such a huge part of her life would no longer be under the same roof. While there had been a distance between them, and Hannah had finally acknowledged to herself that they had little in common, it didn't make being parted from her any easier. But Judith would be safe and happy now. Her need for Hannah was diminished and Judith had finally been able to admit it.

The hardest thing was leaving baby Sarah. Hannah adored the little girl and was sad that she would miss out on seeing her niece growing up. It made her all the more determined to seek out Aunt Elizabeth. It was more than twenty years since Elizabeth had left England. Hannah hoped it would not be so long before she next saw Judith and Sarah.

Hannah was to change trains at Seymour and join the train from Melbourne for the long journey to Sydney.

The train passed through the flat Victorian scenery of orchards and pastures with the ubiquitous gum trees dotted about. The landscape was repetitive, open and enormous. Unaccustomed, even back in England, to the countryside, Hannah felt overwhelmed and insignificant, nostalgic for the bustle and crowds of Liverpool, with its smoke-blackened nineteenth-century buildings – what was left of them. When she and Judith arrived in Australia, they went straight from ship to train and she'd had no chance to explore Melbourne. Tatura was a small country town with little more than one main street. How she hoped Sydney would not disappoint.

When the train crossed a wide river, an elderly man sitting opposite her turned to his wife and said, 'We've crossed the Murray.' He addressed Hannah, asking, 'You're not from round here, are you?'

'I'm from England.'

'Thought so. We've just left the state of Victoria. Welcome to New South Wales.' He leaned forward, evidently keen to chat. 'The lines are different gauges in each state. The bridge has both gauges, but then we all have to get off on the other side and change trains.' He continued to explain the engineering intricacies of the Australian railway system as they changed platforms and trains at Albury, while Hannah tried to feign interest.

The new train set off, travelling on its different gauged track, through seemingly endless grasslands, stopping at stations with strange-sounding names like Wagga Wagga. The landscape was peppered with the ghostly silver-white gum trees and occasional gashes where the rust red Australian soil was revealed. Could she ever grow to love this country? It was all so alien, though the little stations with their fancy ironwork felt very British.

The elderly man, now sitting on the other side of the carriage, called across to her. 'What're you doing in Australia then?'

Hannah hesitated then said, 'I have family here, an aunt. I lost my home in the Blitz, so I've come out here to start again.' She chose not to mention her sister, the death of her husband, nor her brother-in-law in the internment camp.'

The man nodded. 'You'll do fine here. As long as you watch out for spiders and snakes and try not to whinge too much.' He gave a dry laugh and nudged his wife. 'No one likes a whinging pom, do they, Jean?' Smiling at Hannah he added, 'But you don't seem like the whinging type.'

The train stopped at a town called Junee, where the couple got off. The man warned her there would be another delay, while a bank engine was attached to the train to pull it up the steep escarpment. 'Gradient's one in forty so it's a slow old struggle. And you have to wait for the down train to come through first. They're building a second track for the up trains to loop round the mountain but it's solid rock so it'll be years before it's finished.' He gave Hannah a little two-fingered tap of the head in parting. His wife said nothing and Hannah realised she hadn't spoken once, throughout the entire journey.

The train climbed slowly through steep-sided, bare rock cuttings, the struggle up the mountainside a metaphor for Hannah's feelings about her own life. It was all such an effort. And now she must face it completely alone. She remembered what the stranger had said about not whinging and made a silent vow to treat this whole terrifying enterprise as an adventure.

Hadn't her aunt also faced this, twenty years earlier? Elizabeth had been in a worse situation than Hannah. It must have been a catalogue of disasters for her. Entirely alone and penniless. Thrown out of her lifelong home by her own sister, Hannah's mother. Raped by Hannah's father. Pregnant with her first child as a result of that terrible experience. Forced to marry Will's father. Hannah's own experience couldn't compare. Yet, according to Will, Elizabeth had made the best of her unwelcome marriage and had somehow dealt with the loss of her two infant children to diphtheria. If what Miss Radley had said was true, Aunt Elizabeth had eventually found happiness with the man she had always loved and they had a son together.

Perhaps Hannah was living her life the wrong way round? She had found love and happiness very young and enjoyed it only briefly before it was snatched away. So, no happy ending awaited her, but maybe she could find a way to build a future here in this country. Maybe she could concentrate on feeling a connection to Will and try to sense his presence here. This was his birthplace and discovering it would be like discovering him again.

With these thoughts, she drifted off to sleep, lulled by the motion of the train and the gathering darkness outside the windows.

It was early morning when the train reached Sydney.

Hannah walked out of the railway station and enquired of a passerby how to reach the Harbour.

'Jump on that tram,' said the man. 'Get off at the end of the line. Circular Quay.'

The tram went along streets that seemed familiar – red-brick, nineteenth-century buildings, lining streets named after British Prime Ministers and other historical figures. At the end of Loftus Street, all the remaining passengers disembarked and Hannah followed them. There it was. Sydney Harbour. She crossed the road to the waterfront, where the ferries docked at the landing stages, disgorging crowds of people heading to their jobs in the city.

The suitcase was heavy in her hand, but she wanted to drink in the scene in front of her before she tried to find somewhere to stay. To her left, beyond the Circular Quay, were the soaring heights of the magnificent Harbour Bridge. Hannah's eyes welled up. If only Will were here to share it with her.

The morning was warm, cloudless and the sky a vivid blue. She moved along the quayside in front of tall buildings along the right side of the quay, in order to get a better view of the great bridge. The water was as blue as the sky – so different from the dirty grey of the Mersey. Ferries plied their way back and forth and, beyond the bridge on the Northern shore of the Harbour, she could see the giant cartoonish face and twin Art Deco towers of the entrance to Luna Park, a permanent fairground.

Tears dry, she walked to the end of the promontory, drinking in the view of the harbour with its coves and inlets, boats and ships making their way across the limpid waters.

Her heart lifted at the beauty. What lay ahead might be hard, would bring many challenges, but Hannah would meet them head-on. Liverpool was the past. Australia was her future. And wherever she went, Will would always be with her.

She remembered the words Mr Hathaway had said about his beloved Flo – that if the choice had been to live forever but never to have known her, or to die the next day but have had what they'd had together, he wouldn't have hesitated for a second. Grief and sorrow were the price of love.

And it was a price worth paying.

THE END

IF YOU ENJOYED SISTERS AT WAR

It would be fantastic if you could spare a few minutes to leave a review at the retailer where you bought the book.

Reviews make a massive difference to authors - they help books get discovered by other readers and make it easier for authors to get promotional support – some promotions require a minimum number of reviews in order for a book to be accepted. Your words can make a difference.

Thank you!

CLARE'S NEWSLETTER

Why not subscribe to Clare's monthly newsletter? Clare will update you on her work in progress, her travels, and you'll be the first to know when she does a cover reveal, shares an extract, or has news of special offers and promotions. She often asks for input from her subscribers on cover design, book titles and characters' names.

Don't worry - your email address will NEVER be shared with a third party and if you reply to any of the newsletters you will get a personal response from Clare. She LOVES hearing from readers.

As a special thank you, you'll get a free download of her short story collection, *A Fine Pair of Shoes and Other Stories*

Here's the link to sign up - Click below or go to clareflynn.co.uk to the sign-up form. (Privacy Policy on Clare's website)

https://www.subscribepage.com/r4wiu5

ACKNOWLEDGMENTS

This last year has been an interesting and challenging one. I couldn't have got through it without the support of friends.

Thanks to all the gang in The Sanctuary group in particular Liza Perrat who read and commented on the final draft. To my three MIAMI 'sisters', Hilary Bruffell, Anne Caborn and Clare O'Brien.

Thanks, as always, to my cover designer Jane Dixon-Smith and editor Debi Alper. I'm grateful to Margaret Kaine and Joanna Warrington for their comments on the first draft and to Lynn Osborne, Debbie Marmor, JT Carey and Lorraine Morse for proofing. Special thanks to Lina Negri for suggestions to improve my Italian. Any remaining mistakes are mine!

ABOUT THE AUTHOR

Clare Flynn is the author of thirteen historical novels and a collection of short stories.

A former Marketing Director and strategy consultant, she was born in Liverpool and has lived in London, Newcastle, Paris, Milan, Brussels and Sydney and is now enjoying being in Eastbourne on the Sussex coast where she can see the sea and the Downs from her windows.

When not writing, she loves to travel (often for research purposes) and enjoys painting in oils and watercolours as well as making patchwork quilts and learning to play the piano again.

ALSO BY CLARE FLYNN

A Greater World

Love, loss and a voyage into the unknown

Elizabeth Morton, born into a prosperous family, and **Michael Winterbourne**, a miner, come from different worlds but when they each suffer a life-changing tragedy they're set on a path that intertwines on the deck of the SS Historic, bound for Sydney.

Falling in love should have been the end to all their troubles. But fate and the mysterious **Jack Kidd** make sure it's only the beginning.

"Characters readers will truly relate to, root for, shed tears over, and will still think about long after the book is done." (*Readers' Favorite*)

ALSO AVAILABLE AS AN AUDIO BOOK

Storms Gather Between Us

Life can change in the matter of a moment...

Since escaping his family's notoriety in Australia **Will Kidd** has spent a decade sailing the seas, never looking back. Content to live the life of a wanderer, everything changes in a single moment when he comes face to face with a ghost from his past on a cloudy beach in Liverpool.

The daughter of an abusive zealot, every step of **Hannah Dawson's** life has been laid out for her...until she meets Will by chance and is set on a new path. Their love is forbidden and forces on all sides divide them, but their bond is undeniable. Now, they will have to fight against all the odds to escape the chains of their histories and find their way back to one another.

"A wonderful read. Very thought-provoking and emotion-

inducing, with a lovely ending and memorable characters."
(*Pursuing Stacey blog*)

ALSO AVAILABLE AS AN AUDIOBOOK

The Pearl of Penang

Winner of the 2020 BookBrunch Selfies Award for Adult Fiction;
Discovering Diamonds Book of the Month

*"Following the death of my wife, I am in need of support and
companionship. I am prepared to make you an offer of marriage."*

Flynn's tenth novel explores love, marriage, the impact of war and
the challenges of displacement – this time in a tropical paradise as
the threat of the Japanese empire looms closer.

ALSO AVAILABLE AS AN AUDIOBOOK narrated by Victoria
Riley

A Prisoner from Penang

After Penang is attacked by the Japanese at the end of 1941, Mary
Helston believes Singapore will be a safe haven. But within weeks
the supposedly invincible British stronghold is on the brink of
collapse to the advancing enemy.

Mary and her mother are captured at sea as they try to escape and
are interned on the islands of Sumatra. Imprisoned with them is
Veronica Leighton, the one person on the planet Mary has reason
to loathe with a passion.

As the motley band of women struggle to adapt to captivity,
relationships and friendships are tested. When starvation, lack of
medication and the spread of disease worsen, each woman must
draw on every ounce of strength in their battle for survival.

A vivid and moving story of sacrifice, hope and humanity.

*"In this testament to the strength of female friendship and endurance
under the harshest of conditions, Flynn has imagined the unimaginable -
a dazzling achievement."* Linda Gillard, Author of *The Memory
Tree* and *House of Silence*

ALSO AVAILABLE AS AN AUDIOBOOK narrated by Victoria Riley

A Painter in Penang

Sixteen-year-old Jasmine Barrington hates everything about living in Kenya and longs to return to the island of Penang in British colonial Malaya where she was born. Expulsion from her Nairobi convent school offers a welcome escape – the chance to stay with her parents' friends, Mary and Reggie Hyde-Underwood on their Penang rubber estate.

But this is 1948 and communist insurgents are embarking on a reign of terror in what becomes the Malayan Emergency. Jasmine goes through testing experiences – confronting heartache, a shocking past secret and danger. Throughout it all, the one constant in her life is her passion for painting.

A dramatic coming of age story, set against the backdrop of a tropical paradise torn apart by civil war.

"A moving, poignant, involving read." Author Lorna Fergusson

"If you like well-researched historical sagas with depth, you will enjoy this." Deborah Swift, Author of *The Occupation*

"The PENANG trilogy is a testament to human endurance, the triumph of the spirit, but above all, to the love of family and friends." Amazon reviewer

ALSO AVAILABLE AS AN AUDIOBOOK narrated by Victoria Riley

ALL THREE PENANG NOVELS also available as a 3-book digital collection at all retailers.

The Chalky Sea

Two troubled people in a turbulent world.

Gwen Collingwood is an English woman, and **Jim Armstrong**, a young Canadian soldier. Their stories entwine during World War Two in a small English seaside town.

" Flynn's novel is a vivid page-turner that depicts the destruction of war, but it is most notable for its portrayal of the effects it has on individual lives. *(BookLife, Publishers Weekly)*

ALSO AVAILABLE AS AN AUDIO BOOK

The Alien Corn

They faced up to the challenges of war – but can they deal with the troubles of peace?

The follow up to *The Chalky Sea*, *The Alien Corn* is set in rural Canada in the aftermath of World War 2. **Jim Armstrong** has returned to his farm in Ontario where he is joined by his English war bride, Joan. Jim suffers from the after-effects of the horrors he witnessed in the Italian campaign, while Joan struggles to adapt to her new life and family.

"Flynn's novel captures the obstacles faced both by soldiers returning from battle and by those close to them. Readers of the first book will relish the chance to spend more time with the characters, and new readers will find plenty to savor." *(BookLife, Publishers Weekly)*

ALSO AVAILABLE AS AN AUDIO BOOK

The Frozen River

Three strong women make their way in 1950s Canada

The Frozen River completes the trilogy of Canadian novels.

English hairdresser, **Ethel Underwood,** is devastated after the deaths of her family and her wartime fiancé. Widow and single mother of two young daughters, **Alice Armstrong,** receives an unexpected inheritance that will transform her life.

War bride, **Joan Armstrong**, is now mother to four small children.

All three are brought together in a rural Canadian town where they each try to build a future – often in spite of the men in their lives.

Each woman has a different idea of happiness. Will any or all of them achieve it?

AVAILABLE ALSO AS AN AUDIOBOOK narrated by Jenny Hoops

The three Canadian novels are also available as a digital collection, *The Canadians*

Kurinji Flowers

Married to a man she barely knows. Exiled to a country she doesn't know at all.

Ginny Dunbar flees a turbulent past in London, only to discover that her future, married to a tea planter, in a colonial hill station, is anything but secure.

An emotional love story set in the dying days of colonial India.

"A sweeping, lush story - the depiction of India in all its colours, smells and vibrancy is pitch-perfect in its depiction." *(Historical Novel Society)*

Letters from a Patchwork Quilt

A touching story of love, loss and thwarted ambition.

In 1875, 18-year-old would-be poet, **Jack Brennan**, runs away from home to avoid being forced into the priesthood.

Jack's world is shattered when his landlord's daughter falsely accuses him of fathering the child she is expecting, setting his life on a collision course to disaster.

"A heartbreaking and moving tale" *Readers' Favorite*

ALSO AVAILABLE AS AN AUDIO BOOK

The Green Ribbons

A classic Victorian love story, full of twists and turns.

1900. **Hephzibah Wildman** loses her parents in a tragic accident and is forced to leave home to earn her living as a governess at Ingleton Hall.

A gypsy tells her fortune – "Two men will love you – both will pay the price". An impulsive decision by Hephzibah unleashes a chain of events that lead to dangerous consequences.

"Fear, shame and passion in an English setting – reminiscent of Jane Eyre" *Historical Novel Society*

The Gamekeeper's Wife

A gripping tale of love, sacrifice and determination in the aftermath of the First World War.

Martha Walters is the widow of an abusive man. Martha has nothing and is about to lose her home.

Christopher Shipley, the reluctant heir to a substantial family fortune, has more money than he needs or wants, and responsibilities he cannot shirk.

They were never meant to fall in love, but sometimes the wrong person is the right one. Until a terrible secret is revealed to force them apart.

From an English country house to the jungles of Borneo, it will keep you up reading all night.

"One of the best novels of its type I have reviewed for the HNS. Pace. Plot. Emotion." (*Historical Novel Society*)